Praise for the *New York Times* bestselling novels of Diana Palmer

"As a romance follower you just can't do better than a Diana Palmer story to make your heart lighter and smile brighter."
—*Fresh Fiction* on *Wyoming Rugged*

"A fascinating story…. It's nice to have a hero wise enough to know when he can't do things alone and willing to accept help when he needs it. There is pleasure to be found in the nice sense of family this tale imparts."
—*RT Book Reviews* on *Wyoming Bold*

"Palmer proves that love and passion can be found even in the most dangerous situations."
—*Publishers Weekly* on *Untamed*

"The popular Palmer has penned another winning novel, a perfect blend of romance and suspense."
—*Booklist* on *Lawman*

"Palmer knows how to make the sparks fly…. Heartwarming."
—*Publishers Weekly* on *Renegade*

"Sensual and suspenseful."
—*Booklist* on *Lawless*

"Diana Palmer is a mesmerizing storyteller who captures the essence of what a romance should be."
—*Affaire de Coeur*

DIANA PALMER

A LOVE
LIKE THIS

HQN®

ISBN-13: 978-1-335-53465-1

A Love Like This

Recycling programs for this product may not exist in your area.

Copyright © 2021 by Harlequin Books S.A.

White Sand, Wild Sea
First published in 1983. This edition published in 2021.
Copyright © 1983 by Diana Palmer

Fit for a King
First published in 1987. This edition published in 2021.
Copyright © 1987 by Diana Palmer

This edition published by arrangement with Harlequin Books S.A.

For questions and comments about the quality of this book, please contact us at CustomerService@Harlequin.com.

HQN
22 Adelaide St. West, 40th Floor
Toronto, Ontario M5H 4E3, Canada
www.Harlequin.com

Printed in Lithuania

MIX
Paper from responsible sources
FSC® C021394

CONTENTS

WHITE SAND, WILD SEA

For Trudy, Helene, Shirley, Kay,
Cindy, Brenda, Antonia and Nancy

CHAPTER ONE

NIKKI BLAKE FOLLOWED the other four tourists out of the creamy gray walls of Fort Charlotte, touching the weather-worn smooth stone with her fingertips. It was like touching history.

Her eyes darted around the high walls of the massive fort on the edge of Nassau, to the solid cannon sighting over them, to the chains where the "bad boys" once were anchored. The guide had told them that, with a twinkle in his dark eyes. He'd taken them down below, down carved stone steps far below the cannon to a smothering hot underground room, where kerosene lanterns provided the only scant light. He'd plugged in a trouble light in that small room to disclose a rack with a dummy on it, and one beside it—the tortured and the torturer. Nikki had claustrophobia at the best of times, and the underground room had been trying. When she got back to the surface, she dragged air into her lungs as if it had suddenly gone precious, drinking in the thick, flower-scented subtropical air like a beached swimmer.

She barely heard the guide wishing them farewell as she held on to the cold stone as they went back through the tunnel and out over the moat. It had been an exciting experience, one of many during the two days she'd been on New Providence. She'd needed this vacation badly, but if her aunt and uncle hadn't pushed, she'd probably still be in Ashton having nightmares about that last big story she'd covered for her weekly paper.

"Where to next?" she asked the pleasant tour guide, a mountain of a man in a beautifully colored tropical shirt, as he held the jitney's sliding door open for his party.

"The botanical gardens and the flamingos," he told her with a smile. "The flamingo is our national bird, you know."

She did, but the gardens weren't on her part of the tour. She'd opted for the two-hour city tour, not the four-hour one, thinking that the heat would probably smother her if she had to endure that much of it all at once. Besides, she wanted to go back down Bay Street and wander along the straw market and Prince George Wharf, where the passenger ships docked and tourists in colorful holiday clothes decorated the view everywhere the eye wandered.

"You're coming, aren't you?" the lady from Chicago asked with a smile. "You'll love the flamingos. And the flowers…gorgeous!"

"We've looked forward to it all day," the couple from New Jersey added. "It's going to be great fun."

"I've got some shopping to do," Nikki said reluctantly. She'd enjoyed the group so much. They were all pleasant people, very friendly, not a complainer in the bunch. They'd been good company on the winding tour along the narrow paved roads that led them past stone fences behind which island cattle had once been kept, the governor-general's imposing home and the neatly walled little houses out in the country surrounded by tall casuarina pines, hibiscus, breadfruit, banana, golden palm and silk cotton trees.

The island had been an incredible experience from Nikki's viewpoint. A native of Georgia, Nikki lived in a medium-sized town south of Atlanta, and the vegetation there, mostly hardwoods like oaks and flowering trees like magnolias and lots of pine trees, was a far cry from these exotic fruit trees.

This was the first holiday she'd taken in the two years she'd worked full-time for her uncle's newspaper. It had been a necessary trip, not really a luxury: an escape from the nightmares that haunted her, from the sight of Leda's mud-covered body in the pile of debris the tragic flood had left in its foaming path.

Oddly enough the Caribbean didn't bother her, while the sound of running water back home had brought on horrific nightmares. Perhaps it was the very difference of the place that had begun to soothe her.

Nassau itself was quite exciting, from its busy streets to the fantastic jewel-colored water and coral beaches. Her pale green eyes had misted at her first glimpse of Cable Beach, on the way from the airport to the hotel. She'd never dreamed there could be anything as beautiful as the sudden shock of that turquoise water and the white beaches beyond the stand of sea grape and casuarina pines in the foreground. It had literally brought tears to her eyes as she held on to the seat while the rushing jitney swayed to and fro on its winding paved road to the towering white Steel Nassau Inn, a chain hotel overlooking the harbor and one of Nassau's best. Callaway Steel's hotel empire had acquired it several years ago and done extensive renovations.

Everything about the city fascinated her, from the statue of Woodes Rogers and the old cannon at the entrance of a nearby hotel to the story behind them. The people on the busy streets, in the shops, in the hotel itself, were gracious, friendly, proud of their island and their culture. They savored it like aged wine, something impatient tourists had to be taught to do. The first lesson Nikki learned was that in Nassau nobody was in a hurry. Perhaps the subtropical atmosphere had curved time, but the minutes seemed to actually slow and lengthen. Time lost its meaning. The Bahamians moved at a slower pace, took the opportunity to enjoy life a minute at a time, not a day all at once. After the first six hours she spent in Nassau, Nikki put her wristwatch into her suitcase and left it there.

When the jitney let her out at the door of the hotel, she went up to her room and changed into her one-piece white bathing suit with a flowing caftan cover-up in shades of green. The long, carpeted hall was deserted when she opened her door and went back out, with one of the hotel's spotless white towels thrown over one arm. Hotel rules forbade taking towels from the rooms, but Nikki had been too excited to stop and read the signs.

She locked the door behind her and started toward the elevator with the key clutched tightly in one hand.

When she rounded the corner at the elevator, with its huge green palm leaves painted on the metallic walls, the doors were just beginning to close.

"Oh, wait, please!" she called to the solitary occupant, a big, imposing man with faintly waving thick dark hair and eyes that were equally dark and hostile.

He hit the button with a huge fist and stood waiting impatiently for her to get in. She got a brief glimpse of hard features and a square jaw above a very expensive beige suit before she looked away, clutching the forbidden towel tightly against her as she murmured, "Lobby, please."

He ignored her, presumably because he'd already punched the appropriate button. Or perhaps because he didn't speak English. He was deeply tanned and had a faintly French look about him. Nikki had spent the time she'd been in Nassau learning that American-looking tourists were more often than not German or French or Italian.

Back home, being a Georgian was no distinction, because most everyone else in Ashton was, too. But in the Bahamas being an American was a distinction. She smiled delightedly at the irony of it.

"You do know that guests are specifically asked not to remove the bath towels from the rooms?"

It took several seconds for her to realize that the deep, northern-accented English was coming from the man beside her.

She turned and looked at him fully. He was as big as her glimpse of him had intimated, but older than she'd first thought. He had to be in his late thirties, but there was a rigidity about his posture, and those intimidating deep-set eyes, that made him seem even older than that. His face looked as if it rarely smiled, broad and square jawed and expressionless.

"No...nobody said anything yesterday," she stammered. She hated that hesitation in her own voice. She was a reporter; nothing ever rattled her. Well, hardly anything...

"There are signs in the rooms," he replied curtly. "You do read?" he added harshly, as if he doubted it.

Her pale emerald eyes caught like small, bright fires under her thick dark eyelashes, as thick and dark as her hair. "I not only read," she said in her best Southern drawl, "I can write my whole name!"

She hadn't thought his dark eyes could possibly get any colder, but they immediately took on glacial characteristics.

"Your Southern accent needs work," he said just as the doors opened. "Mute the *r*s a little more."

She gaped at his broad back as he walked away. It was one of the few times in her life she'd been stuck for a comeback.

With an irritated toss of her head she bundled up the

towel, holding it against her self-consciously. She hurried in her sandaled feet down the long hall, through the patio bar, which was all but deserted in early afternoon, out past the pool and onto the thick white coral sand, where turquoise water and blazing white foam waves lapped crystal clear against the shore.

Arrogant, hateful man to embarrass her like that, to ruin her pleasant mood... She'd buy a towel, a big beach towel, at her earliest opportunity, that was for sure.

She dragged up a heavy lounge chair and dropped her towel and hotel key on it, leaving the chair under one of the palm-tiled roof shelters that were scattered around the hotel's private beach.

She dragged the green patterned caftan over her head and tossed it on top of the heap, leaving only the low-cut white swimsuit on her softly tanned body. It was a good figure, even if a bit thin. Her breasts were high and firm, if small; her waist flared out into full, rounded hips; and her legs were long, shapely and tanned.

She walked carefully in the thick sand past the other sunbathers to the water's edge, wary of those dangerous pull tabs from canned soft drinks. There were infrequent ones underfoot, despite the valiant efforts of hotel employees who raked the sand constantly to keep it clean.

The water was surprisingly warm, smooth and silky against the skin, like those constant breezes near the water that made the sultry heat bearable. Nikki had learned that an hour of walking up and down the streets called for something cold and wet pretty fast. She was constantly scouring the malls and arcades for tall, glass-chunked containers of yellow goombay punch. And she found that she needed to spend an hour at midday lying down in her hotel room with the air conditioner on full. That was something else Nassau boasted—air conditioners at every window. Apparently everyone was vulnerable to the summer heat, not just tourists who were unaccustomed to the subtropical environment.

She moved out into the glorious aqua water with smooth, sure strokes, savoring the sound of it, the sight of tall casuarina pines across the bay, the huge passenger ships docked nearby. The salt stung her eyes with a vengeance and nagged at a cut on one finger, but it was all so gloriously new and the pace of life was so much slower, that she felt like a small child at a state fair. It seemed odd for her to choose a watery place to relax, after the tragedy that had forced her to take a leave of absence from the paper. But then, the Caribbean wasn't a river, after all, and the whole environment was so different that she didn't think about anything except the present and the pleasure of new experiences.

Her hair was soaked when her strength gave out, and she dragged herself out of the water and back to the yellow plastic-covered lounger to collapse contentedly onto it. She eased up her hips long enough to move the towel, room key and caftan from under her before she stretched back and closed her eyes.

The peace was something she'd never experienced before. Her life at home was full, and hectic most of the time. But this was incredible. To be totally alone in a foreign place, where she neither knew nor was known by anyone. To have dared the trip by herself, to spend two weeks away from her familiar environment and depend only on herself—she knew already that the experience would last her a lifetime.

All her life Nikki had been told what to do. By her parents until their untimely deaths, then by her aunt and uncle. Even by Leda until her marriage.

Nikki sighed. Leda had been her best friend, and she'd wanted Leda to like Ralley Hall. It had been so important that the two people she loved most would get along. And, of course, they had. A month before Nikki and Ralley were to be married, he and Leda had eloped. They'd been married a year and were planning to move back to Ashton when the flood went tearing through the small house they'd bought...

She was suddenly aware of eyes watching her and she opened her own, turning her head lazily on the chair to find the unpleasant stranger from the elevator standing just at the edge of the sidewalk near the swimming pool, looking out over the bay. He was still wearing his suit trousers, but he'd exchanged his expensive shoes for sandals, and doffed his jacket and tie. He looked relaxed, urbane and more than a little intimidating to Nikki, whose experience hadn't included high-powered businessmen. She was used to politicians and city officials, because that was her beat on the paper's staff. But she knew the trappings of high finance, and this man had dollar signs printed all over him. He held a glass of whitish liquid with ice and a cherry in it, quite obviously a piña colada, but the favorite island drink hadn't seemed to relax even one of the hard, uncompromising muscles in his leonine face.

While she studied him, he was studying her, his dark, cold eyes analyzing every inch of her body in the wet bathing suit. She boldly gave him back the faintly insulting appraisal, running her eyes over his powerful physique, from massive chest down over narrow hips and powerful legs. He was a giant of a man with a broad face, an imposing nose, a square jaw and eyes that cut like sharp ice.

Without a change of expression he let his eyes roam back to the turquoise waters for an instant before he turned and walked away, panther-like, toward the patio bar, without having glanced Nikki's way again. She reached for her cover-up and drew it on, feeling chilled despite the heat. Whoever that man was, he had an imposing demeanor and she wouldn't have liked him for an enemy. But there was something vaguely familiar about him, as if she'd met him before. How ridiculous that was, when except for college and the occasional shopping trip to Atlanta, she'd never been anywhere.

She closed her eyes and lay back on the chair, dismissing the disturbing man from her mind. The whispering surf and the murmur of nearby voices, overlaid by a faraway radio playing favorite tunes, lulled her into a pleasant limbo.

The patio bar was beginning to fill up when she started back into the hotel, but the stranger wasn't anywhere around. She glanced longingly at the bar, where the white-coated bartender was busily mixing drinks. She'd have liked to try a piña colada, but she had no head for alcohol, and especially not on an empty stomach. Supper was going to be the first order of business.

She went back to her room and threw on a sleeveless white dress that flattered her dark hair and golden tan, her brunette hair contrasting beautifully with her unexpectedly pale emerald eyes and thick black lashes. She wasn't beautiful. She wasn't really pretty. But she had perfect facial bone structure and a soft bow of a mouth. Her posture was a carryover from ballet lessons, and she had a natural grace that caught the eye when she moved around a room. Her enthusiasm for life and her inborn friendliness attracted people more than her looks. She was as natural as the soft colors of sunset against the stark white sand. But Nikki didn't think of herself as anything more than a competent reporter. When she glanced in the mirror, she saw only a slender brunette with a big mouth and oversize eyes that turned up slightly at the corners, like a cat's, and cheek-bones that were all too obvious. She made a face at her reflection before she left the room, looking quickly around for a fringed white shawl to throw over her bare arms before she went out the door.

She was almost to the elevator when she noticed a tall, dark man in a blue blazer, open-throated white shirt, and white slacks coming toward her down the opposite end of the hall. A man with cold brown eyes.

CHAPTER TWO

SHE FELT A surge of panic at just the sight of him, and her hand pressed the DOWN button impatiently while she murmured a silent plea that the delinquent conveyance would lumber on down from its third-floor layover before the big man reached her.

But it was still hanging up there when the stranger joined her. He lit a cigarette with a lighter that might have been pure gold from the way his fingers caressed it before he slid it back into his pocket. It might have been gold for all she knew, but obviously money, if he had it, hadn't made him happy. She wondered if he'd ever smiled.

She noticed his eyes on the lacy shawl, and remembering his earlier remarks about the towel, she tugged it closer over the very modest rounded neckline of her dress.

"The curtains," she explained, deadpan. "I had a few spare minutes, so I ripped them up and made this simply darling little outfit. I'm sure there was a sign, but I read only Japanese," she added flippantly.

He took a draw from his cigarette, looking infuriatingly indifferent. "All the door signs have Japanese translations," he replied coolly. "Japan is rapidly becoming one of the islands' best sources of tourism." His dark eyes measured her body in a way that made her want to cover herself up even more. "You'd look better in the curtains," he added carelessly. "Your taste in clothes is juvenile."

She was gaping at him, openmouthed, when the elevator arrived, with three passengers speaking rapid Spanish among themselves.

The big man stood aside for her, insinuating himself next to the panel to press the ground floor button.

Nikki wanted to say something cutting back to him, but for the second time that day she was rendered speechless by her own fury.

"Do you always sulk?" he asked with a curled dark eyebrow.

Pale green flames bounced back at him in a face rigid with dislike. "Only," she replied deliberately, "when I'm verbally attacked by strangers with delusions of grandeur!"

"A kitten with claws?" he murmured, and something resembling amusement made ripples in his dark, deep-set eyes.

"*Gatita*," one of the Spanish group, a young man, murmured with a wide grin.

The big, dark man threw a look over his shoulder, followed by a rapid-fire exchange of perfectly accented Spanish. Nikki, with only two dim years of the language to go by, understood little more than her companion's "*buenas noches*," as the elevator doors slid open.

With what she hoped was urbane poise, Nikki moved toward the front entrance of the hotel.

"May I ask where you're going?" the big man asked from behind her.

She stopped as she passed the desk. "To the restaurant on the arcade," she replied involuntarily.

"You're going the long way around," he remarked, indicating a mysterious door across from the elevator, always locked when she'd tried it, which led down a flight of stairs.

"It's locked," she informed him haughtily.

He sighed impatiently. "Didn't the desk clerk give you two keys when you registered?" he asked.

She swallowed. "Yes," she managed weakly, and it suddenly dawned on her which lock that mysterious key was meant for.

"You didn't bother to ask why, obviously," he remarked as she turned and went past him, key in hand, and fitted it into the lock. It opened on the first try.

"I was too busy stealing towels," she muttered.

He followed her down the stairs. "Do you ever read signs or ask questions?" he asked.

She almost laughed out loud. No, she didn't read signs. Most of them only said NO ADMITTANCE, and a reporter's first duty was to get the story, no matter what barriers got in the way. And as for asking questions, boy, was that one for the books!

"Oh, almost never," she replied with her most Southern drawl.

His eyes narrowed as he followed her to the bottom of the steps. "Where *are* you from?"

"Southern Spain," she replied. "*Buenas noches*, you all."

She doubled her pace onto the arcade as she passed the ice cream shop. It, like most of the others, had already closed for the day. There was a sultry, floral breeze, and the arcade took on a fairyland quality after dark. The stone benches in front of the coffee shop were deserted, and tourists wandered to and fro around the entrance to the restaurant and lounge on the bay.

The shawl Nikki was wearing did little more than dress up the outfit that arrogant businessman had dismissed as being "juvenile." She didn't need it to protect her from the chill. There wasn't one.

"Do you make a habit of running off in the middle of

a conversation?" her elevator companion asked suddenly, moving alongside her without rushing at all. His long, smooth strides made two of hers.

She glared at him. "Were we having a conversation? I hardly think constant criticism qualifies."

He lifted his cigarette to his mouth, and she noticed that the breeze was ruffling his thick, slightly wavy hair, giving him a casual air.

"I don't pull my punches, honey. Do you?" he shot back.

She drew the shawl closer while he ground out his cigarette underfoot. "I very rarely get into brawls," she replied conversationally. "My uncle doesn't think it's ladylike to break people's jaws."

She heard a faint, deep sound that could have been anything. "Doesn't he? How about your parents, young lady. Are they mad to let you wander halfway across the ocean alone?"

She drew herself up straight and stared unblinkingly into his dark eyes. "I'm twenty-five years old," she told him. "And I am allowed to cross the street when I want to."

"Hell of a street," he murmured.

"My parents are dead," she added quietly. "I live with my aunt and uncle—it's not uncommon for women to stay at home until they marry where I come from."

She felt his dark eyes on her as they reached the door to the restaurant.

"When did they die?" he asked, placing a huge hand on the door so that she couldn't open it without moving him out of the way—an impossibility.

She studied her sandaled feet. "When I was twelve," she said tightly. Her eyes darted back to his, and before she could erase it, he read the bitter sadness there.

"Have dinner with me," he said shortly, his tone impatient, as if he was offering against his better judgment.

Both her eyebrows went up over emerald eyes. "And be lectured on how I hold my fork?" she burst out.

"Touchy little thing, aren't you?" he asked.

She bristled at him. "Only when I'm being bulldozed by Yan...by northerners." She corrected herself quickly.

One corner of his chiseled mouth quivered, and she could see the smile that died on it flickering briefly in his eyes. "Why don't you say it... Yankees? All right, I'm from Chicago. What about it?"

"I'm from Georgia. What about that?" she countered. Her eyes glistened with emotion. "And for your information, Mr. Accent Expert, I was born and raised in Georgia, and this accent isn't put on. It's real!"

"How to speak Southern in three easy lessons?" he prodded. "Hi, y'all?"

Her mouth compressed angrily. "No wonder they fired off that cannon at Fort Sumter," she breathed. "No wonder...!"

"Peace, Georgia." He chuckled, and something akin to a smile pulled at his hard mouth. "Suppose we raise the white flag over some seafood?"

Her eyes wandered over his broad, hard face. This was insanity...

"Well?" he added curtly.

"All right," she murmured.

He opened the door and ushered her to the entrance of the restaurant, with its huge peacock chairs overlooking the bay where ships and seagulls caught the eye.

The hostess seated them at a window seat and gave them menus to scan.

"Isn't it beautiful?" Nikki sighed, her eyes dreamy

and soft. "Look at the seagulls putting on a show. It's like watching miniature airplanes do spins and barrel rolls."

"You like airplanes?" he asked.

She nodded. "Very much. I took a few lessons before I ran out of time and money. It was fun."

He glanced at the menu. "What do you see that you like?"

"Oh, the clam plate, please." She glared at him over her menu as she added, "And dutch treat. I buy my own meals."

He cocked an eyebrow at her. "Pardon me, honey, but I don't think your body's worth a whole meal. Possibly not a cup of coffee."

Her fingers crumpled one edge of the menu. "I think I'd like to order another table."

"Stay put. I'll reconsider after I've got something in my stomach. It's been a hell of a day." He shifted to tense and then relax the muscles in his big body.

"If my company is so distasteful, why did you invite me to sit with you?" she asked, taking the battle into the enemy camp.

His dark eyes narrowed. "I was lonely, Georgia," he said quietly.

She felt something leap at her heart and collide with it. "Oh." She waited until the young waitress took their order before she spoke again. "Surely you know people here?"

His broad, square-tipped fingers toyed with his napkin.

"I came down on business," he said. "I don't care for the kind of socializing most of my associates go in for."

She folded her hands primly in her lap, easing back into the unexpectedly comfortable peacock chair that seemed to be the style in the restaurant.

"What kind of business are you in?" she asked.

His eyes darkened, narrowed over a cold smile. "Don't you know?" he asked silkily.

She looked away, ignoring that curt tone as her eyes widened on a newcomer in port. "Look!" she burst out. "Isn't that a battleship?"

He followed her fascinated gaze to a dull gray ship flying a French flag, just steaming into the Prince George Wharf. "An escort frigate," he corrected. "French navy."

"I love the docks most of all," she murmured. "I've never been near a seaport in my life. It's just fascinating to sit and watch the ships dock and steam away. And the way those tiny little tugboats pivot them around in the harbor...!" She laughed.

"Are you this enthusiastic about everything?" he asked with a frown.

She glanced at him sheepishly. "It's all new," she explained. "New people, a new environment. I can't help but be enthusiastic about it. This is the first foreign place I've ever seen."

He glanced out the window with a shrug. "I've been here at least a dozen times. It's just another hotel in another city to me."

She drew in a quick, impatient breath. "And that's what's the matter with you," she threw back. "You're too blasé about it. You take everything for granted. Do you realize how many people there are in the world who never leave their hometowns at all? There must be millions who've never been inside an airplane!"

"They haven't missed much," he grumbled. "Damned cramped places, lousy food..."

"I had lots of leg room," she countered, "and the food was delicious. People were nice..."

"God deliver me," he groaned. "I invited you here for a meal, not a sermon."

"No wonder you spend so much time alone," she grumbled as the food was placed before them—her clams and his lobster thermidor. She paused to smile at the waitress and thank her, something he neglected to do, before she launched into him again. "You don't like people, do you?" she asked frankly.

His eyes went cold. "No," he replied.

Her wide-spaced emerald eyes searched his across the table. "We're all alike, you know. Lonely, afraid, nervous, uncertain..."

"I am not afraid," he ground out. "I have never been nervous. And I didn't get where I am today by being uncertain."

"If you were less hostile," she argued, pausing to chew a mouthful of fresh fried clam and murmur how delicious it was, "people might like you more."

"I don't need to be liked." He sampled his lobster and grimaced. "I swear to God, this lobster would bounce if I threw it on the floor."

"Back home, people are eating hog jowl and corn bread, and you're complaining about lobster." She sighed.

He blinked, his fork suspended in midair. "Hog jowl?" he mumbled.

"Jowl of hog," she told him. "Fat. What poor people have to eat because they can't afford lobster."

He narrowed one eye. "Have you ever eaten them?"

Her face tautened. She lifted another forkful of clams to her mouth. "These really are delicious," she commented.

"And an appropriate dish," he observed, waiting for her to get the point.

She shrugged. "I've been poor," she admitted. "I don't like remembering it, and I don't like talking about it."

"You intrigue me," he said over his black coffee. His dark hands curled around the cup, and she noticed a sprinkling of thick, dark hairs on the backs of them—the same hair that peeked out of his open-throated white shirt under the blue blazer. He had a faintly sensuous quality about him, or seemed to. But she doubted if he knew a lot about women. He was as cold as a chilled wineglass, hardly a ladies' man with that rigidity and lack of charm. He seemed to be a lonely man...

"Are you here by yourself?" she asked suddenly.

"Yes," he said curtly.

She studied the tablecloth. "Married?"

He went absolutely rigid in the chair, his eyes cutting. "Widowed."

"Sorry." She added more cream to her coffee and picked at her French fries. "Well, I've got to get back to my room. It's getting dark."

He stared at her blankly. "Do you change into a statue without sunlight?" he murmured.

"Oh, it's not that," she assured him, wiping her mouth with the napkin and throwing down the rest of her coffee. "It's just that I don't like going out at night alone. Too dangerous. Sharks. Man-eating hibiscus. Leering palm trees." She shuddered delicately. Her dancing eyes met his as she gathered her shawl around her and picked up her check. "Thanks for the company. See you around."

"Have you seen the cruise ships by night?" he asked suddenly.

She shook her head wistfully. "They light up, don't they?"

"There's a nice view from the beach. I'll walk out with

you, if you like." He stood up, towering over her, and before she could move, he grabbed her check out of her hand and walked away to the cashier.

"You can't..." she protested behind him.

But he had his wallet out and the check paid before she could finish the sentence. He held the door open for her and followed her outside.

"And that's why I like Southern women," he murmured.

"I beg your pardon?"

"Before you can say *don't*, I already have," he murmured with a laughing sideways glance. "Slow drawls can be a distinct advantage."

She laughed lightly. "Well, thank you for my sup, anyway."

"You were worth it," he replied.

She stopped in the middle of the sidewalk and turned to him, with her short, dark hair whipping around her pixie face. "I...I think there's something we should get straight."

He seemed to take the thought out of her mouth. "I've got all the women I need," he replied blandly. "Of course, if there are ever any openings, I'll keep you in mind."

She couldn't fish out the reply she wanted, so she just kept walking.

The beach was deserted, except for one of the hotel employees, who was dutifully raking the sand clear of debris and a man from the patio bar, who was talking to him. The big man sat down on the concrete sidewalk that led around the restaurant and separated it from the beach. He motioned toward the wharf.

"They light up like Christmas trees," he remarked.

She studied the huge white passenger ships, fascinated. "I'll bet the passengers do, too," she teased with a small laugh.

"Would you like a drink?" he asked.

She shook her head. "I never drink with strangers."

His brows ridged upward. "We've just had dinner together," he reminded her.

"And I don't even know your name."

"Cal," he said after a minute. His eyes went cold. "If you're determined to pretend."

That remark went right over her head. She was too intent on the two passenger ships gleaming like ivory whales wearing strands of diamonds. "I'm Nikki," she murmured. "Short for Nicole."

"I think I like 'Georgia' better," he remarked.

She laughed. "You know, back home it's no big thing to be a Georgian. Most folks are. But over here it's unique to be an American—have you noticed? I've only seen a handful of other Americans since I've been here." She glanced up at him. "Do you still live in America?"

"I live in Chicago. But I visit a lot of places." He drew up one powerful leg to rest his arm across. "What part of Georgia?"

"Ashton. In Creek County," she replied. "It's way south of Atlanta, kind of in the middle of the southern part of the state."

"I'm glad you don't write tourist guide maps," he said dryly. "What do you do for a living?"

"Oh, I'm a reporter for—" she began.

"A reporter?" He stood up in one smooth motion, his body taut with rage, his eyes frightening. "My God, I should have known. I thought I was getting the come-on, but I didn't realize I was being had, as well. How did you find me?"

She couldn't begin to follow him. "I…uh, that is…" she

stammered, surprised to find herself trembling under the cold, quick lash of his voice.

"Can't you damned vultures find someone else to feed on, without tracking me around the world?" he ground out in a tone that lacerated as surely as yelling would have. "Get off my back, honey, or so help me God, I'll stick you and your damned paper with an invasion-of-privacy suit you won't forget!"

She found her voice and stood up, too, flaring like a torch. "And who are you, anyway, that I'd want to follow you around?" she managed, finding her voice at last.

"You don't know?" He laughed sarcastically. "Who put you onto the deal—Ramond? My God, there's nothing earthshaking about the project, nothing faintly newsworthy to the States. So what do you want, honey? More about Penny? That's a closed chapter in my life, and I'm sick of being questioned about her. Is that clear enough, or would you like it in words of one syllable?"

"I don't have the faintest idea what you're talking about," she said tightly. "You may be some kind of super big fish where you come from, but you're just an oversize tadpole to me, Mr. Big Shot Executive!"

"Sure," he said with cutting contempt. His eyes gave her his opinion of her total worth, and she thought she'd never seen such distaste in a face before. "I don't like parasites. From now on keep out of my way. I don't want to have to breathe the same air with you."

He turned around and walked away, his back as stiff as a starched shirt, and Nikki just stood there, shaking. She sat back down on the ledge until her legs felt more stable, feeling sick and hurt and confused. What did he mean about reporters following him all over the world? Why hadn't he let her finish telling him that she worked for a small weekly paper, not some sensational tabloid? And who was he? Who was Penny? Why did he hate reporters?

For the first time she felt small and vulnerable. *More fool me*, she told herself with a bitter smile. *I should have known better.* But what hurt the most was his opinion of her, that he thought she'd picked him up to worm information about some project out of him. She grimaced. How could she have been trying to pick him up when she'd done everything but hire a taxi to keep out of his way? And he'd invited *her* to dinner; she hadn't picked him up.

Tears welled in her eyes. He'd prejudged her and hated her on the basis of her profession, without taking time to get to know her, or to give her the benefit of the doubt. And that was what hurt the most. She'd liked the glimpse she'd had of the man inside that hard shell. She had a peculiar thirst to get to know him better. But that wasn't going to be possible now, she knew.

She stood up, wiped away the tears and started down the sidewalk toward the patio bar. She'd like to have sampled one of those island drinks, like a Bahama Mama or a piña colada. But not at a time like this, when she felt like the end of the world. Drinking was only a crutch for pain, and Nikki didn't like crutches. She swept through the sparsely populated bar on her way upstairs. She wasn't even surprised to find that her dinner companion wasn't among its patrons.

CHAPTER THREE

NIKKI WENT BACK UP to her room overlooking the front of the hotel and stood quietly by the window, looking out over the struggling air conditioner to the streets below, to the horizon. Instead of magnolia trees there were towering palm trees, making a landscape that seemed alien. It wasn't particularly dark on the horizon, as if the island were perpetually lit up by something other than streetlights or the moon. It wasn't anywhere near the pitch darkness of a Georgia moonless night.

She studied the international grouping of flags over the front of the hotel, recognizing one as British, one as American. All around there were people. Hotel employees called greetings to each other as they passed. Tourists got into and out of cabs at a fantastic rate. And there Nikki stood, all alone, her heart down around her ankles, with that arrogant man's words ringing like chapel bells in her ears. *Vulture. Parasite.* She was an idealist, believing that what she did with a typewriter might make some small difference in the world. A story about a child with a disability being honored might inspire another child to try when he or she had given up. A story on an elderly person getting involved in politics might encourage another, more depressed senior citizen to look at life in a brighter way. A story on drugs might keep someone from trying them, might save a life.

That was why Nikki wanted to write. Not to get rich. Not to get famous. Only to help.

But how could she expect Mr. Big Shot to understand ideals? She doubted if he even had any, past getting richer. The flags misted and blurred. Who cared, anyway? She didn't.

AFTER A RESTLESSLY hot night, during which the valiant air conditioner didn't seem to make even a small difference, she rolled over and turned on Radio Bahamas. She listened to a news broadcast followed by a sermon in a delightful British accent, followed by a series of current American top pops and a few golden oldies mingled with the happy calypso beat, the goombay beat, which the Bahamas was famous for. The music made her feel better as it teased her lips into a smile, got into her bloodstream and bubbled. She threw her feet over the side of the bed and got up to dress.

The coffee shop opened at seven each morning, so she hurried down for her egg on a muffin and coffee, and to get ready for another day of sightseeing. Today she was going on a seashell hunt, on one of those tours she'd learned about at the desk. But first she was going to have breakfast and lie in the sun for a while.

The little coffee shop's trade was brisk. She stood in line for ten minutes, and in exchange for her American currency she got a number of beautiful Bahamian coins and a dollar bill with colorful fish and a photograph of Queen Elizabeth. The money here was as colorful as the scenery, as bright and gay and sophisticated as the people themselves. She was beginning to learn the softly accented English the Bahamian people spoke, to understand their fascinating culture. Each morning now, it had become a habit to go down Bay Street and buy the morning newspaper from the blind vendor near the clothing shop. The elderly gentleman had relatives in the States, he'd told her, although he'd never been there himself. She would press the right amount of change into his hand, and he would reply in the West Indian manner, "Thank you, m'dear." Everyone seemed to buy the paper. It was as much a part of the routine as the speedy breakneck traffic of the early morning as workers rushed to their offices and neatly uniformed policemen worked to prevent pileups. The docks were busy, too, as fishermen moved their boats out into the crystal clear water and the straw market began forming with vendors setting up their stalls with bright native handwork, woven purses and hats and other treasures that were gobbled up by tourists.

"Having a good time?" the girl behind the counter asked her with a grin as she handed her the change.

"I love it!" She laughed back, and the joy of the new experiences was in her eyes, her face, her posture as she danced away toward the tables and came face-to-face with the man from Chicago.

Her smile crumbled as she met his cold, contemptuous stare from the table where he was sitting with no breakfast, only a cup of black coffee cupped in his two big hands.

Old habits die hard, and Nikki had been taught manners with her first steps. She gave him a polite, if curt, jerk of her head and made her way to the very back booth, by the door that opened into the back street. She sat down with her muffin and coffee, with her back to the stranger.

It was all she could do to concentrate on her breakfast, which he'd managed to spoil with that steely glare. She was all but shaking with mingled rage and outrage. He knew nothing about her, nothing at all—not that she was conscientious, not that she'd never think of doing anything underhanded to get a story. How dare he judge her! As if

she'd write about a horrible man like him, anyway, whoever he was!

"You'll strain your spine if you don't relax," he said
from just behind her, causing her to stiffen even more with
surprise.

She didn't answer him. She wasn't going to give him
the satisfaction of actually replying. She bit into her egg
and muffin, which tasted like powdered concrete, thanks
to him, and chewed it thirty times before she swallowed.
When she took a sip of her coffee, there was no sound to
indicate that he'd moved an inch.

Curious, she turned her head and jerked to find him
only inches away. He was sitting at the booth behind her,
facing the aisle and watching her with eyes she couldn't
understand.

"If you don't mind," she said quietly, "I'd like to enjoy
what's left of my breakfast."

"There wasn't much of it to begin with," he replied.

"Why don't you go out and take care of your own business?" she asked him coldly. "I came over here for a vacation, not to fight the Civil War after every meal."

She started to get up, unfinished breakfast and all, but
he blocked her by stretching a powerfully muscled arm
across the booth. She collided with it and felt an electric
shock run through her slender body before she jerked back
with a muffled gasp.

He didn't like that betraying little movement; his face
tautened at it. He laughed shortly, "I'm not used to women
running from me," he said. "Especially not women reporters."

"I work for a weekly paper, not a scandal sheet," she said
bitingly. "We have a paid circulation of six thousand, and
we are hardly likely to set the world ablaze with stories on

Jim Blalock's fifty-pound cabbage or our new flood control ordinance."

He studied her face quietly. "A weekly, huh?"

"While we're about it, allow me to blow another hole in your theories," she added angrily. "I don't know who you are. And frankly I couldn't care less. My first impression of you was right on the money. I should have turned around the minute I saw you coming toward the elevator. Next time I will."

She ducked under his arm, tray and all, and stood up.

"All right, I'm convinced," he said, moving in front of her.

"I'm thrilled. Will you get out of my way, please?" she added.

He sighed deeply, taking the tray from her. "We're going to have a rocky relationship if you keep this up."

"You'd be lucky," she returned, but after a minute she sat back down at the table opposite him.

"Not that kind of relationship," he told her. His quiet eyes searched hers. "You aren't hard enough for holiday affairs."

"And you've got all the women you need," she replied with a faint twinkle in her eyes.

"Something like that." He leaned back to light a cigarette while he watched her nibble half-heartedly at her egg and muffin. "Twenty-five is a bit young for me, anyway, Georgia."

"Twenty-six in two weeks," she replied.

There was a long, potent silence between them while murmuring voices from other tables drifted by.

She looked up into dark, searching eyes and felt the breath chased out of her lungs by the intensity of that unblinking stare.

"How long are you going to be here?" he asked gently.

"About ten more days," she managed in a strange little voice. Her heart began to do the calypso in her chest as she returned that long, searching gaze. How odd, it seemed as if she'd known him forever...

Strange sensations wandered through her at the piercing quality of his eyes. He was such an uncommon quantity to her. She felt safe and threatened, all at once, and something in that utterly adult look of his made her feel strangely vulnerable. *If I had good sense*, she thought wildly, *I'd break and run and never go near him again until I was safely on the plane home*. But she was frozen in place. She couldn't force herself to get up and leave him there.

"Don't start looking for cover," he said, reading the apprehension in her taut features. "You don't need to feel threatened with me, little one."

"I'm not little," she said breathlessly.

"Honey," he said, standing even as he crushed out his cigarette, "compared to me, you're tiny."

She stood up beside him, forced to admit the truth in that bland statement. He loomed over her like some dark giant, as solid as concrete, as powerful as a professional athlete. There wasn't an ounce of flesh on him that wasn't firm, no sign of a beer belly or its upper-crust equivalent. His stomach was as flat as her own, his posture not only proud and arrogant, but full of barely concealed vitality. He'd said he'd been married, and she wondered if there were children. But before she could get her muddled thoughts together, she found herself being shuttled out onto the sidewalk.

"But I was going back to my room," she protested, feeling that warm, strong grip on her elbow as he hurried her across the street.

"What for?" he asked without breaking stride.

"To get my swimsuit on."

"You can't swim on a full stomach."

"But I can sunbathe…"

"You'll blister," he remarked, glancing sideways at her creamy complexion against the pale green blouse and white slacks she was wearing. "Or worse, wind up like old leather. Don't fry that perfect skin. It's one of your better features."

"So complimentary," she mumbled. "What do you think you're doing, dragging me along like this?" she added as they dodged other tourists. It appeared that not only did the local people drive on the left-hand side of the road, they walked on the left-hand side of the sidewalk, as well. That had caused Nikki quite a few collisions until she got the hang of walking in crowds.

"I'm taking you under my wing," he replied.

"If you did, you'd crush me," she told him. "And besides, it's too early. None of the shops will be open."

"Which makes this the best time of day to explore," he replied, strolling along beside her like a man without a care in the world. The brown open-necked shirt he was wearing was almost exactly the shade of his eyes, dark against the white slacks on his powerful legs. He was a striking man.

"The beach…" she began weakly.

"Will still be there when you get back," he promised. "Now shut up. I'm rescuing you from certain boredom."

She gave up, falling into step beside him when he released her arm long enough to light a cigarette and send out a great cloud of smoke.

"Do you always capture people this way?" she asked politely.

"Only when it's necessary." He threw her a mocking look. "It never has been before. It's usually the other way around."

"I don't chase men," she informed him. "I'm only a libber where salaries, working conditions and rights are involved. I don't want to brawl or press two-hundred-pound weights, thank you." She gave him a brief scrutiny. "I'll bet you think women should be kept in harems."

"On the contrary," he replied. He took another drag from the cigarette and paused to watch a straw vendor setting up shop on a wide corner as they passed it. "I'm not a chauvinist. The world is changing, and I'm doing my best to change with it." His eyebrow cocked at her. "Although I will admit that harems have their place. God knows what I'd do without mine on cold nights."

"Oink, oink," she murmured.

"Cats, honey, cats. All female, all Siamese. Four of them." He shrugged. "Dogs are all right. I keep one around the grounds for intruders. But it's damned hard to pet a two-hundred-pound Doberman with killer instincts. The cats are friendlier."

"I thought Siamese were vicious," she remarked.

"They fight back," he replied. "But they're loving animals, too. I don't know about you, Georgia, but I can't tolerate people or animals without a little spirit. I hate patronage." His eyes darkened. "God, I hate it!"

She studied his hard face. His gaze was averted, and he seemed to be carved from the same stone the old fort had been. He must be an important man, she decided. He had a quality she'd never seen in any of her contemporaries. Something extra. Magic.

"Is that why you travel alone?" she asked, the words slipping out before she could stop them.

He glanced down at her. "It's one reason. But I don't always travel alone."

A woman. The words flashed into her mind and he read them in her eyes and smiled faintly.

"No, honey, not on a business trip," he murmured dryly, "I'd never be able to think straight with that kind of distraction. I meant, I take Lucifer with me occasionally."

She stopped in the middle of the sidewalk with her mind swimming. "Lucifer?"

"The two-hundred-pound Doberman," he said.

Her eyes searched his. "You said he was a guard dog. Do you need guarding?" she asked, measuring him.

"I can handle myself. But Lucifer is a powerful deterrent, and I have enemies."

"You mean, enemies who might try to kidnap you for ransom?" she asked, all emerald eyes and arched brows.

"Or worse," he agreed. "My, my, what an expression! You are a babe in the woods, aren't you?"

"Cal, what do you do?" she asked bluntly, calling him by name for the first time.

"I'm a businessman," he said vaguely.

"I know, but—"

He lifted a big finger and pressed it to her lips. "Not now," he said gently. "I think I like it better this way for the time being."

"Are you a Russian spy?" she teased. "A Martian scout?"

He chuckled softly, "I'm a hardworking man on holiday."

"You look as though you could use one," she remarked as they walked along the narrow street that ran along the docks. It wasn't really wide enough for cars to park alongside it and still let traffic through, but by some miracle of navigation, the most incredibly large automobiles were able to squeeze through the narrow street. And tourists soon learned how to press back against the buildings to keep from being separated from their toes.

"Isn't this fun?" Nikki laughed.

"Speak for yourself," Cal grumbled, trying to fit his bulk alongside hers as a pink Cadillac slid past them.

"How did you get to be so big, anyway?" she asked him.

"My father was a Dutchman—from Friesland originally, as a matter of fact. A giant of a man from a land of large people. My mother was French."

"How in the world did you wind up in Chicago, then?" she asked, fascinated.

"I was born in the middle of the war," he explained. "My father had left Holland with his division to take part in the Allied invasion of Europe. He met my mother in France. They married and I was born the same year. They came to America because of me, I was told," he added with a dry laugh. "There were no opportunities in Europe after the war, unless you were involved in the black market. My father had the idea that Chicago was as close as he would ever get to paradise. He settled down, got an engineering job with one of the auto makers, made a few minor investments and let himself be talked into some stock in an oil rig."

"And lost his shirt, I imagine," she teased.

"Not quite." He paused at one of the straw vendors' stalls. "This sun's getting hot. How about a hat?"

"Only if you get one, too," she replied. "I don't want to walk around alone in a hat."

"And you call yourself a reporter," he chided. "Where's your spirit of nonconformity? The hell with what people think. Let them worry about what you think, for God's sake."

She flushed uncomfortably, "I'm an introvert by nature," she admitted reluctantly. "Everything past, 'Hi, my name's Nicole!' is pure bravado."

He searched her soft eyes, smiling. "No one would ever suspect it," he murmured. "You're not a bad actress."

"Then why was I turned down for the lead in our school play?" she asked unblinkingly.

"What was your school play?"

She grinned. "*King Lear.*"

He chuckled deeply. "What was the matter—couldn't you grow a beard?"

"You guessed it." She reached out and touched one of the patterned straw hats, done in royal blue and yellow flowers with green petals and little red buds. "Isn't it lovely?" she murmured.

He picked it up and handed it to her, choosing a plain tan one with no frills for himself. He handed the smiling vendor a big bill and waved away the change and the thanks.

"That was nice of you," she said as they walked away, with her new hat perched jauntily on her dark head.

"You're welcome. It suits you," he added with a grin.

"That, too, but I meant letting the woman keep the change. I asked one of them how long it took to make one of those big straw purses, and she said it was a day's work. Most people like to bargain until they get the price down to almost nothing."

She felt his eyes on her, although he didn't say anything. Perhaps he was remembering what she'd left unsaid in the restaurant last night—that she knew what it was to be without.

"Do you like old things?" he asked suddenly.

"I'm hanging around with you, aren't I?" she replied blandly.

He glared at her. "Old things, madam, old things. How would you like to see a fort?"

"I saw Fort Charlotte yesterday," she recalled. "But I don't mind going again..."

"Fort Fincastle," he interrupted.

"Fincastle? Oh, that was the one I didn't get to see," she murmured. "The tour guide didn't want to have to drive up that enormous steep hill. He said it wasn't worth looking at, anyway."

He looked irritated. "It most certainly is. Come on. We'll get one of those picturesque little carriages. You'll like that—it's right up your alley."

"How disappointing that we can't take a jet to it," she returned with a grin. "That would be more your style."

"Keep it up and I won't feed you lunch."

"That," she said, "is blackmail."

"Persuasion," he corrected. "I hope you're up to the climb, you delicate little thing."

"I hope you don't mean we have to do any mountain climbing," she murmured, glancing down at her flat sandals. "These weren't designed for climbing."

"There are steps. Come on, honey, let's get going. I've got a conference at three o'clock with the Minister of Architecture."

"Going to build something, are you?" she asked.

"Mmm-hmm," he murmured, scanning the area for the carriages. "A hotel. The biggest and best the out islands have ever seen, complete with hot tubs, saunas, a built-in spa, lounge and a shopping center."

Strange, he didn't look like an architect. But then, she thought, what did he look like?

He hailed a carriage and helped her in, the conveyance groaning under his formidable weight as he settled in beside her.

"This is how you get the best tours of Nassau," he told her, and settled back as their driver began to give them a brief history of Nassau, highlighting it with stories of pirates and the first governor, Woodes Rogers, who drove them out and made Nassau safe for its residents.

As they passed the Christ Church Cathedral, with its beautiful wrought iron fenced courtyard and masses of tropical flowers in bloom, the guide told them that the first building had been erected in 1670. It was destroyed by the Spaniards in 1684 and rebuilt in 1695. It was destroyed again by invading Spaniards in 1703. The third church, built of wood, was built in 1724 but had to be replaced in 1753 with cut stone. The fifth church, the present one, opened in 1841.

"The tower there," the guide added, "is all that remains of the fourth church."

"It's beautiful," Nikki remarked, and wished they had time to go inside.

"We'll come back," Cal assured her. "The inside is a treat to the eyes."

"You've been inside?" she asked him.

He nodded. But he didn't say anything more, leaving the talking to the guide as they went past a huge silk cotton tree, old buildings, landmarks and flowering hibiscus, bougainvillea, and towering poinciana trees with their wild orange flowers that lined the way to the fort.

Minutes later the driver pulled up in front of a grove of towering trees with limbs almost interwoven to make an arch leading to a barely visible set of steps far in the distance.

Cal helped her out and took her arm to guide her along. Other tourists were gathered at the base of the steps, and Nikki realized with a sense of smothered terror that along with the stone staircase was a waterfall.

Her voice stuck in her throat as Cal, who had no idea what the sound of a waterfall would do to her, carried her along beside him, murmuring something about a water tower at the top of the staircase.

Nikki felt her muscles contract as they neared the steps, as she saw the water cascading down two levels of stone beside the steps, and the sound of it was like no other sound to her sensitive ears.

With that sound came another—the sound of a flood raging over the earthen dam on the river. The sound of the water breaking it, bursting through in a foaming muddy wall to overwhelm the small houses nearby where twelve people, sleeping, unaware of the dam break, would never wake up again.

They were almost upon it now; the water was everywhere. She saw the television film of the flooding, the muddy debris, Leda's open eyes staring up at her...

"No!" she moaned, freezing in place with her eyes mirroring the terror knotted in her stomach.

CHAPTER FOUR

HE TURNED TO HER, catching her by both arms. "You're pale," he said gently. "What is it—the crowd?"

"The...waterfall," she whispered shakenly. "Silly, but I...I can't stand it. Please, let me go."

He turned her with one smooth motion and marched her back off to the carriage, where he put her in back and climbed in beside her with the agility of a much younger man, motioning the carriage driver to go ahead.

She felt a big arm go around her shoulders, felt a shoulder under silky fabric against her cheek as he held her quietly, without asking a single question.

They were back in the city before she got her breath again and moved reluctantly away from that comforting arm.

"Which was it, a flood or a hurricane?" he asked shrewdly, studying her face with narrowed eyes.

"A flood," she replied. "Isn't it insane? I don't mind the surf or the beach at all. But if I go near a waterfall or a river, I get sick to my hose."

"Have you talked about it?" he persisted.

"Only to my uncle," she said quietly. "He's edited the paper for fifteen years. Before that he worked on a big city daily as a police reporter. But the job has made him hard. I don't think he really understood what it did to me."

"Suppose we go back to the hotel, get into our swimming

gear and lie on the beach for a while?" he asked. "And you can tell me all about it."

Her pale eyes flashed up to his and locked there. "Your conference…"

"Isn't for several hours yet," he reminded her. He searched her troubled eyes. "Hasn't anyone ever told you how dangerous it is to bottle things up inside?"

"I'm…" She stared at the passing businesses, the tall hotels. "I'm not used to talking about myself."

"Neither am I, but you've managed to drag more out of me in two days than most of my associates have in ten years." He looked as if that amused him greatly, but his eyes were kind. Dark and full of secrets.

She stared straight ahead at his shirt where the buttons were loose, at a patch of bronzed chest and curling dark hairs. "I could use a swim," she murmured.

"So could I." He chuckled. "It gets hot out here."

"Now, that it does," the driver agreed, glancing back to make sure his passengers were okay. He hadn't made a remark up until then, but Nikki had sensed concern, and now she saw it in his dark eyes.

"I'm fine," she told him. "Just too much sun, I think."

"You get used to it," he replied dryly.

To the sun, yes, she thought, but how about tragedy? Did it ever completely leave? Did the horrible images of it ever fade? She had her doubts.

The beach wasn't even crowded when they laid their towels and robes down on the loungers under the little thatched roof shelter.

Nikki had bought herself a towel in the hotel shop, and apparently Cal had his own—a tremendously big white one with the initials CRS in one corner. She pondered on those all the way down in the elevator. The initials, oil, investments, all of it, added to his unusual parentage, seemed to ring bells far back in her mind, but she couldn't make them into a recognizable melody.

She laid her green caftan on the lounger as Cal stripped off his colorful blue beach shirt. Clad only in white trunks, he was enough to make any woman sit up and stare. His broad chest was powerfully muscled, with a wedge of thick, dark hair curling over the bronzed muscles down to the trunks that covered lean hips and led down to legs like tree trunks. He was the most fascinating man Nikki had ever seen, and she couldn't help the stare that told him so.

He chuckled at the expression on her face. "They do wear swimming trunks in Georgia?" he teased.

"Huh? Who?" she murmured.

"Men."

"Uh, oh yes," she stammered, flushing. She pulled her chair out into the sun and stretched out on it to drink in the warm, bright sunlight.

Cal stretched out beside her on his own chair with a heavy sigh, his dark eyes sliding down the length of her slender body in the clinging white bathing suit.

"That's the only thing I've seen you wear that suits you," he remarked.

She turned her head on the lounger and met his dark, searching gaze with an impact that sent tremors like miniature earthquakes through her body. Without the civilizing veneer of outer clothing he was as sensuous as a cologne commercial.

"I can hardly go around in a bathing suit all my life." She laughed, trying to make her voice sound light.

"That's not what I meant," he replied. His eyes swept over her critically. "That deep, low neckline gives you more fullness, and the color brings out your tan and those fantastic eyes. Your legs are your main asset—long and smooth and delectable."

She swallowed nervously. He made her feel positively threatened. It took every ounce of willpower she possessed to keep from folding her arms across her small breasts.

"Don't look so embarrassed," he said gently. "You've got a good body, small breasts and all, but you could dress it better."

Her face went rouge red. "Cal!" she burst out.

He threw back his dark head and laughed. "My God, talk about repressed areas... Don't you date at all?"

"Well, yes, I do, but most of my dates don't give blow-by-blow accounts of my measurements," she said, exasperated.

"You make me feel a hundred." He sighed musingly.

"How old are you?" she probed gently, her eyes wide and curious.

"Does it matter?" he countered, his eyes watchful.

"No. I'm just curious."

"I'm thirty-eight," he replied, and for an instant time seemed to hang while he waited with impatient interest for her reaction.

"Well?" he prodded shortly.

"What would you like, a rousing cheer?" she asked with arched brows. "Congratulations on having escaped middle-aged spread? An invitation to do a centerfold...?"

His face relaxed into a muffled smile, and he lay back down, shaking his head.

"Better watch out," she warned under her breath. "That's the second time you've smiled in five minutes. Your face may break."

He drew in a deep, relaxed breath and smiled a third time. "You make me feel as if I've only started breathing again, Georgia," he replied quietly. "I'm finding light in my darkest corners."

"It's the atmosphere, not me," she denied, stretching. "You just needed a push out the door."

"I'd like to know about the flood," he said after a minute.

She opened her eyes, riveting them to the curling white foam against that crystal clear aquamarine water, to the swimmers knifing through the silky water.

"We've had flash floods all my life," she began slowly. "But the dam always kept them from amounting to much. It was sturdy and had withstood floods for forty years or more, so nobody worried about heavy rains. Until three weeks ago," she added quietly. "The dam broke in the night, and water shot over it like water over the falls, one man who saw it happen told us later. Tons and tons of muddy water swept along the riverbed, overflowed and washed over a subdivision on its banks. One of the victims was my best friend, Leda Hall. I got there," she said, her voice going light, "just as the rescue people were dragging her out of a pile of debris that had lodged under a bridge downstream." Her voice broke, and she waited until it steadied before she spoke again, with images of that horrible morning flashing like specters through her mind. "She was covered with mud, like something barely human. But the worst of it was when one of the neighbors said that they'd heard screams from under that bridge for hours after the impact. I...I couldn't stop thinking that she might have been hurt, and in pain...but nobody could find her in the dark, you see, in all that debris." Tears rolled down her smooth cheeks. "It haunts me..."

He reached over and caught her fingers in his, pressing them gently. "How in God's name did you ever get into reporting?" he asked quietly. "You don't have the emotional makeup for it, honey. You aren't hard enough."

She wiped the tears on the hem of her caftan and laughed wetly. "I'm not good for much, am I? Not hard enough for holiday affairs, not hard enough to be a reporter..."

"We could work on that first one," he said in a new, different tone.

She turned to find his eyes tracing the soft lines of her face, slow and dark and sensuous.

"Care for a swim?" he murmured.

She nodded, feeling as if she'd had the floor taken abruptly out from under her.

He stood up, waiting for her to precede him into the water before he followed suit.

They swam lazily for several minutes before he surfaced beside her, slinging water out of his eyes. His lashes were beaded with salty water, and she noticed how thick they were, almost as thick as her own.

"Feeling better?" he asked. Standing on the sandy bottom, he towered over her while she tried to keep both feet balanced in the swell of the tide as a powerboat went past with a roar.

"Much." She nodded. "Thank you."

"For listening?" he asked. "Or for taking your mind off it?" he added with a wicked smile.

So it had been a joke, but she wasn't laughing. She bit off a theatrical giggle. "Oh, it did that."

Before she had the words out, his big hands clamped onto her waist and dragged her body fully against his, holding it so that she felt the strength of the powerful muscles crushing her breasts, her thighs. She gasped at the suddenness of the move, at the new angle of seeing his eyes from inches away instead of feet.

"I wasn't teasing," he said quietly. "Could you handle an affair with me?"

She couldn't speak. The contact with his body had drained her strength; the words made oatmeal out of her mind.

"Cal..." she whispered shakenly as her eyes dropped to his wide, chiseled mouth and she wondered achingly how it would feel against hers.

"I didn't mean to let this happen," he whispered gruffly, catching the hair at her nape to jerk her head back as he bent. His mouth caught hers before she could react and ground against it with a hard, uncompromising pressure that seemed to burn brands in her mind.

"Don't fight me," he breathed, pulling away enough to brush his lips softly, tantalizingly, across hers until they parted involuntarily. "That's it..." He trailed off, breaking her mouth open under his, and the world disappeared in swirls of blue and white and pure blinding silver...

His mouth was warm and wise and stirring her senses in ways she'd only dreamed about before. She tasted salt on it, as it demanded response; she felt the powerful muscles of his shoulders tauten as her hands clung to them, her fingers biting into them, her body dissolving against his like melting gold.

He let his lips slide down her cheek to her ear while his arms crushed her close, letting the sea rock them gently in its watery embrace. She heard his quick, rough breath whisper past her ear.

"It's good between us," he said gruffly.

She licked her bruised lips, her eyes closed against the blinding sun, the radiance of that passionate kiss. She felt incredibly weak. "The people on the beach..." she whispered shakenly.

He laughed softly. "They're all stretched out under sunglasses and suntan oil, oblivious to everything. See for yourself." He chuckled, releasing her a little so that she could look for herself.

Sure enough, not one pair of curious eyes had seen them. She couldn't quite look at him. She felt a surge of shyness. Even when she'd been engaged to Ralley, it had never been like this...

"Soft little mouth," he whispered, tracing its slightly swollen contours with one big finger. "I like the feel of it," he whispered, bending to brush his lips softly, briefly against hers. "It's like touching a gardenia petal, smooth and silky and cool against my mouth." He kissed her again, just as briefly, his face beaded with salt water, his body cool where her hands rested on his hard-muscled chest over that curling thatch of black hair.

One hand moved, taking her fingers and working them sensuously into the mat of hair over the silky muscles, in an aching caress.

He drew back and his eyes searched hers while a sudden silence hung between them, warm and sweet and wild.

His chest rose and fell rapidly, and darkness invaded his eyes as she slid her free hand to join the other, discovering the hard, cool contours of that massive bronzed chest with a smoldering excitement. She couldn't recall ever seeing Ralley with his shirt off, or wanting to. But she loved the sight and the feel of this man, the texture of his skin, the tone of the muscles, the faint scent of expensive cologne that clung to him, the magic in those hard, warm lips... She felt as if she were drowning in him, and she never wanted to be rescued.

"Enjoying yourself?" he murmured, watching the lights dance in her eyes, color her cheeks.

With a shock she suddenly realized where she was, whom she was with and what she was doing, all at once. She drew in her breath sharply, pushing away from him to stare up into his eyes with shamed fascination.

That stare said it all. Something dark and quiet lay in his eyes, relaxed the hard lines of his face for just an instant. He smiled—a slow, smug smile that made him look faintly wicked and devastatingly attractive.

"I'll race you to the wall," he challenged, narrow-eyed.

"You'll probably beat me, too," she replied, joining in the game. If he wanted to ignore what had happened, she'd go along. It was probably for the best, anyway.

But long after they'd parted company at the elevator, and she was dressing for lunch, she remembered the hunger in that rough kiss. His wife was dead. But had he been a long time without a woman in his life? That might explain a lot. But it was disappointing, too. Nikki ran a brush through her hair with a long sigh. *Trust me to lose my head over a man I'll never see again*, she grumbled to her reflection. *Just my luck these days.*

Cal had already told her that the conference would most likely last all day. He was having lunch with his associates and would probably have supper with them, too.

But he might have time for a nightcap, he'd added, and if he could manage it, he'd call her. She'd smiled and said that was fine and walked away. But she'd felt like wailing. She hadn't wanted to leave him. She'd wanted to spend the rest of the day with him, sightseeing or swimming, or just talking. She wanted to learn more about him, what he did, what his life was like. She wanted to be kissed again in that wild, hungry way.

She put her suitcase back in the small closet with a sigh. This must be that second childhood she'd heard about. Ri-

diculous to get that nutty about a man she'd only known
for two days.

She went down the hotel arcade to the chain restaurant
for lunch, treating herself to a delicious hamburger and
fries and coffee while she watched the seagulls play over
the water.

Next door was the restaurant and lounge where she'd
had supper last night with Cal. It seemed so long ago now.
They'd learned a lot about each other since then.

When she was through, she wandered back down Bay
Street and browsed through the shops, her eyes sparkling
with curiosity as she saw elegant emeralds, colorful im-
ported fabrics, perfumes and all kinds of exotic imports.
But something was missing. The wonders that had been so
exciting before were just routine now. It wasn't the same
anymore, being alone.

She thought back to the days before Ralley's interest
in Leda became obvious, to things they'd done together.
Strange, she couldn't remember Ralley ever enjoying simple things like window-shopping or strolling down streets.
He was only interested in football games, noisy parties
and talking shop with other reporters. But at the time,
she'd forced herself to like those things, even though it
went against the grain of her own nature. Nikki wasn't a
sports fan. She hated noise, alcohol and people who played
Russian roulette with mind-warping drugs. Her tastes ran
to symphony concerts, the ballet and art exhibits. Ralley
wouldn't have been seen at any of them. She wondered
now what they'd ever had in common, besides infatuation.
Poor Leda. But perhaps she'd shared those interests, too, as
well as being in love with the tall, sandy-haired reporter.
Nikki hoped she had. That one year of happiness was all
fate had allowed her.

And Nikki had been wary of men ever since. The humiliation of sending out wedding invitations and accepting gifts
for a wedding that didn't happen had been a killing blow to
her emotions. She wondered if she could ever trust anyone
else, if she could believe in love again. Simultaneously, she
thought of Cal, and something inside her began to dance.

Nikki went back up to her room around four, ignoring
the beach, because if Cal's conference had ended early, he
just might call. It could be anytime now.

She took a bath and threw on a beige slacks set with
a silky brown patterned matching vest. Then she pored
through the few paperbacks she'd packed, listened to the
radio, stared out the window, paced the floor and chewed
on her nails until six.

In desperation she went down to the restaurant to have
supper alone, her eyes restlessly catching on every tall, dark
man she noticed on the way. But Cal was nowhere in sight.
She rushed through her steak and salad, gulped down her
lemonade and went straight back upstairs, just in case he
called. But when seven o'clock, then eight o'clock, came,
she began to realize that he wasn't going to call.

He'd said he was busy, but hope had died hard. And
maybe it wasn't only business, maybe he did have a woman
with him, in spite of his denials. She'd thought when they
first met that he was a cold sort of man, with hardly the
time to attract women. But she'd revised that opinion dras-
tically. He'd known exactly what he was doing when he'd
kissed her. There was no fumbling, no hesitation, about
it. He was obviously an experienced man, and far beyond
Nikki's small knowledge of men. If anyone had told her a
month ago that she was going to allow a stranger to kiss
her in front of a beach full of people, she'd have laughed

hysterically. But he'd undermined every logical objection she had. And she hadn't fought him. Not at all.

She went back to the dark window and peered out at the streets below. Tourists were still coming and going in droves, and on the street were three young French sailors in their white uniforms with their little red-pom-pommed white caps. She watched them stroll away back in the direction of the docks with a sigh. What would it be like to be a foreign sailor in port, young and single and probably away from home for the first time? She felt a sense of loneliness herself. America seemed a world away from this, and for a moment she missed Uncle Mike and Aunt Jenny. She'd faced all the faint terrors of a tourist alone before the plane landed: What happens if I get hurt? What happens if I get sick? What if someone steals my money and my plane ticket? What if I miss my flight back home...? And the list went on. But she'd come to grips with all those questions the moment she landed and got her first look at the island from the ground. All the fears had disappeared by the time she got through immigration and customs. She'd worry about it when and if it happened. Not until. And she hadn't had a problem so far.

The phone rang twice before she heard it, and then she made a wild dive across the double bed that left her breathless as her hand made a grab for the receiver.

"Hello!" she burst out.

A deep, slow chuckle came over the line, stopping her heart just before it ran wild in her chest and brought a sunstruck smile to her face.

"Cal?" she asked.

"I can't think of anyone else who'd call you at this hour of the night," he murmured, "unless your uncle called to check up on you."

"I thought about calling him," she admitted breathlessly, "but I was afraid of the overseas charges."

"It would cost you more to call Atlanta from your hometown and talk fifteen minutes," he replied lazily. "It's not expensive. Join me for a drink?"

"I'd love to," she said sincerely.

"Meet me at the elevator in five minutes." And the line went dead.

She scurried around searching for her shoes, lost one, called it foul names for the minute it took her to locate it, brushed her hair again, checked her makeup and grabbed her purse. Then she stood watching the clock until four and a half minutes had gone by. She jerked open the door and peeked down the hall.

Seconds later Cal came into view, wearing a tan bush jacket and beige slacks, and she wondered if coincidences like his colors matching hers meant anything.

She closed the door behind her and ran the length of the corridor to meet him at the elevator, her eyes shimmering like jewels underwater, her face slightly flushed, her smile contagious.

"Hi!" she burst out.

He didn't smile. His eyes were narrowed and quiet and he looked down at her for a long time before he spoke. "It's been quite a while since anyone was that glad to see me," he murmured absently.

She flushed scarlet. "Oh...uh, I just didn't want to keep you waiting," she explained.

"Sure." He helped her into the elevator that had just arrived and punched the ground floor button.

"Hard day?" she asked.

"Honey, when you're dealing with any government, they're all hard days," he said with a faint smile. He studied her slender body in the beige leisurewear and the smile grew. "Are we reading each other's minds already?" he mused.

She laughed. "I was going to ask you the same thing," she admitted. Her eyes held his shyly for an instant before the elevator doors slid open.

They passed a smiling, nodding group of Japanese tourists as they walked down the long corridor to the patio bar.

"You sounded breathless when you got to the phone," he remarked. "What were you doing?"

"Watching the French navy," she replied dryly. "Wondering what it would be like to go on liberty in a foreign port."

He cast an amused sideways glance at her as they passed the showcase at the entrance to the bar, where artifacts were displayed—like the old cannonball found in Nassau Harbor by divers.

"What will you have?" he asked as he seated her by the window overlooking the hedged swimming pool and walkways out behind the huge hotel.

"I can't hold my liquor," she admitted sheepishly. "So I don't drink anything stronger than wine usually. But I'd love to try a piña colada."

"Had supper?" he asked, and when she nodded, he added, "It shouldn't give you any trouble. Of course, if you try to get up on one of the tables and do the flamenco, I'll do my best to stop you."

She laughed delightedly. When he stopped being the high-powered executive, he was such charming company. She watched him walk to the bar, all rippling muscle and power. Two older women sitting at a table across the room watched him unashamedly, whispering back and forth, and Nikki couldn't blame them for those intent stares. She liked looking at him, too.

He was back minutes later with two tall, frosty glasses full of a milky substance with cherries in them.

"A piña colada," he said, handing hers to her as he took the seat beside hers. "Coconut rum, milk, pineapple, dark rum and a cherry."

She sipped it and her eyes grew wide. "It's very good," she said, surprised. "I thought it would be bitter, but it's faintly sweet."

"Liquor doesn't have to taste like medicine, you know." He chuckled. "And in this heat, a 'tall, cool one' is almost de rigueur at the end of the day."

She took another sip and sighed contentedly, her eyes going past him to the patio with its neat little white wrought iron tables, where a flower-scented breeze shifted in through the open sliding doors.

"We can sit outside if you'd rather," he suggested.

She was on her feet almost before he finished the sentence. "I was hoping you'd say that," she said, leading him outside into the delicious-smelling breeze. The bay was just visible through the palms and sea grape trees and the hedge around the huge swimming pool.

Cal seated her again and settled down into the chair on the other side of the small table, idly watching the waves curling white and foamy onto the beach beyond.

"Peace," he murmured, "I'd almost forgotten what it was. You've made me slow down, Georgia."

"I just pointed your eyes toward the sights." She laughed. "You slowed yourself down. Mmm, isn't it lovely here?" she asked, closing her eyes to savor it all. The wind ruffling her hair, the scents, the faint buzz of conversation from inside the bar, the swish of the palms.

"It reminds me of Miami," he said.

She opened her eyes and took another sip of her drink.

"I've never been to Miami," she remarked. "Mike and Jenny—my aunt and uncle—flew down for some convention not too long ago. They said it was hot."

He chuckled. "In more ways than one," he murmured. "And crowded. And maddening to get around in. I'd rather take my chances on New York."

"I've never been there, either." She sighed. "I guess before now, the farthest away from home I've ever been is Daytona Beach. And all I remember about it is sun and sand and Leda pushing me in the swimming pool at the hotel with my clothes on." She smiled at the memory. "She was so much fun, always into something…" The smile faded and she took another, longer swallow from the glass.

"Don't look back," he said gently, meeting her eyes across the table.

"It's hard…" she said tightly.

"It gets easier," he countered. "Take it one day at a time."

"Just like that?" she asked.

He reached across and touched her fingers with his. "Exactly like that."

The touch of those warm, hard fingers made her tingle with sensations she hadn't felt since he'd kissed her. She studied the back of his hand, the darkness of it sprinkled with crisp, curling hair, the fingers broad and long.

"Look at me," he said curtly.

She raised her eyes to his and found him watching her. His fingers brushed against hers sensuously, lightly teasing them until they trembled, caressing the soft length of them until they parted and began to respond.

Her lips parted at the awesome surge of emotion the simple action ignited. Her fingers arched under the brush of his, and he eased slowly, sensuously between them in a silence that seemed to cancel out the world and every single thing in it.

He contracted his hand so that it was palm to palm with hers, with all five fingers securely interwoven, and pressed it hard and close while his eyes teased hers.

"Your heart's going like a watch," he murmured lazily. "I can feel it."

"You're not playing fair," she whispered breathlessly. "It's like shooting ducks while they're asleep."

His fingertips were at her pulse, feeling the rough rhythm of it, and his hard mouth was pulled up at both corners.

"Wrong, honey," he said softly. "I'm not playing at all."

She tried to catch her breath, but there was magic in the clasp of that big, warm hand and she couldn't have torn hers away on penalty of death.

"I don't think I could handle it," she protested weakly, her eyes frankly pleading.

"What?"

"An affair," she whispered.

He lifted her hand in his and ran his lips over the back of it with a slow, sensuous pressure. "You've got ten more days to think about it," he murmured. "While I put on the pressure," he added with a wicked grin. "And to pass along a trite expression, 'if you think this is my whole routine...'"

"What...what about your business meetings?" she asked.

"Let me worry about that. Finish your drink. You'll need an early night."

"Why?" she asked, grateful for small miracles when he let her hand go so he could finish his own drink.

"I'll tell you in the morning," he said mysteriously.

Her mind was working overtime all the way out of the lounge. He was interested in her—that was obvious. But she couldn't handle an affair with him; she couldn't. On the other hand, what if he had something more permanent in mind? What if they spent a lot of time together, and he decided that he couldn't live without her? The thought was pure delight. To live with him. To get to know him. To belong to him and have him belong to her, permanently. She glanced up at him as they walked. It couldn't happen this quickly, could it? People didn't get involved so quickly. But she had. She had!

They were just passing the desk when the clerk called out, "Mr. Steel? Mr. Callaway Steel? There's a message for you."

"Thanks," he said. "Wait for me," he told her as he strolled toward the desk.

Nikki stood there like a young fawn confronted by her first hunter. Callaway Steel. More accurately, Callaway Regan Steel, founder and president of the Steel companies, which included such diversified interests as oil, construction, real estate and a hotel empire of which this very hotel was a part. More than one national magazine had featured the first-generation American whose uncanny business sense had amassed a fortune from some old oil shares and two small filling stations.

But that wasn't all Nikki had read about the tycoon. His wife had supposedly suffered a fatal stroke soon after the accident that killed the couple's young daughter, Genene. But one tabloid had brazenly called it a suicide resulting from heavy drug use. All that was two years and more ago, but the press still hounded him, because he was always in the middle of some big business venture. Callaway Steel made headlines wherever he went. And this latest construction project and merger talk would do it again, she was sure.

Her eyes followed him, sad and lost and haunted. Something deep inside her began to wither, like a delicate flower cut off from water and sunlight. There had been such promise in the seedling of their relationship, such gentle hope. And now that was at an end. She was as far out of his league as a B-team football squad was from the Dallas Cowboys. She could never fit into his world, into his life, with all those differences to separate them. And an affair would certainly be all he could offer her, at best. He'd said often enough in print that he'd never marry again.

The evening had held such promise. And now it tasted like warmed-over ashes in her mouth. She saw him nod as he listened to the tall young clerk, turned and walked back toward her with a satisfied look on his face. *Another business triumph*, she thought bitterly. For business was his life now, the only thing that seemed to make him happy.

He stood just in front of her for a minute, reading the sadness in her face, her eyes, and his eyes narrowed in a movement strangely like a·wince.

"You really didn't know, did you?" he asked gently.

She turned and went to the elevator silently, pressing the up button with a slow, steady finger.

"It's been a long day for me," she said quietly. "Thank you for the drink, but I'd better go on up now."

He caught her arm and turned her toward him. "It doesn't matter," he said shortly. "Look at me, damn it!"

She raised her wounded eyes in self-defense. "Doesn't it?" she asked, her voice faintly trembling.

The elevator doors opened to let a party of people out— the same Spanish-speaking group that had ridden down with them once before. One of the men called a greeting to Cal, who returned it politely, but without enthusiasm.

He let her into the elevator first and joined her, his face hard, his dark eyes stormy under a wide swath of dark hair that had fallen out of place onto his forehead, giving him a faintly roguish air.

"Will you listen…?" he began.

"Oh, do wait for me," a small, very cultured voice interrupted, and a tiny, elderly lady in a very sedate navy-and-white suit joined them. Her elegant designer scarf matched the deep blue of her eyes and highlighted the bright silver of her hair. "I thought I was going to get left behind, and I do hate being alone in the lobby at night," she added cheerfully, ignoring the undercurrents between the elevator's only other two occupants, "I'm from Tallahassee," she told them. "Florida, you know," she added. "I just adore the islands, they're so…different. Now, my son would love this. I only wish I could have brought him with me, but he was so busy… Where are you two from?" she added with a tiny pause of breath.

"*No hablo ni una palabra de inglés,*" Cal said in perfect Spanish, and with a faint smile. "*Pero me gusta Nassau por su siempre briliante sol y cielo azul, y mi mujer le gusta también. ¿Y usted?*"

The small woman smiled sheepishly, nodded and replied, "Nice to have met you!" in a loud voice, as if she expected foreigners could only understand English if it was yelled at them.

As the elevator doors opened on the first floor, she moved out of it quickly, nodding and smiling, and looking relieved as she moved off down the hall.

Nikki, who'd been watching the byplay with niggling amusement, darted a glance at Cal.

"What did you tell her?" she asked curiously.

"That I didn't speak English, that I enjoyed the sun and sand, and that you did, too." He ran his eyes down her slender figure. "And that you were my woman," he added.

Her face flushed. "Oh no, I'm not," she said under her breath. The elevator stopped and she ducked past him to get out. "Not now, not ever, Mr. Tycoon. Just put me down as one of your few failed acquisitions."

"And that's something I won't do," he replied, following her down the hall to the door of her room.

She put the key in and turned it, her head bent, her shoulders sagging, her throat filled with tears.

She felt his big, warm hands resting heavily on his shoulders, pressing, holding.

"So I've got money," he said, as if he were searching for the right words, his voice deep and low in the deserted hall. "It pays the bills and supports a few workers. I can go first class when I please. I can afford to run a Rolls and buy a town house in Lincoln Park. But I work hard, Georgia. None of it came easy, and I wasn't born rich. I worked for every dime I've got. I think that entitles me to enjoy a little of it."

She turned, her back to the door and looked up at him sadly. "Oh, I didn't mean that," she said defensively, "I've read about you. I know what a rough road it was to the top. You're quite a success story. But you and I are worlds apart," she added, feeling it was important that she make him understand what she was saying. "Cal, my people have been farmers for three generations. Not plantation holders, not rich people. Except for a fourth cousin who made a million selling lightning rods, I don't even know any rich people. I…I can't cope…"

"You've been coping," he shot back. His eyes darkened in that broad, hard face. "My God, you're the first woman I've ever met who ran the other way when she knew my net worth. Don't you want a mink or a new Ferrari?" he added, his voice lightly teasing.

Her lower lip trembled with sheer fury. Her hand lifted and he caught it, taking it to his chest.

"No, mink wouldn't suit you, would it?" he asked softly. "Neither would strands of diamonds or sports cars. You're a wildflower girl. Daisies and jonquils in carpeted meadows, and the wind in your hair."

She caught her lip in her teeth, trying to stem the tears. She loved those flowers; she picked bouquets of them in season and made arrangements for the table. Ralley had never thought of her that way. He hadn't really considered who or what she was; she'd been more a possession than a person to him.

His fingers went to cup her oval face, holding it up to his dark, gentle eyes while he studied her in a silence rich with emotion.

"Nikki," he murmured deeply, savoring the name on his lips. "Nicole..."

"Cal, it won't work..." she whispered shakily.

"We'll make it work," he whispered as he bent toward her, taking his time about it, fitting his mouth exactly to hers until it touched gently every single curve of her quivering lips. "Kiss me, Nikki," he murmured against her mouth, and she felt his big arms swallowing her as the kiss made a mockery of every other caress she'd ever known. There was a strange tenderness in him as he explored her mouth, a treasuring of it as if it was a fragile, delicate thing that he mustn't be too rough with. He drew back far too soon, and Nikki saw the turbulence she was feeling mirrored in his wood-brown eyes.

"I hope you're properly flattered," he said gruffly. "It's been one hell of a long time since I've been that careful with a woman's mouth."

She was still working on words. Her eyes, her mind, was

full of that dark face above her that had suddenly and un-expectedly become her world. "You're very experienced," she whispered.

"What did you expect? A computer with hands?" he asked dryly. "I was married for twelve years, and I wasn't a saint when I proposed." His face clouded. "Nor since," he added roughly.

"I'm not a sophisticated woman," she told him with a voice that felt sandpapery. "I come from a relatively small town, I've never been a partygoer and I hate what I know of socializing. Cal..." She let her eyes drop to his broad chest. "Cal, I don't think it would be a good idea for me to get...involved with you."

He tipped her face up to his with a long, broad finger. "Honey, you're already involved," he said quietly. "So am I. And we're getting in deeper by the minute. I touch you, and I tremble like a boy. Haven't you noticed that? The same thing happens for you. I'm thirty-eight years old and I've never felt that way before. Don't expect me to walk away from you at this stage."

Her face contorted with indecision, with longing. He was right; he affected her exactly the same way she af-fected him, but she couldn't make him understand what she was talking about. She'd be winnowed out of his society in less than a week; she wasn't strong enough for the kind of people he associated with. She knew nothing about big business, less about entertaining, and she'd only be a hin-drance to him. Physically they were beautiful together, but Nikki had seen too many of her friends' marriages collapse from too much emphasis on the bedroom and too little on the living room. Without a foundation of common interests and friendship, that physical side of a relationship, while wonderful, would never sustain the relationship alone.

"Cal, I'm so confused," she whispered, looking up at him with all her doubts in her eyes.

He drew in a deep, long breath. "Give it time, Georgia," he said, lapsing back to her nickname and the earlier comradeship, his smile kind. "Suppose we spend these next few days just getting acquainted? No heavy petting, no passion on moonlit beaches, no sex, period. And then we'll go from there. Well?"

"I want to," she admitted wholeheartedly. Her hands moved unconsciously on his broad chest over the shirt. "Oh, I want to very much."

"None of that, either," he murmured, stilling her hands. "You did say you couldn't handle an affair with me, and I've got a low boiling point. No fair turning up the heat."

She laughed softly. "All right."

He bent and brushed a gentle kiss against her smooth forehead. "Go to bed. Tomorrow I'm going to rent a car and show you the island. Maybe we'll fly over to Freeport and take in the sights, too."

"I'd like that," she replied, her face beaming.

He watched her, faintly smiling. "Sunshine," he murmured. "Daisies will always remind me of you from now on. You're so natural, Georgia. Nothing false, nothing put on, just a vibrant enthusiasm for life. I've never known anyone like you."

"I've never known anyone like you," she replied, studying him. "Cal…"

"Don't start that again," he said. "You make me feel like a walking checkbook when you look at me like that. I'm a man, Georgia."

"You sure are," she said with a stage sigh, batting her long eyelashes at him.

He chuckled softly, removing his hands from her waist

to jam them into his pockets and stare down his imposing, arrogant nose at her. "I'll pick you up at seven sharp."

"I'll be ready." She opened the door and went inside, smiling at him through the wide crack. "Good night, then."

He smiled back. "Good night. Lock that door," he added firmly.

"Yes, sir!" She got a last glimpse of his amused eyes before she shut the big door and locked it noisily.

CHAPTER FIVE

THE NEXT DAY seemed to go by in a haze. Cal chartered a plane and took her to Freeport on Grand Bahama. She held tightly to his big hand while they wandered through the shops in the International Bazaar and ate in one of the many restaurants there. He bought her a tiny jade elephant, the only thing she'd willingly accept, and she knew she'd treasure it all her life.

Freeport was more spread out than Nassau, with wide boulevards and more sense of space. But privately Nikki liked Nassau best, perhaps because it was more crowded.

"Tired?" Cal asked on the way back, watching her stare down at the turquoise water as they approached the Nassau airport.

"Tired, but happy," she replied, turning to smile up at him. "It was lovely."

"And it's not over," he said with a slow smile. "Feel like some more walking?"

I could get up off my deathbed to walk with you, she thought. But all she said was, "Yes, I do. Where are we going now?"

He stretched lazily. "I thought I'd show you the inside of that church you were so fascinated by." He caught her hand and wrapped it up in his, sending tingles of sensation down her arm. "Then we'll go lie on the beach until it's time for my next meeting."

"Another one?" she asked.

He only laughed. "Honey, my whole life is one big round of meetings, everything from civic ones to board meetings. I don't have time to curse my cats when I'm back in Chicago."

"Do you eat out all the time?" she asked, curious about his lifestyle.

"I have a housekeeper—a wiry, little white-haired thing who can run circles around me," he said with a smile. "Her name's Maggie, and her specialty is giving me hell when I skip dinner."

"A paragon." She laughed.

"Not quite." He scowled. "Maggie has a tongue that waggles at both ends, as the saying goes. That's her only fault, but she's easy to get to, for the press. I almost fired her over that trait once."

She'd have bet it was after his wife's death, but she didn't ask. Prying into old hurts wasn't her privilege.

"Do you ever relax?" she wondered.

He shrugged. "Business isn't work to me—it's play. I enjoy a challenge."

"Is that what pushes you?" she teased lightly.

His face clouded and froze over. "Not quite." He released her hand and reached in his pocket for a cigarette, realized the plane was about to land and put it back again.

"Buckle up, honey. We're going in for a landing," he said curtly.

She did as he asked without another word. She'd offended him, without realizing it. His motivation was surely in some way linked to his dead wife and daughter, and she regretted deeply that unthinking question. Her eyes turned toward the window and she didn't open her mouth again.

They went back to the hotel first, to give Nikki a chance

to change into more comfortable clothes before they went out again. While they were there, Cal exchanged her room and his for a suite of rooms overlooking the bay.

"Don't get any ideas about seducing me, either." He chuckled as he carried her bags into her bedroom. "I've got protection. Genner!"

A tall, graying man with friendly eyes and a taciturn face came ambling out of the sitting room that connected her room with Cal's. "Yes, sir?"

"Genner, this is Miss Blake. Nikki, Genner has been with me for over fifteen years. He smooths the bumps, makes me eat when I don't want to and manages somehow to survive four female Siamese cats who hate him fiercely."

She laughed. "How do you do, Mr. Genner?" she said politely, extending her hand and having it lightly shaken.

"Fine, thank you, miss," he replied. "Would you like some coffee, sir?" he asked Cal.

"That might be a good idea."

"None for me," Nikki said quickly, feeling the heat more than ever, even in the air-conditioned sitting room, "I'd like to lie down for a minute or two, if you don't mind."

"Go ahead," he said gently. "I've got a mountain of work to get through and a meeting on the agenda..."

Nikki thought guiltily of all the time he'd been spending with her instead of his business. "Cal, if you'd rather put the church off until tomorrow, it's fine with me," she lied.

He shifted restlessly, his big hands jammed in his pockets. "I could use a little extra time to study the proposals on that real estate I need for the new hotel," he murmured.

She pasted a smile on her face. She'd had the morning with him, after all... Why should she expect any more?

"Then take it," she said. "I'm really worn out, but I

didn't want to say anything and hurt your feelings. You've been so kind…about the room and all…"

He glared at her. "It wasn't out of kindness and you know it," he growled. "I please myself, no one else."

"You know what I mean," she said gently. "I don't mind about this afternoon. Really, I don't."

He looked hunted for an instant, his eyes pained, his expression one of a man combating a host of conflicting emotions. "I'll call you in the morning, then," he said after a minute.

"That will be fine," she assured him, forcing herself to be cheerful. She glanced around the room. "Why are you staying here in a regular suite?" she added, curious.

Both dark eyebrows went up. "Why not? I own it. I can find out more about its operation from one of the standard rooms than in the executive suite, can't I?"

"Everybody knows who you are, anyway." She laughed.

He shrugged. "It's a well-run hotel," he admitted. "I've known associates to send servants down here with bankrolls to see how efficient the service in their hotels was."

"And…?" she asked. "Have you done that?"

"There's never been a complaint," Cal said with a ghost of a smile. "It isn't the newest hotel on the island, but there's been extensive renovation and remodeling, and the service is second to none."

"I'll agree with that wholeheartedly." She nodded. "It's well-run, all right. But why build another hotel…"

"Not here," he said. "On one of the out islands," he added. "But that's privileged information right now, Georgia."

She nodded. Her eyes flashed up to his and down again. "Well… I'll see you in the morning. Or sometime," she added with a smile and a careful carelessness. It wouldn't do to have him think she was begging for his company. Especially now that they were in adjoining rooms. What more did she want?

He nodded, his eyes narrowed with an absentminded look in them. "Sure. Don't go out at night by yourself," he threw over his shoulder.

"Oh, I wouldn't dream of it," she said.

She went into her room and closed the door behind her. It was silly to cry, but she did.

A cool bath made her feel better. She dressed in white slacks and a sleeveless, V-necked white blouse before she went back out again, in search of the little church.

If only she had someone to talk to, someone she could ask for advice. It would be better if she got on a plane and went home right now, before she got in over her head with Callaway Steel. Apparently he was having second thoughts of his own, because he wasn't all that anxious to spend any more time with her. He'd actually seemed relieved when she suggested parting company.

She sighed, walking along the crowded sidewalk, oblivious to her surroundings. She must have really gotten to him with that remark about what pushed him, and it had been a wholly innocent one. She hadn't meant to dig at him, but perhaps he was used to people who dealt in that brand of sophisticated knife turning.

That kind of loss would be hard to take, those two tragedies so close together. Perhaps he blamed himself. He wasn't a man at peace with himself, nor a man who enjoyed life to any great degree. She suspected that if it hadn't been for his businesses, he wouldn't have made it through until now. The pressure of daily decision-making had probably saved his sanity.

But what kind of life was it? He'd admitted that it had

been a long time since he'd slowed down enough to notice his surroundings, since he'd been able to smile. She was glad she could do that much for the tycoon. But it was the man who interested her, despite the gaping difference in lifestyles that separated them. She'd wanted very much to get to know him, and she knew now that wasn't going to be possible. Callaway Steel preferred people at arm's length, and that was where he planned to put Nikki, despite the closeness they'd shared last night. It must have been the moon and the rum, she thought sadly. Because in broad daylight, Cal had eyes only for the Steel companies.

She stopped at the door of the Christ Church Cathedral, her eyes riveted to the worn stone building with its windows that opened from the bottom and swung out, the courtyard with a black wrought iron fence and hibiscus blooming profusely inside it. It was the most beautiful church she'd ever seen, its history ancient and fascinating.

The interior had a sweeping grace of design, with high ceilings and ceiling fans, mahogany pews and white columns. The walls were lined with marble plaques in memory of deceased persons dating back far into the 1800s. One sad one read:

SACRED TO THE MEMORY OF LOUISA, WHO DIED 6TH JUNE, 1856, IN THE 25TH YEAR OF HER AGE.

Another marked the deaths of the crew of a British ship: crewmen aged sixteen through twenty-nine who succumbed to yellow fever in 1862. Besides the plaques there was an RAF Book of Remembrance listing the officers and men of the RAF who died in performance of their duties while stationed in the Bahamas during World War II from 1939 to 1945.

The silence inside the church was reverent, made more so by the memorabilia of those who had lived and died in the islands so long ago. Nikki wandered down the aisles between the pews, reading the markers, reflecting on what the lives of those people had been like, whether they had been happy or sad, what accomplishments they'd left behind them.

It was a reminder of how fleeting life was, and she remembered Leda, whose twenty-five years had ended so suddenly and so tragically. No one ever expected to die. Death came like a winter storm, so silently, so suddenly.

She clutched her purse tightly in her fingers, staring blankly toward the altar as she remembered, graphically, every minute of the flood she'd covered, Leda's body, the frantic efforts of the rescue people to work around the clutter of reporters and cameras and microphones. It was reminiscent of another flood Nikki's uncle had covered in the mountains, when a dam burst in a heavy rain and shot over a waterfall, killing a number of people, mostly children. That graphic coverage, and the vivid details that had been too horrific to print, had haunted her. The flood that claimed Leda had been added to the other one in her mind, and the combined memories had caused her some serious problems with her emotions.

But now for the first time she felt at peace with herself. This little church was easing the pain in unexpected ways. Perhaps it was the realization that she wasn't alone in grief as she read the wording of some of the plaques, which had been erected by grieving family members and friends so many years ago. Grief was like an heirloom passed down from one generation to the next, and there was no escaping it. One simply had to accept death as a fact of existence, and accept equally the certainty of something better past that invisible barrier that separated life from death. A wisp of verse from Nikki's Presbyterian upbringing lightly touched her mind as she stared toward the altar. "…God cause His countenance to shine upon you, and grant you peace."

Tears welled in her eyes and overflowed, and the tight knot of pain inside her seemed to melt away with the action. Now she could heal. Now at last she could live with it.

She turned, dabbing at her eyes with her hand. She never seemed to have a handkerchief or a tissue when she needed it most. She was almost even with the entrance when a shadowy form took shape just inside the door as she blinked her eyes to force the mist out of them.

"Cal!" she whispered in disbelief.

He shifted restlessly from one huge leg to the other. "I was halfway through a bid when I remembered those," he said quietly, nodding toward the plaques on the walls. "I had a feeling they'd bother you."

She remembered his own losses, his wife, his young daughter, and the tears burned down her cheeks.

He moved forward, pulling out a handkerchief to give her. She pressed it to her tear-filled eyes, catching the scent of expensive cologne in its white softness.

"I'm sorry," she whispered, looking up at him with wide crystal clear eyes. "You hurt, too, don't you?" she whispered, almost afraid to say it.

His face hardened, darkened. He looked away from her, down the long aisle. "Yes," he said harshly. "I hurt."

And he'd thought about her. He'd cared enough to come and see about her, despite his business. She wanted to bawl over that concern, but she forced her scattered emotions back together, sniffed, dabbed at the last of the tears and handed him back the handkerchief.

"I'm glad I came here," she told him, moving past him toward the outside again. "I needed to."

"What denomination are you?" he asked as they moved into the light, and Nikki blinked at the sudden brightness against her sensitive eyes.

"Presbyterian," she murmured.

"Now that," he said with a sideways glance, "is a true coincidence."

She stopped and looked up at him. "You aren't Presbyterian?"

He pulled a cigarette out of his blue-patterned shirt pocket and lit it. "My mother was Roman Catholic. My father was a staunch Calvinist. By some miracle they managed to live together long enough to be convinced that neither was going to convert the other. They became Presbyterians in an attempt to find a common ground."

"That's incredible." She laughed.

"So were they," he returned, his dark eyes soft with memory. "A happy couple."

"Are they dead now?" she asked gently.

"My father is," he replied. "My mother is still very much alive. She's in a nursing home, a good one, and she plays a mean game of chess."

"Do you look like her?"

"My father was blond and blue-eyed," he remarked with a wry grin. "I get my size from him. But the rest is Mother."

"Not quite all of it, surely," she remarked dryly, and then flushed wildly when she realized what she'd said.

Laughter tumbled out of him like wine out of a carafe. "Sheltered little country girl...?" he murmured with a wicked glance.

"Why don't you go back to your bids and your business?" she muttered.

"Hell, I tried. You got in the way." He took a long draw from his cigarette as they walked. "Let's go enjoy the sun for a while. All I've managed to do is give myself a headache."

She smiled. Suddenly the day began to take on a new radiance.

They went to a casino over on Paradise Island that night, where Cal taught Nikki the art of gambling. She'd never even played poker before, and she didn't have a high opinion of gambling in any form, but there was an aura of glamour that clung to this exclusive place.

While the roulette wheel spun and spun, her eyes darted restlessly around the room, finding every sort of apparel imaginable, from evening jackets to sport shirts and everything in between. It was the most fascinating place she'd ever been, despite the fact that she was wearing a long coral-patterned gown when most of the other women were in short dresses or elegant pantsuits. But Cal was wearing an evening jacket and a black tie with his white silk shirt, and Nikki had garnered enough courage over boiled lobster earlier that evening to tell him how devastating he looked.

He'd given her a strange look over that remark, one she couldn't puzzle out. She had the feeling he never knew whether or not people were lying to him, because he was rich. And she was suddenly glad that she wasn't.

"You won," he said into her ear, distracting her from the people-watching habit reporting had ingrained in her.

"Oh, I did?" she murmured vaguely, and asked how much.

He told her, and grinned at the stunned expression on her face.

When they cashed in the chips, she handed half a year's salary to him, which produced an expression that was a cross between incredulity and disbelief.

"What the hell are you handing it to me for?" he asked. "You won it. It's yours."

"Oh no, it's not. You staked me. Here." She caught his big hand and pressed the wad of notes into it.

He stared at it as if it was a dead fish, lying green and lifeless on his palm. His deep-set eyes stared down into hers searchingly. "I assume you aren't independently wealthy, if you work for a newspaper?"

She smiled. "No. My uncle owns the paper, and I wouldn't starve, but my parents didn't leave me anything substantial."

"Then why turn down a sum like this?"

She stared down at it and shrugged. "I don't know. Maybe because it came too easily. I like working for what I get." She tilted her head up at him. "You know, I've seen men go to carnivals and spend a week's salary tossing nickels and dimes for plates they could have bought for a dime apiece. The fever gets into them and they won't quit, and maybe they've got two or three children and a wife at home who'll have to suffer because of that gambling impulse. I may sound idealistic, but I've no use for gambling. Maybe here nobody goes hungry if a player loses two or three thousand dollars. But I've seen the other side of the coin, and it's not pretty."

"You might consider donating it to charity," he suggested.

Her eyes twinkled. "I've got a better idea. Why don't we both donate it to that little church we visited?"

One corner of his hard mouth curled. "Now, that's an idea I like." He pushed it into his pocket. "I'll send a check over in the morning."

"You're a nice man, Callaway Steel," she said as they walked toward the door.

He glanced down at her with a wry smile. "That's a new wrinkle. I don't think I've ever been called *nice*."

"Life is full of new adventures," she told him in her best theatrical voice. "Just think, tomorrow you could be eaten by a shark, or haunted by the ghost of the *Jolly Roger*... I wonder if he was?"

He blinked. "Wonder if who was what?"

"If Roger was Jolly." She frowned. "Hmm, I'll have to give that one some thought."

"You do that," he murmured, hailing them a cab.

The ride back to the hotel was far too short, and Nikki found herself trying to slow her steps as they went past the desk to the elevator.

"You're dragging, honey," Cal remarked.

"Tired feet," she murmured sheepishly.

"Sorry to see it end, Nicole?" he asked wisely, watching her as they entered the elevator and the door slid shut behind them.

She looked up at him, and pain flashed for an instant through her slender body, visible for the blink of an eye in her pale, soft eyes.

"Let's not be serious," she said gently.

He reached out and traced her short, pert nose. "We can't go through life like a couple of clowns. Although you do, don't you?" he added shrewdly. "You use laughter to cover up a lot of hurt."

She looked away toward the neat row of floor buttons on the panel. "And you see too deeply," she countered.

"It wasn't just the flood, was it?" he asked. "Was there a man?"

The elevator door opened in time to spare her an answer, but he wasn't going to let it lie. She knew that by the set of his jaw as he strolled straight and tall beside her toward her room. She'd opened it with her key, but he threw the door back, moved her gently inside the room and went with her, closing the door firmly behind him.

She stared up at him helplessly. She hadn't meant to invite him in; she hadn't wanted to be so alone with him. But it was going to be impossible to throw him out. And apparently he was determined to get an answer.

"Was there a man, Nikki?" he persisted gently, following her as she went into the room with its neatly made double bed, and onto the small balcony overlooking the bay and the beach.

"Yes," she said with a heavy sigh, leaning on the wrought iron railing. "It seems like a hundred years ago now, but yes, there was. Ralley was my fiancé. We'd already sent out the wedding invitations and my friends had given me a shower for the household items when Ralley and Leda eloped and got married across the state line." She smiled sadly. "I did so want them to get along. Leda was my best friend, and it was important to me that they liked each other. Well, they sure did." She laughed, resorting to humor. "They just went a little overboard."

He didn't say anything, but she felt him behind her, felt the warmth of his big body against her back.

"Leda was the one who died in the flood?" he asked after a minute.

She nodded. The wrought iron felt cold and steely under her nervous hands. Being alone with him like this was devastatingly new. Always before there had been people around. But now there were no prying eyes at all.

"Where is the man now?" he asked, moving closer. She felt, with a shock of pleasure, his big hands clasping her waist to bring her back against him.

"He, uh, he lives in a town about fifty miles away from Ashton," she stammered. She felt his warm breath touching her hair, breathed the clean scent of him mingling with the elusive fragrances of his expensive cologne and her light perfume.

His lips touched the side of her neck, running down it to her bare shoulder, where the tiny spaghetti straps held up the blouson bodice of the gown. His dark hair was cool where it touched her face, his mouth was warm and slow and its effect was unexpected.

She turned involuntarily to look up at him, the night sounds of surf and song and voices far away drifted nearby like something from a fantasy while she stared into his eyes and found the missing pieces of her own soul.

"You have the most extraordinary eyes," he murmured absently, scowling. "Just when I think I've got the color figured out, they change. They were emerald, now they're aquamarine."

She smiled softly. "Yours don't change. They're very dark." The smile faded. "Sometimes they're haunted."

"I know." He drew in a deep breath. "I carry my ghosts around with me." His hands moved up to cup her face, warming it, caressing it. "Are you a sorceress, Nikki? Can you exorcise them?"

Her nervous fingers reached up to touch, hesitantly, that hard, square jaw, the shadow where the corner of his chiseled mouth began, the imposing line of his nose. He let her touch him, standing quietly, rigidly, as if she were some small animal creeping up to him, and he was doing his best not to frighten it away. Her fingertips found his high cheekbones, his broad forehead, the silky, heavy brows above his deep-set eyes. Then they drew down the rigid muscles of his cheeks and drew across his warm, firm lips with a slow, whispering touch.

"Are you sculpting me?" he whispered softly.

She shook her head. "Just a low-budget safari," she whispered gently. "It's rugged territory, very dangerous."

"It must be, the way you were touching it." His big fingers speared through the hair at the sides of her head and tilted her face up. "Don't ever be nervous about touching me," he murmured, his eyes solemn.

"You don't seem like the kind of man who'd enjoy it," she said. "I mean, being touched by everyone."

"I don't," he admitted. "But, Nikki, I like it very much when I'm making love to a woman," he whispered at her lips, brushing across hers with his own in a slow, rocking, faintly sensuous motion while his big hands kept her face exactly where he wanted it. "I like being touched, and kissed, and…needed. Don't you?"

She felt the slow, nibbling movements of his lips with an ache that sat up and wailed inside her, coaxing her arms to reach up and hold him, her lips to part and invite something rougher, something more satisfying than these maddening little tortures of kisses.

"What do you want?" he whispered in a low, tender tone, his voice sensuous with triumph, with pleasure.

She realized only then that she was reaching up on her tiptoes, trying to capture that warm, elusive mouth, her eyes narrowed to slits, her breath choking her.

"I want you to kiss the breath out of me," she whispered back, the hunger in her voice, her eyes.

"I may do that," he murmured as he wrapped her body up against his, parting her lips with a curt, hungry pressure. "And then I'll put it back again…"

She was barely aware of the night sounds all around them, of the music drifting up from the patio, of anything except the feel of Cal's big, hard-muscled body against hers, of the massive arms that were swallowing her.

She'd never felt this kind of hunger before, not with Ralley, not with any other man. It was new and devastating, and she wanted the kiss to go on forever, to never stop. All she wanted from life was the hard, warm hunger of that ardent mouth on her own, and the sweet ache it was kindling in her slender body.

His nose rubbed softly against hers as his mouth lifted to nibble at hers. "It isn't enough, is it?" he whispered gruffly.

"No," she murmured, only half-aware of what she was saying. Her fingers tangled in the thick hair at the nape of his broad neck. "Don't stop…" she whispered into his mouth as she brought it back down on her own.

"I was hoping you might say that," he murmured sensuously, and all at once he began to deepen the kiss past her shallow experience, to make of it an intimacy beyond any simple joining of two mouths. Nikki clung to him, moaning softly at the unexpected reserves of passion he was drawing from her with his expertise.

"What kind of men are you used to?" he asked in a tone that mingled amusement with impatience. "For God's sake, don't expect me to do it all."

"Then, you'll just have to teach me, Mr. Steel," she whispered at his lips.

He drew back, staring down at her with narrowed eyes that blazed with unsatisfied desire. "Teach you?"

She sighed, watching his face grow even harder. "I hate to ask, but do you have some deep-seated fear of virgins?"

His chin lifted slightly and his hands contracted where they rested on her narrow waist. "You were engaged, you said," he probed.

She nodded. "I was. But to a man I managed very easily to keep at arm's length through the very few weeks before he ran away with my best friend." She sighed softly, "I'm ashamed to say that I wasn't even tempted."

"You're tempted with me," he said. "More than tempted."

She smiled. "Maybe I'm hoping that once I've got over that hurdle, you'll discover that I'm irresistible and you can't live without me."

He released her with a jerky motion and turned away, ramming his hands into his pockets. "Nikki, the world lost all its color when I lost my daughter," he said quietly. "I don't want to get involved again. I don't want children, and I don't want a woman. Not in the way of loving. I've never met a woman I couldn't walk away from. So let's draw back and do some serious thinking before we take that irrevocable step, Nikki." He turned, his eyes turbulent, and stared at her. "I'd hate to see you hurt," he replied softly.

"Thanks so much for all your consideration," she said with evident sarcasm, filled with hurt and disappointment. She was deliberately pushing him now, and she realized it, but she was somehow powerless to stop. All that monumental control of his, that cool, arrogant confidence, suddenly irritated her. She was offering herself to him—and he wanted to wait?

"Don't do it, Nikki," he warned quietly.

"Don't do what?" she asked innocently. "Don't presume to question you? Excuse me, I'm sure you aren't used to people doing that, Mr. God Almighty Steel. You give the orders, don't you?"

He moved toward her like a springing cat, so quickly that she didn't even see him coming until his rough hands caught her upper arms and slammed her into the muscular wall of his body.

"You only want me so long as you can walk away when it's over," she said deliberately, tingling with apprehension and excitement.

"Nikki," he said, and she watched the control snap, watched the dammed-up fury break loose and darken his eyes, tauten his broad face, knit his heavy brows together.

"What the hell kind of game are you playing?" he asked curtly. "What do you want from me? A commitment? I'm sorry. I'm not looking for emotional involvement of any kind. I've had all I can take of it and survive. Marriage is not in my vocabulary anymore." He sighed roughly. "Nikki, I like being with you. I'd like to have an affair with you, even if only for a few days. But that's all I have to offer, take it or leave it."

She didn't look at him. "I suppose all that talk about getting to know each other was part of the approach?" she murmured.

He shifted his gaze uncomfortably. "I didn't want you to feel pressured. But I'm running out of time. I've talked the Jones Restaurant chain's ownership into a merger with my hotels, and the new hotel's off the ground at last. I don't have any reason to stay down here. I've got work to do. I need to go back to Chicago."

"Don't let me stop you, Cal," she said quietly. She still couldn't bring herself to meet his eyes as she refastened the ties he'd loosened on one shoulder.

"Shut up before you push me over the edge," he added in a tight, angry tone.

"And if I do, what happens?" she breathed, her pale green eyes mirroring the excitement that was whirling like a small tornado inside her.

"You know," he ground out, bending. "Damn you, you know...!"

Her mouth ached under the rough assault of his, and the hunger of it was a pleasure beyond fathoming. His hands moved, stripping her against every hard, warm curve of his big body from her thighs to her breasts, making her feel every inch of him, the warmth, the power of him.

Her fingers tangled in his dark hair, holding his mouth over hers even though it showed no sign of ever wanting to be free. Her mouth opened, tempted, teased his, deepening the kiss shyly until he caught her head in his hands and she felt the expert penetration of his mouth in ardent response.

His teeth nipped her lower lip as he drew away, breathing roughly, his eyes dark and narrow. "Do you want me?" he asked curtly. "Because I'm not a boy, and I don't play juvenile games. For me it doesn't end at foreplay anymore. Another minute of this and you'll sleep with me, because we're both human and we want it too much. Now, do I stop while I still can, or do I start stripping you?"

She sobered, like a drunk thrown headfirst into a snowbank. She drew away from him with her eyes lowered, her face paling.

He drew in his breath heavily, like a man who'd been running. Nikki couldn't meet those accusing dark eyes; she didn't try. She felt as nervous as a child taking a shot, and her heart hurt her with its desperate beat.

"You can make me want you, that's very obvious. But

so can a dozen other women. I'm not impotent," he said in a voice that made her feel two inches tall.

She folded her arms across her breasts and stared down at the floor. "I'm sorry," she whispered. "It was a stupid thing to do."

"At least we agree about that," he muttered. He lit another cigarette. She hadn't seen him smoke that much in the time they'd known each other. She had a feeling it was something he did when he was angry or upset. He seemed to be both right now.

"I, uh, I think I'll go to bed," she said, feeling acutely embarrassed by her own behavior. She turned to go inside, but he didn't try to stop her, or say a word. He hadn't moved when she closed the door.

SHE SLEPT FITFULLY, awaking the next morning with a headache and a sore heart. She didn't know how she was going to face Cal after the spectacle she'd made of herself last night. She still couldn't understand why she'd pushed him that far, unless it had been hurt pride. No, that wasn't all it was, she admitted quietly to herself. It was his refusal to get involved, to commit himself, that had caused her to react that way. She'd wanted more than he was prepared to give, and something inside her had wanted to prove to him that he wasn't immune to her as a woman. She laughed under her breath as she put on white slacks and a matching tank top. No, he wasn't immune to her physically, that was for sure. But what she wanted was the kind of feeling she had for him, the need to be with and comfort and give…

She stepped into her low-heeled beach sandals and barely paused to run a brush through her hair before she squared her shoulders and went into the sitting room. She hadn't bothered with makeup, and she didn't care. Cal wouldn't notice. He'd probably send her home this morning, anyway, and she was half hoping he would.

It was nine o'clock, and she'd imagined that he was still in his staff meeting, but when she went out into the sitting room, he called to her from the balcony.

Her heart shifted nervously at his deep voice, but she walked calmly through the sliding door with none of her apprehension showing.

A lavish breakfast was spread out on the wrought iron table. Cal was buttering a biscuit over a plate dotted with eggs, sausage, ham and grits.

"I heard you stirring around, so I had breakfast sent up," he said as nonchalantly as if nothing at all had happened last night. "Coffee's in the pot. Help yourself."

She sat down and automatically poured herself a cup, lacing it with cream and a spoonful of sugar. She took a piece of toast, but no eggs or meat, an omission he noticed immediately.

"Not eating won't make it go away," he said shortly. "We're not going to talk about last night, now or ever. It didn't happen. Eat your breakfast and we'll go down to the aquarium and watch the dolphins perform."

"I thought you came down here on business," she murmured quietly.

"I did," he growled. He looked up from his plate. "But right now I think I'd do anything to see the light back in your eyes again."

"I just didn't sleep very well," she said.

He reached across the table and caught her hand in his, swallowing it in a warm, possessive clasp.

"Shall I be blunt?" he asked gently. "Nikki, what you feel is a mild case of infatuation."

She went red from her hairline to her chin, but she met

his eyes bravely. "I didn't realize it showed," she said unsteadily.

"I read you very well, Miss Blake," he replied, and his voice was kind. "Nor am I blind. You aren't old enough to build fences around your emotions to hide them. Especially with me. Nikki, you run to me, haven't you ever noticed?" His face clouded. "I'm trying to be as gentle as I can, but I'm hurting, and I can't help it. I want you to understand that it's only the newness of it—I'm simply that, a new experience. Once that edge blunts down, we can be friends. But until it does, you're going to have to keep from putting temptation in my path. I do want you very much, despite everything."

She didn't care about the dolphins, or sightseeing, or breakfast. Her blank eyes met his.

"If you don't mind terribly," she said in a ghost of her normal voice, "I think I'll go home."

His fork was halfway to his mouth. It never made it. He put it back down and leaned forward on his forearms with a heavy sigh, studying her with unnerving precision.

"I wanted you, too," he said gruffly. "I still do. My God, I ache to my heels every time you walk around the room, but, Nikki...damn it!" He shot back the chair and got to his feet, jerking around to grasp the balcony rail and stare down at the crowded beach. "Nikki, you're not ready for that kind of relationship with a man. Not yet, not with me. Men build houses for women like you. They sweat blood to make a decent living, and they look forward to children playing in a fenced-in yard out back somewhere. I've had that. But you haven't. The way you live, where you live, is a world apart from mine. I like my women experienced and unemotional, because an affair is all I want to offer. But the kind of man you'll marry one day isn't going to want that kind of woman, and you know it. He'll want something untouched. A vibrant, happy young woman with a sunny disposition and a body that she'll give to him first, last and always." He stared at his big hands on the railing and sighed. "Honestly, the thought of fathering another child terrifies me," he said. It was in his voice, in those few words: the fear of caring deeply, the fear of losing another child, of losing a woman he loved. He'd chosen the simplest solution.

He wouldn't love again. That way he couldn't be hurt.

She felt the same pain, but for a different reason. He knew she cared for him. That was frankly embarrassing. But at least they were taking care of all the obstacles at once. Perhaps friendship was better than nothing. She'd be with him; she'd get to know him. In time the ache might even be manageable. And in the meantime she could make his loneliness bearable for him; she could erase some of those hard, hurting lines in his face. She could…take care of him.

She stood up and moved to join him, watching the blue water wash lazily up on the beach in white foam.

She nudged against him playfully. "I thought we were going to see the dolphins," she murmured. "If you're going to stand here and leer at half-naked women on the beach, I'll go by myself."

He glanced down at her. Miraculously all the hard, deep lines that had been cut into his face began to relax, to give way before a whisper of a grin.

She smiled to herself. It was good to see those melancholy eyes light up. Even if it was only laughter, and not love, that was the cause.

THE HUGE SEA WORLD complex was like a small dose of marine biology, fascinating to Nikki, who'd never been in one before. She went from tank to tank, staring wide-eyed behind thick glass at huge sea turtles, sharks and a variety of colorful, fascinating creatures, which included dolphins and a baby whale.

"Aren't they beautiful?" she whispered, watching the sleek, elegant dolphins slice through the water. "But how terrible to keep them confined like this, to deny them the freedom of the ocean."

"Is anything ever free, Nikki—even people?" Cal asked from beside her, his dark eyes narrow and brooding.

"Not completely," she agreed. "But I do hate cages. I hate zoos more than anything in the world."

"Most of the animals that live in them grew up there," he reminded her. "It's the only environment they know. Put them back in the wild and they'd starve, if civilization didn't get them first. Wildlife is dwindling, honey. Haven't you noticed? We're paving it out of existence."

"Maybe you're right," she said quietly. "I don't know. I only know how I'd feel if someone locked me up and wouldn't let me go where I pleased. Even if it was in the name of protection."

"Marriage is a kind of prison," he remarked.

"With the wrong person, yes, it must be," she agreed, her mind idly going to Ralley and the unpleasant prospect of the marriage fate had spared her. "But there are happy marriages."

He laughed cynically. "When you put a rich man and a poor woman together, perhaps, so long as she's stacked and—"

Nikki turned on her heel and walked toward the steps that led up to the big tank where the dolphins were scheduled to perform any minute.

"I didn't mean it that way," Cal said tightly, catching her arm as he followed her up the steps.

"You warned me at the beginning that you don't pull your punches," she said quietly, "I'm not that sensitive."

"Then why did you walk away from me?"

She made an odd gesture with her shoulders, shrugging off the slight wound she wasn't going to let him see. "Oh, look," she enthused as they joined the crowd around the tank. Two dolphins leaped into the air in unison to take fish from the outstretched hands of a trainer on a high platform.

Nikki's eyes watched them as they went back under the water and swam feverishly side by side, to jump up and rush backward on their tails. Their faces seemed to wear an eternal smile.

"I'm sorry I don't live near the ocean," she murmured under the applause of the other tourists, "I'd love to learn more about dolphins and whales. I've never missed a Jacques Cousteau special yet."

"Intelligent creatures," Cal agreed, following her fascinated gaze to the black-and-white baby whale opening its huge mouth to receive a fish. "Have you ever heard the recordings of whale songs?"

She nodded, smiling. "Haunting. Beautiful. Like a symphony without music. Did you know that dolphins may be more intelligent than we are?" she added with a grin.

"I'd believe it." He laughed. "They haven't built machines to pollute themselves out of existence."

"No," she said sadly, "we've done that for them. The days are coming when all animals in the wild will be competing with man for space. I saw a special the other night on the Kalahari, and it was really sobering. So little vegetation, with animals and men competing for it..." She turned her face up to his. "Can it really happen? Can we wind up in a world where the only wild things are kept in cages and on reels of film?"

"Dinosaurs are extinct," he said noncommittally. He shifted his broad shoulders. "I don't know, honey. That's a question for a scientist, not a businessman."

She frowned up at him. "Didn't I read somewhere that you were right in the middle of that wilderness controversy?" she murmured.

He chuckled softly. "I like trees," he told her.

"And contributed to a foundation that's pouring money into finding a way to protect dolphins—a research project on some Caribbean island with protected coves…and there was that wildlife preserve…"

"I told you I had cats," he muttered, looking faintly embarrassed. "So I like animals, too. So what?"

She only smiled.

They had dinner at a Chinese restaurant, where Nikki ate sweet and sour pork until she felt as if she'd pop. She was lingering over a cup of black coffee when she noticed Cal's eyes following a particularly lovely waitress. Jealousy surged up in her like bile, and she kept her eyes down so that he wouldn't see it. If she'd been sure of him, if she'd been able to expect anything more than friendship from him, it was an emotion she'd never have known again. Because once he committed himself, Nikki knew he'd never look at any woman but the one to whom he gave his heart.

But he wasn't committed; he was a free agent. And pictures of him with other women invaded her mind, wounding her, hurting her. Of course he wasn't going to live like a monk because they were friends. He wouldn't feel the necessity for those kind of limitations. She shouldn't expect him to. After all, she was equally free, wasn't she? Or was she? Just the thought of being held, being touched, by any other man was frankly repulsive to her.

"Through?" he asked suddenly.

She looked up at him quickly and down again. "Yes. Where to now?"

"Back to the hotel," he said, his eyes idly following that waitress to the counter. "Wait for me here. I'll get the check." He picked it up and she watched him move toward the counter out of the corner of her eye. The older girl's eyes sparkled as he approached and she smiled; a smile Cal answered. They talked for what seemed a long time, and Nikki felt as if a whip had cut into her flesh by the time he came back and helped her out of her chair.

"Do you have anything planned for this afternoon?" she asked, resolutely concealing the jealousy that was eating her alive. She knew that he'd made a date with the other woman; she knew it as surely as if he'd shouted it.

"No, why?" he asked, frowning curiously.

She went through the door he'd opened, leaving the comfortable air-conditioning behind. A wave of hot sea air hit her body like a caress. "I thought I'd spend the afternoon on the beach," she said, stretching with a plastered-on smile.

He walked lazily along beside her the short way back to the hotel. The streets were busy with cars and tourists. Most everything was within walking distance on Bay Street.

"You don't look like you're dying to get on the beach," he murmured, seeing that wildness reflected in her eyes, her face.

She looked up at him innocently. "What do I look like?" she asked.

"I don't know," he said. His dark eyes searched her face. "It's a look I haven't seen in you before. Feel all right?"

"Sure!" she said brightly, and laughed, "I'm having a great time. I'd just like some of that delicious sun. Of course, if you'd planned something..."

"In fact, I had," he murmured with a faint smile. "A meeting with two out-of-town oilmen. They're staying on the floor below us, and we've got some problems at one of the rigs that I'd like to discuss. I was going to wait until tomorrow, but this may work out better." He eyed her curiously. "But that isn't going to leave us any time tonight," he added slowly. "I've got to entertain one of the food chain representatives tonight. I may be out all night."

She hadn't dreamed that anything could hurt so much. Food chain representative? Only if a pretty waitress could be loosely classified that way, she thought with shameful bitterness. But she only shrugged and smiled harshly.

"I wouldn't mind an early night," she lied. "I brought along some material to work on a story with. It will give me just enough time to get it written. I hope you have a great time *entertaining* your *representative*. She sure looked eager enough to me!"

Before he could reply, she took off at a run and didn't stop until she got to her suite of rooms. For the first time, she locked the door between it and the sitting room. Then she threw herself down on her bed and let the tears scald her hot cheeks.

She heard Cal enter the sitting room minutes later. While she sat up, rigid and nervous, she heard other sounds. A door opening and closing. The sound of a shower. Minutes later, the door opened and closed again. Sounds came into the room. A phone being dialed. A muffled deep voice. Footsteps that paced, coming close to her door for an instant. A hesitation. Then a muffled, harsh sound, followed by footsteps moving away, a door jerked open and being closed angrily. Then silence. A long, stifling silence.

Only then did Nikki begin to breathe again. She wasn't going to worry about mending this wall between them. Not now anyway. She was going to get on her bathing suit, go downstairs, and lie on the beach until the aching stopped. And then she'd think about going home. She could catch a flight back to Atlanta and have Mike meet her. She could always leave a note for Cal. Not that he'd mind, she was sure. It wouldn't bother him that much to lose a *friend*. And no doubt the pretty waitress could console him...

She got up and put on the black-and-white striped swimsuit she'd brought along, sliding her arms into a white beach robe. Maybe the sun would get her mind off her chaotic feelings.

The beach wasn't crowded, probably because most of the tourists were still at lunch, so Nikki picked a place near the water. She lay down on her stomach on the wildly striped beach towel, pausing to unclip the halter of the two-piece suit so that she wouldn't have a line across her back from the suntan. Then she closed her eyes, wiped everything out of her mind and let the warm sun and watery sound of the surf relax her into a sweet, light sleep.

She awoke to the sound of children laughing nearby. To the murmur of voices. And to a sensation like blistering all over her back.

Her eyes flew open and the sensation got worse by the second. Her back felt stiff; as if her skin had been violently stretched to the point of bursting. There was the feel of a giant blister to it, and she knew before she eased the halter clip painfully together that she'd made a terrible mistake in letting herself go to sleep.

The backs of her legs were red, too, but a glance over

her shoulder told her belatedly that her back was in much worse shape. With a faint moan, she picked up the towel, slipped into her beach shoes and went back up to her rooms.

She stripped off the halter and backed up to a full-length mirror in the bathroom, wincing when she saw what she'd accomplished with her impulsiveness.

"Leave it to you," she muttered at her pouting reflection. One side of her face was redder than the other, too, and already she was wondering how she was going to be able to bear anything against her back. She felt faintly nauseated, as well. If only she could get some cream on that blistered skin. But how was she going to reach behind her? And worst of all, how was she going to get home? It would be absolute torture to try to sit in an airplane seat— assuming that she could get a dress on over it.

She took the tube of suntan lotion and squeezed out a glob of it, easing it over the portions of her back that she could reach. She winced even at her own light touch. What was she going to do now?

With a muffled sob at her own stupidity she walked back into her bedroom, a towel clutched to her breasts, and lay facedown on the quilted coverlet. It looked as if she might have to spend the rest of her life that way.

A few minutes later there was a light tap at the door, followed by Genner's polite voice. "Miss Blake?" he called.

She relaxed. She'd been afraid that it was Cal, but she might have known that he'd never tap lightly at anyone's door. In the mood he'd been in earlier, he was more likely to kick it down.

"Yes, Genner?" she called back, her voice weak.

"May I bring you anything, madam?" he replied. "I'm

sorry I wasn't here sooner, but as I explained to Mr. Steel, I was delayed at the post office."

"No, thank you, Genner," she replied. "I...I just thought I'd lie down for a while. I've been on the beach and I'm... tired," she added.

"If I can be of assistance, please call," he told her, and his footsteps went away.

Nothing short of new skin on her back would be of any immediate assistance, but she couldn't tell him that. What was she going to do?

She got up and fished a couple of aspirin out of her suitcase. With her susceptibility to medicine they'd knock her out for at least a couple of hours and spare her that much pain. She swallowed them with a glass of water and lay back down on the bed. Minutes later she fell asleep.

A deep voice cut through her restless dream and woke her up, along with a far from gentle touch on her arm.

She gasped, half rising from the bed before she realized that there was nothing protecting her bare torso from Callaway Steel's dark, angry eyes.

With a gasp she dropped back down onto the bed, her face matching color with her back.

"Where did you come from?" she asked drowsily.

"That's a long story," he replied. "What the hell have you done to yourself? Do you realize that you've got a second-degree burn on your back? You little fool, I could beat you!"

"Anywhere but on my back, please," she whispered, with a weak attempt at humor. "I didn't mean to go to sleep in the sun..."

He was unscrewing the cap on some cream while she spoke. He noticed her pointed glance at it. "It's an analgesic cream, to take some of the sting out. If you're not better by the morning, you'll see a doctor. Now grit your teeth. This is going to hurt like hell."

She chewed on her lip instead, wincing at even the gentle touch of his big hand as it smoothed the cool cream against the angry burn on her back.

"You crazy idiot," he growled as he smeared it on, taut anger in every hard line of his face. "Why the hell didn't you stay in your room and throw things? There are kinder ways of getting back at a man."

"I wasn't getting back at you," she ground out. "I'm not that petty that I'd do myself in just to get at you," she informed him stiffly. "I just went to sleep, that's all."

"Well, you won't sleep much now," he said with venom in his deep voice.

Tears welled up in her eyes. "And it will serve me right, won't it? Why don't you smooth some vinegar on it...?"

"That's enough." His tone was uncompromising and full of authority. He finished rubbing in the cream. "Genner, bring me a cold, wet cloth."

"Yes, sir," Genner replied from somewhere near the doorway, his pleasant voice concerned.

"What are you going to do, choke me with it?" she asked tearfully.

"Wipe your face," he said quietly. His fingers moved up to smooth the disheveled hair away from her temple. "Want some aspirin?"

The tenderness was her undoing. She couldn't hold back the tears. She told him, tearfully, what time she'd taken the last two, and he calculated when she could have two more. Genner came back with the cloth and went out again, closing the door gently behind him. Cal bathed her hot face with the cloth, his hands tender, his eyes out of sight.

"I'm sorry," she whispered with her eyes closed. "I feel like such a fool. I do want to go home, Cal."

"Like this?" he murmured, and there was amusement in his deep, slow voice. "You'd scandalize the airline."

She tried to smile. "There isn't much to scandalize them with," she managed weakly.

His fingers ran over her soft hair. "There's more than enough," he murmured gently. "You have a lovely body. Exquisite."

She felt the heat in her cheeks, remembering that first surge of consciousness when she'd risen up without thinking and given him a brazenly clear look at her bareness.

"Another first, Nikki?" he whispered gently. "I wasn't disappointed." His fingers moved down to the curve of her shoulder, tracing the inside of it with a touch that made her tremble. "My God, you're perfect."

"Don't…" she choked.

"Too intimate?" he asked slowly. "Do you want me to pretend that I closed my eyes? I didn't, Nikki. I couldn't. I wanted to look at you."

Her eyes opened straight into his, and she felt tremors in the very fiber of her soul as she met that dark, quiet gaze.

"How fortunate for you," he said under his breath, "that you're half-fried, Miss Blake. Because if you weren't, nothing in this world would save you from me right now."

Her lips parted on a gasp that never got past them. Her heart felt as if it were going to strangle her with its wild beat.

Cal bent, brushing his mouth lightly, tenderly, over her eyes, her small, pert nose. There was a tenderness in the caress that she'd never expected from a man like him.

His fingers traced her soft mouth and he sighed heavily.

"My God, you're tangling me up like seaweed. Do you realize that?" he growled.

"I'm not trying to," she replied, forcing a smile. "I won't get in your way. I'm sorry about this afternoon. I promise, it won't ever happen again. Okay?"

"It didn't even dawn on me what you meant until I got back to my room," he murmured, ignoring her little speech. "About my meeting. Nicole, that waitress used to work for me in this hotel. She left to marry the man who opened the restaurant. She's just helping out today because one of their regular girls was sick."

She looked thunderstruck. "Oh," she managed.

His face clouded. "And despite the opinion you seem to have of me, I don't seduce the hired help. When I want a woman that badly, I can afford one who knows the score. I don't have to resort to pickups."

She felt ashamed, of her suspicions and her unfounded jealousy. "I'm sorry," she said genuinely. "It was none of my business, and I had no right—"

His finger pressed against her lips. "You want me," he said quietly, putting it bluntly. "That gives you the right."

"Cal..."

"And I want you," he added, his hard face, his eyes, enforcing every word. His fingers contracted in her hair. "Oh my God, I want you, Nicole!"

Her lips trembled. She couldn't find the words to answer him.

He drew in a harsh breath and stood up, bending his dark head to light a cigarette. He moved deliberately away from the bed, staring at the carpet.

"I don't know what to say," she murmured miserably.

"There's nothing to say. I've tried every way I know to ward it off, but it's like a damned tidal wave." He made a contemptuous gesture, blowing out a cloud of smoke as he turned to face her. "I don't want marriage," he ground out.

"I'm not asking you for anything," she said, her eyes as soft as the words.

"If we spend much time around each other," he replied, "I'm going to ask you for something. I'm going to ask you for that perfect body that you've never given to a man. And you won't lift a finger to stop me. Will you, Nikki?" he added curtly.

She eased onto her side with a sigh, drawing the towel against her like a security blanket, her eyes sad as they looked up into his. "No," she admitted painfully. "I'd welcome you. You knew that from the beginning. But afterward..." Her eyes lowered.

"Twenty-five years of conditioning don't go away easily."

"I realize that."

She shifted, wincing as the sunburned skin protested. "What do you want, then?"

He laughed shortly. "That's a hell of a silly question."

She smiled in spite of herself. Her eyes traced every line of his body, his face almost worshipfully, loving the hard, smooth lines of it. He scowled at the look.

"Don't worry." She laughed gently. "It's just infatuation. Or desire. Or both. I wouldn't know how to trap you."

"I feel trapped," he said shortly. He finished the cigarette and stubbed it out in an ashtray. "It might be a good idea if we don't see each other for a while. Are you sure you want to cut your vacation short?"

"Yes," she agreed sadly.

He glanced at her. "Your birthday's coming. I'll pick you up in Ashton. I want to take you to New Orleans for some Creole food. As I remember, you told me that was your favorite."

That shocked her, that he should remember something so trivial. But she was learning that he remembered a lot of things that most people dismissed as too trivial. Small, dreadfully important things that endeared him to his staff. To her.

"I'd like that very much."

He smiled half-heartedly. "Are you going to be all right? Genner will bring you a tray."

"That would be nice. Yes, I'll live. I've had burns like this before," she said with a laugh. "The last time I sunbathed, in fact."

He searched her dark green eyes, dark with pain and the pleasure of looking at him. "Are you in love with me?" he asked suddenly, curtly.

She flushed, but she didn't look away, "I'm infatuated," she replied tightly. "Remember? Or maybe I just want an ermine coat and a sports car."

He only smiled. "No, honey, not you. But if you did, you could have them." His eyes narrowed, the amusement left his face. He looked surprised. "You could have almost anything you wanted, with no strings attached. All you'd ever have to do is ask."

"I've got everything I need," she lied. Without him she'd be poor all her life.

"I haven't," he murmured, his eyes sweeping over her body like a tangible caress, dark and hungry and bold. His chest rose and fell heavily, his jaw tautened. He turned away with a quick, graceful movement.

"That business meeting I mentioned was on the level," he said shortly, turning at the doorway. For the first time, she noticed the handsome gray suit he was wearing, the delicately patterned silk tie that complemented it. "There aren't any other women, Nikki. Not now."

His tone implied that there would be, and she managed a faint smile. "Don't work too hard."

"I'll check on you before I turn in. Genner can find me if he has to." His eyes narrowed. "Honey, we can get a doctor…"

"Really, I'll be fine," she promised, touched by the very evident concern.

He nodded curtly, even though he didn't seem convinced.

She was half-asleep when she heard her bedroom door open. The pain had subsided enough to let her drift off, and she was lying on her side with the sheet around her hips, to keep it away from her back. The cream Cal had smoothed over the burn earlier had taken most of the sting out of it, but the sheet was still abrasive.

She felt rather than saw someone at her side, and she opened her eyes drowsily.

"Hello," she murmured sleepily, with a lazy smile as she saw Cal standing there in a black robe.

"Hello, yourself," he replied. His eyes drank their fill of her small, high breasts and the bare curve of her waist before she came fully awake and realized that she was uncovered.

Her fingers reached to jerk up the sheet, but he sat down beside her, stalling the instinctive movement.

"No," he said quietly.

She met his searching gaze levelly, shy with him as she'd never been before, faintly embarrassed at the newness of letting him look at her.

"You have lovely breasts," he said gently, studying them.

Her breath came quickly, unsteadily. The room was dim,

and the sound of the sea nearby was like a lullaby. Her own eyes went to Cal's broad chest, clearly visible where the robe had fallen away. It was short, only midthigh, and as robes went, it was of little value as a cover. Almost all of his massive hair-roughened chest was visible, abrasively masculine with its rippling bronzed muscles. His broad thighs were barely covered, either, as dark as his chest and sprinkled with curling hair. Nikki had never wanted anything as much as she wanted to touch him. She burned with the hunger, so intent on the sight of him that she missed the narrow appraisal of his eyes.

He reached out and caught her hands, bringing them slowly to the single loop in the belt around his waist.

She looked up, the question, the hesitation, in her wide, pale eyes as time seemed to hang between them.

"You may be disappointed, Little Miss Curiosity," he said with a flicker of humor in his dark eyes. "I'm pushing forty."

While he spoke, he guided her hands, helping them to unfasten the robe. With a single, smooth motion he let it fall to the floor and watched her stunned, absorbed face with patient amusement.

Her eyes fell helplessly to the full, blatant masculinity of his big, powerfully muscled body. She couldn't help staring. It was the first time she'd ever seen a man without clothes at this range, and Cal would have been devastating to an experienced woman. There wasn't an ounce of flab anywhere. He had the conditioned physique of a professional athlete, all darkly tanned flesh and rippling, sensuous muscle under a rugged carpet of curling hair as dark as that on his head.

Her eyes ran over him, then back up to meet his quiet

gaze. "I didn't know that a man could be beautiful, until now," she said in a hushed whisper.

His chest rose and fell heavily as he stared at her. "I've been called a lot of things in my time, but never that."

She sat up, her fingers hesitantly, nervously, touching his shoulder, his chest where the dark hair made a wedge against the powerful muscles.

"Do you mind?" she asked breathlessly.

He shook his head, watching her closely. "Did you go this far with him?"

"With Ralley?" she asked. She shook her head with a wan little smile. "Leda came along before he really wanted to that badly. And honestly, I never wanted to at all. I was never curious about him like this. I never ached to touch him…" She paused, realizing just how much she was confessing as her eyes levered back up to his.

"I'll let you touch me any way you want to," he said in a deep, husky whisper. His eyes darkened. "But I'm not superhuman, and I do want you like hell. If things get out of hand…"

She leaned forward, touching her mouth very gently to his as her hands eased down his massive body and she felt the tremor that rippled under her hands.

"Nikki…" he ground out, catching her wandering hands to press them roughly, possessively, against his body and she gasped at the urgency in the motion.

Her eyes opened, looking straight into his, reading the tearing hunger that shadowed them.

"I want to," she whispered shakily. "I want to please you. I want to lie in your arms and feel your body against every inch of me."

"You sweet little fool, you don't even know how to take precautions, do you?" he growled unsteadily, even as he lowered himself onto his back, bringing her down with him. "I hope to God I can keep my head long enough… Come here, Nikki. If you want me, show me how much."

She let her body melt down against his, her soft breasts crushing onto his hard, hair-matted chest, gasping at the sweetness of the contact as she ran her hands through the cool, dark hair at his temples.

"Don't let me hurt you," he murmured as his hands traveled gently down her back to her hips and eased them fully over his.

"Cal…!" she gasped, stiffening.

His smile was fully male, predatory, his eyes narrowed with calculating amusement. "And this is only the beginning." He laughed softly. "Kiss me, Nikki."

With a soft moan she burrowed her mouth into his, trembling at the feel of his warm, hard fingers brushing gentle patterns on her tender back, her legs, the inside of her thighs, as he deepened the kiss sensually and made of it something erotic beyond words.

He eased her onto her side so that his mouth could smooth the skin of her throat, could take full, aching possession of her taut breasts in the thick silence of the room—a silence broken sporadically by the rasp of skin against skin, by the sharp, shocked little cries that tore out of her throat.

Time seemed to throb into oblivion as he roused her to a point beyond bearing, whispering urgently, coaxing, guiding her until she could feel the tremors racking her body echoed back by his.

"Now," he whispered roughly, lifting her over him with hands that were at once gentle and urgent. "This is what… making love…is," he ground out, and as his mouth took hers, she heard a strange, sweet cry echo in her mind while the world spun golden floss as it whirled away into the throbbing darkness...

Dawn was filtering in through the blinds when she opened her eyes and realized where she was. Her head was pillowed on a man's warm shoulder, and she could see the wall across a broad, bronzed chest covered with curling black hair.

Her fingers tangled idly in that carpet above a deep, regular heartbeat, and she smiled, shifting her pleasantly aching body with a feline grace.

Her eyes traced the broad masculine face so close to hers, lingering on the imposing nose, the chiseled mouth, the faint shadow of beard on his square jaw. He was good to look at, to lie with. Her cheek gently nuzzled against his shoulder as she drank in the masculine scent of his body that mingled with the remnants of his expensive cologne.

I love you, she thought, looking at him. *I love you more than life, and if this is all I can ever have with you, it will be enough. I'll cradle the memory of the night in my mind like a lighted candle, and on lonely nights, I'll take it out and unwrap it and live it all over again. I'll live on loving you until the day I die...*

His eyes were suddenly open, watching her. "Good morning," she said hesitantly.

His fingers touched her mouth. "Come here and do it properly," he murmured, smiling. She moved, letting her body fit into the now-familiar contours of his. She smiled under his hungry mouth.

"Better?" she teased.

"Much better." He traced the straight line of her nose and smiled into her soft eyes. "How's your back?"

"It doesn't feel blistered anymore," she admitted.

"How about the rest of you?" he murmured.

Her fingers tangled in his thick, dark hair. "The rest of me never felt better," she whispered, leaning forward to brush her mouth against his. "I never dreamed it would be like that," she breathed.

He chuckled deeply. "How did you think it would be?"

She shrugged, nuzzling closer. "I thought it would hurt," she said honestly.

"It depends on the man, my love," he murmured at her ear, "and whether he cares enough about his woman not to hurt her." His fingers tightened at the nape of her neck and he sighed roughly. "My God, you can't imagine how it felt, Nikki," he growled unsteadily. "To hear those wild, sweet little noises you made and to know while I was having you that I was the first man, the only man…" His arms hurt suddenly as he drew her breathlessly close. "There's never been a night like that for me."

"You… I know you've had women," she murmured.

He drew back and looked down into her misty eyes. "I've never had a virgin, Nikki," he admitted quietly. "So, you see, last night was a first for me, too."

"Did I really please you?" she asked, her eyes telling him how important that was.

"Yes," he replied. His finger traced the long, sweet line of her lips. "Couldn't you tell, you repressed little thing?" he chuckled.

Her mind vaguely recalled a harsh groan, accompanied by the sound of her name being repeated like a litany while he shuddered uncontrollably under her own taut body. Her eyes closed and she nestled against him.

"Yes," she breathed. "Oh yes, I could tell. I wanted to give you even more…"

He drew her close, and his mouth burned against hers

in a long, sweet kiss that left her aching with new sensations, new hungers. She looked up at him, pleading.

"No," he whispered, pressing a finger against her lips, and the smile had gone from his face. "By some miracle I managed to keep my head enough to protect you last night. But I want you even more this morning, and I'm fresh out of magic."

"Would you hate it so much if I got pregnant?" she asked daringly.

His face darkened. He drew away from her and got out of bed, stretching his huge frame jerkily. "You'd better get some clothes on," he said as he pulled on his robe. "We're flying out about nine this morning."

She sat up in bed, gaping at him. "But you said we'd be here at least—"

He rammed his hands in the pockets of his robe and glanced at her, his eyes hot and possessive on the unconscious nudity of her torso. "I only have so much in the way of self-control," he ground out. "If we stay here another day…" He turned away, muttering a curse under his breath. "Don't argue with me."

She watched him until he disappeared into the bathroom. Her green eyes misted with unexpected tears. So it had only been a means to an end. He'd wanted her, so he'd brought her here to make it easier. She closed her eyes and chewed unconsciously on her lower lip as a wave of humiliation washed over her. He wouldn't have forced her, she knew that even now. But she'd given in without a struggle, poor little green fish, and now there was nothing left in her that he wanted.

She dragged herself out of bed and began to get her clothes together. When he came out, she'd have a bath, she told herself, making the thoughts come mechanically.

She'd pretend that nothing had happened; she wouldn't ask for what he couldn't give. Tears bled helplessly down her flushed cheeks. What a stupid fool she'd been!

CHAPTER SIX

NIKKI SHOWERED AND changed into a yellow sundress that left most of her back bare, a concession to the blistering that was still uncomfortable. With Cal she tried to pretend that nothing had happened, that things were the same as they had been the day before. But she didn't realize how brittle her voice was, or how false the smile pasted on her lips looked.

"Nikki," he began as they started to get into his small corporate jet, holding her back with a gentle hand, "I want to explain something to you."

"You don't need to," she said with all the bravado she could muster. She even managed a smile. "These things happen. There had to be a first time for me. I'm just glad it was with you."

"You're making it sound cheap," he ground out. His fingers tightened. "It wasn't a one-night stand for me. Will you believe that?"

She shifted restlessly. "You told me at the very beginning that you didn't want commitment," she reminded him. "I haven't asked for that, have I?"

He laughed bitterly, studying her wan face. "No, you haven't asked for a damned thing," he agreed curtly. "But I've cut you up pretty badly, haven't I? You look like a ghost of the laughing woman I brought down here."

She shrugged. "I'll get over it."

"Will you really?" His eyes cut into hers. "You're in love with me."

"Infatuation, remember, Mr. Tycoon?" she shot back, her cheeks flaming with sudden color. "I'll outgrow it, you said."

He moved a step closer, and just the warmth of his big body was intimidating, intoxicating. She felt herself beginning to sway toward him, hating her own helpless reaction.

He bent, letting his chiseled mouth stop barely an inch above hers. "Will you...outgrow it?" he whispered sensuously. "Come here, Nikki. Kiss me."

With a muffled sob she reached up to drag his mouth down against hers. "Oh damn you, Cal," she breathed into his demanding mouth as he kissed her roughly, hungrily, crushing her slenderness to him.

He was breathing heavily when he let her go, and his eyes were darkly blazing down at her. "I touch you and it's the Fourth of July," he said unsteadily. "Every sane thought goes out of my head, and I want nothing more from life than the brush of your body against mine in the darkness. What happened last night, I didn't plan. But it wasn't casual and it wasn't cheap." He drew in a deep, steadying breath, "I'm taking you home because I've got meetings I can't cancel, and it's impossible for me to think when you're with me. I'm not walking away from you. I don't even think that's possible anymore."

She stared up at him, dumbfounded, her eyes telling him everything she felt, without a word being spoken.

He traced her trembling mouth with a finger that wasn't quite steady, his broad face somber and dark in the early-morning light. In the gray suit and dark blue tie he looked every inch the conservative businessman. Her fingers rested on his thin white silk shirt, through which the dark shadowy wedge of hair was faintly, sensuously visible. She remembered suddenly how it had felt under her fingers last night while he taught her how to touch him…

"I think I'll wither away from you," she whispered achingly, her eyes searching his. "Like a flower out of the sun."

His fingers caught her by the waist and held her in front of him lightly. "Don't forget, we've got a date. Your birthday."

She smiled half-heartedly. "I'll be ready. But you don't have to—"

"Haven't you learned by now," he murmured deeply, "that I don't waste time doing things that don't please me?"

She studied his dark face. "Do I please you?"

"What a ridiculous question. Get in the plane, you funny woman, before I leave you here."

"Yes, Your Worship," she murmured, dashing in ahead of him as his dark brows arched threateningly.

Genner sat in the jet while Cal walked Nikki toward the airport office so that she could call Mike to pick her up.

Her steps involuntarily dragged, her eyes glancing off the tall, massive figure beside her. She'd dreaded this moment ever since she'd fallen for Cal, dreaded the parting long before it came. And the hurt wasn't lessened by knowing its inevitability.

He glanced down at her and his face seemed to harden. "It isn't goodbye."

"No, of course not," she agreed with a weak smile.

"Your birthday is a week from Friday, isn't it?" he asked quietly, and she nodded. "I'll be here at five o'clock. Make a note and we'll fly down to New Orleans for dinner. All right?"

Her poor crumpled heart lifted a little, and she managed a brighter smile for him. "I'll look forward to it," she said gently.

His eyes dropped to her mouth and lingered on it so intently that it made her lips part in response.

"I wish small towns weren't hotbeds of gossip," he said huskily. "I'd like to break your mouth open under mine and kiss you the way I did last night. I'd like to hold you so close that you could feel how hungry I am for you. And that might shock a few people."

"I'm going to miss you," she said without thinking.

"How do you think I feel, for God's sake?" he ground out. His dark eyes glittered at her. "If I took you with me, we wouldn't get out of the damned bed for a week. I've got too many irons in the fire to risk it right now, too many people depending on me for their jobs."

Her breath caught in her throat. "Do you want me that much?" she asked.

His chest rose and fell heavily under her fingers. "Until it's almost beyond bearing," he replied solemnly. "But I don't start things I can't finish. I told you how I felt about commitment, didn't I? I haven't lied."

"I know that. I won't ask for something you can't give." She moved closer, her heart in the soft eyes that looked up into his. "Your terms, Cal, all the way."

He scowled. "Don't you want anything?" he asked suddenly.

Her eyebrows arched. "Like what?"

"A car. A fur coat…"

She felt a surge of compassion so strong that it almost shook her. Her fingers pressed gently against his warm, hard mouth.

"I'd rather have the memory of last night," she said quietly, "than all the mink coats in the world. Does that answer your question, Mr. Steel?"

He drew her close and held her for a long moment before he spoke.

"I'm glad I made it something you'd want to remember," he said at her ear. All at once he chuckled softly.

"What's so funny?" she prodded.

"The look on your face when I pulled you over me last night," he murmured, drawing back enough to let him see the faint embarrassment that lingered in her face.

She laughed in spite of herself, remembering her own stunned surprise, his faint amusement even in the throes of passion.

"Quite obviously, you weren't aware that it was possible in that position," he whispered. "But it was the only way I could protect your back, you little witch. I'm no lightweight."

She looked into his eyes with a wild excitement making her knees weak as the memory of the long, achingly sweet night pricked her mind. "It was…so beautiful," she whispered slowly.

His nostrils flared with a sudden, harsh breath. His fingers tightened on her shoulders. "It wasn't just sex," he said unsteadily. "It was a beginning. Do you love me, Nikki?"

"Yes." Her voice broke on the word, but it was in her eyes, in her face, in her hands that clung helplessly to his waist.

His eyes closed, his jaw tautened for an instant before he suddenly let her go. "Go call your uncle," he said heavily, turning away to light a cigarette. His eyes met hers one last time. "And remember one thing, Nikki. You belong to me now, just as I belong to you. We're not playing games."

She searched his hard face, but not a trace of emotion showed in it. "Cal…"

"Keep away from that guy Hall. He had his chance. Now it's mine. So long, Georgia," he added with a last, satisfied appraisal before he turned away and strode back toward the jet. He didn't look back when he climbed into it. Somehow that stuck in Nikki's mind, even when she watched him take off.

CHAPTER SEVEN

UNCLE MIKE MET her at the airport, his deep blue eyes worried, his stocky frame restlessly pacing the concourse. He moved forward the instant he saw her coming toward him and caught her in a bear hug.

"Welcome home, honey," he said with a quick smile. "Are you okay? What happened? Why are you back so soon?"

She laughed nervously and tried not to cry. "Nothing terribly important, Uncle Mike, just a mix-up, that's all." She bit her lip and smiled through a mist, "I'm okay."

He searched her pale eyes and nodded. "We'll talk about it when we get home. Bill Hastings flew me up to meet you. We'll ride back with him in the Cessna."

"Jenny didn't come with you, I don't suppose?" she asked, clutching her single suitcase tightly until he calmly reached down and took it away from her before they started down the concourse.

"The flower club was meeting." He laughed. "Madam President couldn't relinquish her gavel for the trip. But she was as worried as me. Almost," he added dryly.

"I just cut the trip short, that's all."

"So you said." He threw a protective arm across her shoulders and grinned at her. "Welcome home, pilgrim," he repeated. "We missed you."

"I missed you, too," she said wholeheartedly, hugging

him back. It would be all right now. Everything would be all right; she was home.

But all the way to Ashton she only listened half-heartedly to the shouted conversation between her uncle and the pilot while her thoughts were back in Nassau with Cal. It seemed like someone else's trip, not her own, now that she was back. Time, which had slowed to a crawl on New Providence, was back on schedule again, and in the airport everyone had seemed to be in a maddening rush. The landscape below the four-place plane looked strange, too, because she'd become accustomed to the sight of palm trees and sandy beaches. Perhaps that would help, the fact that she wouldn't have the island to remind her of Cal with every step she took.

An hour later they landed at the Ashton airport and Mike's big Thunderbird was a welcome sight. Nikki slid in, leaning back contentedly against the black velour upholstery in the white car's interior. Even in the blazing heat of a Georgia July, it was comforting.

"I need to get an update on the planning committee's recommendations for upgrading this airport," Mike muttered as he cranked the car and turned on the air-conditioning. "That might be a good one for you, Nikki," he added as he backed out of the parking spot and headed the car toward the highway.

"I've still got the background material you loaned me to do that last update with," she replied absently. Her eyes were staring blankly out the window at the flat landscape with the thick hardwood trees far on the horizon. Closer was the imposing skyline of Ashton.

Ashton was older than the Civil War, having been founded in 1850. It had flaunted its own proud company, the Ashton Rifles, as part of the Confederate army. Two of Nikki's great-uncles had been members of it, one of whom died at the battle of Cemetery Ridge. The other survived to a ripe old age in Ashton.

A statue of a Confederate soldier stood guard over the town square, while dozens of small businesses huddled in a neat, wide circle around it amid clean air and pretty little trees. The square boasted a large park with benches and sidewalks and masses of flowers donated and cared for by the Ashton Garden Club.

Although Ashton wasn't technically a small town, it wasn't a big city, either. It was a nice medium-sized city with a small-town personality: plenty of parking space, good police and fire departments, a daily newspaper, two radio stations and the weekly newspaper that Mike Wayne's family had founded sixty-five years before. And it was one thing more. It was Nikki's home.

Her eyes lingered on the newspaper office, tucked between the Ashton Pharmacy and the Clinton brothers' five and dime store. It was an unimposing little office, with the bulk of its operation tucked away in the back, and Nikki had her own office, next to Mike's. There was one other reporter, "Red" Jones, a typesetter and an advertising representative.

"Missed it, did you?" Mike asked shrewdly, watching her eyes scan the block for the office.

"I missed a lot of things," she said with a smile. "The refrigerator, mostly."

He chuckled. "For the ice, no doubt."

"And the water. And the soft drinks. And the food." She sighed. "I didn't think I'd ever be cool again. But it was a lovely trip, and I'll be your friend for life if you won't ask me any more about it."

There was a brief pause before he answered. "Okay, honey, if that's how you want it. Now, let's see if we can get enough together to make some sandwiches with before your aunt gets back from her meeting. Then," he added with a grin, "we'll go back to work. Suit you?"

"Oh yes, it sure does," she said enthusiastically. "Ridiculous as it may sound, I've missed my job, too."

"You love it." He shrugged. "People should enjoy what they do for a living, Nikki. Life is too short to work for the paycheck alone. Money isn't the bottom line."

"To some people, it is," she said sadly.

He glanced at her curiously, but he didn't say anything. Mike Wayne was a veteran reporter, and he read his niece well enough to know that something had upset her pretty badly. But he knew, too, that he'd never be able to pry it out of her. In her own good time, and when she felt ready, she'd talk about it. That was the best part of having Nikki around, that she never tried to hide things from them. She'd been a pitiful little girl, all nervousness and thin limbs and uncertainty. God knew he'd loved her like his own, and Jenny had, too. Maybe they didn't have kids of their own, but Nikki sure felt as if she were. He'd wanted to adopt Nikki years before her parents died. If they'd really wanted her, they had a strange way of showing it. They'd been too wrapped up in each other to care much about Nikki. They never seemed to say more than a few words to her, or to touch her or smile at her.

The Waynes had always gotten along well with Jenny's brother and his wife, but Mike hadn't taken to them privately. He resented their treatment of Nikki, their thoughtlessness. He remembered one Christmas when she was about ten; her parents hadn't even bought her a present. Christmas Day, at the family dinner, her father had handed her a five-dollar bill and told her to go get what she wanted. Mike had wanted to get up out of his chair and deck him.

But for Jenny's sake he'd bitten his tongue almost through and finished his turkey.

Now, holidays and special occasions always got remembered; Mike saw to it. He liked to think he'd made up some of those dark years to that lonely little girl.

The Wayne home was neoclassical in styling, with deep blue shutters around its windows and a fanlight above the front door, which tempted the imagination with its intricate, delicate pattern. The grounds were lushly green and shady, as dogwoods, pines and pecan trees mingled around the dark green hedge that separated the circular drive from the house and grounds. Azaleas were in full, glorious bloom, along with the crepe myrtle and wisteria. Jarrat Wayne had built the house the same year he opened the newspaper for operation sixty-five years before. Nikki loved every line of it, and the history it imparted. It was a copy of a much older house Jarrat had seen in the eastern part of the state. His wife had fallen in love with the design, so Jarrat had it copied for her.

"I just had the swimming pool cleaned," Mike told her as he drove the car up to the front walkway and cut off the engine. "Go on in, honey. I'll bring the suitcase."

"Left the door unlocked again, did we?" Nikki teased as she opened the car door and got out.

Mike looked uncomfortable for a minute, sweeping a hand through his silvered black hair. "Well, hell, I only flew to Atlanta and back..."

"Someday," she echoed Jenny's eternal argument, "some happy burglar is going to come and carry away every single possession you and Jenny have."

"Every single possession we have wouldn't bring ten dollars," he scoffed. "You know I'm not stupid enough to keep valuables in the house. I don't even buy cheap original paintings anymore."

"How about that antique table that belonged to your great-grandfather's aunt in the West Indies, made of mahogany?" she asked, waiting for him to catch up with her. "And how about the grandfather clock in the hall that Uncle Cecil brought over from Ireland? And how about..."

"So I'll start wearing the key to the house around my neck on a chain," he grumbled, gripping the suitcase tightly as he stomped up the steps and threw open the door for her. "Nag, nag, nag..."

She laughed delightedly, feeling her old self for the first time since she'd left with Cal. It was good to be home.

"Don't you feel like a swim?" Jenny asked later, when they were relaxing on the patio after a huge supper. "It's a hot night."

Nikki glanced toward her tall, well-endowed aunt, who was still dressed in slacks and a tent blouse in a shade of green that matched the eyes she and Nikki shared. Nikki's late father had eyes the same shade.

"I don't see you beating any paths toward a bathing suit," Nikki murmured, laughing at her over a tall glass of sweetened iced tea.

"My figure loses something in the translation." Jenny Wayne laughed. She leaned forward, resting her forearms on her knees, and studied Nikki's slender figure in the casual white sundress. "You look lovely in white, dear. You should wear more of it. By the way, did Mike tell you the news?" she asked, and her tone made Nikki feel apprehensive.

She sat up straighter in the wrought iron chair. "What news?" she asked.

"That's what I thought," she muttered. "Leave poor old Jenny to do the dirty work while he hides in the bathroom."

"What news?" Nikki repeated.

Jenny took a deep breath. "That Ralley's back."

Bad luck seemed to come in bunches, Nikki thought as she sipped her iced tea and tried to look nonchalant. "Is he?"

"Oh, don't play it cool with me," Jenny grumbled. "Who sat up with you all night the day he married Leda and patted you while you cried? Remember me? Long-suffering Aunt Jenny, who loves you like a daughter?"

Nikki had to smile at that. She gave her aunt a quick glance. "Okay, long-suffering aunt. I heard you. I just don't know what to say. I thought I loved Ralley, but now I'm almost sure I didn't. I was just in love with love. He's a good reporter, and Mike's lucky to have him back. But as to how I feel about it." She sighed, shrugging. "I don't feel anything. I'm just too numb."

"Not over the flood," Jenny said with a shrewd glance over the troubled pixie face, the downswept thick dark lashes. "So what went on in Nassau?"

Nikki's fingers curled around the frosty, sweating glass. She rocked it gently, listening to the soft, musical tinkle it made. "I met someone," she said.

"You come home looking like a dog whose owner was just run over by a van, with shadows under both eyes and a bitter little smile that says more than you think, and all that boils down to three words. Okay, fair enough. Who, what, where, when, how and why?"

"I forgot that Mike found you doing rewrites for a daily newspaper." Nikki laughed with a sparkling emerald glance.

"I could have won a Pulitzer," Jenny said haughtily. "I

just didn't want to deprive the other staffers of all that opportunity."

"Which means, translated, that after you covered your first wreck, you decided the rewrite desk was a nicer memory to take home to supper," Nikki replied. "Right?"

The older woman made a face at her. "Now, if you're through trying to drag red herrings across my feet, how about telling me the truth? If you're ready to, of course. Never let it be said that I tried to pry."

"It's nothing, really," she replied quietly, her eyes faraway and sad. "I met a very nice man, we went sightseeing together and had a great time. But he was really out of my league. I doubt anything'll come of it."

"Nothing!" Jenny threw up her hands. "What do you mean he was out of your league? Was he rich? Famous?"

"Oh no," Nikki lied. She didn't want anyone to know Cal's identity, much less Mike and Jenny. Love her they did, but Mike wouldn't be above calling up Callaway Steel to give him a piece of his mind if he knew who'd upset the apple of his eye. And Jenny had no secrets at all from Mike; it was one of the reasons their marriage was such a good one.

"He was just an upper-crust man," Nikki said finally, "with an oversize ego."

"Not going to tell me a thing, are you?" Jenny laughed at the expression on Nikki's face. "Don't worry. I won't try to pump you. I know what a sucker you are for tears." She smiled gently. "You really fell for him, didn't you, honey? It happens like that sometimes. I saw Mike, and I knew. Just that fast."

Nikki's pale green eyes clouded. "I wouldn't have believed anyone could care so much, so soon. Oh, Jenny, it hurts so!"

Jenny got up and took the shorter woman in her arms, rocking her, comforting her, as she had years ago when her mother died of a brain tumor and, six months later, when her father ran his truck into the river. She was good at giving comfort to Nikki, she thought sadly; the girl had gone through so much tragedy in her life. Leda's death had been the last straw. She was glad Nikki had found someone to share a few smiles with on that trip. God knows she'd needed it desperately. And if a few tears were the price, they were surely worth it. Nikki's pride would heal, and so would her heart. It was her memories that worried Jenny. She held Nikki closer and stroked her hair.

RALLEY HALL WAS tall and blond and blue-eyed, and Nikki had loved him with all her heart. But when she walked into the office and found him sitting behind the newspaper's editorial desk, she didn't feel anything at all except a friendly warmth and sympathy.

"Hello, Ralley," she said gently, shaking his hand while Mike Wayne watched nervously. "How are you?"

He shrugged. "Coping," he replied with a faint smile. "I sold the house and moved back here," he added. "The memories were too much. Even the job reminded me of her." His face contorted, and she saw the sadness in it for an instant before he erased it. He'd looked like that at the funeral.

"You'll enjoy being back," she assured him, trying to keep her memories out of the way. "Mike might even let you do the update on the airport, if you bribe him with a fifth of bourbon."

Ralley jumped right in, staring over Nikki's shoulder at the older man. "Really?" he asked with arched eyebrows.

"Depends on the brand," Mike said with a grin.

Ralley mentioned a well-known one, and Mike nodded.

"It's yours. Just as well—Nikki doesn't know the fuselage from the altimeter."

"I do so!" she said indignantly. She tossed back her short, dark hair with a haughty hand. "I'll have you know I could have been the poor woman's Wright brothers with just a little more training."

"Remember that airplane model I got you for Christmas two years ago?" Mike asked her. "The one you put the wings on upside down?"

Her face flushed. "They weren't marked."

"Most people know what they look like."

"I got the propeller in the right place," she reminded him. "One out of two isn't bad."

"Weren't you going to interview the mayor on that new water system we're getting federal funds to build?" he asked her.

"Right!" she said, backing out of the office. "You bet. I'm on my way. Good to have you back, Ralley."

Ralley smiled, and it was genuine. "It's good to be back," he said, and meant it. It was in his whole look.

"Pictures," Mike reminded her.

She made a face. "I'll forget to put film in the camera again," she protested.

"I already loaded it. Bye!"

She shook her head as she walked toward her own office. "Oh, the perils of being a journalist..." she mumbled.

The next few days went by in a rush. Nikki forced herself to keep busy, not to think about the past at all. She and Ralley were still a little distant with each other, but she was beginning to understand Mike's reason for bringing the reporter back. Ralley was a good editorial writer, one of the best. He got his facts straight, and he wasn't afraid to state them, despite the flak. He wouldn't pass the buck to Mike, either. If an irate reader called, Ralley talked to him, soothed him, explained his point of view and listened to the reader's. He'd matured a lot in the past year, ever since Leda's death. But what Nikki had once felt for him was gone forever.

On the other hand, Ralley was noticing Nikki in a way he hadn't before, even when they were engaged. She'd just been someone to go around with back then, pretty and cute and sparkling. But Nikki had changed, too; she was much more of a woman now, and Ralley found himself regretting his impulsive elopement with Leda. Not that he hadn't cared for Leda; he had. But no one knew how strained the marriage had become in the past few months. Leda and he had been perfect together physically. She'd given him something that Nikki had never tried to give. Where Nikki was chaste and reserved and unresponsive, Leda had been a veritable volcano. She'd captivated him, and he'd let himself be led to the altar. But once the first few weeks of marriage had dampened those high-burning fires, he'd begun to notice things about Leda that he hadn't noticed before the marriage. She was lazy. She didn't like housework, she hated to cook, she wanted to be with him constantly. He couldn't even escape her in the evenings; she followed him around like a puppy. In desperation he'd suggested that she might enjoy a job of her own, but she'd refused flatly to go to work. She had a husband to do that. All she needed to do was look beautiful and make sure his clothes went to the cleaners once a week.

Probably they'd have wound up in divorce court eventually, but Ralley wasn't sharing that tidbit with anyone. Let them think it was the perfect marriage; it would be better for all concerned, especially for him. If Nikki felt sorry for him, he might have a chance of winning her back. This new

Nikki was exciting, and he sensed a new maturity in her. And since there was obviously no other man in her life, she'd probably never gotten over him. He'd smiled secretively at the thought. How sweet of her to pine over him. Perhaps he wouldn't have to try too hard after all.

It should have gotten better. She should have been able to put Cal in the back of her mind and finally blot him out of it entirely. But each day the wanting was worse, the ache was worse, until she wound up awake until two and three o'clock every morning, pacing, pacing, like a caged little animal.

Her mind fed on him, on bits and pieces of memory that she threaded and sewed into a silken veil to clothe the raw wound inside her that being without him had caused. She went to work mechanically, she did interviews, she wrote stories, she took pictures, she helped make up the paper, she stripped in corrections and wrote headlines. But nothing she did gave her any pleasure. She grew melancholy and pale, and even Ralley began to notice how dull her emerald eyes had become, how her steps dragged. She barely ate at all anymore, drinking cup after cup of black coffee and walking the floor at night.

Cal was probably out with a new woman every night, she told herself, and cried just at the thought of another woman holding him, touching him, caressing him with her eyes as Nikki had, loving him...

She was literally mourning him, and nothing eased the pain, nothing lessened the gnawing hunger for him.

Late on Friday night she was reluctantly watching a police drama with Mike when Jenny went to answer the phone.

"Nikki, it's for you," Jenny called, and there was a note in her voice that puzzled the younger woman.

Nikki lifted the receiver and said, "Hello," bracing herself to fend off Ralley one more time.

"Hello, yourself," came a deep, unmistakable voice from the other end of the line.

She felt a tingle of excitement the length of her body and had to sit down because her knees buckled. *Easy, girl*, she told herself. *Easy.*

"How are you?" she asked politely.

"How the hell do you think I am?" he growled. "You don't sound so good yourself."

She cleared her throat. "I've been working hard," she told him.

There was a muffled curse. "Look, meet me at the Ashton airport in an hour."

It was like an electric shock, lifting her from the chair. "Do what!" she burst out.

"You heard me. One hour." And the line went dead.

She sat there looking at the receiver with the same expression a fisherman would have on his face if he threw in his line and pulled out a chicken dinner.

"Well, was it him?" Jenny and Mike chorused, watching her from the doorway of the living room.

She nodded.

"Is he coming here?" Jenny asked, poised to grab a broom and a mop and head for the stove to cook.

"I think so. He said to meet him at the airport in an hour."

"He's coming." Jenny took off like a shot.

"I'll put some ice in the cooler for drinks," Mike murmured, following her.

Nikki clutched the receiver against her, cradling it, rocking it, while she finally let the tears loose.

She was sitting at the airport in Mike's T-bird fifteen

minutes before Cal was due, with the doors locked and the CB unit on as Mike had made her promise, since the airfield was deserted. The airport manager's family lived in the mobile home just beside the apron, and their lights were still on. Mike had probably called them, too, Nikki thought with a smile. He and Jenny were like a couple of mother hens with a chick over her. It was good to have people care about you, even if they did carry it to extremes. Nikki didn't know what her life would have been like if it hadn't been for them.

A droning sound caught her attention. She straightened her white shirtwaist dress and primped in the rearview mirror under the dome light, making sure her face looked its best with the hint of soft pink lipstick, her dark hair curled toward her face in a soft style that she hoped suited her. Her fingers trembled as she nudged it into place; her heart was shaking her in its fury.

A small jet dropped down onto the runway with precision point landing, coming easily to a stop to turn and taxi onto the apron. On the side was painted STEEL AVIATION.

Nikki was already standing on the pavement, her eyes straining to see the door opening in the spill of the nearby streetlights.

A tall, big man in a pale suit came quickly out of it and stepped decisively toward her. Before he made another move, she was running to him, her arms open, her eyes blurring him as tears veiled them.

"Cal!" she cried.

His arms opened as she reached them. He caught her, lifted her, crushed her against him, finding her mouth with his in one smooth, rough motion to take it as if it had belonged to him since time immemorial. She clung, giving him back the kiss, holding him, sobbing wildly as the world melted away in her mind and there was only the feel of his arms and his mouth, the scent of him, the reality of him. It was like coming home after a long, lonely journey.

"Am I hurting you?" he whispered huskily against her mouth. "Nikki, am I hurting?"

"No." She kissed him back hungrily. "Oh no! Cal, I've missed you…"

His mouth broke against hers again and again, tasting, touching, demanding. There had been a slight chill in the air, but she was warm now, wrapped up so closely against his massive frame, safe and protected in the circle of his big arms.

She gave him everything that she had in the way of response, holding back nothing. Her body seemed to burn everywhere it touched him, aching, clinging to the powerful lines of his.

"I'll always belong to you," she whispered breathlessly. "Whether you want me or not…"

"I want you," he said in a deep, rough tone.

She leaned her forehead against his chin, fighting to catch her breath. Her body felt molten, liquid, and she clung to him for support.

His breath came with as much difficulty as hers. He stood quietly, holding her until his hard, heavy pulse calmed, until the faint tremor went out of his powerful arms.

"My aunt's in the kitchen, cooking," she whispered. "Can you stay?"

"Only the night," he murmured quietly, "I'm due in Panama City by six o'clock tomorrow night for an early meeting with some of my staff. I just stopped by to see you."

"Oh, I see." She took a small, hurting breath.

"No, I don't think you do." He smiled.

"Would your pilot like to come along?" she asked, glancing back toward the plane.

He eyed her with faint amusement. "I founded Steel Aviation and you're asking who flew me?"

Her eyes went from the plane back to him. "I thought it was oil."

"Oil came first. When I had the money, I went into hotels and aviation." He smiled at her confusion. "I like airplanes, don't you?"

"Oh yes, but I don't think I could fly a jet. Even a baby jet."

"I'll teach you." He slid an arm around her shoulders and pulled her close against his side. "Oh God, you feel good to me," he murmured, brushing his mouth against her temple. "I didn't know how lonely I was until I left you. I'm sorry this has to be such a short visit. But I'll be back again in a week—on your birthday. Don't you forget. I'll be at your house at 5:00 p.m. sharp to pick you up. Okay?"

She smiled up at him, her face brightening. "Okay." He held the car door open for her, but when she sat behind the wheel, he slid in and pushed her aside with his bulk. "Move over," he said. "Nobody drives me except me. Not even you."

"Well, I like that!" she said indignantly, giving him just enough room to fit under the steering wheel. He slid the seat back to allow his long legs room enough to fit under the wheel and lifted an eyebrow at her.

"Woman's libber," he accused.

"Male chauvinist pig," she came right back.

He laughed as he pulled the car away from the airport. "You color the world for me," he murmured. "I think I'd forgotten how to laugh, how to play, until you came along."

She lowered her eyes, the memory of that night between them, but she smiled. "I'm glad you think so."

"Well, direct me, unless you want to drive around in circles all night!" he teased, and she turned her attention to getting them home.

When they arrived at her door, she got out of the car in a fog, allowing herself to be escorted up the steps and into the house.

"Don't they ever lock this door?" Cal asked when he discovered that he didn't need the key Nikki had handed him.

She laughed softly. "Uncle Mike forgets. Someone constantly nags him about it, but I think it's gotten to the revenge stage now."

"I like this architecture," he murmured, studying the entrance hall and the staircase. "Neoclassical, isn't it?"

"Yes, and there's quite a story behind it. Remind me to tell you someday." She took off her light jacket and tossed it on the back of the sofa in the living room. Mike and Jenny were nowhere in sight.

Cal took off his suit coat and loosened his tie. "God, it's hot here," he murmured.

"We used to have air-conditioning," she said apologetically, rising to turn on the big window fan, "but Mike got a horrible allergy to it and we had to take it out. Fortunately it doesn't stay this hot year-round, and he isn't allergic to heat. Don't you want to change into something..."

"More comfortable?" he suggested with a grin.

She flushed, glancing away from his wicked gaze. "I thought that suit might be hot."

"It is. Care to help me take it off?"

She opened her mouth to speak, but he was having such fun at her expense, it seemed a shame to spoil it.

She walked over to him and began to unfasten, slowly,

the buttons on his silky vest. Her eyebrows levered up at the expression on his broad, dark face. "You asked for help. I'm only trying to be hospitable."

His big chest rose and fell roughly under a skirl of deep, pleased laughter. "Imp," he murmured, reaching down to jerk her body against him. "Delightful, little pixie." The smile vanished, and his eyes were lonely, still. "My God, I've been lonely, Nicole!"

It was like coming back to life after being buried. All the weight of depression lifted, floated up, soared away, and her eyes burned on his face like pencils making sketches. He was so good to look at, to touch, to be held by. And she'd missed him unbearably. She recognized that loneliness in his eyes, because it was a mirror of her own.

"Cal, I've missed you, too," she whispered fervently. She bit her bottom lip, searching his face, his eyes, hungrily. All at once her arms went up to him and he lifted her, crushed her against his big, warm body. "Kiss me..." she pleaded, her voice breaking, splintering as his dark head bent and his mouth took hers.

He was rough this time, as if the waiting had worn him, tried his patience, as if he'd never expected to see her again in this life.

"I missed you," he repeated against her eager, soft mouth, his voice deep, husky, his arms hurting as they crushed her into his huge frame. "You took the sunlight with you, the music... God, Nicole, I've been lonely before, but never like this."

She went up on tiptoe to give him back the kiss, all sensation, all woman. She felt him tremble in her arms with a sense of wonder at her own power.

"Come home with me," he groaned. "It's a huge town house. There's more than enough room..."

"And be what, Cal?" she asked quietly, searching his eyes.

"My woman," he said.

She shook her head with a sad, hurting smile. "There's another name for a woman who lets herself be kept by a man. I don't want it." She drew away from him. "Besides," she said, staring out the dark window, "I have my own life here, a job I enjoy, roots… We did agree not to make any commitments, didn't we?"

He was silent for a long moment before he spoke. "I guess we did," he said curtly. His eyes were accusing as they met hers. "I knew you were going to be trouble the minute I laid eyes on you," he added.

She smiled despite the heartache that was eating at her. The temptation to give in was great. But not as great as her own self-respect, and she couldn't sacrifice that to become an expensive plaything. She went back to him, reaching up to kiss him again. "Let's live one day at a time, okay?" she asked softly.

He grimaced. "I suppose we'll have to. Flying visits, like this, phone calls…" His mouth crushed down against hers. "Never mind, just kiss me and ease the ache a little."

Mike and Jenny came in together a few minutes later, exchanging smug glances when they found Cal and Nikki deep in conversation in the living room. Nikki looked up, only just realizing that they must have gone for a drive to give her some privacy with Cal, and she flushed as she met Jenny's eyes.

She made the introductions, noticing the easy way Cal was with her aunt and uncle, as if he'd known them for years. He and Mike spent the rest of the evening discussing stocks, bonds, politics and aviation, while Jenny and Nikki murmured and listened.

"How about some more coffee?" Jenny asked finally, "I've got a pie in the refrigerator..."

"None for me, thanks," Cal said, rising. "It's been a long day for me, and if you don't mind an unsociable visitor, I think I'll have an early night. I'll have to fly out tomorrow afternoon for a meeting in Panama City."

"Mike will show you which room," Jenny said with a smile. "We're glad you could stay, and I'm sure Nikki is," she added.

Cal smiled at Nikki, his eyes possessive. "I hope so," he murmured. "Good night, honey."

"Good night, Cal," she murmured.

"Oh, you've got tomorrow off," Mike called over his shoulder. "You can't leave Mr. Steel to sit around the house alone."

"Cal," their guest corrected. "I'm only Mr. Steel to my enemies." And, with a grin, he left the room.

"Now," Jenny began when they heard a door close upstairs, "do tell me all about that nice small businessman you met in Nassau. Remember, the one with the oversize ego..."

"I should have his ego," Mike moaned as he rejoined them, dropping down into his big armchair by the dark window. "A corporate giant, in my home."

"Reach for your pad, and I'll strangle you," Nikki said mutinously. She stood over her uncle with hard eyes. "He's a guest, not a walking news story. Okay?"

Mike grimaced. "Nikki..."

"Promise me, Uncle Mike," she wheedled, "or I'll tell Aunt Jenny about that blonde stewardess..." she added in a whisper.

His jaw dropped. "That was completely innocent!" he whispered back.

"It won't be when I get through with it. Well?" she asked.

His face pouted, his blue eyes met hers accusingly. "I may never forgive you," he reminded her.

"It won't be the first time, either," she said gaily.

"I do occasionally read financial magazines," Mike said. "Callaway Steel is something of a legend among tycoons, you know."

"He is something, period." Jenny sighed. "Oh, if I were a few years younger, and Mike wasn't so sexy..."

"He's a good bit older than you are, Nikki," Mike said gently.

She sighed. "I know. But it doesn't matter. We're only friends, Mike." Her voice was more wistful than she knew.

"He looks like he'd be dynamite," Jenny murmured.

"He is." Nikki sighed, walking right into the trap.

"And don't hand me that 'just friends' routine," Jenny added with a wink. "He didn't come all this way just to say hello. By the way," she added, patting Nikki's cheek as they went into the hall ahead of Mike, "your lipstick's smeared."

Nikki wouldn't have touched that line with a shotgun. "Good night," she called as she raced up the stairs.

"Is IT ALWAYS this quiet?" Cal asked lazily as he and Nikki lounged by the private lake under a towering oak tree on the grassy lawn the next morning.

"Most of the time," she agreed. She was lying on her stomach in a bright yellow sundress, watching Cal, who was stretched out on his back wearing slacks and an unbuttoned brown plaid shirt. His thick, dark hair was mussed and fell into unruly patterns on his broad forehead. It made him look younger, but those hard lines in his face were still very much present.

She tickled his imposing nose with a blade of grass,

laughing when he caught her wrist and pulled her over so that she was propped up on his broad, partially bared chest.

"I like you in yellow," he murmured, opening his eyes to study the peasant-blouse styling of the dress. "It suits your personality."

"Mushy?" she asked with arched brows.

He frowned. "How did you get that?"

"Well, you said it reminded you of my personality, and butter is yellow but mushy..."

He chuckled softly. "Your mind would fascinate a research scientist."

"Umm," she murmured. She only half heard him; she'd just discovered a faint dimple in his chin, and her fingers were tracing it.

"What I meant," he murmured back, linking his hands behind her, "was that you're sunny."

She smiled. "Thank you."

His dark eyes searched hers. "Life hasn't been kind to you," he said gently. "Neither have I, in a lot of ways. It's hard for me to trust people, Nikki."

"I know. It's hard for me, and I'm not rich," she said gently. Her soft eyes searched his. "Did you really think I was after you because of who you were that first day?"

"Yes," he admitted. He looked up through the leafy, sun-patterned branches of the oak. "It's an old ploy with women to pretend indifference to get a man's attention. You caught mine that first day, with that bathing suit tantalizingly visible under that next-to-nothing cover-up. You have gorgeous legs, Miss Blake."

She laughed disbelievingly. "But you were horrible...!"

"Self-defense," he said softly. "I wanted you on sight. I thought if I made you mad enough to stay away, I'd forget about you. Then you started running, and that old hunting instinct took over, in spite of my misgivings. When I found out you were a reporter, it all blew up in my mind."

"You don't trust reporters, I gather."

He met her eyes. "Nikki, I've been harassed to death by the press." His dark face seemed to stiffen. "You've heard about what happened, I gather? That my daughter was killed in an automobile accident and that my...wife died a few months later? The media had a field day with it. And every time I read another story speculating on Penny's death, I had to relive it all again."

"Penny was your wife, wasn't she?" she asked quietly.

He nodded. "A beautiful woman. Blonde, blue-eyed, utterly gorgeous. But it was only skin-deep. She hated me, she hated the idea of a child, she hated anything that took her away from her mirror and her admirers. She had two lovers the first year we were married." His jaw tautened. "I didn't love her. The marriage was more of a merger than anything else. But after Genene was born, I told her if I ever caught her with another man, if there was a breath of scandal, I'd cut her off without a cent and she'd never see Genene again. It was very effective, in one sense. She gave up men. But she substituted drugs for them."

"Didn't she care for you?" she asked, incredulous.

"No, honey. She gave what little affection she was capable of to Genene. There wasn't anything left over for anyone else. The night of the accident I was away at a conference. Penny decided to leave Genene with her grandmother so that she could go on to a party. She was high when she left the house." He took a slow breath. "She never made it. I'll never forget how I felt when the call came. It was just as well that it took me four hours to get home. I wanted to wring Penny's neck."

She could imagine how it must have been for him. Under

those layers of reserve he seemed to be a deeply emotional man; the kind who'd love completely, not holding anything back.

He flexed his broad shoulders, shifting. She started to get up, but his grip was formidable. "Penny sobered up pretty quickly after that, but she couldn't live with the guilt, not without some anesthetic. It kept taking more and more, and every time I'd send her off to be dried out, she'd start again. It reached the point where I couldn't even reason with her anymore. One night she took a few pills too many. It was already too late when the maid found her."

She searched his dark eyes. "And ever since, you've been asking yourself, 'What if...?'" she murmured.

He looked faintly shocked. "You don't miss much, do you?"

"I know how it is," she replied. "My mother died of a brain tumor—there was no help to be had. But my father and I had just had an argument the night he was killed." She dropped her eyes to the pattern of his shirt. "You know how kids can be. He and my mother were devoted to each other. They never had time for me. After she died, it was even worse. I'd gotten the lead in our school play, and it was the night we were putting it on. Dad refused to go, or even to drive me there. I ranted and raved about it until he slapped me." Her eyes closed on the memory. "I didn't say another word, and neither did he. He walked out the door. Thirty minutes later Uncle Mike came to get me." She sighed. "They said he was driving too fast for conditions. But it was suicide. He didn't want to live without Mother."

Cal's big arms swallowed her, drawing her gently down against him, comforting her, soothing her. His fingers worked in her hair in a slow, rhythmic motion, and she could feel the steady, strong beat of his heart against her breasts.

"What was your daughter like?" she asked softly.

His chest rose and fell slowly against her. "Like me, strangely enough," he murmured. The words came hesitantly, and Nikki sensed that he hadn't talked about it to anyone until now. Perhaps there wasn't anyone he could talk to, unless it was his mother.

"Dark?" she prompted.

"Dark hair, dark eyes. Tall, for her age. All legs and big eyes." He laughed gently. "She liked to climb trees, which horrified her mother. Ladies weren't supposed to do that, but Genene was a tomboy through and through. I bought her a horse and Penny went up like a rocket, but Genene was a born rider. We'd get up early every morning and go riding before I went to the office." He laughed shortly. "Once I walked out of a board meeting in the middle of a proxy fight to take Genene to a birthday party."

"What happened?" she asked.

"I won." He chuckled. "The deciding votes came from a stockholder who was delighted at the sight of a man willing to give up an empire for a birthday party."

She laughed with him. "But you didn't do it for that reason, I don't imagine."

"No, I didn't. Hell, anytime they think I'm not showing enough profit, they can throw me out with my blessing. But that hasn't happened, and it won't happen." His arms tightened. "I had cake and ice cream with the kids. Genene won a prize for pinning the tail on the donkey. You'd think she won the Nobel Prize, the way she beamed." He drew in a short breath. "A week later she was dead. I've thanked God on my knees ever since that I didn't tell her I was too busy to take her to that birthday party." He sighed heavily. "If only I'd been at home…"

She drew away far enough to look down into his dark, sad eyes. She laid a finger across his hard, chiseled mouth. "You couldn't have prevented it if you'd been standing across the street," she said gently. "Any more than I could have taken my father's foot off the accelerator, or stopped my mother from getting a brain tumor… Cal, I don't pretend to know all the answers. But God sees farther down the road than we do. Perhaps He's protecting people from something we can't foresee by drawing them to Him." She smiled quietly. "I like to think of it that way, at least."

Her fingers traced his mouth; her eyes lingered on the chiseled curve of it. Impulsively, she leaned down and brushed her lips over it, feeling a delicious shiver of sensation at the light contact.

"Do you mind?" she whispered achingly.

His chest rose and fell quickly, heavily. "I need it as much as you do, Nikki," he replied in a deep, taut whisper. "I need you…"

His arms brought her down to him, and he made a harsh, muffled sound as her mouth opened over his. The action tightened the arms around her bruisingly as he whipped her across his big body and onto her back in the lush, green grass with the weight of his broad chest crushing her down into it.

His mouth was hungry, rough, slow and achingly thorough on the petal softness of hers. She felt the nip of his teeth against her full lower lip before his tongue drew a sensuous path over it, past it, in a sudden, sharp intimacy that dragged a moan from her throat.

Her arms slid under his, her hands easing past the hem of his cotton shirt to caress his warm, bronzed back over his hard, silky muscles. Her fingers dug into his back, tested its strength, as his mouth became more demanding on hers.

He levered away from her all at once, his eyes dark with unsatisfied desire, his jaw as taut as the muscles in his powerful arms as they supported him.

"No more, Nikki," he said in a husky voice. "We're getting in over our heads."

Her fingers lingered on the damp flesh of his back, her eyes mirroring the conflict that was going on inside her. She thought ahead involuntarily, to the end of the day when she'd watch him fly away and she'd stand on the runway and feel an emptiness like death inside. The thought took the light out of her eyes, the smile from her face. How was she going to manage life without Cal in it? Would the memories be enough?

He took a long draw from the cigarette he'd just lit and turned, his face more composed, his eyes calm if a little dark.

"It's just as well that we aren't still in Nassau," he said with a wry smile.

She made a face at him. "I used to think I had loads of willpower until you came along," she admitted shyly. "With Ralley, I was always reserved, very cool. He used to complain about it."

He didn't like that reference; she read the distaste in his dark eyes. "Ralley?" he asked.

"Ralley Hall. He, uh, came back to work for Uncle Mike this week," she added reluctantly.

Cal's dark head lifted sharply. "How convenient."

She hated the ice in that deep voice. She scrambled to her feet with worried eyes. "Cal, it was over long before the flood," she told him. "I gave him up the day he and Leda married, and I never wanted him back. I still don't."

His taut features relaxed a little. He took a long draw from the cigarette and studied its orange tip.

"Did you ever let him touch you the way I have?" he asked suddenly, staring straight across into her eyes.

"No, Cal," she replied. "Not ever."

He moved forward, dropping a careless big arm across her shoulders in a gesture that was more comradely than lover-like. "I'd like to see where you work," he said as they walked back toward the house.

Which meant, she thought nervously, that he wanted to see Ralley. At least he was that interested in her. But was it only a physical jealousy, or was he beginning to care?

She wasn't going to sacrifice her hard-won peace of mind to that kind of reflection, she decided firmly.

"Suppose we drive by the office then?" she asked pleasantly.

He nodded. "That suits me."

Now, if only the police would arrest someone important so that Ralley would have to leave the office to cover the story...

She should have expected to find her former fiancé in his office, poring over the week's columns to check them for errors and make sure they'd fit the space he'd allowed.

He stood up when Nikki walked in with Cal at her side. Cal had exchanged his casual clothes for a dark blue blazer with an open-necked white silk shirt and white trousers. He looked like a fashion plate, and Nikki wanted more than anything to show him off. He was so good to look at.

But if she thought so, Ralley didn't. His blue eyes turned cold when they met Cal's, and that dislike was reflected in the older man's dark, piercing eyes.

"How do you do?" Ralley asked as if he couldn't have cared less, when Nikki introduced them.

He held out his hand, but Cal hesitated a few seconds before he took it, treating it like dead meat.

"This is the editorial office," Nikki said, jumping in. "Ralley is our news editor. He does most of the editorial writing and substitutes for me at city and county council meetings when I'm tied up elsewhere. He edits column copy, too."

"Nikki's never needs editing," Ralley murmured, giving Nikki his most ardent look. He came around the desk to slide an arm affectionately around her shoulders, grinning when she stiffened in shock. "She's a super little writer," he added, "and I tell her so twice a day, don't I, darling?"

Cal didn't say a word; the expression on his broad face didn't change. But something in the gaze he pinned on Ralley's face made the younger man remove his arm and back away.

"I'll show you around," Ralley volunteered. "Thursdays aren't too hectic, except for phone calls protesting what people read when the paper comes out on Wednesdays. The really bad day is Tuesday, when we go to press. That's when we all scream and tear our hair out and curse the telephone."

"It rings like mad all day long," Nikki added with a tight smile. Cal was as remote now as if he'd been shot to the moon. She couldn't understand Ralley's brazen move any more than she could understand Cal's reaction to it. Surely he didn't believe there was anything between her and Ralley? Surely Ralley didn't think she still cared…!

"This is where the type comes from," Ralley told Cal, indicating a computer with a screen and a keyboard like a typewriter, with two extra narrow keyboards on either side. "It's a computerized system, brand-new, just like the big-city papers have. Reporters mostly set their own copy, but we have Billie to set the filler stuff and the legals," he added with a wink at the petite blonde behind the computer.

"Is the newspaper printed here?" Cal asked quietly.

"No," Nikki told him. "We have to carry it all the way to Mount Hebron, thirty miles away. At that, it's still less expensive than buying the setup we'd need to do it here. We do all the makeup and paste-up, get our own ads and make them up—everything, in fact, but the actual printing. Mike drives the paper down there Wednesday morning and we get it back by that afternoon. Then we all rush to the back, run the papers through the mailing plate machine to put the names on the local papers, bag the single wraps, and get it in the mail. It's in the boxes Thursday morning."

"And nobody comes by the office on Thursday and Friday, because they don't want to bother us while we're working on the paper," the redheaded reporter, aptly named Red Jones, piped in, pausing to introduce himself and short, dark Jerry Clinton to the newcomer.

"Nobody realizes that we do that on Monday and Tuesday." Clinton grinned. "It's a deep, dark secret."

"These two handle the police beat and the advertising, respectively," Nikki said. "We're all interchangeable, of course, and we all do makeup and paste-up."

"And Jenny keeps the books," Mike broke in, joining them. "Came to see if I was working, huh?" he teased Nikki.

Cal arched his eyebrows at the neat, orderly operation. "I expected to find a desk buried under reams of paper and old journalism books and yellowed back issues stacked on shelves. I'm impressed."

"You should have seen the place when my father was alive." Mike chuckled. "He used to inspect the office once a week wearing white gloves. God help the staff if he found dust. Care for some coffee? We have our own snack bar in the back."

"No, thanks," Cal replied before Nikki could open her mouth, "I've got some phone calls to make."

"See you at the house, then," Mike murmured, sensing undercurrents.

"Nice to have met you," Cal told the rest of the staff, his eyes stopping short of Ralley.

They echoed the polite remark. Ralley, seeing opportunity slamming at his door, moved forward and tugged a lock of Nikki's hair in an old, affectionate intimacy.

"See you later," he said, keeping his tone uniform with the gesture. "Take care of her, Mr. Steel," he added with a curt smile.

"Goodbye, Ralley," Nikki said, her glowing eyes promising retribution at the earliest opportunity. "Thanks for all your help."

Ralley ignored the sarcasm. No way was he going to let that big-shot outsider swipe his girl. He'd seen Nikki first, and he wasn't giving her up. He didn't plan to let her slip through his fingers this time. He'd been a fool to let her go, but Leda's charms had blinded him. He was older now, and wiser, and he wasn't going to hand Nikki over to some expensive stranger. She couldn't be serious about that big man, anyway; God knew he was years older than she was. Mike had mentioned something about him being a tycoon, but Ralley was skeptical. After all the guy could have been pretending. But even if he did have all that money, it wouldn't take the place of love. Nikki still loved him, he told himself smugly. All he had to do was prove it to her. He walked back into his office whistling.

"ARE YOU GOING to ignore me for the rest of the day?" Nikki asked as she and Cal sat down alone to a small lunch.

Cal glanced at her, dark-eyed and unapproachable, over his coffee cup. He'd been pleasant enough since that visit to the office, but it was all on the surface.

Cal was just as remote as he'd been on the drive home, and she wondered if a sledgehammer would dent him.

"I won't be here for the rest of the day," he said quietly.

"You're leaving?" she asked, her eyes wincing, her disappointment almost a physical ache.

"I'm a businessman. I've got too many irons in the fire to stay here." He finished his coffee.

She'd noticed that he'd changed into a beige suit, with a matching tie, that he was dressed for travel, not recreation. But she hadn't wanted to believe it. Now she had to.

She wasn't sure, but she thought she knew the reason he was leaving. If she was wrong, it was going to be horribly embarrassing. But if she wasn't, she'd have been a fool to keep quiet.

She laid her napkin beside her plate and drew in a steadying breath. "I am not having an affair with Ralley Hall," she said quietly. "I am not involved with him in any way. I can't explain why he put on that show for you, but that's all it was. A show."

"That isn't what he told me," he replied curtly, and his eyes were cold.

She frowned slightly. "But he didn't talk to you…"

He put down his own napkin and stood up. "I called him while you were fixing lunch." He shot back the cuff of his shirt and checked his watch. "I won't be able to wait until your aunt gets back from her shopping trip. Tell her I appreciate her hospitality very much. I've already thanked your uncle and phoned for a cab to take me to the airport."

She caught his arm hesitantly. "Cal, what did he tell you?" she asked, fearing the worst.

He looked down at her with the cruelest expression she'd ever seen. "Come on, honey, don't give me that. No wonder your conscience bothered you about your friend. Did she know you were seeing her husband behind her back?"

Her heart fell over in her chest. Ralley had told him that! How could he, how *could* he!

"It's not true!" she burst out, horrified. "Cal, you've got to believe me!"

He removed her hand from his jacket, gently but firmly. "I don't know what to believe anymore." His dark eyes searched her face narrowly. "You wanted him before he married your friend. You loved him, you said. Well, nothing's changed except that she's dead and he's free."

Nothing? she wanted to say. Everything had changed. And it hadn't been love she'd felt for Ralley—she knew that now for certain. It hadn't torn her heart out by its roots when Ralley had left; it had only hurt her pride. What she was feeling now made that remembered agony less painful than a pinch. Losing Cal was a little like dying. She didn't know how she was going to breathe when he was gone.

"Why won't you believe me?" she asked sadly. "Is it because you don't want to? Does it give you an excuse to keep from getting involved? You didn't have to worry about that. I wasn't going to try to trap you." She turned away and sat back down at the table. "I learned a long time ago that you can't make people want to be with you, any more than you can force them to love you." Her fingers reached for the half-full cup of coffee in front of her; she swallowed it down quickly and got to her feet, dabbing at her mouth with her napkin. "It was nice to see you again. If you'll excuse me, I'm already late for work."

She didn't look at him as she went out the door, hiding the tears that threatened to spill over onto her pale cheeks. Neither of them said a word about work, although they both knew Mike had told her she didn't have to come in.

As she drove with determined calmness down the driveway, she didn't even look back. She was hurting too much.

Ralley looked up sharply when she walked into his office and slammed the door behind her, shutting them off from the rest of the staff.

"Why?" she asked venomously. Her eyes were still red from the tears; her voice shook with controlled fury.

He knew what she meant. He got up from behind the desk with a conciliatory smile on his handsome face. "Now, honey, don't get all up in the air. He's an old guy, much too old for you."

"Is that what you told him?" she asked.

"Sure. It was the truth," he said defensively. He approached her, but she backed away, her eyes openly hating him.

"What else did you tell him?" she persisted.

He stopped, leaning his back against the desk, not so confident now. "That you loved me," he said hesitantly. "You do, don't you? You always did, even when I married Leda. I knew it. Nikki, I missed you," he said softly, leaning toward her. "Leda was a lovely girl, a sweet girl. But she wasn't you. If I'd just kept my head and waited, it would have blown over. We'd have got married..."

"And made each other miserable for the rest of our lives," she finished for him, certainty in her pale green eyes as they cut into his. "I was infatuated with you. God help me, I'd probably have gone through with the wedding if you hadn't eloped with Leda. But it's all over, Ralley. You're beating a dead horse. It's too late."

His lower lip protruded. "You're just upset," he said soothingly. "But you'll get over it," he added smugly, smiling at her before he went back to sit at his desk. "When you're calmer, we'll talk some more. You haven't got over me yet, Nikki. I'll show you."

"The only thing I want to see is your back walking away," she grumbled.

"Don't pretend you cared about the big man," he said sarcastically. "Maybe he had a fat wallet, but he was years too old for you. Besides," he added shrewdly, "what would a man like that want with a small-town girl like you? Maybe you were a novelty for a while, but you wouldn't fit into his kind of society and you know it."

She did, and it cut like a double-sharpened knife. She turned around and walked out of the office without bothering to reply. There was nothing she could say, anyway.

For the next week Ralley did everything but sit on her doorstep and play a flute to get her attention. He followed her to the local drugstore at lunch and sat with her until she started going home in desperation. She couldn't seem to move without bumping into him. When she heard the phone ring at night, she knew before she answered that it was Ralley with another invitation. He'd invited her out every night since Cal left, and she'd turned him down every time. She was too raw inside at what he'd done to want his company again, ever. But Ralley was persistent. It was what made him a good reporter. He never gave up.

"You're looking pale," Jenny remarked gently one day over a ham sandwich. She'd served it on the patio with the remark that Nikki needed some fresh air.

"It's from running," she replied lightly. "Ralley thinks he can get me back if he's persistent enough."

Jenny watched her closely while she bit into her sandwich. "Can he?" she murmured.

Nikki shook her head. She stared into her cup of black coffee, leaving all but one bite of the sandwich on her plate untouched. "I told him it was over, but he wouldn't believe me."

"What, exactly, did he tell Mr. Steel?" Jenny asked after a minute. "You haven't talked about it, and I haven't asked. But it's going to explode inside you if you don't let it out."

"I don't know all of it," she admitted bitterly. "He told him he was too old for me, and that I'd been seeing Ralley while Leda was alive, too, apparently."

Jenny ruffled indignantly. "Why didn't you tell Mike? He'd have thrown him out the door!"

"That's why," came the dry reply. "Ralley's a good reporter, Jenny. He only wants me because I'm not available. That was why he chased me the first time, years ago." She laughed softly. "Funny, I didn't like him at first. Now I don't like him at all." Her face fell. "Cal wouldn't believe me when I told him Ralley was lying."

"Then maybe he cared more than you knew," Jenny murmured. "He'll be back, honey. Just calm down."

"He won't be back." Nikki got to her feet. "Thanks for the sandwich. I've got to cover an emergency services meeting at city hall, then I'll be at the office."

Jenny only nodded, watching her niece walk stiffly away.

But being calmer didn't help to sort anything out. As the days went by, she found herself under siege again by Ralley, who seemed more determined than ever to get her back. She didn't flatter herself that it was love causing his acquisitive spurts. Ralley simply had a dogged determination to obtain anything that resisted him. It made him a good reporter—but a nagging suitor.

"I'm afraid to sit in the living room," she wailed to Jenny as they sat by the pool. "I expect to find him leering at me from behind the potted plant!"

"Won't give up, huh?" her aunt teased.

Nikki leaned forward, propping her chin on her hands. "Never. I'm so tired of dodging him. I seem to have done little else since I came back from Nassau." She laughed mirthlessly. "Funny, isn't it? There was a time, when he was sneaking around to see Leda, that I'd have given anything to make him care. And now it doesn't matter at all."

"Because now you're in love with someone else," came the wise reply.

She nodded. "Desperately," she admitted with a wan smile. "The question is, where do I go from here? I'm not kidding myself that Cal will ever want to marry me. He and I move in different circles, and he's told me himself that the thought of having another child terrifies him. He doesn't even want a commitment. He told me so." Her eyes clouded. "He hasn't even called me."

"You said he was going to be up to his ears in meetings," Jenny reminded her.

She laughed bitterly. "And that shows you the place I occupy in his thoughts, doesn't it? I'm not even as important as a board meeting. Do you know he walked out of a board meeting in the middle of a proxy fight to take his daughter to a birthday party?" she asked her aunt.

"It sounds like something he'd do," Jenny replied, smiling. "And remember, he came quite a long way to spend a day with you."

"But that was before…" She turned away. "It doesn't matter."

"I don't want to raise your hopes too high, my darling," the older woman said gently. "But he had the look of a man deeply in love."

Nikki sighed. "But, then, so did Ralley…once," she reminded Jenny with a faint smile. And before the subject had the chance to come around again, she got Jenny off on recipes.

Friday finally came. Her birthday, and Nikki had been nervous all day, wondering if Cal would remember his promise to take her to New Orleans. Mike had given her the afternoon off, swearing that she was of no damn use in the office except for wearing ruts in his floor. Ralley had overheard the conversation, and Nikki had the oddest feeling that he was up to something. But of course, he wouldn't have the opportunity to disrupt her plans again. She'd see to that.

Jenny had gone to visit friends, and Mike had to drive to Atlanta for a conference on an editing workshop he was helping with, so Nikki had the house to herself. In a way that was worse than having it full of people. She dressed in a two-piece white knit suit that showed her tan off to advantage and white strappy sandals. Then she paced the floor and bit her lip, eyeing the clock every few minutes and wondering.

Cal had said that they belonged to each other. But wasn't that pretty much what a man said when he'd been with a woman for the first time? He hadn't wanted the relationship to get that involved; he'd said so often enough. But he'd given in to his own hunger, and perhaps it was guilt that had caused his remarks. He'd been the first, and he knew it, and he was sometimes pretty old-fashioned in his outlook. He might be permissive, but he still harbored feelings of responsibility, and it wasn't inconceivable that he could be that way about Nikki.

She stared at the clock again. It was only ten minutes until five. If he was coming, he'd be there on time. Cal was nothing if not punctual.

Only ten more minutes and she'd see him again. Maybe only five more minutes. Her heart quivered madly in her taut body. It seemed like years since she'd seen him, held him. Centuries! It didn't matter if he didn't love her, as long as she could be with him for even a few minutes, see him, touch him. Oh God, she loved him so!

A sound caught her attention and she froze in the middle of the room. It was a car coming up the driveway. It was Cal!

She ran for the door as the car pulled up at the steps and she peered blindly through the curtains, trying to see through the layers of gauzy fabric...

She gave up and opened the door just as a tall man bounded up the steps. Her heart sank. It was only Ralley.

"What are you doing here!" she burst out.

"I've got to pick up something for Mike—if you don't mind," he added sarcastically.

"Oh, all right, but will you please hurry?" she ground out, peering around him toward the deserted driveway.

He went into the study and ruffled through some papers on the desk. His narrowed eyes studied her quickly.

"Uh, it sure is hot out there," he murmured, tossing her a brief glance. "Do you think I could have a small glass of wine—just to take off the top layer of heat?"

"Ralley...!"

"I know Mike keeps a bottle of port chilled." He grinned. "Come on, Nikki, have pity on a poor, hot reporter."

"All right, but just one glass," she muttered, running for the kitchen. "I'm going out."

He murmured something, but she didn't stay around long enough to hear it.

Her ears strained for the sound of a car as she poured him a glass of the chilled port from the refrigerator and raced back to the study to hand it to him.

"Umm," he murmured, sipping it. "That's delicious. Thanks, Nikki."

She was literally wringing her hands. Why didn't he go? The sound of a car caught her attention.

"It's Cal!" she burst out. But as she moved, so did Ralley, and seconds later, the port was all down the front of her white knit suit.

"Oh, Nikki, I'm so sorry!" he burst out, grabbing a handkerchief from his pocket. "Here…"

"That won't do, you idiot, I've got to change!" She couldn't let Cal see her like this! "Ralley, tell Cal I'll be right down!" she told him, and dashed up the stairs.

The minute she was out of sight, Ralley began to take off his clothes. By the time the doorbell rang, he was down to his briefs. He walked calmly to the door, with the wineglass still in his hand, ruffling his hair in the process. He wiped the smile off his lips just as he jerked the door open.

Cal, dressed in dark evening clothes with a shirt that probably cost more than Ralley's entire wardrobe, seemed to implode at the sight of the younger man.

"Where's Nikki?" he asked in a deep, softly dangerous tone.

"Upstairs, waiting for me, of course," Ralley drawled, lifting the empty glass. "She'll be sorry she missed you…"

"Cal!"

They both turned as Nikki gaped helplessly at the tableau below, dressed in nothing but her slip, the dark stain of the wine just faintly visible where it had seeped through. Her face contorted in something like agony. What Cal obviously believed was in his taut expression and she saw immediately that it was going to be useless to plead her case. Ralley smiled insolently, and Nikki wanted to strangle him with her bare hands.

"Hello, darling, look who's here." Ralley laughed.

Cal's huge fists clenched at his side. He didn't say a word to Nikki, but his dark eyes spoke volumes. He turned to Ralley and with a move so quick that Nikki missed it, he threw a shattering punch at the younger man. Ralley didn't have time to dodge it. It caught him square on the jaw and sent him sprawling sideways on the polished wood floor.

Cal's blazing eyes went from the fallen, groaning man on the floor to Nikki, frozen on the staircase.

"Excuse me for breaking up the party," he said in a voice that dripped ice water. "I thought we had a date, but obviously I was mistaken."

He spared Ralley a final, contemptuous glance before he opened the door and stormed out.

Tears bled down Nikki's pale cheeks. She couldn't remember a time in her life when she'd hurt as much.

Ralley dragged himself to his feet, gingerly touching his jaw. "He's got a punch like a mule," he groaned.

Nikki only stared at him, hurting like she'd never hurt before.

Belatedly he looked up and saw her face. He stood there, watching her with eyes in which comprehension began to shine. "You really love *him*, don't you?" he asked quietly.

She didn't even answer the question. "Please get dressed and go away," she said in a ghost of her normal voice. "You can't imagine how silly you look."

She turned and went back into her bedroom, closing the door firmly behind her.

There was a faint knock at the door.

"Nikki…" Ralley called through it, his voice sad, faintly embarrassed. "Nikki, he wrote telling you he was coming. I…I intercepted the note at the office. I'm sorry."

But she didn't answer him. She was crying too hard.

CHAPTER EIGHT

NIKKI WENT DOWNSTAIRS an hour later, when she'd had a bath she didn't need and put on a beige pantsuit and blotted her eyes for the tenth time. She'd cried until her eyes were raw. But all the tears in the river wouldn't bring Cal back, and she knew it.

Ralley had gone home, and it was beginning to get dark outside. Nikki poured herself a glass of wine and dumped it down her throat. She still felt miserable, so she refilled the glass and drank it down. Damn Ralley—when she got herself together enough, she was going to kill him. On second thought there must be something worse than that she could do to him. Perhaps she could write a false exposé on the police chief and publish it under his byline. She remembered the size and temper of the public official and smiled half-heartedly. Ralley would be turned into chili powder. Unfortunately so would Mike, who would be blamed for it. With a sigh she refilled the glass once more and sat down on the sofa.

It was just as well, she told herself. Cal lived in a different world. She'd never have been able to cope. Her eyes teared again and the hot, bright dots rolled pitifully down her cheeks.

Her mind went homing back to Nassau, to that unexpected night with Cal. All over again she could feel his hands, so tender, so wary of hurting her, his mouth blazing on her bare skin while he whispered words that still could make her blush.

She got up, almost tripping over the rug, and walked the floor, sipping at the red wine. She'd never see him again. She'd grow old and spend her miserable life trying to make do with memories. And it just wasn't going to be enough. All the memories on earth wouldn't amount to one minute with Cal.

"I always seem to love the wrong men," she grumbled, tossing off the rest of the wine. She stared into the empty glass, frowning slightly. Where had it gone so fast? Perhaps she'd spilled part of it. She remembered Ralley pouring the glass of wine down the front of her white outfit and her lips pouted wildly. Without thinking she flung the empty glass at the fireplace and watched it splinter. Good enough for it. It wouldn't stay full, anyway.

Bells sounded in her ears. She blinked. Surely she wasn't that drunk? She shook her head and listened. There it was again, that funny chiming... Of course, she thought with an off-center smile, it was the doorbell. Mike must have forgotten his key. Or it could be Ralley again...

She made her way toward the front door. If it was Ralley, she was going to kill him. She was debating on methods when she opened the door and found a ghost standing there.

Cal was still wearing his evening clothes, but his tie was untied and the top buttons of his expensive ruffled white silk shirt were undone. He looked tired, angry and exasperated, all at once.

Her lower lip trembled. "Oh, Cal," she whispered brokenly. Without thinking she held out her arms, wondering vaguely if he'd push her away.

He moved forward like a conquering army, jerking her against his big body to lift her while his mouth crushed down on hers. She felt the tremor shake him even while he deepened the kiss, his tongue penetrating, his breath sighing raggedly against her cheek as his arms contracted painfully around her.

Tears rolled helplessly down her cheeks when he finally paused long enough to take a breath. Her fingers caressed his broad, darkly tanned face, trembling.

"It wasn't true, it wasn't..." she whispered unsteadily.

"I know." He kissed her again, letting her body slide down his until her feet touched the floor, "I'm so sorry, darling," he whispered roughly. "God, I want you...!"

Her arms linked around his neck and they swayed together wildly, so lost in each other that they were aware of nothing else. Her thighs trembled against the hard muscles of his, and she thought wildly that if she died right now, it would be enough that she'd held him, kissed him, one last time.

"I love you," she whispered into his devouring mouth.

He trembled convulsively at the words, drawing back to look into her misty, wide eyes. "I love you, Nikki, for always," he whispered back, his voice shaky, his eyes punctuating the incredible statement.

"But...you said..." she faltered.

He smiled faintly. "I know. But that was before I tried to function without you." He drew in a steadying breath, taking time to reach behind him and close the door.

"You were so angry," she whispered, searching his dark, soft eyes, "I was afraid you were gone for good. Ralley intercepted your note—I never even saw it—and he staged that whole scene. He spilled wine on me and when I went upstairs to change..."

He smoothed the hair back from her tearful face. "Hush, darling, it's all right, I'm here now." He bent and kissed the tears from her eyes. "I remembered when I got to the airport that there was a wine stain on your slip and an empty glass in his hands. And along with that, I remembered something else."

"What?" she asked, smiling wetly.

He brushed his mouth across hers. "That you loved me," he said simply. "So I came back."

Her lips trembled, her eyes widened. "You could have gone away, and I'd never have seen you again…"

"That's not likely." He lifted her, carrying her easily into the living room, to sit down in Mike's big armchair with Nikki in his lap.

She nuzzled her face into his warm throat. "I wanted to kill Ralley…"

He chuckled softly. "Hush, it's all over. I'm here, and I love you."

"That's the second time you've said it," she whispered.

His big arms tightened. "If I keep saying it, perhaps you'll begin to believe it." He eased her head back on his shoulder so that he could see her face. "Didn't you hear what I told you before I left the last time? That we belonged to each other?"

"I thought it was just because you were the first…"

He sighed deeply. His fingers toyed with the hair at her ear. "Nikki, all the time I was spouting those clichés about not wanting commitment, I was making plans. Hundreds of them, and they all included you. Vacations in France, buying a house outside Chicago, buying furniture none of which I could picture without you. And something else, something more " He tilted her eyes up to his. "Nikki, the next time we make love, I'm not going to hold back. I want a child with you."

That was the final surrender, she thought wildly, that was total commitment.

Her fingers traced the lines of his hard, chiseled mouth, "I'd like very much…to give you a child," she whispered softly. "Very, very much."

"Then suppose you put this on," he murmured, drawing a box out of his pocket, "and we'll go somewhere and discuss it."

She turned the black velvet box in her hands curiously before she opened it over a blaze of emeralds. Her breath stopped as the two rings filled her gaze. An engagement ring and a wedding band ringed around with emeralds and diamonds. She looked up at him.

"Cal…?"

"I'm good in bed," he reminded her. "And I don't have many bad habits."

She laughed through her tears as she buried her face against him. "Oh, I love you so!"

He laughed gently. "When do Mike and Jenny get home?" he asked.

She drew back and sat up. "Oh, not for three or four hours at least," she murmured, peeking up at him through her lashes.

Without another word he got up, lifting her with him, rings and all, and started up the staircase. She clung to him, her eyes full of emeralds and babies and the long, sweet years ahead.

* * * * *

FIT FOR A KING

For parrot people everywhere…

CHAPTER ONE

THE KING-SIZE BED felt strange to Elissa, which was no surprise, really, since it wasn't her own. It belonged to Kingston Roper, and it was a good thing they were friends or she'd never have done him this "little favor" on a minute's notice. Elissa's own safe, single bed was in her little cottage on the white Jamaican beach near Montego Bay, only a short walk from King's enormous villa.

In the past two years Elissa knew she'd gone from being just an irritating neighbor to the only friend King had. And *friend* was the word; they certainly weren't lovers. Elissa Gloriana Dean, for all her eccentricities and uninhibited appearance, was an innocent. Her missionary parents had given her a loving but restrictive upbringing, and not even her budding success in the sophisticated world of fashion design had liberated her in any physical way.

This trip down she'd been on the island only since that morning, missing King, who wasn't at home, and halfheartedly working on her newest collection of colorful leisure wear for the boutique that carried her exclusive designs. Then, just an hour ago, King had phoned her with this wild request and had hung up without a word of explanation the moment she'd agreed to help him out. She couldn't imagine why he wanted her to be found in his bed. He didn't seem to be dating anyone. But then again, maybe he was being hounded by some bored socialite and wanted to show her that he was already involved. This tactic did seem a bit drastic, though, especially since King was adept at speaking his mind. He never pulled his punches, even with people he liked. Oh, well. All the wondering in the world wasn't going to give her any answers. She'd simply have to wait to hear what King had to say.

She stretched luxuriously in his huge bed, the smooth satin sheets feeling cool and sexy against her skin. She was wearing a nightgown, but it was made of the finest cotton and slit to the hips on both sides. In front, it made a plunge to her navel. The daring pink negligee was part of her fantasy life, she admitted to herself. In some ways she might be repressed on the surface, but in her mind she was a beautiful siren who lured men to their dooms.

Only with King could she safely indulge that fantasy woman, however, because he never approached her physically. With King, she could flirt to her heart's content. Although she was friendly to most men, she was careful not to tease. The instant a man mistook her playful friendliness for a come-on, she retreated into her shell, the fantasy shattered. It was one thing to pretend to be sexy, but quite another to follow through. A frightening experience in her teens had left her extremely wary in that regard.

King was safe, though, Elissa reminded herself. Over the past two years he'd become a friend and a confidant, and she wasn't afraid to let down her guard with him. She wouldn't have dreamed of wearing this revealing gown in front of anyone else. But despite their sometimes flirtatious camaraderie, King scarcely even seemed to notice that she *had* a body, so this little charade held no danger. She smiled to herself, feeling womanly and sexy and wildly come-hitherish. She would put on a great act for whoever this persistent female was, and later King could tell her all about it.

Kingston Roper, she mused. He could be such an enigma at times—like now. He was a big-time businessman, she knew—oil and gas and a few diversified interests, as she recalled. He'd inherited interest in the family company, which had been on the verge of bankruptcy, and had used his business savvy to make a fortune. Apparently his half brother, whose father had left the business to both sons, had been competing like mad to overtake King ever since.

Although they talked frequently and freely, she and King didn't spend a whole lot of time discussing everyday details about themselves, and as a result, she now realized, she didn't know all that much about his family. His half brother, Bobby, was married, and King had said something about expecting him and his wife for a visit. But that was at about the time she'd had to go back to the States to oversee her latest collection as it was assembled.

She smiled again as she thought about the success of that collection, which allowed her the luxury of spending time in Jamaica. Her name was her label—*Elissa*—and she catered to a unique clientele. Her sportswear was exotic, and its fantasy flair was designed to capture the eye as well as the imagination. She favored dramatic combinations of red and black and white, with the emphasis on cut and silhouette. Her styles had taken some time to catch on, but now that they had, sales were booming, and she was making a nice living. The cottage had been a godsend—she'd bought it at a terrific price when she'd been on a rare vacation—and for the past two years, whenever she needed rest or inspiration, she left the small Miami house she shared with her parents and came to sunny Jamaica.

She'd led a sheltered but happy life, one of the consequences of being the only child of former missionaries. Her parents were highly individualistic and encouraged

Elissa to be the same—except in one respect. They were extremely moral people, and they had instilled that same morality into their daughter. As a result of her upbringing, Elissa was something of a misfit in the modern world, but in most respects—even in her wild designs—she was an individual.

When she came to Jamaica, she relaxed by watching out for King, who seemed to be in almost permanent residence these days. Two years ago she'd taken him on as a social project, since he kept so much to himself, never smiled and seemed to think about nothing except business. Gradually, she reflected, he'd thawed a little. She grinned, then tensed, listening carefully to the sounds coming from the next room. Realizing it was only Warchief mumbling to himself in his covered cage, she relaxed.

The big yellow-naped Amazon parrot belonged to Elissa, but she'd never taken him to the States. He belonged on his tropical island, and she loved him too much to risk disturbing his delicate immune system with the stress of international travel. King seemed to like him well enough, since he let the five-year-old parrot stay with him when Elissa was away. Warchief had had a bad cold when she'd arrived in Jamaica this time, and to avoid upsetting the bird with a move while he was still sick, King was letting him stay at the villa until he recovered. He'd be well soon, though; already he was as feisty as ever.

It had been Warchief who'd first introduced them, she remembered fondly. Elissa had nearly drained her bank account to buy the big green bird from his previous owner, who'd been moving into an apartment. Warchief definitely wasn't an apartment bird. He heralded dawn and dusk with equal enthusiasm, and his ear-piercing cries did sound like a Native American warrior of old on the attack. Hence, his name.

At the time, Elissa had been thoroughly ignorant of birds and hadn't known about this particular trait of Amazon parrots. She had taken Warchief to her cottage, and promptly at dusk she'd discovered why his former owner had been so enthusiastic about selling him.

Covering the cage had only made the parrot madder. She'd frantically thumbed through one of the old bird magazines she'd been given to an article on screaming, biting birds. Don't throw water on them, the article cautioned. If you do, instead of a screaming, biting bird, you'll have a *wet*, screaming, biting bird.

She'd sighed worriedly, gnawing on her lower lip as the parrot began to imitate a police siren. Or could it be the real thing? Perhaps her new neighbor in that big white villa had called the Jamaican police?

At that point a loud, angry knock on the front door had startled her. "Hush, Warchief!" she'd pleaded.

He'd squawked even louder, rattling the bars of his cage like a convict bent on escape.

"Oh, for heaven's sake!" she'd wailed, holding her ears and peeking out the curtain before she opened the door.

But it hadn't been the police. It was worse. It was the cold, hard, mean-looking man who lived in that huge white villa down the beach. The man who looked as intimidating as a stone wall and walked like a bulldozer hunting hills. He seemed furious, and Elissa wondered if she could get away with pretending she wasn't home.

"Open this door, or the police will," a deep, Western-accented voice boomed.

With a resigned sigh, she unlocked it. He was tall, whipcord lean and dangerous looking, from his tousled dark hair and his half-opened tropical shirt to the white shorts that emphasized the deep tan and pure muscle of his long legs. He had a chest that would have started fires in a more liberated woman than Elissa. It was very broad, with a thick wedge of black hair that curled down past the waistband around his lean hips. His face was chiseled-looking, rough and masculine, with a straight nose and a cruelly sensuous mouth. There wasn't an ounce of fat on him, and he smelled of tangy cologne—expensive, probably, if that Rolex buried in the thick hair on his wrist and the big diamond ring on his darkly tanned hand were any indication of material worth. He made her feel like a midget, even though she was considered tall herself.

"Yes?" She smiled, trying to bluff her way through his obvious animosity.

"What the hell's going on over here?" he asked curtly.

She blinked. "I beg your pardon?"

"I heard screams," he said, his very dark, almost black, eyes staring intently at her face.

"Well, yes, they were screams, but—" she began.

"I bought my house specifically for its peaceful location," he broke in before she could finish. "I like peace and quiet. I came all the way here from Oklahoma to get it. I don't like wild parties."

"Oh, neither do I," she said earnestly.

At which point Warchief let out a scream that could have shattered crystal.

"Why is that woman screaming? What in hell kind of company are you keeping here, lady?" The man from Oklahoma spared her a speaking glance before he pushed past her into the cottage and began looking for the source of the scream.

She sighed, leaning against the doorjamb as he strode

into the bedroom, then the small kitchen, muttering about bloody murder and the lack of consideration for the neighbors on this side of the island.

Warchief began laughing in an absurd parody of a man's deep voice, and then he screamed again, his tone rising alarmingly.

The Oklahoman was back, hands on his narrow hips, scowling. And then his eyes found the covered cage.

"Helllllp!" Warchief moaned, and the man's eyebrows shot up his forehead.

"The wild party," she informed him calmly, "is in there. And *wild* is really a good word for that particular party."

"Ouuuuut!" the parrot wailed. "Let me out!"

The Oklahoman pulled off the dark cover, and Warchief immediately began making eyes at him. "Hello!" he purred, leaping from his perch ring to the cage door. "I'm a good boy. Who are you?"

The tall man blinked. "It's a parrot."

"I'm a good boy," Warchief said, and he laughed again. As an encore he turned upside down, cocking his head at the man. "You're cute!"

Cute wasn't exactly the word Elissa would have used, but that parrot had style—she'd say that for him. She covered her mouth with her hand to keep from laughing.

Warchief spread his tail feathers and ruffled the rest of himself, dilated his pale brown eyes in what bird fanciers call "blazing" and let out a beaut of a wail. The stranger from Oklahoma raised one heavy eyebrow. "How would you like him," he asked darkly, glancing at her, "fried or baked stuffed?"

"You can't!" she moaned. "He's just a baby!"

The parrot let out another bloodcurdling scream.

"Down, boy!" the man growled. "I don't have my ears insured."

Elissa muffled a giggle. "He's terrific, isn't he?" she asked gleefully. "Now I see why his owner had to sell him when he moved into a small apartment building. I didn't realize it until the sun started going down."

The intruder stared at the pile of bird magazines on the glass-topped coffee table. "Well? Haven't you learned yet what to do about his screaming?"

"Of course," she replied, tongue in cheek. "You cover the cage. It works every time. This expert—" she held up the magazine "—says so."

He glanced at the cover of the magazine. "That issue is three years old."

She shrugged. "Can I help it if bird magazines aren't exactly the going thing on the island? The owner gave these to me along with the cage."

His eyes told her what he thought of the magazines, the cage and the bird in it. Her, too.

"So he screams a little," she defended, shifting under that hot glare. "Basically he's a nice bird. He'll even let you pet him."

He eyed the bird. "Want to show me?"

"Not really." But at the man's baleful glance, she moved closer and held out her hand. The parrot cackled and made a playful swipe at it. She jerked her hand back. "Well, he'll almost let you pet him," she equivocated.

"Care to try again?" he challenged, folding his darkly tanned arms across that massive chest.

She put her hands behind her. "No, thanks. I've kind of gotten used to having ten fingers," she muttered.

"No doubt. What in heaven's name do you want with a parrot, anyway?" he asked, clearly exasperated.

"I was lonely," she said bluntly. She glanced down at her bare feet.

"Why not take a lover?" he returned.

She looked up and saw that his eyes were full of what looked like mischief. "Take him where?" she asked glibly, hiding the uncomfortable reaction his suggestion evoked from her.

A corner of his firm mouth seemed to twitch. "Cute."

"You're cute!" Warchief echoed, and he began to strut in a circle, fluffed up like a cat in a dryer, screaming his lime-green head off. Even the streak of yellow on his nape seemed to glow.

"For Pete's sake, boy!" the man burst out.

"Maybe he's a girl," Elissa commented. "He sure seems to like you a lot."

He glared at Warchief. "I don't like the way he's looking at me," he commented. "I feel like an entrée."

"His former owner promised he wouldn't bite," she faltered.

"Sure he did." He held out his hand, and Warchief seemed to actually grin before he reached through the wide cage bars for it.

He wasn't a malicious bird; he just liked to test his strength, Elissa rationalized. But the man from Oklahoma had strong fingers. He let Warchief bear down for a minute before he leisurely removed the big beak and firmly said, "No!"

He picked up the cage cover and put it back in place. And to Elissa's amazement, the parrot shut up.

"You have to let an animal know who's boss," he told Elissa. "Never jerk your hand back if he starts to bite, and don't let him get away with it. You'll only reinforce his bad behavior."

She blinked. "You seem to know a lot about birds."

"I had a cockatoo," he told her. "I gave it to a friend of mine because I'm away so much of the time."

"You're from Oklahoma, you said?" she asked, curious.

He cocked an eyebrow. "Yes."

"I'm from Florida," she said with a smile. "I design sportswear for a chain of boutiques." She peeked up at him. "I could design you a great sundress."

He glowered at her. "First the parrot, now this. I don't know which is worse, lady, you or the last woman who lived here."

"The woman I bought the cottage from?" she recalled, frowning. "What was wrong with her?"

"She liked to sunbathe nude when I was swimming," he muttered darkly.

She grinned, remembering the woman very well. She was about fifty years old, at least a size twenty and only five feet tall.

"It's not funny," he commented.

"Yes, it is." She laughed.

But he still didn't smile. Despite his earlier flip remarks, he looked like a man who hadn't much use for humor.

"I've got three hours of work left before I can sleep," he said curtly, turning away. "From now on, cover that bird when he starts whooping. He'll get the message sooner or later. And don't keep him up late. It isn't good for him. Birds need twelve hours each of daylight and dark."

"Yes, sir. Thank you, sir. Anything else, sir?" she asked pertly as she skipped along beside him to the door.

He stopped short, his dark eyes threatening. "How old are you, anyway? Past the age of consent?"

"I'm a candidate for the old folks' home, in fact." She

grinned. "I'm pushing twenty-six. Still about twenty years your junior, though, I'll bet, old man."

He looked stunned, as if no one had ever dared speak to him in such a manner. "I'm thirty-nine," he said absently.

"You look more like forty-five." She sighed, studying his hard, care-creased face. "I'll bet you take five-hour vacations and count your money every night. You have that look, you know." His eyebrows shot up, and she wiggled hers. "Rich and miserable?"

"I'm filthy rich, but I'm not miserable."

"Yes, you are," she told him. "You just don't realize it. But don't worry. Now that I'm around, I'll save you from yourself. In no time you'll be a new man."

"I like me fine the way I am," he said tersely, glaring down at her. "So don't pester me. I don't care to be remodeled, least of all by some bored textile worker."

"I'm a designer," she shot back.

"You can't possibly be old enough." He patted her on the head, the first glimpse of real humor she'd seen in him. "Go to bed, child."

"Mind you don't trip over your long beard, Grandpa," she called after him.

He didn't look back or say another word. He just kept walking.

And that had been the beginning of an odd friendship. In the months that followed, Elissa had learned precious few actual facts about her taciturn neighbor, but she'd gleaned a great deal about his temperament. His full name was Kingston, and no one called him King. Except Elissa. He spent most of his waking hours on business. Although he traveled extensively, his home base was Jamaica because few people, except those who really needed to, knew how to get in touch with him there. He liked his privacy and avoided the social gatherings that seemed de rigueur for the Americans in their exclusive part of Montego Bay. He kept to himself and spent his rare free time walking on the beach, alone and apparently liking it. He might have gone on for years that way. But Elissa had saved him from himself.

Although she didn't trust most men, she instinctively trusted King. He seemed totally uninterested in her as a woman, and when weeks went by without his making a suggestive remark or a pass, she began to feel totally safe with him. That allowed her to indulge her fantasy of being the sophisticated, worldly kind of woman she liked to read about in novels. It was an illusion, of course, but King didn't seem to mind her outrageous flirting and sometimes suggestive remarks. He treated her much like a young girl, alternately indulging and teasing her. And that was fine with Elissa. She'd long since learned that she wouldn't fit easily into the modern world. She couldn't bring herself to sleep with a man just because it was the fashion. And since most men she dated expected that courtesy, she simply withdrew. She never took a date home—not anymore, at least. There had been a nice man when she was twenty. A real jewel, she'd thought—until she took him home to meet Mom and Dad. She'd never seen him again.

For all her religious outlook on life, her parents were characters. Her father collected lizards, and her mother was a special deputy with the sheriff's department. Odd people. Lovely but very odd. Since she'd given up on expecting tolerance from the opposite sex, she couldn't imagine a male friend really understanding her delightful family. So it was a good thing she'd decided to die a virgin.

Fortunately, King had no designs on her whatsoever, so he was good company and a hedge against other men when she was on the island. He was the perfect safe harbor. Not only that, but he needed a little attention to keep him from becoming a hermit. And who better to draw him out than Elissa, given her somewhat evangelical background?

At first she contented herself with leaving little notes for him to find, exhorting pithy things like "Too much loneliness makes a man odd" or "Sunstroke can be hazardous to your health." She put the notes on his front door, on the windshield of his car, even under the rock where he liked to sit and watch the sunset. From there, she took bolder steps. She baked things for him. She put flowers on his doorstep.

Eventually, he came over to tell her to stop—and found her waiting for him with an elaborate meal. Clearly it was the last straw, and he gave up trying to ignore her. After that, he came to eat at least once a week, and sometimes they walked on the beach together. Despite her outgoing approach, she was a little wary of him at first, until he proved by his attitude that he wasn't going to try to get her into the nearest available bed. And then he became her friend. She totally relaxed with him and looked forward to their times together. He seemed pleased enough with that arrangement himself, talking to her as if she were a sister.

When she went back to the States to work, he generously offered to keep Warchief. She'd been delighted, and King had given the bird a nice substitute home. When he was out of the country on business, he even hired a woman to look after the house and the bird. For all his hardness, he had a soft center—if one looked closely enough. He was still impatient and demanding with most people—Elissa had once had her ears curled listening to him chew out a subordinate—but he seemed to tolerate her better than he tolerated others.

The only puzzling thing about him was his lack of a love life. He was devastatingly handsome and physically near perfect. At his age, she'd have expected him to be married. But he wasn't and evidently never had been. He dated occasionally, but Elissa never spotted him bringing a woman home overnight. Even in her innocence, Elissa knew it was rather unusual for a man who was so much a man to spend so much time alone. She wondered about it frequently, and once she even got up enough courage to quiz him on the subject. But his face had closed up, and he'd changed the subject. She hadn't asked again.

Despite her innate curiosity, she was relieved that he'd never once made a pass at her. She had some hang-ups from an experience that her parents didn't even know about, thank God. One wild party, attended without their knowledge, had cured her of any wanton imaginings. She'd barely escaped with her innocence intact, and she'd gleaned a very unpleasant, threatening picture of the aroused male. She'd been careful ever since.

She was only grateful that her parents weren't in any danger of dropping in at the Roper villa. If they'd seen her in King's bed... Then she laughed, remembering how they were. They knew her so well that they'd have asked what was the joke. How marvelous having parents like hers, idiosyncrasies and all.

King was due any minute, and Elissa's part in this practical joke was simply to lie back and look loved. She wasn't sure why he wanted to give that impression, or to whom, but he'd once saved her from the unwanted attention of a very persistent insurance salesman, so now she was saving him. From something. Really, though, he was going to owe her a steak dinner for all this bother.

She heard the front door open, and voices drifted down the hall. She recognized King's, and for one wild second she let herself pretend that she was waiting for him as a lover. The thought didn't terrify her, and that puzzled her. In fact, her body began to tingle in the oddest ways, and that *really* puzzled her.

Then the bedroom door opened, and King stared at her over the head of the most beautiful blonde Elissa had ever seen.

The blonde wore a look of helpless longing and unholy torment. And King's expression was a revelation as he glanced down at her. For a face that rarely gave away a trace of emotion, it was suddenly explicit with tender interest. Who was the woman? Elissa wondered. And why would King want to discourage her when he was so obviously attracted to her?

Elissa was so confused that she almost forgot to play her part. This vulnerability in King was so unexpected. But there must be a reason he wanted that lovely woman with him to think he was involved with someone else, and this was obviously no time to ask questions.

"Well, hello, darling," Elissa said in her best husky voice. She tugged the covers up demurely and yawned delicately. "I fell asleep again," she added meaningfully, and she waited for the blonde to react.

CHAPTER TWO

THE REACTION WAS almost instantaneous. "Oh!" The woman faltered, stopping beside King as if frozen to the spot. She stared at Elissa with huge, soft eyes, clearly struggling to find words, and her delicate skin colored, making her even more beautiful. "Ex-excuse me."

"I didn't expect you to still be here, Elissa," King said with a smile that was obviously forced.

Elissa played her part to perfection, letting her eyes droop sleepily. "I'm sorry if I've overstayed my welcome."

"Don't be absurd," he replied. "There's no reason you shouldn't stay if you like. Bess, do you mind...?" he asked the blonde. "There's a guest bathroom just down the hall."

"I'll...I'll use that one, of course." She looked totally flustered, Elissa noted sympathetically. "Excuse me," she whispered, her voice almost breaking. She turned and nearly ran down the hall.

King closed the door and leaned back against it, his face without expression, his dark eyes looking at Elissa without really seeming to see her. He never gave away much, but that hard face was faintly pale under its rugged tan.

Elissa climbed out of bed, oblivious to her state of undress. He wasn't looking, anyway. He paid very little attention to her as a rule, and if she'd wondered why in the past, she now had a suspicion. She went to stand in front of him, her head back, her eyes curious.

"Okay," she said. "Why don't you tell me all about it. I'm a clam when I need to be, and you look as if you need a friend pretty badly."

His jaw tightened. He looked down into her blue eyes, and she could see his control waver, just for an instant, before he got it back. "That's Bess," he said finally. "My brother's wife," he added significantly. After a pause, he continued tonelessly, "He'll be along in an hour or so. He's still in a business meeting."

She remembered his mentioning Bobby and Bess, and she also remembered that he never talked much about them. Now she had a sneaking hunch she knew why. Her eyes narrowed as she took in his look of utter dejection.

"Is one of you in hot pursuit of the other?" she conjectured, smiling gently at his faint surprise. "Since I'm guessing, *she's* after *you*, I imagine, and that's why I was shanghaied into decorating your bed."

"It isn't quite that simple," he murmured, searching her wide eyes.

"Why don't you try telling me about it," she suggested softly.

Still gazing intently at her, he seemed to consider that possibility, took a deep breath and then began. "They came down month before last while Bobby was working to get a hotel complex started. He's been deeply involved in negotiations, and now he's finalizing the subcontracting bids," he explained. He paused.

"Go on," Elissa prompted gently.

"Bess has been lonely, so instead of going back to Oklahoma, she's been depending on me for amusement." He stopped, then continued haltingly, "But a couple of nights ago, the amusement did a disappearing act, and things started to get serious." Again he stopped, then rushed on.

"So I started grasping at straws and told her I was involved with you. If you hadn't sent me that letter asking me to get the utilities on, I might still be in hot water. But I knew you'd be in tonight, so I made sure Bess would come over. To catch you in a compromising situation, that is."

"Too bad I wasn't stark naked instead, then," she said lightly, trying to cheer him up. She gave him a wicked smile. "Just picture it, gorgeous me in my birthday suit sprawled out on your satin sheets. That would have really caught her eye."

Oddly enough, that picture made King go hot all over. He suddenly realized he'd never really thought of Elissa as a woman before. She was so young, so naive, so trusting. She was like a little sister to him. But now, as his dark eyes wandered over her, he realized with a start that she was pretty sexy in that gown, and he wasn't thinking brotherly thoughts at all. He blinked. Maybe he was getting old and his glands were going crazy. Either that or his confusion over Bess was getting to him. In an effort to ground himself in reality once more, he reached out and clasped her shoulders. It was a mistake—they were bare.

Elissa started. It was a rare thing for King to touch her, and she was amazed at the pleasure the feel of his hands on her bare skin gave her.

"I think this will do it," he mused, even more confused yet relieved he could still find voice to respond to her joking remark. "Temporarily, at least. How about joining us for drinks, just for an hour or so? Just until Bobby gets here?"

He sounded almost desperate, and Elissa grinned. "Sure. What are friends for?" she said easily. She wondered how much he really cared for Bess and if his only motive in the charade was to ward off his sister-in-law. Perhaps he needed a barrier against his own impulses, too, to keep himself honest. Hard to tell; he could be such a poker face. At times she wondered if she really knew him at all. She searched his dark eyes, frowning slightly. "King, is she in love with you?"

"I don't think she knows, Elissa," he said, his voice quiet and tense. "She's lonely and bored—maybe a bit afraid, as well. Bobby leaves her alone too much. I'm not sure if she's really interested in me or just using me as a ploy to get Bobby's attention."

In fact, he was afraid to take a chance on Bess's developing any real feelings for him, since he was having a hard enough time resisting her now. But he wasn't admitting any of that to Elissa.

He'd always had a soft spot for his sister-in-law, he acknowledged. Few people in her current social circle knew how rough she'd had it, what with a father who drank and kept her mother pregnant all the time. Bess hadn't even owned a decent dress when Bobby brought her home and announced that they were getting married. King had formed an immediate affection for the shy little blonde, and that tenderness had held on for the past ten years. Now it was hard to decide whether it was still brotherly affection or something more. Bess had never actively encouraged him before now.

Elissa caught the wistful look in King's eyes. Her lips pursed. "Did you ever have something going with her, maybe before Bobby did?" she probed gently.

He shook his head. "She was just eighteen when they married. They were the same age, in fact." He shrugged. "I was already eleven years her senior. Besides, Bobby saw her first." He laughed, then instantly sobered. "They were close in those early days, when Bobby was working his way up in the business world. But now, with their years of living high on the hog and with the oil industry depressed, money's gotten a little tight." He frowned, studying her. "You know, I think maybe Bobby's working himself like crazy because he's afraid Bess won't want him if he can't support her in the style she's gotten accustomed to. And because he's ignoring her in his pursuit of new building contracts, she thinks he doesn't care."

"What a mess." She sighed.

"You aren't kidding. And guess who's smack-dab in the middle of it?" he asked ruefully. "They've gotten along pretty well the past ten years, but then, there was always lots of money. Bess used to joke about leaving him if he ever lost his shirt. She said she never wanted to be poor again. I don't think she really meant it about leaving him, but Bobby tends to take things literally, and they don't seem to talk much anymore. Anyway, I helped Bobby make some real-estate contacts here in Jamaica, and two months ago they came down to get things started. Bobby's been hellishly busy, so for the past few weeks Bess has turned to me—out of boredom, I'm sure. At first I suspected she wanted to use me to get Bobby to notice her again—you know, make him a little jealous. But it's getting complicated now." He shrugged, smiling faintly. "She's always been special to me, and I'm only human, if you get my meaning. But I don't want anyone to get hurt. That's where you come in."

"I'm going to run interference, I gather?" she murmured.

"That's it," he agreed pleasantly. "By the way, you've been in the States for the past few months because we had a quarrel. But now we've patched it up, and we're quite serious about each other."

"I'm beginning to see the light," she mused, grinning. "So we're lovers, is that it?"

He chuckled. "Can't keep our hands off each other," he agreed. "Mad to be together."

"What fun." She smiled. "Now explain my missionary parents to her and how you so easily led me into a life of sin."

He groaned. "Don't, for heaven's sake, even mention your parents to her. Well, not what they do for a living, at least."

She sighed. "I hope she doesn't pin me down and start asking embarrassing questions."

"I'll try not to leave you alone with her. You've got to save me," he murmured drily, although there seemed to be something serious behind the gibe. "Bobby and I are getting along better than we ever have. I can't come between him and the one thing in life he really values."

She sighed. "Okay. I'll play along. But I have to go back to the States in about three weeks, so you'd better get her convinced fast."

"They'll be going back any day now, I hope," he said. "Otherwise I don't know if I can stand it much longer. It's a good thing I saw your lights on before Bobby got me to pick up Bess at their villa. I barely had time to pressure you into cooperating before I had to leave."

"Lucky you," she agreed with a grin. "I hadn't planned to come back for two more weeks."

He groaned. "I'd have been in over my head by then, for sure."

She glanced up at him. "Well, don't you worry. I'll save you." She frowned, moving away from the disturbing touch of his hands. "Let's see now, what did I do with that red cape—you know, the one with the big *S* on it?"

"Never mind the Superwoman cape," he said. "Just hold my hand."

"The one with the Rolex and the diamond ring?" She pursed her lips. "Careful I don't steal them. I'm not rich yet, you know."

He laughed. "You will be," he said. Then he glanced toward the door. "Get dressed, will you? I'll wait for you."

Heavens, he had it bad, Elissa thought, if he was afraid to face the other woman without reinforcements.

"Chin up," she said lightly. "I know karate. If she makes one move—just one move—to undress you, I'll defend your honor with my very life."

He chuckled. Once, he'd thought his new neighbor was a complete eccentric. He still did, actually, but she could be quite a gem at times, too. And right now she was saving his neck. "You're a nice girl," he said playfully.

She winced. "A nice girl? Thanks awfully. I like you, too."

She turned, picked up her clothes from the chair and headed toward the bathroom.

"You can't dress in front of me?" he asked unexpectedly, watching her from his relaxed position against the door.

She glanced up at him. "No," she confessed with a somewhat wobbly laugh. "I'm not quite as liberated as I might seem. I—I've never undressed in front of a man in my life, except for my family physician."

The confession seemed to shock him. "Never?" he asked.

"Never," she emphasized, knowing exactly what she was revealing to him.

He scowled. Because of her physical aloofness, he'd somehow taken it for granted that she'd been hurt in love somehow. To think of her as a virgin was vaguely disturbing.

"Why?" he asked with characteristic bluntness. "Did something happen to you?"

"My father's a minister, remember? And he and my mother were missionaries to Brazil when I was growing up. Try being Ms. Liberation in that kind of atmosphere. I dare you."

He was learning more about her in minutes than he'd learned in two years. He studied her intently, his gaze taking in what he could see of her body in that very revealing gown. Her breasts were full and firm-looking, her minuscule waist flared into nicely rounded hips, and she had long, nicely shaped legs. Her face was lovely. And that teasing, provocative air of hers, he realized, was pretty false at times. Remembering that he'd seen her actually back away when men came too close physically, he regarded her thoughtfully.

"No wonder," he mumbled.

"No wonder what?" she echoed.

"Well, I'd always thought of you as sophisticated," he mused, thinking of her occasional flirtatiousness. "You certainly don't act like a virgin. And yet—"

"How does a virgin act, for heaven's sake?" she broke in. "Stand on the edge of a volcano and jump in?"

Despite the seriousness of his current predicament, King found himself laughing, and it dawned on him that he laughed more with Elissa than he ever had in his life. But then, his path hadn't been an easy one. Part Native American, he'd grown up fighting two worlds. Most people didn't even know that he and Bobby had different fathers. Bobby's was a Texas oilman who'd left his business equally to both boys. King's father was a full-blooded Apache whose ill-fated attempt to fit into his wife's social set had been a disaster. A marriage of rich and poor might make good novels, but it was hard work in real life. Eventually, King's father had walked out the door in the middle of one too many cocktail parties and vanished. King had never seen him again. His mother had remarried, and when Bobby came along, there seemed to be little affection left for the elder son. He learned to fight his own battles, because he got no coddling. He'd spent his whole life fighting. He guessed that in many ways he was still fighting.

"You almost never laugh," Elissa pointed out, holding her jumpsuit against her breasts.

"Oh, now and again I do. With you." He smiled. "Go get dressed, walking sacrifice. I'll wait out here."

She studied him quietly, curious about the worn expression on his face. More than Bess was troubling him, she sensed. She wondered briefly if being the product of two worlds ever bothered him. She knew about his Native American ancestry; in her typical outspoken fashion she'd once asked him why he was so dark. He'd given her the answer abruptly and changed the subject, clearly unwilling to discuss it. She sighed. What an enigma. She smiled back at him and went into the bathroom to change.

She put on one of her own creations, a slinky black jumpsuit with a red bodice and single strappy sleeve, and ran a brush through her long hair. She probably wouldn't wear the outfit around anybody except King. Another part of her fantasy life, she thought, and grinned at her reflection. She realized then that her lipstick was in her purse, so she went back into the bedroom to get it.

"Oh, fudge," she muttered, fumbling through the contents. "I don't even have a lipstick." She lifted her eyebrows in a speaking look, expecting him to read her mind, as usual. And he did.

"Sorry, I never use the stuff myself," he said drily. "Do you really need one?" he asked, shouldering himself away from the door, a cigarette in his hand. He didn't often smoke, but tonight was unsettling him.

"Your sexy sister-in-law will be sure to notice if I don't make myself as beautiful as possible," she teased.

He came close to her, towering over her and letting his eyes wander with uncharacteristic boldness down her slender body. "If you'd put lipstick on," he murmured, "probably I'd have kissed it off by now, don't you think?"

Her heart jumped up into her throat at the unfamiliar look in those dark eyes. They searched her face, only to drop and linger on her full breasts, and suddenly she wished her neckline were a bit higher. He hadn't seemed to notice her body in the very revealing nightgown, but he was unusually attentive now.

"We shouldn't keep your sister-in-law waiting," she said. For the first time, he was making her nervous. Eyeing him warily, she walked around him, her composure starting to shatter. As usual, when a man came on too strong, she began to draw into her shell.

His lean hand shot out unexpectedly, and he drew her toward him, clamping her waist so that she couldn't move away.

That proximity was new and a little frightening, and she looked up into his dark eyes uncomprehendingly. "What are you doing?" she asked nervously.

"Trying to ruffle you a little," he murmured darkly. "You're too neat and pretty to go out there and convince Bess we're lovers."

"All right, then, how's this?" She ran her hand roughly through her hair.

He shook his head. "Not good enough." His eyes dropped to her soft mouth, and for the first time in their relationship he wondered how it would feel to have that soft mouth under his lips.

She felt his strong fingers bite into her waist, and her eyes widened. "Hold it, now, big fella," she cautioned gently. "I'm not on the menu, remember?"

His eyebrows rose curiously. "Are you afraid of me, tidbit?" he asked in a tone he'd never used before. It was deep and slow and sultry, like the look in his dark, faintly amused eyes.

"That doesn't enter into it," she replied. "I won't let you use me for real. I won't substitute for your sister-in-law, King."

His face hardened. "I don't recall asking you to," he returned curtly, releasing her.

"Good. As long as it's just an act, we'll get along fine," she said sweetly, although her legs were wobbling from his unexpected nearness. She could almost drown in that heady, expensive cologne of his, which clung to her skin from just that brief contact with him. The situation was far too intimate, and she quickly changed the subject to divert them both. "Is Bobby anything like you?" she asked. "I've never met him, you know. They were always back in Oklahoma when I was down here."

"We don't look a lot alike," he mused after a minute, finishing his cigarette. "You'll see for yourself soon enough."

She forced a smile. "Don't worry so much," she said, attempting to ease his obvious anxiety. "They'll leave soon, and you'll get your life back together."

With a rough sigh, he put out the cigarette and stuck his hands into his pockets. "I hate being in this position," he said unexpectedly, glaring toward the door.

"Doesn't your brother pay her any attention at all?" she asked quietly.

"He's very competitive," he replied. "He doesn't like running a close second to me. He never has. With the oil glut bringing the price of crude down, we've both had to diversify. But I've done it with more success than he has. Now he's going to catch up or kill himself. Unfortunately, Bess has become a casualty."

"Do they have children?"

He grimaced. "Bobby wanted to wait until they were completely secure."

"Aren't they, by now?" she probed gently.

He glanced at her. "They're comfortable, but they've gotten used to credit in a big way. Bess has diamonds and a sports car, but it could all go up in smoke tomorrow. That's how close they're living. Bobby's scared, and with good reason. This Jamaica project will either pull him out or break him, and he knows that, too."

Elissa didn't say anything, but she felt sorry for Bess. For a wife, the worst thing in the world must be having a husband who never noticed her. Elissa's parents were always together at home, even if they were doing different things. They might be apart physically, but when they looked at each other, you knew that they were always one.

"Talking about it won't solve this problem," he said after a minute. "You don't mind carrying out the charade?" he added, raising his eyes.

"Not at all," she said, smiling gamely. "I've always wanted to try my hand at acting." She struck a pose, the back of her hand across her eyes. "I vant to be alone!"

"You imp." He chuckled. He shook his head on a sigh. "You're a puzzle, little miss designer," he murmured, watching her narrowly. "I'm amazed that no enterprising young man has ever seduced you."

She shrugged. "Most young men don't like seducing a

minister's daughter," she said pertly. Her eyes twinkled. "I almost got in trouble one time, defying my folks. It hurt my conscience and frightened me a little, but I bounced back."

"Did you really?" he mused. "Then why are you still a virgin?"

"Because you don't undo twenty-five years of conditioning overnight," she replied easily. She searched his dark eyes. "If I ever did let a man seduce me, though, I'd want him to be like you."

His heart stopped. He couldn't think of a single thing to say as the thought worked on him and made his body react in a shocking way.

She shifted, embarrassed at her own boldness, although his stony face didn't give away a thing. "Sorry. I didn't mean to embarrass you. I just meant that you're a special kind of man. I know you'd never have to hurt a woman to feed your ego." She sighed. "I guess you've probably forgotten more about sex than I've ever learned."

"I guess I have, honey," he said, studying her down-bent head with a slight frown. He caught her hand in his—offering a small measure of comfort, he told himself. "We'd better go out."

At his strong, possessively warm touch, which set her palm to tingling, she looked up and met his searching gaze. It was like electricity. Startling. Unnerving. Her very breathing seemed to be affected by it.

"Yes," she said absently. His mouth was beautiful in a very masculine way, and she couldn't seem to stop looking at it.

He touched her long hair gently, his eyes still probing hers. She was trembling, he noticed in amazement. Then he looked down at the bodice of her jumpsuit and was surprised to find her nipples hard against the fabric—very obviously there was no bra beneath it. Suddenly he wanted to smooth his hands over her breasts. He wanted to taste her warm mouth and feel her body yield against the strength of his. His eyes narrowed at his own disturbing thoughts.

"I wish you wouldn't look at me that way," she said with that irrepressible honesty that had always intrigued him. "It...it makes me feel shaky."

His eyes rose to hers once more. "When I look at your breasts, you mean?" he asked gently.

Her lips opened on a shocked breath. He'd never spoken to her that way.

He could have bitten his tongue. What in hell was wrong with him? This was Elissa; they'd been friends for a long time. It was Bess who was getting to him. He sighed, wondering why he'd never before really noticed this little imp with her exquisite body and lovely face.

"I didn't mean to say that," he said vaguely. He dropped her hand, turned away from her abruptly and lit another cigarette. "I'm in a hell of a situation. I guess I'm more disturbed than I realized. Come on. Let's get it over with."

"All right." She followed him, her mind whirling. Had he been drinking? Would that explain his odd behavior? Perhaps wanting Bess had worked on his mind long enough to disorient him. That had to be it. He'd looked at her and he'd seen Bess. It was nothing to worry about.

"You're sure about this?" he asked before he opened the door.

"Of course," she assured him.

He sighed. "Well, let's see if we can carry it off." He held out his hand again.

She slid her slender fingers into it, a hesitant, but trusting "Okay." She looked up, batting her lashes. "Oh, Kingston, you're so sexxxxxxy!" she drawled.

He laughed unexpectedly. "Cut it out. You're supposed to convince her."

"I guess I can try." She sighed. "You lead, I'll follow."

Bess was sitting on the edge of a chair, glancing toward the hallway when they emerged. The blonde's very blue eyes narrowed and there was real hostility in them for an instant before she skillfully erased it.

"I didn't know King had a...a girlfriend," Bess said, deliberately hesitating over the word. She smiled with sleek sophistication. "He said you'd had a quarrel and went back to Florida. But you seem to have made up."

"Oh, in the most delicious ways, too, haven't we, darling?" she asked King with a fluttering of her long lashes.

He chuckled. "I guess so," he mused, but he didn't look at Bess.

"Where in Florida do you live?" Bess continued.

"In Miami, most of the year," Elissa replied. She let go of King's hand and smiled at the older woman. "I understand you're married to King's brother?"

Bess glanced down at the drink she'd poured herself. "Yes. I'm Bobby's wife."

"You're cuuuuute!" Warchief burst out, circling his cage with appropriate whistles and clicks.

Bess stared at the big parrot. "You flirt," she accused the bird, forcing a smile.

Elissa relaxed a little. Bess wasn't so bad; at least she liked parrots. "He likes women," she explained, "but he's really in love with King. When I take him home, he mourns."

"Oh. He's yours?" Bess asked.

"Yes. He stays with King when I'm in the States, and I've only been back since this morning."

King glanced at her quickly. "Want a drink?"

"Yes, thank you," Elissa said. She read him very well.

He was warning her not to let too much slip. She smiled. "Do you have pets, Bess?"

The other woman shook her head. "No pets. No kids." She sounded oddly wistful. She laughed, a hollow, haunting melody. "No nothing. It's just me and Bobby—when Bobby's ever home."

"Hard times, Bess," King reminded her. "If he doesn't keep on the ball, you'll have to give up your diamonds."

"It wasn't the diamonds I married him for, but he won't believe that," Bess replied. She looked up, her eyes searching King's face with what looked like pure longing. "Remember how it used to be, in the old days? Bobby and I would go to amusement parks and spend hours on the rides. Sometimes you'd take an afternoon off and come with us, and we'd stuff ourselves with ice cream and cotton candy..."

"It isn't wise to look back." He handed a vodka and tonic to Elissa.

"It isn't wise to look ahead, either," Bess replied miserably. "All I do is sit in hotel rooms these days...or sit at home alone." She glared at her drink. "It's a miracle I'm not an alcoholic."

"Don't you have a job or anything to keep you busy?" Elissa asked without thinking. At Bess's obvious chagrin, she hastily added, "I'm sorry, that sounded like a criticism, but honestly it wasn't. I just meant, if you had a project or a hobby, it might be less of a strain to be alone at times."

"I don't know how to do anything," Bess said sadly. "I married fresh out of high school, so I never really learned how to do much...besides be a wife."

The irony of Bess's situation wasn't lost on Elissa. "We can all do something," she said gently. "Paint or write or play an instrument or do crafts..."

"I used to play the piano," Bess replied. She looked down at her hands. "I was pretty good, too. But Bobby resented the time I spent practicing." She laughed bitterly. "How's that for a reversal?"

"I've always wished I could play," Elissa said enthusi-astically, glancing at King's set, solemn face and hoping to alleviate the tension Bess's comments were feeding.

"You design clothes, don't you?" the other woman asked curiously, her eyes faintly approving the jumpsuit. "Did you design that?"

"Yes, do you like it?" Elissa asked eagerly. "I haven't shown this one to my parents. They'd be—" She stopped short, jamming on verbal brakes as King glared at her. "They'd be delighted," she concluded weakly.

"Of course they would. They're very proud of you," King said quickly.

"What do your parents do?" Bess asked politely, raising her glass to her lips.

Elissa gnawed her lip. "They... They're into ancient history," she said truthfully. Wasn't the Bible a record of human history, after all?

"How interesting." Bess finished her drink, tossing back her hair as she glanced at the diamond-studded watch on her slender wrist. "Bobby's late," she muttered. "Another business meeting that ran overtime. Or so he swears," she added under her breath. "Too bad I'm not a briefcase. I'd be swamped with affection these days."

"It's a difficult time, Bess. Subcontracting can be ex-tremely time-consuming," King reminded her. "Jamaica desperately needs outside investments, and the hotel Bobby's planning will employ a lot of people, help the economy. But it has to be properly built. These things take time."

"It's been months already," Bess muttered dispiritedly.

"It will be over soon," King said, "and you'll be back in Oklahoma City."

Bess looked up. "Yes, I suppose I will. What a trip to look forward to. Instead of staring at hotel walls, I can stare at my own for a change," she said dully. Her eyes searched King's. "You never visit us anymore, Kingston. You spend most of your life here."

King swirled the Scotch in his glass and stuck his free hand into his pocket. "I like Jamaica," he said. He glanced deliberately at Elissa. "A lot."

Bess took an audible breath and drained her glass. "Pour me another, would you, please?" she asked, handing it to King.

"I think you've had enough, Bess," he replied. He took the glass and put it aside, gazing down at a chastened-looking Bess. She merely folded her hands in her lap and looked defeated.

Elissa was trying to decide what to do to cheer them all up when a car came up the winding sandy drive from the main road. A horn sounded, and seconds later, a car door slammed.

"It's Bobby," Bess said dully.

King strode to the door to meet him, and Elissa found Bess staring after him with quiet misery in her eyes.

Elissa watched Bess watching King. "What's your husband like?" she asked, diverting her.

Bess blinked, looking startled. "Bobby? He's… He's a businessman. He doesn't look much like Kingston, even though they had the same mother. Kingston's father was Native American," she added.

"Yes, I know." Elissa smiled at her. "You're very pretty."

Bess's eyes widened. "You're very frank."

"It saves thinking up lies." She cocked her head at the other woman. "How did you and Bobby meet?" she asked.

Bess laughed softly. "You're so unexpected! Bobby was our star quarterback, and I was a cheerleader."

"King says you've been married about ten years, yet you never had children," Elissa mused aloud. "Didn't you want any?"

Bess sighed, looking at her shoes. "When would Bobby ever have time? He's always at the office or on the phone." She pushed back her hair angrily. "I never thought it would be like this. I thought— Anyway, who wants kids?" she murmured, avoiding Elissa's eyes. She shifted restlessly on the couch. "They just clutter up people's lives. I would love to go back to studying piano again, though. But my practicing would disturb Bobby when he's trying to work at home."

"How sad," Elissa said, and meant it. "I think a woman needs fulfillment as a person, just as a man does."

Bess frowned. "It floored me when you asked if I did anything. You know, I never realized that I might be able to do something with myself..."

Elissa heard male voices; King and Bobby were approaching, much to her relief. She was finding this hard going. It shouldn't have bothered her that King was in danger of falling in love with this bitter, confused woman, but it did. It bothered her a lot.

"How long have you and Kingston been...been together?" Bess tried to sound casual, but there was pain in her voice.

"Well..." It was extremely difficult for her to fabricate, and Elissa was grateful that King and a shorter man suddenly appeared in the doorway.

"There you are. Finally," Bess said as the younger man

came in a step ahead of King. She looked at him and then averted her eyes. "Did you get what you went for?" she asked. The question sounded innocent enough, but Elissa sensed something in the blonde's voice, something faintly accusing. Perhaps she wondered if Bobby's "business" was really business.

"Of course," Bobby replied. He gave his wife an intent appraisal, his gaze both searching and faintly defensive.

He wasn't anything like King, Elissa decided. His hair was dark blond, and he was blue-eyed. He wasn't a bad-looking man at all, and he was slim but well built. He had a nice mouth, and he seemed pleasant enough altogether. But he looked weary and worn, and there were deep lines in his face.

"Your husband has approved the subcontractors," King announced with a grin. "And the bids were well under budget. He'll make you a rich woman yet, Bess."

"How lovely," she said carelessly. "I'll run right out and buy a new mink."

"You'd better get a strong cage and some thick gloves," Elissa said with a mischievous smile.

Bess looked up, clearly puzzled by the remark. She frowned. "Cage? Gloves?"

Bobby got the joke and burst out laughing, instantly looking years younger and more approachable. "I'm afraid you've got it wrong," he told Elissa. "She doesn't want a mink kit. She wants the real thing—a ready-made coat."

"Oh, a fast-food mink, in a manner of speaking," Elissa agreed. "Got you."

King's eyes sparkled as he watched her, his firm lips tugging up in a smile. "Watch this girl," he cautioned his half brother. "She's got a quicker mind than I have."

"That'll be the day, you old—I mean, darling," she

drawled at King, winking. "I happen to know that yours is a genuine steel trap, always set and ready for business."

"A better description I haven't heard," Bobby agreed. "You must be Elissa. Kingston's told me so much about you over the past couple of years that I feel as if I know you already. Tell me, how in the world do you put up with him?"

"Why, there's nothing to it," Elissa said, glancing wickedly at King, and oddly pleased to hear that he talked about her at home. "I got commando training by watching that television show about professional mercenaries."

"I guess that's telling you," Bobby said with a chuckle, winking at King.

"I guess it is," she agreed.

"Kingston isn't all that bad, surely," Bess interrupted, smiling gently up at him. "He's kept me from vegetating on this island for the past two weeks. I don't know how I'd have managed without him."

Bobby laughed, failing to see Bess's intent look at his brother. He seemed to be too busy looking at Elissa. "Good thing, too, considering how little free time I've had," he tossed off to his wife. "You know, Elissa, you're every bit as delightful as Kingston said you were," he added.

Elissa smiled, murmuring a polite reply. She was totally unprepared for the shock and sudden irritation in Bess's eyes.

CHAPTER THREE

BOBBY SPARED BESS a faintly curious glance before his attention went back to Elissa. "I'm glad you're back," he told her. "Kingston's been a royal pain these past few days."

King frowned, but he didn't rise to the bait.

"So you did miss me." Elissa batted her lashes at King. "How nice!"

"Of course I missed you," he said curtly. "Bobby, what will you have to drink?"

"Nothing," Bess said quietly. "I'd like to go back to the hotel now," she told her husband with a cool stare. "I'm tired."

"Try sitting in a board meeting for four straight hours and see how relaxed *that* leaves you," her husband challenged. "Look, Bess, we're leaving tomorrow, and I may not see Kingston again for weeks. I want to talk over a new project with him."

"You can use the phone, can't you?" Bess asked, exasperated, as she got gracefully to her feet. In three-inch heels, she was almost her husband's height. "Lord knows you find time to talk to everyone else, but heaven forbid it should be me. Maybe I should make an appointment."

"You just don't understand, do you?" her husband said with a resigned sigh. "Never mind, babe. We'll go." He glanced apologetically at King and Elissa. "Thanks for the invitation, even if I don't get the drink. I'll call you in the morning, big brother."

"Fine," King replied.

"We could go for a ride," Bess murmured to Bobby as he joined her.

"A ride? Are you crazy? I still have to go over bids!" Bobby snapped.

Bess started to speak, then seemed to give up. "Yes, of course." She led the way to the door, calling over her shoulder, "Good night, Kingston, Elissa." She didn't look at either of them. She just kept walking out into the sultry evening breeze.

"I don't know what in hell's gotten into her," Bobby apologized. "She's been worse since we came down here. I can't very well stop working, can I? I don't have time to entertain her. The oil market is too depressed to support us. If we hadn't diversified a few years back into real estate, we'd be living in public housing by now!" He glanced at King. "She's so bored with everything lately. Suppose I let her stay with you for a week or so while I fly back to Oklahoma and catch up at the office?" he asked King in all innocence.

Elissa, standing at the door beside King, could feel him tense against her. "Elissa and I are going to spend a few days with her people in Florida," he replied unexpectedly, his quick glance daring Elissa to deny it. "Not that Bess isn't welcome to use the house..."

"No, I don't want her here alone." Bobby sighed. "It was just a thought. So your people live in Florida?" he added, smiling at Elissa.

"Yes, in Miami," she replied. This was unexpected. Surely King was hedging, but the thought of taking him home with her made her nervous. Her parents didn't approve of her fashions; they certainly weren't going to approve of her friendship with a man like King. They'd think he was a playboy. And for King to actually spend time around her eccentric parents! Her heart almost stopped. But then she reminded herself that he was only playing for time, of course. He wasn't serious.

"What do they do?" Bobby persisted.

"My father is a min—" She caught it just in time, even before King unobtrusively pinched her. She jumped. "He's in ancient history," she bit off, glaring at King. "And my mother is a housewife."

Bobby nodded. "Any brothers or sisters?"

She shook her head gladly. "No. Just me."

"You'd better get going," King interrupted, as if he didn't like the interest Bobby was showing in her. "Bess will take the car if you don't."

"She will at that," he agreed. "Well, good night."

"Good night," King replied.

Bobby left, and a minute later the car roared angrily down the driveway.

"They don't seem ideally suited, do they?" Elissa asked quietly, watching the taillights disappear among the palms.

"They used to be," King replied. "When times were hard, they were always together, doing simple things like window-shopping or just walking. Then, when the money started coming in, Bess was like a kid in a candy shop. She had to have all kinds of expensive things." He sighed. "And Bobby wanted her to have them. He worked harder and harder to give them to her, but it kept him away from home a lot. When the oil market fell, he went into partnership in a small construction firm back home."

He paused, as if thinking, then continued pensively, "Bobby's always felt obliged to compete with me. In recent years, he's tried even harder. That means Bess spends too much time alone, and she isn't the kind of woman who can just sit. She isn't even domestic. Too bad she and Bobby never wanted children."

He turned, missing Elissa's sharp glance. Didn't he know that Bess was just hiding what she really wanted? Elissa was sure that the other woman did want children, very much. He poured himself another Scotch. "Want another?" he asked as an afterthought.

She nodded. "Yes, thanks. Why does he want to compete with you?"

"It's the way he's made, I guess. The second brother isn't going to be second best. He's twenty-eight now, and I think he wants to best me financially before he gets to be my age." He poured Elissa's drink before he opened the sliding doors to the beach. He stood there, tall and unapproachable, the breeze running like fingers through his thick black hair as he watched the surf crash white and frothy onto the hard-packed sand beyond the patio. "He doesn't like the fact that his father allowed me to inherit," he added. "His father and I got along pretty well—in a business sense at least—and I think Bobby somehow felt threatened by that."

"He's your half brother, of course," she said hesitantly, remembering how little King liked to talk about personal matters.

"That's right." He lifted his glass to his lips with a bitter smile. "He's not a duke's mixture—didn't you notice?"

She glared at him. "Neither are you," she snapped. "You're part Apache, which is something else entirely."

He cocked an amused eyebrow at her. "Thank you for clarifying the situation for me," he murmured drily, and he went back to contemplating the outside world.

For a few minutes they sipped their drinks in silence, and

Elissa wondered at the sense of freedom the liquor gave her. She hadn't had more than a small glass of wine in a long time. But the vodka seemed to be doing strange things to her, making her extremely aware of King, diluting her inhibitions. She felt light-headed. Reckless. Her body burned with new temptations. She put down the empty glass, and her hand seemed to move in slow motion. King was close to finishing his drink, too. Was it his third? She couldn't keep track. Bess had gotten to him, all right. Elissa wondered if he was completely sober.

"Do you have other family?" she asked after a minute, joining him in the doorway.

"Bobby's father died some years back. Our mother is in a nursing home," he added simply. "Alzheimer's disease. We visit her, but she doesn't know us anymore."

"How terrible for you. And for her."

"It is that," he agreed. He took a long swallow. "I don't know about my own father. He got sick of my mother's rich friends and left us when I was just a boy." He studied his glass. "He was from New Mexico, but he worked on oil rigs in Oklahoma. That's where he met my mother." He glanced at her. "She was blonde and blue-eyed, like Bobby, and she loved the good life. Money was everything to her. My father had simpler tastes."

"I wouldn't have asked," she replied quietly. It startled her that he was willing to share such a personal thing with her. Either he was extremely upset by Bess, or the alcohol was affecting him.

She stared at his shirt where he'd unbuttoned it and removed his tie. Against the white fabric, his skin looked even darker than usual. Her eyes were drawn to the thick mesh of hair over hard, bronzed muscle.

As if he sensed that rapt stare, he turned toward her

and his eyes caught hers. He didn't look away. While her heart went wild, with deliberate slowness he tossed away the cigarette he'd just lit and took a step toward her, bringing her totally against him, so that her breasts touched his chest where his shirt was open. She wasn't wearing anything under the jumpsuit, and she could feel her nipples harden at the contact with him. Tensing away from him, she wondered uncomfortably if he felt them, too.

"Anything sexual disturbs you, doesn't it?" he asked softly, well aware of the tension in her body. "Well, I'm safe—you said so yourself. So why don't you cut your teeth on me?"

"I can't!" she gasped. He had her with her back to the sliding glass door, so that she was trapped between its coldness and his warmth, her breasts wildly sensitive against his hard chest.

"Shh," he whispered at her temple. "Don't panic. I won't hurt you." He smiled softly. The drinks had done the trick; he was finally feeling relaxed and slightly muddled, which was a relief from all the heavy thinking he'd had to do lately. He couldn't have Bess, he reasoned now, but Elissa was fair game, wasn't she? Shy and virginal—how tempting to a man. What would it hurt to give her a little experience? He cared about her, in a way. And who better to deal with her repressions? She'd almost admitted earlier that she'd let him.

"Why are you doing this?" she asked in a high-pitched tone. Her fingers started to push him away, but when her hands encountered warm, hair-roughened skin, they stopped struggling and flattened against him. She realized she didn't feel like resisting, anyway. The alcohol had done something to her willpower. She felt more like relaxing against King than fighting him; his proximity was having a throbbing effect on her body.

"Because I need something to occupy me, to keep me out of trouble. So you're going to be my hobby," he said.

"I don't want to be your hobby," she protested weakly. Her legs felt trembly.

"I was yours at the beginning," he reminded her. "You've no one to blame but yourself."

"That was different. You were repressed," she said defensively. He was too close. She was inhaling the tangy, clean scent of him, and it was intoxicating her more than the vodka had. His bared chest was hard under her fingers, and between seeing him and smelling him and feeling him, she was adrift on sensation, her heart pounding. All that devastating masculinity, so close.

"*I* was repressed?" he asked with an amused smile.

"You were all alone," she said quietly, avoiding his eyes. "I felt sorry for you. I was alone, too. I… Well, I thought it would be nice to have a friend."

"You had Warchief," he pointed out, grinning. "Speaking of Warchief…" He glanced around. The big parrot was on his perch ring, one foot drawn up, his eyes closed. "Unusual, his going to sleep without being covered. Is that antibiotic working, do you think?"

"He isn't sneezing or rasping," she said, grateful for the change of subject. "He's better. He's just sleepy. He always goes to sleep at dusk, when you're not around." She grinned. "He's in love with you."

"I think he's a she," he laughed. Then he turned his attention back to her, looking down at the bodice of her jumpsuit with narrowing eyes. He moved experimentally, rubbing his chest against her, and she gasped at the sudden, sharp pleasure the friction produced.

She flushed to the roots of her long dark hair. "King!"

"Shocking, isn't it?" he asked, lifting his narrow gaze to hers.

Her eyes searched his, curiosity momentarily displacing her nervousness at this new intimacy.

His gaze held hers while the hands at her waist began to move her in a sensuous circle against his hard, warm chest.

The only sounds she heard were the hoarseness of the ocean against the sand and the wildness of her own breathing. She couldn't bear to look at King as sensation overwhelmed her, and she lowered her forehead to his shoulder. He was breathing heavily, too, his heartbeat audible.

His thumbs edged under her arms, brushing at the sides of her breasts, feeling her softness, feeling her begin to tremble with the newness of physical pleasure.

"You aren't wearing a bra, are you?" he whispered, his voice deep and soft at her ear. "That silky thing is so thin that it's like holding you naked in my arms."

The power of the erotic suggestion was such that Elissa bit her lip to keep from crying out. Her nails dug into his shoulders, and her legs threatened to buckle underneath her. She shuddered.

"Elissa," he breathed roughly.

She could smell the Scotch on his breath, but even that was oddly exciting. His arms suddenly lifted her into an embrace tight enough that she could feel his ribs digging into her. She clung to him, her face buried in his throat, breathing in the exquisitely male scent of him, her head spinning, her body aching for something it had never known, her breasts crushed against hard muscle. He bit her ear, then ran his tongue around its soft curves, an intimate gesture that she'd never realized could have such a profound effect.

Her arms tightened around his neck, her face fiery with unexpected passion as he held her. Was she mistaken, or was there a fine tremor in the arms so fiercely holding her?

His cheek brushed against hers. "Your breasts feel swollen," he whispered, once more moving her body against him. "Do they ache?" he whispered knowingly.

"Yes," she gasped mindlessly. "Oh, King!" Her curiosity outweighed her caution, outweighed the fear that had always come with the threat of intimacy, and she reveled in the feel of his slick, damp skin against her tender breasts.

"I can make them stop aching," he whispered huskily. His lips traveled down her face to her throat, his breathing harsh and rapid. "Here…"

His mouth slid over the silky bodice and suddenly pressed, open and hot, right against the soft curve of her thinly veiled breast.

She cried out at the pleasure it gave her, and her back arched to give him access.

But the sound had shocked King into realizing what he was doing. His head jerked up, his eyes wide and frankly stunned. "Dear God," he said harshly. He hadn't expected this. Hadn't expected to want her. He hadn't known it until now, hadn't dreamed… He felt the tautness of his body and suddenly released her and turned away, not wanting her to know what she was doing to him.

She gaped at him. He was breathing harshly as he reached over to pick up his nearly finished drink from the table. His hand seemed to tremble a little as he lifted the glass to his mouth and drained it. "I'm sorry," he bit off, setting the glass down hard on the table. "I didn't expect that to happen."

He was apologizing, she registered, but for what? For wanting her? "I don't…mind." She said it and was amazed to find that it was true. She didn't mind having him want her. It was heady and wildly exciting.

He turned, his dark eyes glazed and questioning. "Why not?"

She shrugged helplessly. "I don't know." Her eyes fell to his chest. "I still... I still ache," she whispered shakily.

His lips were parted, as if he was finding it difficult to breathe. "Have you felt like that with anyone else?" he asked, distressed to realize it was suddenly deeply important that he know.

"No," she confessed, her voice soft, gentle.

He couldn't decide what to do. Should he send her home or pick her up in his arms and take her into his bed and show her how sweet he could make it for her? Damn. How could just a couple of drinks make him so addled?

She looked up at that moment and saw the indecision in his eyes, and she knew exactly what had caused it. Her face colored. "I—I can't sleep with you," she whispered huskily. "I...like what you just did to me, but... I can't deal with that kind of easy intimacy. Not even with you."

His dark eyes roamed down her body, the sight of that sweet softness he'd known so briefly making him ache. He caught her eyes. "I can make you want it," he said in a stranger's sensuous voice.

"And after?" she asked.

He drew in a slow breath. "My God, what am I saying?"

"It's been a hard night for you," she said, forcing herself not to take it too seriously. He was frustrated, that was all, and she was handy and he'd forgotten all the reasons why not. "I wish things were different."

"So do I." He rammed his hands into his pockets. "Believe me, so do I." It was the truth. His body fairly throbbed with wanting her. How odd, his muddled brain mused, to have this kind of reaction to Elissa when it was Bess he'd been afraid of wanting. Could it be misplaced desire? Lord, he couldn't even think straight.

"I'd better go home."

He turned. "I'll walk you."

"No. It's all right. You can watch me out the door," she said quickly—too quickly.

"I can't help it, you know," he said softly, accurately reading the apprehension in her lovely face and smiling in spite of himself when she colored. "A man's body will give him away every time. But I trust you not to take advantage of it," he added with dry humor.

She stared at him, then gasped with helpless laughter, "You horrible man!"

"Well, I'm vulnerable," he commented as he opened the front door and stood aside to let her pass. "A man has to look out for his honor, after all. I might marry someday. She'll want to be the first."

"I'm sure she'd be at least the fifteenth," she chided, laughing at her own boldness. Now that the heart-shattering truth of just moments before had passed, it was once again easy to talk to him, even about the intimate things.

"Not quite that many," he mumbled as they walked, the breeze, warm and salty smelling, ruffling the fronds of the palm trees.

"Well, you didn't learn what you did back there by reading a book," she observed.

He cocked an eyebrow and laughed faintly. "No, I didn't." He stopped, tilting her chin up. "God, it was sweet."

Her lips parted, and her breath caught in her throat. Then he laughed softly, angrily, as he took her arm, almost roughly, and propelled her along the moonlit beach.

"I must be drunk," he muttered. "You'll have to overlook a few things about tonight, I guess. I haven't been myself."

Which was absolutely true. Even speaking was hard for him right now. He needed a cold shower—badly. And for some reason, he didn't want Elissa to know what he was feeling, to know the extent of this bizarre aberration in his thought processes. It shocked him, the sudden hunger he felt to strip her out of that jumpsuit, throw her down on the beach and make her his. He remembered how she'd looked in that sexy nightgown, and he almost groaned out loud. He had to be drunk all right, he told himself. How could he even imagine a union between them? She with her hang-ups and he with his impossibly confused feelings for Bess. Was this what people meant by love on the rebound? Or had he always wanted Elissa and refused to acknowledge it in the face of her physical reticence?

"You're very quiet," she said when they reached her door.

"I'm shocked at my own behavior," he said curtly.

"It's been difficult for you," she returned, unable to meet his eyes. "It was just the alcohol."

"Yes. It must have been. We'll forget it happened."

"That might be best," she said lightly, forcing herself not to show the disquiet she felt.

"You don't need to make it sound so damned easy," he said, unreasonably irritated and finding himself on the verge of spewing out exactly what he'd wanted to keep silent about, yet unable to stop himself. His self-control was shot. "Do you know how much I want to lay you down in the sand and have you? Do you?" he demanded harshly. "And because of that, you'd better stay away from me until I get myself together." Hurting, and lashing out because of it, he straightened to deal the killing blow. "Because anything I did right now would be because of Bess—wanting Bess—and you'd better remember it."

It was a lie—he was too confused to know his own mind right now—but he reasoned that enough people stood to get hurt by Bess's recent interest in him, and he didn't want Elissa to become a casualty, too. Anything—anything at all—that would keep her at arm's length would ultimately be for her own good. She didn't need to compromise her innocence because of his confused longings. So he'd have to be cruel to be kind, even though she wouldn't realize it right now. Someday, however, she'd thank him for what must seem like callous behavior.

She clenched her teeth. He hadn't exactly shocked her with the admission—she'd suspected she'd been a stand-in for Bess—but had he needed to be so blunt? "Then I'll say good-night."

"Say it, and go inside." He jammed his hands into his pockets.

"What a sweet-tempered man you are," she muttered. She turned to unlock the door, then glared at him over her shoulder as she went inside. "Thanks for a lovely evening. I did so enjoy it."

He glared back. "Including the way you threw yourself at me back there?" he asked with a cold, mocking smile, pushing her that last step.

He was asking for a hard slap. She tried to remember that he'd been drinking, but all she wanted to do was push him into a coral reef and whistle for a passing shark! "I was drinking," she admitted, "and so were you."

"Well, I won't make the same mistake with you again," he returned coldly. "Obviously you can't hold your liquor." He didn't know why he was goading her—why didn't he let her go inside, where she'd be safely away from him?

"Said the pot to the kettle!" she threw back, fuming. "You were the one who started it!"

"You weren't fighting very hard," he pointed out.

She clenched her fists. "Next time you need help with your love life, find another pigeon. I'm not playing second fiddle to you and your sister-in-law!"

"Stop shouting," he grumbled.

"I'll shout if I like. And I want my bird back!"

"When he's well, with my blessing," he shot back.

Her lower lip trembled. She was near tears. With her fists clenched at her sides, she felt herself shaking with mingled rage and frustration. Here she was yelling things she didn't mean but couldn't help saying, and she didn't know what to do about it. She'd never felt like this before, and she didn't even understand what was wrong.

"I hate you!" she wailed.

He took his hands out of his pockets and moved close, cupping her head in his lean fingers, holding her firmly. "Do you, Elissa?" That's what he'd wanted, wasn't it? To protect her from himself? But as he gazed down into her wide, glistening eyes, he felt a wave of emotion crash over him, engulfing him in frustrated desire. He was only human, after all.

"In lieu of a cold shower…" he said under his breath, and he bent his head.

Elissa's mouth felt bruised from the sheer force of his hard lips, and he didn't spare her. His mouth lifted for an instant, only to come down again more intimately, his tongue pushing into her mouth, his fingers biting into her to tilt her head and give him better access to her lips.

She moaned, and he caught his breath. "Open your mouth," he ground out, his hands at her throat, lifting, coaxing. "Oh, God, Elissa, open your mouth…"

She did, shuddering as he deepened the kiss. Her knees weakened and threatened to collapse, but the instant her body relaxed against the rigid strength of his, he seemed to come to his senses. His lips lifted slowly, delicately probing, brushing. He felt her breasts, so smooth and hard tipped, press against him, saw her expression soft with confused desire. Elissa. He blinked, his mind in limbo. He wanted her. His body ached to have hers, to press it into the soft sand beneath his, to feel her skin warm and welcoming under his hands...

Elissa... He cursed under his breath and stopped abruptly, feeling outraged at his lack of control. He hadn't meant for this to happen. That damned Scotch! What was he doing? He went rigid and suddenly all but threw her away from him.

"Was that what you wanted?" he demanded, wanting to hurt, to make her pay for that lapse in his control. "Now you know, so go inside, little girl. You'll have to get the rest of your experience with someone else. I don't initiate virgins."

She swallowed. He wasn't making any sense at all; he was being totally erratic. His fists clenched, and she saw the shudder ripple through his powerful body. *Too much to drink*, her mind registered. *Dangerous*.

"Who asked you to?" she shot back. She hated him. She hated him! With shaking hands she opened the door, went inside and slammed it behind her, locking it, as well. Outside she heard a harsh muttered curse.

She collapsed against the wall with an unsteady sigh. She hadn't expected that. As a matter of fact, about the *last* thing she'd expected after his outburst was for him to kiss her. He'd never kissed her before tonight. Come to think of it, they'd never argued before. She felt a lump in her throat as she realized that she'd just lost a good friend and she didn't even understand why.

His footsteps died away, and all she heard was the gentle wind off the Caribbean. She touched her lips, feeling their swollen fullness with wonder. Her tongue touched them and tasted him.

It all seemed like a dream. For some reason King had stepped completely out of character, and for that matter, she had, too. But none of it made any sense. Surely if King were pining away for his sister-in-law, he wouldn't be capable of that kind of passion with another woman. Or would he? She cursed her ignorance of men and their basic makeup.

Trying to sort things out, she concluded that if King needed to use her as a shield, he must have some kind of special feeling for Bess. The tender look in his eyes when he'd gazed at his sister-in-law had afforded Elissa a rare glimpse behind the mask of cool reserve King usually wore. Apparently, Bess had always been special to him, and now, maybe for the first time, he was confronting her in a new way—as a desirable woman, not just as a relative.

Elissa sighed, remembering with guilt her own delicious abandon in King's arms. She was sure the drinks had influenced her. They'd obviously influenced him, too. She went into her bedroom and flicked on the light, quietly removing the jumpsuit and putting on a long, plain cotton nightgown. King had reminded her that anything he did to her would be only out of desire for Bess. Was that completely true? she wondered. There were so many puzzles now. Their uncomplicated friendship had turned into a mental wrestling match.

She brushed her long hair and crawled into bed. But once she turned out the light, she could feel all over again the warmth of King's lips on hers, his tongue pushing into her mouth in a kiss unlike any she'd ever experienced. She felt her face go hot as she remembered just how involved he'd gotten. And he'd accused *her* of throwing herself at *him*! Incredible, how much his sharp words had hurt. Of course, she'd been spared his temper for the past two years. She might never have seen it if he hadn't made such a blatant pass at her in the first place. Men!

Well, her sexy nightie was still lying on his bed, she remembered; she hoped it gave him nightmares. She rolled over and closed her eyes, counting waves and praying for sleep. *You can just hold your breath until I do you another favor, King Roper*, she thought furiously.

CHAPTER FOUR

IN HER WILD and confusing dreams, Elissa felt King's hands caressing her, molding her curves, teaching her new movements, new sensations. She could see his face taut with passion, feel the ripple of his muscles as he began a pagan rhythm with his body...

She sat up straight in bed, drenched with sweat and trembling from the effects of those sensuous and disturbing dreams. Her own reactions shocked her. Were all those years of suppressing her sensuality about to explode in her face? Last night her old fears of intimacy had dropped away, and she'd felt straightforward desire for the first time in her life.

It was the vodka, she thought stubbornly, trying desperately to get her delinquent emotions under control. After all, how could she forget that King had accused her of throwing herself at him?

"Sure I did," she muttered as she went into the living room that overlooked the beach. "Sure I did. I forced him to hold me like that and kiss my..."

She swallowed, ignoring the instant hardening of her nipples. This was outrageous! Where was her pride?

She made herself a cup of coffee and opened a packaged pastry, nibbling at it halfheartedly as she began to scribble ideas for new designs on her big sketch pad. Unfortunately, nothing appealed to her. She stayed with her work for a few minutes and then gave up, walking out onto her small patio. Her long hair and wildly colorful caftan fluttered in the eternal breeze from the sea, and she let the sound of the surf soothe her as she gazed appreciatively at a big sailboat on the horizon.

Jamaica was the stuff of dreams, she mused. Pirate legends and fascinating people. Her eyes turned toward a distant hill, at the top of which the structure called Rose Hall perched. If legend was fact, its long-ago owner, Annie Palmer, whom the locals had dubbed the White Witch of Rose Hall, had murdered three husbands and several lovers there, in addition to practicing voodoo and brutalizing her slaves.

Once, after a tour of the spooky house, Elissa had had nightmares for days. One night, she recalled, she'd awakened screaming, and she'd heard a pounding at her door. King, his pajama bottoms peeking out above the waistband of his trousers testifying to his haste in rushing to her cottage, had, upon assessing that nothing was wrong, laughed at her indulgently and cradled her like a child. Even then, she reflected, sitting on the edge of her bed and holding her, he hadn't seemed to notice her as a woman. There had been nothing remotely sexual about the comfort he'd given her. And yet now, after last night, it was impossible to think of him in a nonsexual way.

She stepped down onto the beach and saw that King's car was gone. Where was he? she wondered briefly. Deciding it was really none of her business, she brushed back her hair and turned once again to watch the big sailboat in the distance wend its way seaward. Her cottage was too far off the beaten track for much contact with city life, and she liked it that way. All the same, it must be fascinating to live in Mo' Bay, as everyone called Montego Bay, and see the people who visited the island from those grand oceangoing hotels.

With her coffee cup in her hands, she sat down on the warm sand and watched the graceful casuarina pines blow in the wind. It was heaven here. So peaceful and quiet and exquisitely unpolluted.

Her eyes drifted closed, and suddenly she envisioned herself on the beach with King, in the moonlight, making wild, passionate love, with the surf crashing around them…

Her eyes popped open, and she jumped to her feet so quickly that she almost upended her coffee all over herself. Dazed by her wayward thoughts, she stumbled back inside and went straight to work. And this time she did three designs that satisfied her creative instincts.

It was the longest day she could remember. At dusk she heard Warchief go off like an air-raid siren and wished that she could get him and bring him home, but it was misting rain and he was better off where he was for the time being. She was feeling unaccountably lonely, and she missed having him on his big T-stand perch in the living room, chattering away and begging scraps when she broke off work for a snack or a meal. She almost always ended up sharing fresh fruits and vegetables and bread, which he ate with evident enjoyment.

She sighed, turning away from the window. She missed her bird. She was going to miss King even more. After last night, she was sure he wouldn't have anything else to do with her. She still found it amazing that he'd wanted to take her to bed. She was glad she'd had the sense to refuse, but she still flushed thinking about what she'd let him do to her by those sliding glass doors. Best to put such errant thoughts out of her mind, she chided herself.

Just after dark, she was puttering around the kitchen in

shorts and a long-sleeved man's shirt when she saw King drive up to his villa, accompanied by Bobby and Bess. She frowned. Weren't they supposed to have left that morning?

Minutes later, her phone rang.

"I'm home," King said in a deep, sexy tone that she knew instantly was a ruse. "Why don't you come over and have a drink? Bess and Bobby are staying the night with me."

She fished for excuses. "I have to feed the hermit crabs and put out lobster pots…"

"I'll see you in five minutes," he said, ignoring her feeble attempt at humor, and hung up.

She glared at the telephone. She wanted to call him back and tell him what he could do with his overbearing attitude, but now that she'd begun this horrible charade, she felt obliged to go through with it. Why, she didn't know.

After changing into a strappy little black dress, hose and high heels, she tramped across to King's house.

Warchief went into raucous ecstasies of welcome at her arrival. "Quiet, sweet thing," Elissa scolded playfully, nodding to Bobby and a subdued Bess as she went to pet her parrot.

Evidently he'd lost his inclination to bite. He blazed his eyes, docilely bent his head for her to scratch and cooed, "Hello, pretty thing."

"I've missed you, too, you horrible bird," she murmured, nuzzling her nose against his head.

"I wouldn't put *my* nose that close to him," Bess gasped.

"Wise decision," King remarked easily. "He's totally unpredictable. He won't let anyone except Elissa that close."

"Now go to sleep," Elissa whispered when she'd scratched his green head enough to satisfy Warchief and his eyes were nearly closed.

She busied herself covering his cage, uneasier around

King than she'd ever been in the two years she'd known him. She couldn't even manage to meet his eyes, she was so confused.

"I expected to find you already over here," Bess remarked. Dressed in flowing yellow lounging pajamas that suited her blondness, she leaned back on the big white sofa.

"I had some designs to work on," Elissa replied.

"She works better at her own cottage, where there are fewer distractions," King remarked, his dark eyes narrow on her averted face.

Bobby hadn't said a word, except to greet Elissa warmly. He was bent over financial reports spread all over the coffee table, seemingly oblivious to the world around him.

Bess gave him a weary glance before she turned back to study Elissa and King. "So what's with you two? You barely seem to be speaking," she observed. Her eyes openly flirted with King.

King cleared his throat and stared hard at Elissa. "How astute of you to notice, Bess. Actually, Elissa and I had a little tiff, but it's nothing, really."

"Yes," Elissa began, glaring at him. "I simply lost control and threw myself at—" Suddenly she found herself being grabbed by the hand and dragged into a bedroom.

"Rape!" she yelled, and Bobby surprised everyone by bursting out with laughter.

King closed the door behind them, his face livid. He leaned back against the door, watching her retreat to the window.

"Stop that," he growled. "You're slitting my throat!"

"Good. I'll bet you bleed ice water," she returned, her eyes wide and accusing.

"I shouldn't have said what I said last night," he began slowly. "I'm sorry. I can't begin to explain why I did it."

"You were drunk and so was I," she replied to save face.

His eyebrow made an arch. "On three drinks?"

"I'm not used to liquor of any sort," she defended herself. "And unless I'm mistaken, you don't drink much, either."

His powerful shoulders rose and fell. In his white slacks and a red-and-white knit shirt, he looked impossibly handsome. His dark eyes ran up and down her body, and she knew he was remembering, as she had, how it had been between them. Her heart pounded once again at the sheer impact of that memory.

"Bobby postponed his flight until tomorrow morning," he said a few moments later. "He thought it would be fun if the four of us flew back to the States together."

"I can't," she protested. "Warchief—"

"I've got a sitter, as usual," he returned. "I can't stay here or Bess will get a migraine or find some excuse to stay with me. Bobby, as you can see, is immersed in his work. He doesn't even realize what's happening."

"You poor man," she said coolly.

He glared at her. "Do you think I can help it?"

"No." She sighed, turning away. "I don't suppose she can help it, either."

He came up behind her, his warm, strong hands clasping her arms. She trembled at their touch, so aware of him physically that it made her ache.

His fingers contracted rhythmically, as if he liked the silky feel of her skin. His breath in her hair was warm and not quite steady.

"We can fly to Miami, and then I can drive you to your parents' house. That will accomplish two things—satisfy my sense of honesty and get Bess out of my hair."

So he wasn't planning to stay, thank God. But what would her parents say at this unexpected visit? They were

bound to wonder why she'd cut her vacation short and why
King was with her. This entire situation was totally ludi-
crous. Yet, despite herself, her heart went out to King in his
predicament, and she reasoned it wouldn't hurt her work
any to touch base in Florida. Maybe her parents wouldn't
have to see King, and they'd never know that anything
was amiss.

"All right," she agreed. "I'll go."

"Good girl."

She turned and looked up at him. "Yes, I am," she said
quietly. "Try to remember that the next time you decide to
make a pass at me."

He searched her soft blue eyes. "You and I are an ex-
plosive mixture, aren't we?" he asked, his voice deep and
measured.

Her nails were making quiet patterns on his shirtfront
while she looked at him. "Until last night, I never really understood why women couldn't stop men from making love
to them," she confessed. "It's very hard to stop, isn't it?"

He smiled indulgently. "Well, a woman *can* tease a man
until he's desperate to have her."

"I tease sometimes," she admitted slowly, searching his
darkening eyes, "but I don't really mean it. Not as a come-
on." She lowered her gaze to his throat. "I've always wanted
to be more like Bess," she said. "Sophisticated and worldly
and very desirable. But the minute a man comes too close,
I freeze. All those old inhibitions rear up, and I run. But I
don't mean to be cruel. It's…like a fantasy."

He tilted her face up to his. "I think I've always known
that, Elissa," he said quietly. "And I know you weren't teasing me. Not deliberately, anyway," he added with a smile.
"Though you did get a little wild."

She blushed feverishly.

"What I'm trying to explain," he continued, tracing her cheek, "is that I was frustrated and I couldn't do anything about it. I ended up saying a lot of things I didn't mean."

"So did I," she replied. "I—I ached."

"Not half as much as I did," he said with a mock groan. He pushed her long hair away from her face. "I lay awake half the night, picturing you nude, on the beach, your arms open for me," he said huskily.

"Why, that's just what I—!" She stopped, her mouth open, horrified at what she'd admitted.

"There's nothing to be ashamed of," he said gently. "You're human. So am I. We had a little too much to drink, we quarreled—that's all."

"King, you—you won't try to seduce me?" she asked, afraid that he might out of frustration over Bess and knowing from last night's experience that he wouldn't meet much resistance.

"Could I?" he asked in a smooth, sensuous tone, searching her wide eyes.

"Yes," she admitted, lowering her gaze.

His own reaction startled him; it was instantaneous and overwhelming, and he caught his breath as his body tautened. He saw her blush scarlet at the awareness of what was happening to him, and he muttered unsteadily, "This is absurd."

"King?" she whispered, her body throbbing wildly from the knowledge of what her response had done to him.

"Oh, what the hell," he breathed, and he bent to her mouth.

His lips came down on hers and opened them sensuously, while his arms lifted her against him, savoring her soft weight. He carried her to the huge king-size bed and placed her carefully on the black silk coverlet. Then he slid alongside her, his look lazy, his eyes dangerous. Lowering his head, he trailed a string of warm, moist kisses from her temple to her throat.

"Does this untie?" he murmured, searching her shoulders for the ends of the straps.

Her lips parted. She thought she wanted to protest, but her body was singing to her, her blood raging in her veins. She wanted his eyes on her, there, his mouth, she wanted...

"You have bedroom eyes," he whispered. His fingers found the tiny bows just behind her shoulders, and he untied them very slowly. "When I look in them I can see what you want."

"What do I want?" she whispered, her voice husky and unfamiliar to her own ears as she lay beneath him.

"My eyes," he replied, drawing the bodice of her dress down just to the soft beginning slope of her breasts. "And my mouth." He bent his head to her creamy skin, running his lips just beneath her collarbone in slow, sensuous sweeps. His hands were on her rib cage, smoothing the black crepe, his thumbs just under her breasts, touching them as if by accident.

Her fists clenched beside her head, and her breath caught. He lifted his head, looking at her.

"You're trembling," he breathed, reaching for the top of the bodice.

"King," she moaned helplessly.

"Innocent," he whispered. He held her eyes as his hands moved, and she felt the cool night air on her breasts as the fabric fell to her waist.

"Oh!" she whispered softly, arching her body gently.

His gaze moved slowly down to her breasts, their small pink nipples aroused and hard, her body shuddering a little with the newness of this kind of intimacy.

"The first time," he said under his breath. "My God, they're exquisite." His lightly calloused fingers brushed them, tenderly tracing their contours, touching the hard nipples just lightly enough to make her shudder with pleasure.

She couldn't even speak; her throat was tight with exquisite tension.

"Now," he whispered, bending. "Now, Elissa, now..."

His hand cupped her while his mouth opened on her, and she cried out. Then his mouth caught hers, stifling the tiny sound while his hand possessed her, savoring her silky warmth.

"I could eat you," he ground out against her eager, open mouth. "I could eat you like candy."

Another sound tore from her, and he lifted his head, looking dazedly past her to the radio. His hand trembled as he reached for the volume and turned it on to a heavy reggae beat.

"Now," he murmured, "you can make as much noise as you want."

Her lips opened to voice a protest, and his crushed down over them, his tongue moving into her mouth with a slow, hungry rhythm, his knee easing between her legs.

She felt her fingernails digging into the nape of his neck, reveling in the feel of his thick dark hair. Her body was on fire for him; she'd never in her life felt anything as explosively sexual. She wanted fulfillment; she wanted to be part of him, rock with him, writhe under him.

Her moans grew sharper when his mouth traveled down over her breasts to her waist, her stomach. She moved helplessly in his embrace, feeling his strength, loving his hands, loving the ardor of his warm mouth.

He paused, breathing raggedly, to strip off his shirt, and she gasped at the sight of him like that, looming over her, his chest thick with dark hair, the bronzed muscles rippling, his face dark with passion, his eyes almost black. She could feel the heat of his body, see the fine tremor of his arms.

"Come here," he commanded, kneeling before her.

She rose to her own knees, and he pulled her to him, pressing her breasts hard against his hair-roughened chest and making her shudder with the fierce pleasure of it. He held her there, kissing her deeply and shifting her against him in the process until her nipples were so sensitized that they burned and her nails dug into his back.

"I want...you," was dragged out of her throat. She buried her face in his neck and clung to him, her hips against his, her thighs trembling. "I...want...you."

His hands went to her hips, grinding her into him, and a burning sensation shot through her lower body. She shuddered helplessly, gasping with pleasure and barely contained desire.

"Lie down," he whispered shakily. "Lie down under me. I'll make you stop shaking. I'll make you part of me..."

"The door... Is it locked?" she asked huskily, feeling his weight come over her, his hands urgent on her body.

"Locked?" His hands stilled, and he looked into her feverish eyes. "Elissa?" He swallowed, his bare chest rising and falling with the force of his heartbeat as he looked down at her. "Elissa... I could make you pregnant."

She was hardly able to breathe. His eyes were the world. She loved him, and she hadn't known. He was more than her friend. He was everything. And to have his child—the thought was too wonderful for words.

Her eyes went down his body possessively, loving its long, powerful lines, loving every inch of him with sweet abandon. Her hips moved sensuously under his, eliciting a groan from him.

"No, honey," he whispered, stilling her impatient movements. "Don't make me. We've got to stop while we can."

"Why?" she asked dazedly.

"We can't make love with Bobby and Bess sitting in the next room." He laughed brittlely. "I must have been out of my mind to let things go this far."

His hands cupped her head, and he dropped a hard, quick kiss onto her lips. Then he sat up, smoothing his hands blatantly over her breasts, his eyes appreciative and boldly possessive. "God, you're something," he said. "As hot and wild as I am. We'd set fires together," he added with what sounded like regret.

She sat up, too, more than unsettled by the confusing sequence of events and moods. Feeling uncomfortably exposed beneath that frank stare of his, she tugged at her bodice, but his hand prevented her from tugging it up.

"Not yet," he murmured. His hand went to her back, arching her over his arm, and his mouth opened, taking her breast inside the moist darkness.

She shuddered, biting her lip to keep from crying out. It was the sweetest kind of ache he made there, his tongue rubbing lazily at her nipple, his lips tugging at her. She clutched the back of his dark head, holding him there, while his free hand came up just below his mouth and cupped her sensuously.

It was a long time before he lifted his head, and he clearly liked what he saw when he looked at her. "I'd like to have you on the beach, just the way I dreamed of."

She flushed to the roots of her hair at the image that had haunted her all day, too.

His hand moved over her soft breasts. "You're very pale here," he said. "I'd like to teach you the delicious pleasure of sunbathing nude. Swimming nude."

"You do," she said without thinking, her voice breathless sounding.

He lifted his head, smiling slowly. "Yes. You've watched me sometimes at night, from your kitchen window, haven't you?"

The flush got worse, but she didn't look away. "I was curious," she confessed softly. "There was moonlight once, and you came out of the water very close to the cottage... I never knew a man could be beautiful." She faltered, blushing furiously. "I didn't think you'd know I was watching."

He brushed his mouth over her eyes. "I knew," he murmured. "I don't mind if you look at me."

She was still trembling when he got to his feet and pulled her up with him, slowly retying the straps at her shoulders.

"You look loved," he said unexpectedly. He brushed her tangled hair away from her damp face, then turned away to pick up his shirt.

To Elissa's amazement, her hand reached out to protest when he started to put it on.

He looked up in surprise, then gently drew her hands to him. "Go ahead. Indulge yourself."

"You don't mind?" she asked, savoring his hair-roughened skin with hands that had never known a man's body.

"Mind? Not in the least," he returned. "Come here. I'll teach you how."

She hadn't known there was a right and wrong way to touch a man, but with his hands showing her how, urging her mouth to his skin, teaching her what excited him, what pleased him the most, she felt her confidence grow, and with it a new sense of womanly power. She didn't protest, not even when he guided her hands and let her experience him in a way she'd never dreamed of.

Finally he emitted a low groan and slid her arms around his waist.

"Sometimes I forget how innocent you are," he said in her ear. He bit it, laughing softly, and his cheek nuzzled hers. "You make me forget," he whispered. He drew his mouth across her cheek, then raised his head to search her eyes. "You shut out the world while I'm holding you."

He kissed her gently then, and she understood. She blotted out his hunger for Bess—that was what he meant.

But I love you, she wanted to say. *I love you, and I want so much more of you than this.* Two years of friendship, and it had never occurred to her just how necessary he'd become to her, just how possessive she'd become of him. Nothing he'd done to her was unwelcome. She realized she could lie with him and give herself and live on it for the rest of her life, despite all her hard-won principles. Was that lust? Or was it the natural hunger for oneness, for total knowledge?

With his mouth still over hers, she frowned and opened her eyes, only to find his eyes open and watching her. Her heart went wild. His tongue penetrated her mouth, his hands came up under her breasts, and she couldn't sustain the look a second longer. She closed her eyes with a hungry moan, and he kissed her deeply, thoroughly, before finally releasing her and putting her from him. She straightened up and smoothed out her dress as best she could.

"Don't brush your hair," he said when she reached for a brush on his dresser just as they were about to leave the room.

"Why not? I must look a mess."

"Because I want her to see you like this," he said gruffly. "With your mouth swollen and your hair in a tangle and your skin glowing. I want her to know that we've been making love."

"That's cruel," she whispered.

"I have to be cruel, don't you see? My God, Elissa, he's my brother," he groaned.

"Yes, I know." She stood in front of him, reaching up to smooth away his frown. She smiled gently, drowning in new fantasies, brimming over with her new knowledge of him, new memories to put under her pillow and cherish.

"Too bad you're such an innocent," he said with a sigh.

"What would you do if I weren't?" she teased gently.

"I'd take you into my bed and work Bess out of my system with a vengeance," he said honestly. "And I could, with you. I've never wanted anyone so much in all my life."

"I wish I could let you," she replied. "I think I'd like sleeping with you, King. Lovemaking is more beautiful than I ever realized."

"I'm glad you think of it that way, and not as something to satisfy a passing physical urge," he said. "Ideally it is an act of love. With you," he added quietly, bemusedly, "it feels like it. I don't understand…"

She drew in a slow breath and went to turn the radio off, flushing at the reason it had been turned on. She looked across the room and found him watching her.

"There's no need to blush," he said quietly, once again reading her mind. "You did my ego a world of good— believe me. If it hadn't been for our houseguests, I wouldn't have given a damn if you'd yelled the place down."

"It's embarrassing to feel like this," she whispered. "They'll see…"

"Yes," he agreed tersely. "Thank God."

She couldn't answer that. She opened the door and walked ahead of him.

Bess wasn't there. Bobby looked up with a sly grin. "Bess has gone for a walk on the beach," he murmured.

He cleared his throat. "I guess you two settled your differences…"

Elissa blushed to the roots of her hair. King laughed delightedly and slid his arm around her. "It wasn't anything serious," he said, chuckling. "I'm sorry if we embarrassed you."

Bobby shrugged. "Not me. But Bess is unusually sensitive, I guess." He put down his pen. "She and I used to be like that, but she's grown away from me. So many parties and teas and girls' nights out—I hardly see her when I'm at home."

"You might try spending more time there, now that you can afford to," King suggested pointedly.

"I might. I think I'll stroll out and join her."

"We'll make some coffee," King said, and he led Elissa toward the kitchen.

"She was hurt," Elissa said as she filled the coffeepot.

"I know." His voice was deep and curt, and he was staring out the window at Bess watching the waves.

She plugged in the pot and went to him, touching his chest lightly where the shirt was unbuttoned. "And so are you," she said gently. "I'm sorry. I feel as if I've failed you."

"How?" he asked, smiling.

"I couldn't give myself."

"The hell you couldn't." He chuckled wryly, then linked his arms around her waist and looked down at her. "*I* stopped us. You didn't. Not even when I mentioned pregnancy."

She lowered her eyes to his chest. "I'm not so afraid of it."

"Aren't you?" He studied her. No, she didn't seem to be.

And he was shocked to learn that he wasn't, either. That intrigued him. Shouldn't he have been?

He turned to gaze out the window once more.

CHAPTER FIVE

"ARE YOU SURE Bess doesn't want children?" Elissa asked abruptly, disrupting his disturbing thoughts.

He turned back toward her. "She says not," he replied. Hands in his pockets, he leaned against the counter. "In the beginning, I think it was because she didn't want to be tied down. Her mother had seven children." He smiled sadly, remembering. "Bess was in the middle, but she did her share of looking after the little ones. She had a rough time of it, and so did the other kids, for that matter," he murmured, remembering how Bess's father drank and terrified the children. "Anyway, children don't necessarily guarantee a good marriage. I've seen happy marriages destroyed by them."

That sounded very private. "Have you?"

He frowned. "My mother often said that she and my father were happy enough until I came along and spoiled things," he said quietly.

"What a horrid thing to say to your own child," Elissa muttered, her face taut as she arranged cups and saucers and cream and sugar on a big silver tray.

"My mother was a devoted socialite," he said. "She didn't much care for children. If my stepfather hadn't insisted, Bobby probably would never have been born. Odd how things turn out. She was a vivacious, beautiful woman with a quick mind. And now she's a shell of her former self."

"Do you visit her very often?"

"As often as I can," he said. "She doesn't know me, of course."

She studied his hard face while the coffee finished perking, thinking how difficult his childhood must have been. She felt a burst of sympathy for the boy he had been.

"It wasn't that rough," he said after a minute, clearly reading her expression. "Besides, it was an incentive to show them all what I could do. Hasn't anyone ever told you that revenge has produced a hell of a lot of successful men?"

"I suppose so. Is that why you've never married? Because of your own childhood?" she persisted gently.

He sighed. "Oh, Elissa," he murmured, smiling. "You're one of a kind, honey."

"I just wondered," she said.

He watched her pour coffee into the elegant floral china cups, thinking how sweetly domestic she seemed at that moment. She could cook like an angel, she looked exquisite in anything she put on, she had a gentle and loving nature, and physically she made the top of his head fly off with the uninhibitedness of her response to him.

"If I ever married, I suppose it would be you," he said unexpectedly.

Her hand trembled, spilling coffee. She put the pot down with shaky fingers and reached for a dish towel to mop up the mess.

"That was unkind," she told him.

"I meant it, in fact," he said lazily, moving closer. "There's not much hope of marriage in my life, with things the way they are. But I think I could enjoy living with you. You're quiet and amusing, and I covet your body."

He was openly leering at it, in fact, and she burst out laughing. It was a joke, of course. After all the time she'd known him, occasionally it was still difficult to tell when he was joking.

"I covet yours, too, but I'm not that kind of girl," she reminded him primly.

"That doesn't stop you from looking out windows at nude men at night, I notice," he said, tongue in cheek.

She threw up her hands. "Well, if that's the attitude you're going to take, I'll find some other nude man to ogle!"

"What was that?" Bobby asked from the doorway, laughing. Behind him, Bess was glaring at them both.

Elissa flushed. "Now see what you've done? Your brother will think I'm a voyeur."

"Well, aren't you?" King grinned.

She handed him the tray. "I hope you drop it on your foot," she said sweetly.

"Vicious woman," he muttered. "Open the door, honey," he told Bess.

Bess flushed, and the two of them exchanged a look that made Elissa want to throw herself off a building. Fortunately, Bobby had gone ahead and didn't see it. Elissa wished *she* hadn't. King might want her body, but what she saw in his eyes when he looked at Bess was something she'd have died for. It was a sweeping kind of hunger, mingled with tenderness.

Bess curled up on the sofa to drink her coffee, pausing now and again to glance at Elissa, who knew that everything she and King had done probably showed in her lack of makeup and tangled hair.

"I hope we're not intruding by staying here tonight," Bess said quietly. "But the hotel was so crowded, and you're much closer to the airport than we were, way up in Ocho Rios."

"You're not intruding at all," King replied. He glanced

at Elissa. "Elissa will need tonight to pack and get the cottage squared away, won't you, baby?"

"That's right," she said. It was hard to talk when he called her "baby." "And I'd better get to it if we're leaving in the morning. What time is it?" she added, rising.

"You'll need to be ready by eight," he said. He got lazily to his feet. "I'll walk you home," he said with a meaningful smile. "Don't wait up," he told the other two.

"I need an early night myself," Bess said coolly. "I expect I'll be out like a light in no time."

"I wish I could say the same," Bobby muttered over his paperwork. "I won't finish before dawn, at this rate. I guess you wouldn't care to help?" he asked Bess.

Her eyes widened. "Me? Heavens, I can't add one and one."

"Too bad," Bobby said. He seemed about to say something else, but he shrugged and bent his head again. "See you in the morning, Elissa."

"Sleep well," she told them, clinging to King's hand as he led her out into the darkness.

He lit a cigarette and smoked it during the short walk to her cottage, not saying a word. It was a warm, pleasant night, even with the misting rain around them.

At the back step of her cottage, he ground out the cigarette. "I'm sorry about this trip, but I couldn't think of another way to do it that didn't involve you."

"It's all right. I'm not doing so well with the new designs, anyway. I'll let them go for a week or two and touch base with some of my contacts back home."

"You still live with your parents, don't you?" he asked.

"Well, there's been no reason not to," she reminded him. "They'd be hurt if I wanted to live alone in Miami, and New York is pretty far away. We've been close all my life."

"I wouldn't know what that kind of closeness was," he admitted. "I like Bobby well enough, but we've never been really affectionate. I've never felt that way about any of my family."

"I'm sorry, because it's a special feeling."

"I suppose it is." He bent and brushed his lips carelessly over hers. "I'll go for a walk before I head back. Don't answer the phone for the next hour, in case Bess calls to see what's going on over here."

She tugged at his shirtsleeve as he turned. "I could make you some hot chocolate," she said shyly.

He lifted her hand to his mouth and kissed its warm palm. "I could take you to bed, too."

She looked up at him in the light from her kitchen. "King…"

His face went taut. "Elissa, I enjoy making love to you. I could make a banquet of your body. I even like you. But if I seduced you, what would we do?"

She blinked. "I don't understand."

He cupped her face in his hands. "Listen to me, little one. Sex is a loaded gun. Once you have it with someone, it involves you in ways you might not realize. I can't become involved with a virgin."

"After the first time, I wouldn't be a virgin," she reminded him.

He sighed angrily. "After the first time, you might wish you still were," he said bluntly. "You've been raised to think of sex as a sin outside marriage. How are you going to feel about yourself and me if I let that happen? Besides which," he added, "there's always the risk that you could get pregnant. And that's a complication neither of us is ready for."

She smiled wistfully, shaking her head.

"What does that mean?" he asked.

"I was just picturing you, your first time with a woman, going through all that with her," she said on a grin.

He cocked his head a little and smiled slowly. "My first time," he said in a loud whisper, "was so damned fast she hardly knew what was going on."

Her face slowly went scarlet, and he laughed. "Did you expect that the first time is always good for a man?" He grinned. "Men aren't born knowing how to make love. It takes experience to make bells ring and the earth move. After my first fumbling attempts, I had to work up the courage even to try again."

"I can't quite imagine that," she mused, smiling.

He nuzzled his forehead against hers, sighing. "Funny, I can tell you things I've never told anyone else," he murmured. "I must feel safe with you."

"I feel safe with you," she echoed. "That was why I latched onto you at the very beginning. You never tried to put the make on me."

"Until now," he corrected, lifting his head to search her eyes. "Are you sorry I didn't let things go on as they were?"

"No," she said almost at once. "Even though I can't imagine lying with any other man like that, I know I'd have let you do anything you wanted to," she admitted, "and I would have gloried in it. I don't even have enough pride to refuse you. It's too wonderful."

His eyes narrowed in pain, and his hands tightened on her oval face. "You shouldn't be quite that honest," he teased gently. "I'm only human. I might lose my head one night."

Her lips parted on a soft sigh. "I'll bet you're very good in bed," she whispered shyly.

"So I've been told," he said, laughing. His hands caressed her shoulders. "Look, we have to stop talking about sex," he murmured, "or we'll both be in trouble." He sighed. "What a mess. What a hell of a mess."

"It will all work out," she said. She stood on tiptoe to touch her lips to his eyelids. They closed tremulously, and she drew her mouth over them, amazed at the sudden stiffening of his body, the catch of his breath. She drew away, but his hands caught her waist and held her there.

"Don't stop," he breathed roughly. "I like it."

"Do you?" She repeated the soft little caresses, then instinctively smoothed kisses over his thick eyebrows, his lean cheeks and high cheekbones, down to his very sensuous mouth.

He was breathing rapidly, and she liked that. She remembered what he'd said to her that first time, driving her wild, and with her lips poised near his, she whispered, "Open your mouth."

It was like setting a match to dry wood. He seemed to go up in flames. His arms lifted her, crushing her against him, and his mouth invaded hers with a sensuous insistence. He was trembling, and his loss of control inspired both fear and wonder in her.

"Yes," she whispered when he backed her up against the door and fit his body to hers. "Yes!"

His rhythmic movements should have shocked her, but they were pure delight. She arched into them, her pride gone with her inhibitions, her arms curved around his neck, her mouth smiling under his as she gasped with pleasure.

She felt his hands moving on her body, gliding down to her hips, easing up the skirt of her dress. His urgent fingers felt cool on her hot skin, so welcome, so right. She moaned.

He lifted his head for an instant to breathe, his eyes frightening, his body shuddering. "Crazy child," he ground out, glaring at her. Then he moved against her, deliberately. "Feel that! Don't you know what you're asking for?"

"Heaven," she whispered, feeling deprived when he pulled away from her and turned his back.

"Heaven," he chided. He lifted his head, gulping in deep breaths, hating his loss of control and almost hating her for causing it. He'd never let a woman affect him so deeply. He fumbled for a cigarette. It was because she was a virgin, of course. She didn't know what she was doing. She was experimenting, and her innocence caused her to do things that a more experienced woman would know better than to try.

"Damn you!" he burst out, half laughing, half groaning.

She was still leaning against the door where he'd left her, breathless but smiling. He was as vulnerable to her as she was to him, she knew now. That was encouraging. Perhaps he did feel drawn to Bess, who was more or less using him to salve her tortured ego, but his emotional involvement with the other woman wasn't total. It couldn't be, or he wouldn't hunger so for Elissa. For perhaps the first time in her life she consciously felt a surge of pride in her own womanhood, in her ability to reach him. Her love life had been strictly fantasy until now, but King made her feel fiercely female and totally unafraid of him or anything he might do.

"Chicken," she purred.

He whirled, his black eyes narrowed in a face that was drawn with pain.

"What in hell are you trying to do?" he demanded.

"Lure you into bed with me," she said softly. "Come on. I dare you," she taunted with her newfound confidence.

He just stared at her. He had the cigarette in his lips now, but lighting it was another matter. He couldn't seem to hold the flame steady, and that brought a string of bitter curses to his lips.

She only smiled, coaxed the lighter from his lean fingers, flicked on the flame and held it to the cigarette.

"Proud of yourself?" he asked coldly. He smiled, but not happily.

"Proud of what I can do to you, yes," she confessed gently. "You seem so reserved at times, so unapproachable. It's nice to know you're human."

"You almost found out exactly how human," he muttered.

Her eyes searched his, and she sighed softly. "I tingle all over. That was so sweet."

"Not for me," he said through his teeth.

She watched his face, frowning a little. "I don't understand."

"I know." He took a deep draw from the cigarette and turned away, walking down the beach.

She followed, puzzled. "Can't you talk about it?"

He reached out, drawing her gently against his hips. His voice at her temple was slow and thick with discomfort. "I ache for you," he whispered. "Badly. Have you forgotten what we talked about, how after a certain point it's difficult to pull back?"

"I wasn't going to stop you," she reminded him.

"We couldn't very well make love on the beach in full view of my family!" he burst out. "Where's your mind tonight?"

"I don't know." She sighed. "I ache in places I never knew I had, I'm burning up with desire, and here you are, fully capable of putting out every fire I've got, and you're complaining that you're in pain."

He couldn't help it; he burst out laughing. "Oh, my God," he moaned.

She threw up her hands. "I offer you myself, no strings attached, and you walk off in a snit."

"Your parents would be ashamed of you," he pointed out.

"My parents don't expect me to be superhuman," she shot back. "God made bodies, you know, so I guess he expected that people would want to enjoy them occasionally."

"Although you'd rather do so with a ring on your finger," he prodded.

She shrugged. "Yes. But that doesn't cool me off any."

"Cool, the devil." He flung the cigarette away and lifted her suddenly, carrying her into the surf. "I'll cool you off."

He dumped her into the next wave. She spluttered and struggled to her feet, her dress plastered to her body, her hair in strings down her back.

"Wild animal!" she raged.

"Sexy baggage," he returned. "Want to hit me? Come on. Try it."

She took a swing at him. He sidestepped, and she went down again, and before she could get up he was in the water beside her, holding her down.

There was a look in his eyes that she'd never seen, and the sheer strength of his hands excited her. "You can't very well wear it like that, can you?" He laughed softly as he felt her bedraggled dress. "Let me help you out of it."

"You can't! Not here!" she gasped, looking around wildly.

"Yes I can," he shot back, and he began unfastening the soaking dress.

The surf crashed around them while he undressed her, and she reveled in the contrast between the cool water and her heated flesh, in the lazy contact of his hands, in the look on his dark face as he uncovered and savored every soft inch of her, his eyes lingering on her full breasts.

"God, what a beauty you are," he whispered. "I ought to strangle you for doing this to me."

"I'd like to point out that you're undressing me, not vice versa," she choked.

"You've seen me without my clothes," he said softly, searching her eyes.

"Yes." Her lips parted as she looked at him. "I wish we were alone. Totally alone."

"Stop tempting me," he whispered. After a minute, he reluctantly fastened the dress again and, with a heavy sigh, picked her up. His arms were strong and comforting against the night breezes. She snuggled closer, feeling unutterably cared for, and he bent to kiss her gently as he carried her up the beach. "You need to change and get some sleep. And in case you want to know, I'm leaving you at the door."

"Why?" she moaned against his lips.

"Sex makes babies," he whispered back. "I don't have anything to protect you."

She moaned again. "I don't care," she wailed.

"You would in the morning." He carried her to the door and set her slowly on her feet, taking a minute to run his hands over her and make her tremble with wanting.

"Sexy," he murmured. "Sexy and sweet, and I want to bury myself in you. Now you'd better get inside and try to sleep."

"Don't go," she whispered. "You're soaking wet, too."

"I can't very well walk home without my clothes." He chuckled. "Go to bed."

She shivered. "I can't."

"Why not?"

"My house key is in my pocketbook. Inside," she added with a faint flush. "Well, I forgot when I locked the door..."

He looked heavenward. "Women!" He searched until he found the spare key she hid under the hibiscus bush. "Here. I remembered, even if you didn't."

She looked up at him, her heart shaking her. He was so much man. So big and capable and strong, and just for once she liked being dependent, letting him take care of her. She thought about how it would be, having him beside her in the darkness, holding him through the night. Just holding him would be enough, she realized suddenly. What she felt was overpowering but not entirely physical. It was so tender, so sweet and new. If only he could feel it for her.

He unlocked the door and opened it, glancing down at her expression curiously. "What's wrong?" he asked, pressing the key into her palm.

"Nothing, really."

He reached in and switched on the light, then looked at her, drinking in the contours of her body now clearly visible through the dress plastered wetly to her skin. He shook his head. "You'll be the death of me one day. I'll have a heart attack trying to be noble."

"I won't take the blame," she said pertly.

"I won't take *you*," he whispered, bending to brush a chaste kiss on her forehead. "Now go to bed, siren. We've got an early flight."

"All right."

He handed her a shawl from the hat rack, watching her wrap herself in it. "Why do you want me all of a sudden?" he asked gently. "You've spent two years keeping me at arm's length. What's changed?"

"I never knew how devastating it could be," she said shyly.

"It shocks me a little, too," he said honestly. "You're not exactly my usual kind of woman."

"Maybe that's why you want me," she essayed.

He sighed. "I don't know. All I know is that for the past twenty-four hours, you're all I've thought about. But I can't afford to lose my head. Your conscience would torment you to death."

"But I don't want to lose you. You're my friend." Her eyes filled with unshed tears at the thought.

"Don't cry," he ground out. "I can't stand it."

She lifted her face. "Sorry. I was looking ahead. One of us will eventually marry, I guess," she added, thinking that it would probably be King. "And that will be the end of us, anyway."

He studied her, scowling. It hadn't occurred to him that he might ever have to lose her. But she was right: she would probably marry eventually, and her husband might not take kindly to their unusual friendship. There would be no more long walks along a Jamaican beach, no more phone calls at two in the morning just because he needed someone to talk to, no more laughing Elissa leaving him notes under rocks...

"I'll miss having you to talk to," she confessed softly.

He shifted restlessly. "I was thinking the same thing," he said quietly. "I'm alone except for you." Before she could reply, he turned and opened the door. "I'll see you in the morning."

He closed it and left her standing there.

Alone, in the harsh light of reality, she was astounded at her behavior. Letting fantasies take over, she had offered to... Her face flamed, and she caught her breath. She'd acted like a total wanton with King.

She got out of her wet things, put on a caftan and dried

her hair, troubled by the direction her life was taking. If she truly became King's lover, would she be discarded when he tired of her? She loved him, but she knew he merely wanted her. She had to get her perspective back, and she couldn't do that around King. All in all, it was best that she was going home.

Unbidden, the memory of what King had said before leaving came back to her: "I'm alone except for you." What had he meant by the statement?

She was still puzzling over it when she went to bed.

CHAPTER SIX

RIDING TO THE airport was an ordeal. Although Elissa sat in the front seat with King, his eyes kept darting to the rearview mirror. He talked to Bobby, but it was Bess he was exchanging eloquent looks with.

The one thing it did accomplish was to make Elissa see clearly what a fool she'd been to daydream over his exquisite lovemaking. He'd only been toying with her; there hadn't been anything serious about it on his part. Probably he'd made love to dozens of women without feeling the need to commit himself. Men weren't like women, she told herself; they didn't need emotional involvement to find fulfillment. But it saddened her all the same. She'd just begun to realize how much she cared about him, how much a part of her life he'd become. She'd looked forward to coming to Jamaica, not because of the island itself but because of the man who lived next door. And she felt possessive about him.

That possessiveness had reared its ugly head the instant she saw Bess. It hadn't taken much effort to realize how appealing King's sister-in-law must be to him. She wasn't a shallow flirt just out for a good time. She was beautiful and vulnerable and unhappy, tied to a man she cared about who never paid her any attention. How terrible that must feel, and how much King must want to comfort and protect her. But how terrible, too, for King to be torn between his feelings for Bess and for Bobby and his sense of what was right. What a mess.

And what a pity, Elissa thought, that she herself couldn't be one of those superficial people who enjoyed life without really considering consequences. But she knew herself too well to think she could survive a casual affair with King. Her principles were too firmly embedded in her personality, and despite her abandon when she was with him, he was right that her conscience would kill her if she fell into his bed. Besides, she thought miserably, would he still feel the same about her once he'd been intimate with her? She didn't think she could stand to have him and then lose him.

And what about Bess? Did she really want King, or was she attracted to him because he was safely unattainable and no real threat to her marriage? Elissa sighed, staring at the passing sea-grape trees and tall casuarina pines that partially veiled the blinding white beach and the incredible blues and greens of the Caribbean. What a ridiculous question. Her eyes turned to King, adoring his profile. He was handsome and rich, and what he didn't know about women wasn't worth knowing. Who wouldn't want him for keeps? She looked away quickly and closed her eyes on a wave of pain. If he and Bess wound up together, they would undoubtedly marry and have children. How that thought hurt!

Time crawled while they got through the long line of customs and immigration before boarding the plane. Bess eased into the seat next to King's on the enormous jumbo jet, and Elissa, on his other side, couldn't help but notice the way Bess clutched his hand as the plane prepared for takeoff.

"Frightened?" King asked his sister-in-law in a tone so tender that it hurt Elissa.

"Not now," Bess whispered, her heart in her eyes.

Elissa looked away, unable to bear the tender smiles they were exchanging. Across the aisle, Bobby, once more buried in his paperwork, hadn't even noticed.

When they touched down in Miami, Elissa breathed a sigh of relief. Sitting next to King and Bess had been utter torment, but now she could escape. She could go home to her parents and try to forget all about this. She didn't ever want to see the two of them together again. If that meant selling her cottage, well… The thought was horrifying. She couldn't bear it if she never saw King again! Her eyes filled with hot tears, and she swallowed them down before he could see them. How had this happened? They'd been friends. She almost wished he'd never touched her. She could almost hate him for making her so aware of him, of her feelings for him.

They cleared customs and immigration again, and Elissa stood a little apart while King said goodbye to Bobby and Bess.

"We need to get going," he told them, "so we won't wait to wave you off. I'll be back to the ranch in a week or so. Check with Blake Donavan and make sure everything's all right. He's supposed to be looking out for me while my foreman's on vacation."

"Imagine Donavan having time to do that," Bobby said with a laugh. "The last I heard, he was up to his ears trying to hold on to his own place after his uncle died. All those greedy cousins of his, filing lawsuits…"

King chuckled. "Donavan won, didn't you hear? Hell of a businessman."

"And a dish," Bess said playfully, glancing surreptitiously at Bobby. "He's never married, either. I wonder why not. Do you suppose he's nursing some hopeless passion for someone?"

No one responded to Bess's musings, but Elissa saw King's face harden. Then he forced a smile as he shook Bobby's hand. "Take care of yourself and Bess."

"Sure, sure. Thought we might find some time to go horseback riding this weekend," he added with a grin at Bess, who looked amazed. "Bess and I might pack a picnic lunch."

"You on a picnic?" Bess murmured. "Do you go with or without your pocket calculator?"

"Don't be catty, you sweet little thing," Bobby said, chuckling. "See you, Elissa. King will have to bring you out sometime and show you the place."

"That would be nice," Elissa murmured politely.

Bess didn't say goodbye to either of them, except to force a smile and wave as she walked ahead of Bobby down the terminal.

King watched her, his heart in his eyes. Elissa couldn't bear that, so she picked up her carryall and began to walk toward the exit.

"Where the hell do you think you're going?" he demanded, falling into step beside her to reach for her bag with an impatient hand.

"Home," she replied. "There's no need for you to come with me. You're perfectly safe now. You can check into a hotel somewhere and—"

"I said I'd take you home," he reminded her, his tone cool and authoritative. "Sit over there while I arrange about a car."

She did, angrily, still wounded by having watched him with Bess. She had to get herself under control, she thought. It wouldn't do to let him see how deeply involved with him she'd become.

She gave a brief thought to her parents and how they

were going to react to having her home so unexpectedly. At least she didn't have to worry about King's meeting them; he'd probably be glad to let her off at the gate of their modest house outside Miami and rush off.

But when King pulled up at her parents' beachfront house and surveyed the surrounding dunes and the waves of the Atlantic rolling lazily to shore behind it, he seemed in no hurry to leave. He gazed at the hibiscus lining the front walk, along with the graceful palms and a banana tree her mother had planted years before, took in the white front gate and the lounge furniture on the porch and remarked, "It reminds me of your cottage in Jamaica."

"They're similar. Well, thanks for the ride." She started to get out of the car, but he clasped her wrist, then her fingers.

His eyes were very dark, looking into hers. Puzzled. Faintly disturbed. "You've been quiet. Too quiet."

She shifted restlessly. She didn't want him asking questions or making assumptions. "My parents aren't expecting me," she muttered. "I'm trying to figure out what to tell them."

"Tell them a hurricane blew over your cottage," he suggested, tongue in cheek.

"What a cheerful man you are," she replied, staring at him. "Why don't you go into comedy for a living?"

"Stop fighting me," he murmured as she tugged against his firm but gentle hold. "You'll hurt my ego."

"It could stand a little deflation," she said crisply, glaring at him.

Comprehension took the playful expression from his face, leaving his eyes narrow and glittering. He dropped her hand. "She can't help it any more than I can," he said, his tone cold and cutting.

"So I noticed." She reached for the door handle. "Good thing for you both that your half brother is blind as a bat and keeps his nose stuck in his papers. Those quiet types are the ones who go for their guns without asking for explanations. You and Bess would look lousy on the front page of the tabloids, full of bullet holes."

"Would we?" he asked with surprising mildness. "You seem to find the idea satisfying."

She grabbed her carryall and slammed the door, about to add something cutting. But just as she opened her mouth, her mother, clad in a flapping red-splashed muumuu, came rushing through the gate like a barefooted, white-haired tornado.

"Darling!" she enthused, grabbing her daughter up in a fierce hug, her blue eyes dancing with glee. "Oh, what a delicious surprise! Your father will be overjoyed! He's just bought another crawly for his collection and wants to show it off to someone— Who are you?" she added, staring over Elissa's shoulder as King came around the car.

"Kingston Roper," he answered easily, studying the tall, thin woman. "You must be Elissa's mother."

"Yes, I am. I'm Tina Dean." Her mother withdrew a little, her blue eyes confused and a little curious. "Is something wrong?"

"King is my neighbor in Jamaica," Elissa said. "He was kind enough to offer me a lift from the airport. We flew over with his brother and sister-in-law." She could see that Tina Dean was quietly sizing him up, taking in his tailored suit, his hand-stitched shoes, his silk tie and expensive accessories. She could almost hear her mother's mind clicking, sorting through what Elissa had told her of her friendship with King and trying to put two and two together about what this obviously wealthy man was doing with her daughter.

"I have some iced tea in the kitchen," she remarked. "Would you like some, Mr. Roper?"

"King has to get back to Miami," Elissa said firmly, staring up at him. "Don't you?" she emphasized.

"Not at all," he replied with a maddening smile. "I'm in no hurry."

"Delightful," Mrs. Dean said with a grin. Her eyes twinkled. "How do you feel about reptiles, Mr. Roper?"

"Well, I used to have a pet horned toad," he began.

"Oh, Mother, no," Elissa moaned, putting her face in her hands.

King gave her a curious glance before Mrs. Dean took his hand and led him into the house.

Elias Dean was in his study, where he kept his collection of exotic lizards. He looked up, his thick silver hair slightly receding from his broad forehead, his eyes covered by thick spectacles with wire rims. At the sight of his daughter, he beamed and greeted her warmly. Then he turned his attention to their new visitor.

"Well, hello, who's this?" he asked pleasantly, rising from a terrarium with a big frilled green lizard in one hand.

King offered a hand, apparently unruffled by the "crawlies." "Kingston Roper." He grinned. "You must be Elissa's father."

"That I am. Do you like lizards, Mr. Roper? This is my hobby." He sighed, looking around him contentedly at terrarium after terrarium. "I can't ever seem to get enough, you know. It's up to ten curly-tails now, several spring lizards, newts, salamanders... But this is my pride and joy." He reached for a door and opened it. Inside was an enormous pool with potted tropical plants all around it. On a rock in the pool under a fluorescent lamp was Ludwig, a four-foot iguana who looked like a dinosaur. He stared at them with total boredom and closed his eyes.

"Iguana?" King asked, clearly interested.

"Yes. Isn't he beautiful?" her father asked. "He was only a baby when I got him. I had to force-feed him the first week with a big syringe, until he took fruits and vegetables on his own. I like frogs, too. I want one of those huge African frogs—they weigh ten pounds. She doesn't like frogs," he added with a miserable glance at Tina.

Tina laughed. "You're just lucky I don't mind lizards, Elias. Although I did draw the line at that ball python you were ogling. Snakes disturb me." She shuddered. "Lizards are bad enough."

"I have to have a hobby, my dear," he reminded her. "It could be worse. Do you remember that witch doctor we met down the Amazon, the one who collected heads?"

"I withdraw every objection," Tina promised, hand over her heart. "Would you like tea, darling? I'm going to pour some for Elissa and her...and Mr. Roper."

"I'll be out directly," Elias promised. "I have to feed poor old Ludwig."

"Poor old Ludwig," Tina chuckled as they made their way back down the hall to the kitchen, where sliding doors opened onto a deck facing the ocean. "He takes him walking down the beach on a leash. It's a good thing we have such a loyal congregation." She shook her head.

"Father is eccentric," Elissa said quietly, glancing worriedly at King.

He cocked an eyebrow. "My father collected rocks," he remarked. "And I had a great-uncle who could forecast the weather with jars of bear grease. Compared to that, keeping lizards seems pretty sane."

Elissa leaned back in her chair. "Go ahead, Mother, tell him what you do in your spare time," she dared, watching Tina pour amber tea into tall glasses of ice.

King frowned slightly and turned to Tina. "What do you do in your spare time?"

Tina set the glasses on the small kitchen table. "Well, I'm a special deputy for the sheriff's department."

"Now, that sounds interesting," King said, and he seemed to mean it.

"It's very interesting," she agreed. She got her own tea and sat down. "I have so much experience as a missionary, you see, it gives me a little insight into people. Some of the folks we arrest are women, and I seem to deal with them better than the men do." She smiled wistfully. "I've been on drug busts and in shoot-outs and stakeouts, and once I jumped a fence and wrestled down a young pusher and held him for the deputies. Yes, it's exciting and very rewarding. I often look up the people later and try to get to know them." Her eyes softened. "I've managed to get several of them to come to services on Sunday. And we baptized one just last week," she added, her voice a little husky. "I suppose this sounds pretty saccharine to a worldly man like you."

"But I'm not," King said, surprising even Elissa. "I was raised a Baptist in Jack's Corner, a small town outside Oklahoma City, near my ranch. My father was Apache, but he bowed to some white customs. He found church fulfilling for a time."

Elissa was stunned at how easily King related to her mother. He'd even volunteered information about his heritage, which he was usually so prickly about.

"Apache," Tina said, studying him more closely with totally innocent curiosity. "Yes, your eyes are very dark, and you have high cheekbones…"

"Mother," Elissa groaned, "he's not an exhibit."

King chuckled. "Elissa is remembering that I can get touchy about my ancestry," he remarked with a smile in Elissa's direction. "I don't mind honest curiosity. I don't suppose you see many Native Americans in this part of the country."

Tina grinned. "I guess I don't look it," she told him, "but I'm part Seminole, on my mother's side."

King's eyebrows rose. "You never told me," he murmured to Elissa.

She shrugged. "You never asked about my ancestry."

He frowned. That was true. They often shared their thoughts and feelings and dreams, and he'd even told her about his family, but he'd never bothered to ask about hers. He felt oddly guilty about that now and inordinately curious to know more about this little spitfire.

"My grandfather had a Seminole name, which he changed," Tina continued, looking at King. "Is Roper your father's real name?"

King smiled and told her the Apache word for Man Who Throws Rope. "That's why he changed it to Roper," he added.

"Do you like to fish, Mr. Roper?" Elissa's father asked, coming into the kitchen.

"If you mean deep-sea fishing, no," King replied. "But if you mean dipping a worm on a hook into a creek, yes."

Mr. Dean grinned. "My sentiments exactly. There's a nice little swamp about two hours' drive from here, where you can get some of the biggest bream and crappie you ever saw."

"We have a spare room," Tina Dean added, smiling at him. "It's quiet here. We're off the main drag. I see that Elissa looks horrified, but we won't let the lizards eat you, and if you're as tired as you look, the change might do you good, Mr. Roper."

Elissa went red. She'd forgotten how outspoken her mother was. She did look horrified. She felt horrified. *Don't do this to me*, she wailed silently. *He's in love with another woman, and I want to get away from him.*

King turned toward Elissa and saw that look on her face. "If you don't want me to stay, I won't," he said gently.

The soft tone made her toes curl. What could she say? "I don't mind," she murmured.

"I must look tired if it shows that much," he said, winking at Mrs. Dean. "Yes, I'll stay, thank you."

"Wonderful!" Mr. Dean chuckled. "We'll find some lazy projects to keep you relaxed."

"I'll fatten you up," Mrs. Dean seconded, giving him a critical glance. "You look undernourished."

Elissa could have laughed. He might look trim, but he was very muscular under his shirt. She flushed, wondering what her parents would say if she confessed that she'd watched him swim in the nude from her cottage window. She forced a smile and finished her iced tea while her mother asked about his work. He replied that he was in oil and gas. It didn't dawn on Elissa until much later how her mother had interpreted that remark.

"To think, a handsome man like that working in a garage," Mrs. Dean sighed as she made supper.

"What?" Elissa asked sharply.

"Well, he's in oil and gas," she explained patiently, "and despite the nice-looking suit he's wearing, which he might have borrowed, I think his watch and ring are only copies of expensive ones. He's trying to impress us, darling, to show us that he'd be a good catch for you. I'm very flattered. I like him. So does your father. And there's nothing wrong with working in a garage. His parents probably own it, you know, and that's probably their home in Jamaica. They must just let him use it."

Boy, had her mother gotten it wrong. But Elissa bit her tongue. This was better. They didn't need to know how rich King really was; it might inhibit them. She liked their response to him, and his to them. She couldn't bear to spoil it. She'd tell them later, after King was gone.

Her eyes closed. Despite her trepidations, it was marvelous to have him in her home, to savor being with him away from Bess's influence. She was in heaven. Even if he stayed only overnight, she'd love the house forever afterward, because she'd see him in every nook and cranny of it. And if he married Bess, well, her dreams wouldn't harm the two of them very much.

CHAPTER SEVEN

AFTER SUPPER, KING and Elissa went for a stroll along the beach. It was very much like Jamaica at night, the white-caps rolling onto the beach with a foamy whisper.

"You don't mind that I'm here, do you?" he asked casually.

"No." She had changed into shorts and a long-sleeved shirt, and she was enjoying the feeling of the cool white sand on her bare feet. She tossed back her long hair and sighed, drinking in the peacefulness of the setting.

He was still wearing his slacks, but he'd unbuttoned his shirt halfway down and was wearing thongs instead of shoes. He looked very casual, not at all the elegant millionaire he really was.

"I didn't know you'd been raised a Baptist," she commented, turning her eyes seaward.

He glanced at her. "And I didn't know that you had Seminole blood."

She smiled. "I've got a little Irish, too, and a trace of German."

"I've got some Irish myself." He stopped her, gesturing toward a hermit crab diving into a hole in a small sandy bank. "I had one of those for a pet once. They're cute."

"With those claws?" she groaned.

"Claw, woman," he chided. "Well, one big one and one much smaller one. They don't pinch that hard."

"You wouldn't feel it with hands the size of yours, I guess."

He slid his hands into his pockets, stretching the expensive fabric of his slacks against the powerful muscles of his legs as he walked. "I like it here," he said lazily. "I like your parents, too. I can see now why you're such an independent little cuss. They're very open and honest."

She laughed softly, enjoying his company and the cool breeze and the solitude. "You'd really think so if you'd heard what my mother said about you."

He stopped, looking down at her. "What did she say?" he asked with interest.

"She says that you're very handsome to work in a garage, which your parents must own, and that that's their villa in Jamaica. They just let you use it. Your watch and ring are copies of the real thing, to impress them. Oh, and you probably borrowed that expensive suit you're wearing."

His eyebrows shot up, and he began to laugh, but not in a sarcastic or mocking way. It sounded like pure delight. "They think I'm a grease monkey?"

"You told them you were in gas and oil," she reminded him. "My parents don't know any oil magnates but they know a lot of mechanics."

"Well, I'll be damned," he mused. "I think I like that. Yes, I think I do. I haven't been treated like a normal human being in my adult life. At least not since I hit it big."

"You have so," she retorted. "Do I treat you like a big fish?"

He pursed his firm lips, then smiled at her, his white teeth gleaming in the pale light of the half moon. "Not really," he admitted. "That was one of the things I liked best about you. After I realized that you weren't chasing after me because I was rich," he added.

The cynicism in his voice touched her. "Did you really think that's why I kept hounding you?" She laughed. "How surprising."

"Women had chased me for years," he replied. "Once or twice I let myself be caught, but mostly I didn't give a damn for that kind of woman. It didn't take me long to learn that you weren't the least bit interested in my bank account. Then," he added with a wicked glance as he started walking again, "I decided it was my body you wanted."

"How conceited," she remarked airily.

"If you remember, I made one very subtle pass at you, right at the beginning," he said. "And you backed away with a look in your eyes I'll never forget. I didn't understand why you shied away from me. I thought you'd had some bad experience and were afraid of men. That made me even more protective, and I gave up any ideas of seducing you."

"Until a few days ago," she muttered.

His head jerked toward her. "Don't put all the blame on me, honey. You were giving as good as you got in my bed that night."

She was glad the darkness hid her blush. She stiffened a little as she shuffled along the beach beside him, oblivious now to the clamoring surf. Her legs were getting cold, but she didn't want to suggest that they go inside. Every second she could spend alone with him was a delight, even if it had to be spent in the middle of an argument.

"Thank you for that sterling assessment of my morals," she said lightly, forcing back a surge of fury. "I suppose that makes me what men call an easy—King!"

He jerked her around none too gently and shook her by both arms. "No, it doesn't make you easy," he said, his voice cold and curt. "Stop trying to make yourself sound cheap."

"Isn't that what you're trying to do?" she asked, hating the slight wobble in her voice.

His lean fingers tightened on her arms, exciting and strong through the flimsy sleeves of her oversize shirt. "I don't know what I'm trying to do," he said surprisingly. His hands relaxed, became caressing. He breathed slowly, deliberately, and drew her into his arms. He wrapped her against his taut body, enveloping her in his spicy cologne and his warmth, and laid his cheek on her dark hair.

It was, she thought suddenly, as if he needed comforting. And perhaps he did. He didn't say a lot about his feelings for Bess, but she was sure that he was confused and wounded by what was happening. He was willing to sacrifice his own happiness to keep from hurting Bess and Bobby, so he'd subdue what he felt for Bess or ignore it if he could. But with the woman tempting him and, as he'd said, with his being only human, perhaps he did need comforting. And at the moment, Elissa was his anchor, his safety net, his life jacket. She didn't mind; it was enough to do what she could to help him through a difficult time. Love made you vulnerable. She knew, loving him as she did.

She slid her arms around his hard waist and pressed her cheek over his heart, enjoying the heavy, measured beat of it in the darkness. "We all want things that we can't have, from time to time," she began softly. "Like me, living a fantasy. I'd give so much to be like those women in the nighttime soap operas who have their fun and never have to suffer for it. But I'm too much of a coward to try it. I'd always worry about consequences and about hurting other people." She closed her eyes, breathing him in. "I always felt so free with you. I could tease, and you never took me seriously. I could try my wings, I could fly, without any danger of falling."

"Until one night you flew too close to the flame and singed your pretty wings," he murmured drily. "Were you shocked?"

"Oh, yes," she confessed. "I didn't expect it, you see. And I didn't realize how vulnerable I might be."

"I did," he replied. His arms tightened. "We were both holding back for different reasons, bottling up our passions. Inevitably, it was going to get away from us one day. It just happened to be with each other. And I'm damned glad about that," he added curtly. "Another man might have taken advantage of it and seduced you for real."

She colored softly. "I can't imagine letting any other man do those things to me," she said honestly.

He actually shuddered. "Don't say things like that. I'm more vulnerable than you realize."

"Because she's gone."

He paused for an instant, and when his voice finally came, it was cold and measured. "Yes. Because she's gone. I did warn you that anything I did to you would be out of desire for her. Didn't you hear me?"

"I was too busy kissing you." She laughed gently.

He laughed, too, despite himself. "Imp," he muttered, tightening his arms and then loosening them to step away from her and look down into her quiet eyes. "You seemed to like kissing me."

She tossed back her head, living the dream all over again. "You have a nice mouth. Very slow, very experienced."

"Yours isn't bad, either," he murmured, dropping his eyes to it. He touched her cheek and traced her lips with his thumbs. "I'm sorry we're so close to the house. We could strip and go swimming."

"My father would let Ludwig eat you," she said with a laugh.

He sighed. "It was just a thought. I'd give a lot to see you out of your clothes, pretty thing."

That was embarrassing and a little exciting, all at once. "Well, you haven't missed much," she said.

"Not from the waist up, anyway," he agreed too readily, and laughed at her shocked little gasp. "God, you're sweet to tease. I'd forgotten that women could be shocked. Women in my set tend to be pretty blasé about sex."

"Probably because there isn't a lot they don't know about it." She tried to step back, but he caught her long hair and held her there in front of him.

"You're nervous of me," he murmured. "Why should you be? You could always scream for help."

"Yes, I know." She tugged at his hand. "I don't want to stand in for Bess, King."

"You told me that in the beginning. I haven't forgotten." He hesitated for a minute before he reluctantly let her go. "You sound positive enough about it."

His voice gave nothing away, but she thought he sounded a bit irritated. She tossed her hair and laughed up at him. "How would you feel if I kissed you and pretended you were some sexy man I wanted?"

His blood surged. "I'd break your sweet neck," he said without a second's hesitation.

She laughed even louder. "You see? Tit for tat, big man."

He made a swipe at her behind, and she barely sidestepped in time.

"If you hit me," she threatened, "I'll tell my daddy."

"Go ahead," he challenged. "I dare you."

"You ought to be shaking in your shoes," she replied. "He's got friends in high places."

He got her meaning and grinned, all his bad temper gone. "You know, I laugh more with you than I've ever laughed in my life," he remarked as they wandered back down the beach toward the brightly lit cottage.

"I don't think you even knew how to laugh at the beginning," she recalled. "You were a little frightening. All business and cold as ice."

"Cold on the outside," he said softly. "Never on the inside."

That was a blatant insinuation, and she ignored it. "Are you and Dad going fishing tomorrow?"

"Yes, we are." He glanced her way. "Are you coming with us?"

"I'd like to, but I've got to get in touch with Angel Mahoney and tell her I'm going to need another week on those new designs. Angel is vice president of the Seawear collection, and she bought my designs for the chain of boutiques Seawear owns. I thought they were too strange for anyone," she confessed, "but Angel thought they were deliciously outrageous and very salable. And she was right. I'm making all kinds of money these days."

"It doesn't show," he said abruptly with a speaking glance at what she was wearing.

She lifted a haughty eyebrow. "I wouldn't waste my exquisite wardrobe on a mere friend," she informed him.

His dark eyes narrowed. "Is that all I am?"

"It's all I'm going to let you be," she said gently, looking away from him. "Would you like—"

"Why?" He was behind her in the shadow of the house, his hands around her waist pulling her back against his tautly muscled body.

"You know why," she ground out. The warmth of those hands was driving her wild.

"I can't have Bess," he whispered in her ear, drawing her even closer, "but I can have you. You can have me."

She trembled and closed her eyes as the tempting pictures rambled shamelessly in her mind. She gritted her teeth, because there was only one possible answer to the blatant seduction in his voice. "No."

"Tell me you aren't tempted, Elissa," he dared.

She pulled away from him, taking a few seconds to get her composure back. "How about some coffee?"

He hesitated at the back door, then sighed and gave in. He didn't understand himself lately. Elissa was suddenly in his blood, and he wanted her out. He hoped he wouldn't one day lose control with her. The thought frightened him a little. Yet he seemed to totally forget Bess when he touched Elissa. That was somehow frightening, too.

He followed her inside, his face thoughtful, to find her parents waiting to join them around the coffeepot. He smiled at them, relieved to find something to keep his mind occupied. It was having a field day with memories of Elissa, her dress disheveled and pushed down to her waist.

THE NEXT MORNING, King and Elissa's father set off before daylight. By the time Elissa and her mother were up, the men were long gone. Tina fixed a small breakfast for them and then set about her housework, while Elissa went down to the beach for a swim. Afterward, she set to work on her designs with a fierce determination to work off her frustrations on paper.

It worked, too; she came up with some totally new looks, very innovative and sexy and cool. She took a break for lunch and some lazy conversation with her mother, and then went back down to the beach, a flowered patio skirt over her one-piece black bathing suit, and stretched out on her towel to scribble some more.

The sun kept going in and out of the clouds. She closed her eyes with a sigh as it began to cool down, and she was almost asleep when a shadow fell over her.

She opened her eyes to King's dark face, his eyes narrow and speculative where the skirt had fallen away from her long, tanned legs. Her bodice had slipped because of the shoulder straps, almost baring one breast.

"Sexy as hell," he murmured, and there was irritation in his voice. "You look like a beached mermaid, and you'd better thank your lucky stars your parents are within earshot."

"Oh, promises, promises," she laughed drowsily, only half taking him seriously. She stretched, and his jaw tightened.

He unbuttoned his shirt, watching her the whole time, seeing how her attention suddenly became riveted on the hair-covered muscles he was revealing. When he stripped it off, her eyes widened on his torso, and he felt a surge of desire so strong that it almost knocked him to his knees. She liked looking at him. She was too inexperienced to hide her own longing, and the sight of it made him all too vulnerable to his own hungers.

"I thought I might go for a swim," he said huskily as his hand went to his belt.

Her lips parted. "You...can't," she began, thinking of her parents.

"I'm wearing trunks," he said. He unhitched the belt and slowly moved the zipper down. She was breathing quickly by the time he finally peeled the jeans down his long legs and discarded them, along with his sneakers.

"Why did you do that?" she asked in a strange, high-pitched tone when he turned to her.

"I like the way you look at me when I'm undressing," he said quietly, meeting her hesitant gaze. There was no mockery in his eyes, no teasing. He moved closer, looking down at her for a long instant before he caught one of her hands in his and put it against his chest. The hard muscles surged against it as he breathed, feeling the soft, silent searching of her cool fingers against his heated skin.

"My...my father?" she whispered, glancing down the beach.

"He's cleaning fish," he replied, searching her eyes. "Your mother is cooking."

"Oh."

He eased down alongside her, deftly unbuttoning her skirt. He pushed it aside, baring the smooth, exquisite lines of her body in the bathing suit. His hand went to the shoulder strap that was already almost off. He traced it down the fastening under her arm and, holding her shocked eyes, unhooked it.

"You mustn't, King," she said shakily. She caught his wrist, but it didn't even slow him down. He stared at her bodice, peeling it aside with steady, strong fingers, his thumb blatantly caressing her swelling breast and making her jerk with a sudden spasm of pleasure.

"Go ahead," he murmured curtly, bending his head. "Lie to me. Tell me you don't want this."

"What about...Bess?" she groaned, pushing at him.

He said something harsh and explicit that she only half heard, and then his head was against her body, his mouth taking her breast inside the warm darkness, teasing it with his tongue.

Her whimpers excited him. She didn't know how to hold back, and that was delicious. He slid his hands under her, smoothing her soft skin, lifting her closer to his ardent mouth.

She was trembling now, too far gone to protest anything he did to her. He moved one hand up her side to explore the exquisite softness of her breast while his mouth gently teased it. He lifted his head just enough to look, to watch his subtle tracing shatter her composure and bring a mist of tears to her blue eyes.

"Don't cry," he whispered, bending to touch his mouth to her eyelids and taste the salty moisture there.

"I hate you," she whimpered huskily.

He smiled indulgently. "No, you don't. You hate being vulnerable. So do I. But we enjoy each other too much to deny ourselves this pleasure. And it is pleasure, isn't it, Elissa?" he whispered over her mouth. "Such wild, sweet pleasure."

"But—"

He covered the word with his lips, brushing her mouth open with lazy, expert movements that made her body burn. She tried to protest, but he kept at it, slowing his movements, deepening them, tormenting her with little shivers of sensation that made her wild. He'd never kissed her like this before. It was as intimate as lovemaking. More intimate. She moaned, the sound as intimate as the kiss, as revealing as her shudders.

His free hand came up to her chin, cupping it, holding it firm. Above her, his body blocked out the sun, and his face was a stranger's, hard and faintly flushed, his eyes almost frightening.

"Yes," he whispered gruffly, continuing the subtle torment of her mouth, watching it open, feeling its aching sensuality. "Yes, you're ready for me, now, aren't you? Soft and submissive...oh, baby..."

His tongue penetrated her mouth in one slow, sharp thrust, his lips crushing down on hers.

She cried out, her trembling hands clutching his hair, her nails digging into his nape. She arched, shuddering, her body in sweet anguish as he felt her need and answered it, his hand swallowing her breast, softly cradling it. Her tongue tangled with his; her breathing seemed to stop. It was the most incredible sensation she'd ever felt in her life. Like flying into fire. Burning up. She was trembling all over and she couldn't stop, totally vulnerable and powerless to hide it from him.

She began to cry, tears rolling down to their feverishly joined mouths, sobs tearing from her throat, and still she clung, arching her body toward his hand.

"Elissa," he whispered in a tone he'd never used—achingly tender, almost loving.

He moved completely onto her shaking body, his weight exquisitely satisfying, his mouth tender now, his hands... He was doing something to her bodice, and then she felt his chest against her bare breasts, the hair on it tickling, the warm muscles gently spreading her swollen softness against them.

"Hold on tight," he whispered at her lips. "Hold me."

She couldn't stop crying. She buried her lips in his hot throat, shuddering under his weight, devastated by the feel of his body in such intimacy. He was aroused, and she felt that, too, and moaned.

"Sweet," he whispered at her ear, his fingers biting into her back. "Sweet, sweet Elissa!"

She bit his shoulder, a helpless reaction that she didn't even understand, and made a sound in her throat that curled his toes.

"Shh," he murmured. His fingers came to her cheek and

soothed it, smoothing back her damp hair. His hand slid down to her waist and caressed it gently, while he whispered to her, tender little encouragements to relax, to lie still, to be quiet.

By the time she stopped shaking and could feel his taut body relaxing and losing its frightening hardness, her face was drenched in tears.

He rolled beside her then, still holding her, and onto his back. He pillowed her head on his shoulder, his arms betraying a fine tremor, while he stared blankly up at the sky, where seagulls dived and called to each other against the gray clouds.

"I have to leave," he said after a minute, his voice harsh. "We can't go on like this any longer."

She knew that instinctively. He'd gone almost too far to stop, and so had she. She wasn't thinking anymore. Her body had a will of its own, too strong to fight. She closed her eyes and felt that she'd die if she couldn't have him just once.

"I know," she whispered. She sat up, her breasts swollen and slightly red from the pressure of his lips.

"Oh, baby," he breathed, looking as she covered them, his eyes blazing. "I could look at you forever."

"Don't." She closed her eyes, and he sat up, too, fastening the straps for her with hands that were a little unsteady.

"I don't know what's wrong with me lately," he confessed, forcing her to look at him. "I want you to the point of madness. You, Elissa. Not Bess." He looked down at her shoulders, delighting in their creamy perfection. "I don't understand why I feel this way, but if I don't have you, I think I'll die."

She understood that, because she felt the same way. "I want you just as much," she said quietly. "But afterward,

I'll hate you," she added, looking up at him. "All those years of conditioning don't just vanish. I'll hate you, and myself, and I don't know how I'll live with it. But," she confessed shyly, looking at his chest, "I don't know how I'll live without it."

He got to his feet, pulling her up with him. His face was serious now, intent. "Come back to Oklahoma with me."

She moved restlessly, frightened of what they were discussing.

"Come with me," he repeated gently. He tilted her eyes up to his. "I promise I won't make you pregnant. I can't stop what's going to happen, but I'll make sure you're protected."

"No, I...I'll do that," she faltered. She looked toward the sea. "But how will we explain to my parents that I'm going back with you?"

He sighed wearily and touched her hair. "If it's any consolation, it bothers me, too." His fingers trailed down her cheek to her mouth, and he stared at it until her lips parted. "We'll tell them we may be getting engaged, and you're to stay with my family."

She looked up at him with stunned delight in her eyes, and the sight of it made him suddenly possessive. He jerked her against him.

"The hell with it—let's get married," he said suddenly. "I can't have Bess, and I've got to have you. Let's do it by the book."

She almost screamed "Yes!" at him, but she held back, sobered by the certainty that Bess would surely find some way to get to him eventually. It wouldn't do for Elissa to marry him and create even more problems. No matter how much it hurt, she was going to have to sink her pride and principles and give him the physical ease they both ached for. She loved him. If she had nothing else, she could have this. She could belong to him for a few ecstatic days, and then she would have to pay the piper. Somehow she'd survive the future. She and her memories of him.

"I won't marry you," she whispered gently. "But I'll go with you."

He frowned. "I don't mind—"

She put her fingers against his mouth. "You would, someday. Marriage should be a total commitment, a sacred thing, not just a legalization of desire. I hate what I feel for you, I hate what I'm going to do, but I think we'd regret marriage a lot more."

"It would ease your conscience afterward," he said tersely.

"And destroy yours," she countered. "Bess may...may be free someday. How would you feel if you were tied to me by then?"

His grimace gave her the answer. "It isn't fair, asking this of you."

"Life isn't fair sometimes," she said with a sigh, fighting tears. She looked up at him with the anguish of love in every line of her face. "Oh, King," she whispered softly, "I want you, too."

His hands tightened on her arms. "Come to see the ranch," he said, feeling guilty but unable to stop himself. "Just that. Maybe we can fight it."

That gave her a little hope. It would make it easier to explain to her parents if she wasn't definite about things. She smiled. "Okay."

He loved the way she smiled. Her eyes brightened, her face relaxed, she looked...beautiful. She *was* beautiful, inside and out. His body made an emphatic statement about its feelings for her, and he laughed in spite of himself.

"I'd better get dressed," he murmured drily, turning

away. He hadn't even been in the water, but he was drenched with sweat anyway.

She found her patio skirt and put it on, watching him pull on his jeans. It didn't embarrass her anymore when she knew he wanted her. It was so natural, as if she were already an extension of him, a physical part of him. She loved him to distraction.

He glanced at her, frowning at that rapt expression. She didn't seem to be afraid of him or nervous about giving herself to him. Why? Did she care for him? That made him tingle, and he turned to scoop up his shirt with a feeling he didn't understand. When he was dressed again, he took her hand, clasping it close in his without a single twinge about Bess.

"If it happens," he said without looking at her, "I'll make sure you never want to forget what we do together."

"I never would, whatever happened," she said solemnly.

He drew in a steadying breath and linked his fingers with hers. She made him feel ten feet tall. He couldn't understand this compulsion to make love to her; it wasn't only sex, but he couldn't puzzle out what else it was. He glanced down at her slender body, already picturing the very fluid way it was going to become part of him. He felt a flush of warmth from head to toe, and it got worse when he happened to drop his gaze to her flat stomach and involuntarily wondered what she'd look like with a baby in there.

His fingers clasped hers until they hurt, and she caught at them with curious laughter.

"What is it?" she asked breathlessly, wondering if he was thinking about Bess.

He searched her eyes. "Elissa... Do you like children?" he asked slowly.

Inexplicably, she felt deliriously happy. He'd never asked

a question like that. It gave her a little hope. She smiled, turning back toward the house. "Yes, of course. I'd like at least two someday. Why?"

He didn't answer her. His eyes were dark and troubled the rest of the way home. Bess said she didn't want children. And he was shocked to discover that he did. But he wanted them with Elissa.

He was totally withdrawn while he waited for the women to get supper together, electing to watch television with Mr. Dean. A telephone call he made a little later gave Tina the chance to ask Elissa what was wrong.

"He's asked me to his ranch," Elissa said with a smile. "I think he's worried about telling you and Dad."

Tina searched her daughter's face. "You're very much in love with him, aren't you, darling?"

Elissa sighed. "Yes. But he… I'm not sure he feels that way about me."

"He wants you." Tina smiled, but her eyes were solemn. "Be sure, honey. It's all too easy for a man to be physically infatuated, with no lasting emotion to hold him to a woman. I like your young man very much, but then, he's no threat to me."

Elissa put her head in her hands and leaned over her coffee cup, feeling lost and miserable. "I don't know what to do," she confessed. "I don't know if I can live without him now."

"My poor darling," Tina said quietly. She leaned over and kissed her daughter's forehead. "You have to find your own way, you know. I love you, and nothing you do will ever change that. I know your father and I must seem very old-fashioned to you, but we believe in what we do, and the way we live has to reflect that. Earthly pleasures are fleeting. Love is immortal, and it goes beyond satisfying some fleeting physical hunger. In other words, sweetheart," she explained with a grin, "sex won't make up for the lack of love, no matter how good it is."

"You hussy, talking like that," Elissa teased.

"That's me," Tina agreed. Her eyes twinkled. "You don't realize how much the world has changed in recent years. When I was in high school, girls could get expelled for wearing a skirt an inch above the knee. That was considered vulgar." She pursed her lips with a smile. "Life is so violent these days that I sometimes wish we were back in the Amazon," she muttered. "I felt safe there."

"I can help you out," Elissa said. "I'll bring Warchief over here to live with us and he can make you feel you're back in the jungle."

Tina, who'd heard volumes about the big parrot, frowned. "We have neighbors with sensitive ears."

"Our nearest neighbor is a mile down the beach," Elissa pointed out.

"That's what I mean. Sound carries. Besides," she groaned, "parrots fly. I have enough trouble with little bitty mosquitoes. Imagine something that has wings and bites and weighs a pound."

Elissa had never thought of him as a giant green mosquito. She laughed. She'd have to remember to tell King. King. Her gaze softened. What was she going to do?

Tina patted her hand. "Life generally goes on," she reminded her daughter. "And God loves us. Even when we're naughty little girls and boys."

That was a comforting thought. Elissa got up and began to set the table.

CHAPTER EIGHT

ELISSA'S FIRST SIGHT of the Oklahoma plains drew a helpless sigh from her. Oklahoma City, where King had claimed his big gray Lincoln at the airport parking lot, was beautiful and intriguing for its rising oil derricks within the huge city itself. But the rolling plains, sweeping toward the horizon as far as the eye could see, brought tears to her eyes.

"I've never, ever seen anything like it," she breathed, her expression mirroring total delight.

King swerved the car as he darted a glance at her, fascinated. "I thought you'd hate it," he replied. "You live on the coast."

She wasn't even listening. "The Plains Indians—did they come down this far? The Sioux and Cheyenne?"

"Well, honey, Oklahoma was where they sent the Five Civilized Tribes back during the Trail of Tears, during the late 1830s and 1840s. Some of them fought for the Confederacy during the Civil War—a few were slaveholders, you see—and because of that, the government forced them to sell their western lands at a sacrifice. We have Chickasaws, Choctaws, Cherokees, Creek—and Seminoles," he added after a pause.

Her face brightened. "No wonder it seems like home. Don't they say something about an ancestral memory? Perhaps some of my ancestors came here."

"The Seminoles were fierce warriors," he agreed easily. "They fought the government to a standstill."

"The Apache were pretty fierce, too, I hear," she murmured. She smiled at him and then turned her attention back to the undulating hills. "How beautiful. There's so much space, King."

"That's what I like about it. No crowding yet. Plenty of room. Oil and gas and cattle."

"The oil industry has been hard-hit, though."

"Bobby and I had to diversify," he agreed. "But good business management will spare us too much grief. There it is." He indicated a dirt road leading to a grove of trees and a sprawling white frame house with huge porches. There were outbuildings and endless fences and herds of white-and-red cattle everywhere.

"The ranch?" she asked, excited.

"The ranch." He chuckled at her expression as he pulled off the main highway onto the winding dirt road. "Like it?"

"Oh, I love it," she said softly, drinking in the lush greens and the wildflowers that seemed to be everywhere. "Those are sunflowers!" she exclaimed.

"You'll find a lot of unfamiliar vegetation," he said. "We don't have sea grapes and palms out here. We have water oaks and hickory trees… Of course, we have some fascinating animals here, too. I doubt you've ever seen a moose."

"I can hardly wait."

"You shouldn't be this enthusiastic," he murmured drily, remembering how much Bess had hated the ranch when she and Bobby married. Of course, Bess had grown up in dirt-poor surroundings, and he supposed she'd had her fill of roughing it. She'd probably longed for something completely different, more refined. But Bobby, like King, had loved the plains, loved walking the hills in search of arrowheads—one of King's favorite childhood pastimes. "You're a city girl, remember?"

"I'm a country girl," she argued. "Just because I work near Miami doesn't make me citified. I like wide-open spaces, like the beach and hills. Can I go walking when I feel like it, or are there…"

"Wild Indians?" he suggested with a wicked grin.

She hit him. "Wolves," she replied.

"Only this one," he murmured, winking at her.

She gave up, shaking her head. She didn't remember the reason he'd brought her here. The real reason. He still wanted her. It was in his eyes, in the way he smiled at her. And Bess was somewhere nearby…

"Where does Bobby live?" she asked suddenly.

The smile left his face. "There." He indicated a modern split-level house in the distance. "Almost in Jack's Corner. Bess used to spend a lot of time in Oklahoma City, but Bobby said she's started getting interested in local society." He frowned. "Too bad it's only tea parties and such. She sure could do a lot of social work if she had a mind to."

He drove the Lincoln up to the front steps, and Elissa sighed over the big green rocking chairs and the porch swing. "I love it!" She grinned. "Can we sit in the swing?"

"Presently," he promised, climbing out to open her door and help her, with old-world courtesy, to the ground.

The screen door swung open, and a middle-aged woman stomped onto the porch. Margaret Floyd, the housekeeper, was a big, buxom woman in her sixties with white hair and dark eyes and a mean-looking expression.

"Well, it's about time," she said, parking her hands on her broad hips. She was wearing a pale yellow print housedress with purple bedroom shoes, and a splattered white apron hugged her ample middle. "You're an hour late. What did you do, get hijacked on the way back? I've ruined dinner, you'll be glad to know, and who's that?"

Elissa was being dragged up the steps and pushed forward like a shield before she had time to catch her breath.

"This is Elissa Dean," King said, holding her there firmly, even though she wasn't struggling.

"Well, glory be!" Margaret's broad face brightened like a sunflower. "Finally!"

She rushed forward, and Elissa found herself engulfed in the smell of flour and apples.

"I thought he'd never get enough sense to bring you home," Margaret gushed. "Idiot, chasing after them stupid city women." She glared at King before turning back to Elissa. "You look like a nice girl. He says you still live at home," she added with unashamed curiosity.

"Well, yes," Elissa stammered. "My folks wouldn't have it any other way."

Margaret looked as if all her prayers had been answered. "Lordy, child, do come in and let me feed you. I've got a delicious pot roast, even if I do say so myself, and a pan of homemade rolls, and I baked him an apple pie."

King went back to get the luggage, muttering things it was just as well Margaret didn't actually hear. Margaret was a wonderful cook, had a mind like a steel trap and didn't feel the least bashful about asking the most intimate kind of questions.

King finally ran her off so they could eat their meal in peace. Elissa's face was beet red by then, and he looked a bit put out himself. Elissa couldn't know that over the years, only Bess had ever been afforded such courteous treatment by the housekeeper. Margaret had always found not-so-subtle ways of showing her disapproval for the type of woman King had entertained so frequently in his younger days. Bess had been different, because Margaret knew her background and was frankly sorry for her.

"It's a lovely meal," Elissa said finally.

"Lovely," he muttered.

She didn't attempt conversation again. She finished the food and allowed Margaret to whisk her upstairs to unpack.

King was called out the minute he left the supper table to attend to sixty things the foreman—Ben Floyd, Margaret's husband—hadn't been able to, despite neighbor Blake Donavan's help.

Elissa found herself alone after Margaret went to her own small house below the stables, and when King didn't come back by midnight, she went to bed. Her first day on the ranch had been an experience.

The next morning, she awoke to strange noises. Cattle lowing. A rooster crowing. The barking of a dog. Clatter from downstairs. She sat up in bed with a lazy yawn and drank in the sweet, clean country air. It wasn't so far removed from the Florida coast, after all. Country was country, except for the noises.

She got up and dressed in jeans and a short-sleeved blouse, feeling as summery as the weather. She left her hair down and her face clear of makeup.

Downstairs, King was sitting at the breakfast table with a brooding look. But it wasn't the King she'd become accustomed to. This was a Westerner with a capital *W*. She stood stock-still in the doorway, just staring.

From his faded jeans and dusty boots up over a blue-and-white Western shirt to his dark hair, he was a different man. It wasn't only the clothing; it was something in his face. A different look. A naturalness. A man in his native setting.

He looked up from his newspaper and cocked an eyebrow. "Well? Aren't you hungry?"

"Of course." She sat down beside him, her eyes curious.

"You've seen me in jeans before," he reminded her, amused at her expression.

"You never looked like this before," she faltered. Her eyes searched his.

He winked at her. "Did you sleep well?"

"Beautifully." She sighed. "How about you?"

"When I finally got to sleep," he muttered darkly, "it was soundly. Ben had five hours' work waiting."

"Wasn't some neighbor supposed to be watching things for you?"

"He was, and he did," came a deep, amused voice from the doorway, "but only Kingston can sign Kingston's name to his checks."

Elissa turned to find the voice. The man she saw made her shiver. He looked dangerous, a wild man with unruly black hair and pale green eyes set in lashes as thick and black as his eyebrows. He was lithe and lean and sported a scar down one cheek and a nose that looked to have been broken once too often. Somehow he didn't look like the kind of man King would call a friend, and Elissa wondered how much else there was to learn about the enigmatic man she'd fallen in love with.

"Blake Donavan," King introduced him. "This is my houseguest, Elissa Dean."

"I'm glad to meet you, Mr. Donavan," she said hesitantly.

He gave her an indifferent appraisal and nodded. "Same here." He turned his attention to King. "If you've got everything you need, I'll head back home. I've got those damned lawyers waiting. At least this time it's for something productive. My signature goes on a document, and the suit's settled once and for all."

King lifted his coffee cup. "I hear Meredith Calhoun just won an award for her latest book."

The green eyes kindled, and the lean face seemed to close up. Obviously this writer, whoever she was, was a touchy subject for Blake Donavan, Elissa noted. Had King brought up the name deliberately? she wondered.

"I've got work to do," Donavan said tersely. "See you, Roper. Miss Dean," he added, touching the brim of his hat, and was gone.

"Who's Meredith Calhoun?" Elissa whispered, mindful of the open door.

King sighed. "That's a long story," he replied, apparently unwilling to delve into it.

"He's a hard-looking man," she ventured.

"Pure diamond," he agreed, "and it goes straight through. If he looks hard, it's because life made him hard. He was illegitimate, and his mother died in childbirth. He was taken in by a crusty old uncle who adopted him and gave him his name. The uncle died last year, and Donavan's been in a hell of a court battle for the property ever since."

"I can see why he won," she remarked, shivering slightly and wondering anew at King's ready compassion for life's unfortunates. Of course, that compassion was what had made him so vulnerable to Bess... "He's younger than you, isn't he?" she said weakly, dragging her thoughts back to the present.

His dark eyes narrowed on her face. "Yes. Eight years. He's almost thirty-three. Why? Does he appeal to you?"

She blinked. That sounded amazingly like jealousy. Why on earth should he feel possessive about her when it was Bess he loved?

Without waiting for her reply—besides, she was too

stunned and confused to offer one—he got to his feet. "I've got a full day's work ahead of me."

"Not in your office, I gather?" she fished.

"On my ranch," he said, leaning down to press a hard, warm kiss on her parted lips. "This is how I relax, tidbit—by keeping busy. Manual labor built this ranch."

"You look like a cowboy," she mused, surprised by the ardent kiss.

"I am a cowboy," he replied, searching her blue eyes. "I can travel first-class and buy damned near anything I want, but what I like best is a horse under me and open land around me and a night sky to sleep under."

"Do you?" She reached up to him, and amazingly, he came to her, letting her have his mouth. She kissed him warmly and was stunned by the softness of his lips, by his eager participation in a caress that had nothing to do with sex.

"Want to come see the calves later?" he asked as he lifted his head. "If you're good, I'll even let you pet one."

"Yes, I'd like to," she said, smiling lazily.

He drew in a slow, pleased breath as his eyes drank in her lovely face. "Fairy face," he whispered. He bent again, brushing her mouth with his. "I'll see you at lunch. Don't let Margaret talk you to death."

"I like Margaret," she murmured.

"Margaret likes you, too, baby doll," Margaret said from the doorway with a platter of eggs in her hand. She grinned toothily at King. "You lucky man, you."

King actually flushed. "I've got work to do," he mumbled, and he left them both there, pulling his hat down over his eyes with a jerk as he strode noisily from the room.

"Only walks that way when I've annoyed him," Margaret assured her, grinning even wider. "But you're the first girl he's brought home to me to visit in a long, long time, so I reckon he's in pretty deep. But you watch him, he's no choirboy. He can be right dangerous in full pursuit."

Elissa burst out laughing. "Oh, Margaret, you're a jewel," she said, and meant it. "He doesn't love me, you know. I'm just his friend, that's all."

Margaret nodded as she sat down. "That's right, and I'm a Halloween pumpkin," she agreed. She helped herself to a cup of coffee and folded her hefty forearms on the table. She stared straight at Elissa. "Now, tell me about yourself. I hear you design clothes."

It was like the Spanish Inquisition. By the time Elissa was allowed to escape and go exploring around the house, Margaret knew her favorite perfume, her entire family history— she'd hooted with delight upon learning King had brought home a minister's daughter—and as much as possible of her potential future.

The ranch itself was a new experience. There were well-kept stables housing beautiful Appaloosas, cattle everywhere and a bull who seemed to have his own building and a full-time caretaker. He was red and white, like most of the cattle, and as big as a house. When King came home at lunchtime, he found her at the barn, staring at the creature.

"His name is King's Pride 4120," he informed her smugly, hands in his pockets. "He's out of the foundation herd of Herefords Bobby's grandfather began here, but I've improved the strain with selective breeding."

"Why does he have a number?" she asked. "Has he been arrested or something?"

"That gets complicated." He threw an affectionate arm around her shoulders and led her back to the house, explaining things like embryo transplants and daily weight-gain ratios and all the intricacies of breeding superior beef cattle.

The technical information rattled around in Elissa's head like marbles, but it was fascinating all the same.

"Margaret's making beef-salad sandwiches for lunch," she told him on the front porch, where the big green swing and several rocking chairs faced the open plains.

"How much has she dragged out of you so far?" he asked with a raised eyebrow and a dry smile.

"Before or after she got to the color of my underwear?" She laughed.

He just shook his head.

Lunch was quiet. Margaret went off to listen to the news while she worked in the kitchen, and King didn't seem inclined to talk. Afterward, he saddled a horse for her with the ease of long practice and helped her into the saddle. This, at least, was familiar. They'd gone riding together in Jamaica several times over the past two years. She glanced at him under the brim of her borrowed straw hat, thinking how everything about him was familiar to her and yet subtly different these days.

He caught her glance and grinned. "Remember the day we rode down the beach hell-for-leather, and you fell off in the surf?"

"I'm holding on tight this time," she retorted, wrapping the reins around her hand. "Lead on, cowboy. You won't lose me."

"Let's see."

He took off, nudging his Appaloosa gelding to a quick lead. She followed on her mare, laughing delightedly at the open land and his company and the sunny afternoon.

The calves were Herefords, and not newborn as she'd expected. The calves started coming in February and March, he told her, to coincide with his breeding program. They were fattened up and then sold when they reached the desired weight.

"It's so sad to think of eating them," she mused while she scratched a white-topknotted head above soulful brown eyes. "Isn't he cute?"

He leaned against the fence post, his hat pushed back, his eyes watchful. "They tell stories about the cattle drives in the old days and how close the cattle got to their drovers. They say that sometimes the cowboys had to actually go with the cattle into the abattoirs, to keep them from stampeding. They bawled when the drovers started to leave them."

Tears sprang to her eyes. She was vaguely embarrassed at her sentimentality and tried to hide her reaction, but he saw her tears. He caught her gently by the shoulders, turning her. He bent, lifting her into his arms, and carried her back to the horses.

"I'm sorry," she whispered.

"You softhearted little greenhorn," he whispered back, and he smiled as he brought his mouth with exquisite tenderness to hers.

He'd meant it to be a sweet, comforting gesture, but her mouth opened beneath his, and his breath stopped in his throat. He hesitated, but only for a second. Then he carried her away from the horses and laid her down in the tall buffalo grass, his lean body settling completely over her.

"King!" she gasped.

"Elissa," he breathed huskily. He kissed her hungrily, giving in to the aching need, the long nights of wanting her. He reached under her to catch her hips and drag them lazily against his, letting her feel the evidence of his need. And for long, exquisite moments, they enjoyed the touch and taste and feel for each other.

Then, when it was almost too much, he groaned and rolled onto his back. Not since his teens had he felt so damned helpless to control himself. And she could see how much she aroused him.

She sat up, her eyes like saucers, and he held her rapt gaze.

"This never happens to me," he whispered, his voice deep and husky and gruff. "Never this quick or this completely with any woman but you, damn it."

Her lips parted on a smile as she looked at him, not with triumph but with love. "Do you mind if that makes me proud?" she asked softly.

He drew in an unsteady breath. "I guess not." He sat up, bending over his upraised knees. "I can't imagine how I've lasted this long."

She touched his hand where it rested on his knee. "I'm sorry," she said softly, searching the dark, tormented eyes that met hers. "But it pleases me that even if you don't love me, at least you want me."

He brought her hand to his mouth. "Do you want me to love you?" he asked quietly. "Because that may come in time. Marry me, Elissa."

She lowered her eyes to his hand. "I'll have to think about it," she said finally, biting her tongue to keep from screaming yes. She had to be reasonable. She couldn't let her love for him influence her; she had to think of what was best for him, too, since obviously he wasn't thinking at all.

His fingers tightened. He started to speak and then seemed to decide against it. "All right."

She looked up. "Does Bobby know we're here?"

"Yes," he said finally. "I called him a few hours ago. Bess is in Oklahoma City until tomorrow morning. He invited us to go riding with them."

"When?"

"Tomorrow afternoon." He tilted her face up. "Don't decide now. You've got one hell of a big decision to work up to by bedtime."

Her lips trembled. "I...I care for you," she whispered.

His hand touched her cheek, and he wished he could read her mind. He felt guilty and uncertain, but he cared for her, too, in his way. "Then marry me," he said, feeling oddly certain that it would be the right thing for them both. "Say yes."

She managed a quiet sigh. Logic went out the window. "Yes."

He stared into her eyes for a long time, feeling electricity arc between them. He wanted her. He was fond of her. She cared for him. It would be enough. And it would be a final, permanent barrier between him and Bess.

He bent to her mouth and kissed her very gently before he helped her to her feet and back into the saddle. He didn't say another word all the way home.

CHAPTER NINE

ELISSA SPENT THE afternoon helping Margaret in the kitchen. King had gone out again, presumably to finish his ranch work. Margaret kept throwing the younger woman speaking glances, and Elissa knew she must look troubled.

"Out with it," Margaret said finally. "What's wrong?"

"He wants to marry me," Elissa replied, scouring a pan they'd used to fry steak for lunch.

"Hallelujah!"

"It isn't that simple," she said with a rueful smile. She turned back to the pan. "He doesn't love me."

"Men don't know what love is until they're in too deep to climb out," Margaret observed, chuckling. "I've seen how he looks at you. There's enough there to build on—you mark my words."

Elissa tingled. Yes, he did look at her as if she were a sumptuous dessert. But there was still Bess to consider. She sighed.

"Don't worry about it," the older woman coaxed. "Just say yes, and I'll take care of everything. Let's see, invitations and the reception, and champagne and hors d'oeuvres," she murmured.

Elissa didn't say anything else. She was too worried.

They sat down to supper alone, and after cleaning up, Margaret finally went home, bubbling with happiness. Elissa arranged a plate for King and covered it, and she was just wiping up a spill on the floor when King walked in the back door.

He looked at little dusty and very tired. He studied her from under the wide brim of his Stetson, taking in the picture she made in a loose gold-and-white caftan, kneeling there against the spotless cream linoleum.

"You're a picture, do you know it?" he mused. "All that long, sexy hair and big blue eyes, and your tan looks pretty good with white and gold."

She stood up, smiling. "You look like a cowboy," she replied.

His eyebrows arched. "Is that a compliment or a criticism?"

She lowered her eyes shyly. "I like cowboys."

"Where's Margaret?"

"Gone home. I've fixed you a plate, if you're hungry."

He looked faintly sheepish for a minute, steadying his dusty boots. "Well, Jim was up at the cow camp with us," he began. "Jim's the cook when we're working. He rustled up a pot of chili and some tortillas and a pudding that I expect to dream about for days." He cocked his head at her. "Don't tell Margaret, will you? I'll get burned biscuits for a week if she finds out. Could you dispose of that plateful of stuff without her knowing?"

She laughed delightfully. "Of course."

"I'll be down directly, once I clean up, and I'll thank you properly," he murmured, lowering his voice an octave.

She felt her heart skip at the look in his dark eyes as he went by her. He winked on his way into the hall, and she watched him go, feeling strangely quiet and contented yet delirious with anticipation.

He paused on the middle step and looked down at her.

"How about making some coffee?" he asked. "I'll come back down and we'll share a pot while we talk."

His eyes fell to her body and lingered. She felt weak in the knees. He wanted more than just talk, and she knew it. They were so much on the same wavelength that she could almost feel him breathing.

"I'll do that," she said, her voice husky.

He nodded. His eyes smiled. "And I could do with a piece of cake, if there's any left," he added.

"There's enough. I'll slice it. Don't drown in the shower," she teased.

"I can swim." He grinned and continued up the stairs.

Elissa made coffee and carried the silver service into the living room, curling up on the sofa to wait for him. Minutes later he joined her, dressed in clean denims and a half-unbuttoned blue-check shirt. His hair was damp, and he smelled of soap and spicy cologne. Elissa could hardly take her eyes off him as he eased his tall, powerful frame down on the sofa beside her.

"I'll pour," she said. She sounded, and was, flustered. To disguise it, she moved to the floor in front of the coffee table so that she was just in front of him. It was all she could do to get the coffee out of the heavy silver pot into the white china cups.

"You're nervous. Why?" he asked quietly.

She laughed. "I don't know."

He reached down, turning her so that she was kneeling between his legs. His fingers traced her flushed cheeks, and his eyes were steady on hers. Everything she felt was in her face—it was like reading a book—and his reaction to that blatant adoration shocked him. He felt a surge of possession strong enough to knock the breath out of him, and his body was suddenly, achingly hungry for hers. Not for sex alone but for something more. He frowned. He'd never felt that need before, not with any woman. He wanted to… to join with Elissa. To know her in every way there was.

He felt oddly young as he bent toward her, and the first touch of his mouth against her soft one was tentative. He drank in the floral scent of her, drowned in her shy, eager response. It was always like this with her, like flying, like bubbles in champagne. She was his from the moment he touched her. But now it felt as if he belonged to her, as well.

With a long, aching sigh, he brought her up against him, easing her onto his lap as he deepened the slow, tender kiss. She felt his kiss with wonder, because it had never been like this before. She relaxed into him, looping her arms around his neck, her mouth parting, opening under the sweet ardor of his.

She felt his hands at her waist, tracing her rib cage, then delicately touching the soft contours of her breasts. Under the caftan, she wore only pale yellow briefs, and when he felt her skin so close, his breath caught.

Her body began to tremble as he stroked it, his fingers deft and sure and faintly insistent. His mouth hardened on hers, and her ears were filled with the harsh quickness of his breathing and her own faint gasps when he touched her more intimately.

Her soft blue eyes looked up into his when he lifted his head, and she saw a strange expression there. "What is it?" she whispered unsteadily.

He watched his fingers tracing her breasts, watched the involuntarily movement of her body at the pleasure he gave her. "I want you," he breathed. "But not…like I've ever wanted anyone else." His dark eyes went back to hers. "I want to join your body to mine. I want oneness…"

Her lips parted. "Yes." Even as she thought the word, she

said it, because this might be the only time. She might lose him, but this once she could belong to him. He knew she was a virgin. It would be special. It would be everything.

She slid the zipper of the caftan down to her waist, and his chest rose sharply. He searched her eyes for a long moment before he eased the fabric out of the way and looked at her. After a moment, he bent, and his lips began to touch her in reverent adoration. Her breasts, her belly and her hips burned under his mouth. She moved helplessly as he touched her in ways he never had, and long before he eased her out of her caftan and briefs, she was lost.

She moaned when he moved away long enough to strip off his own clothing, his eyes dark and sensual and full of desire. There was a faint tremor in his powerful body as he sat back down on the sofa and eased her gently over him, so that she was sitting facing him. She gasped at the first touch of skin against skin, light against dark, hard muscle against softness.

"There's nothing to be afraid of," he whispered, brushing her body in agonizingly slow movements against his, her breasts just barely touching him, her hips trembling against his blatant masculinity.

Her hands gripped his hard arms, and she leaned her forehead against his chest so that he wouldn't see the fear. "Is it going to hurt?" she whispered.

"It's going to be beautiful," he whispered back, his hands on her hips. "Give me your mouth."

She lifted her face and saw the soft affection in his eyes. Her heart was his. She loved him so. It was magic, the way it felt, to be this way with him, to be intimate with him. Her mind was beyond right and wrong, in thrall to the budding demands of her own womanhood.

His hands explored her waist and hips, gently caressing, softly arousing. He moved her hips against his, and she bit back a moan. She clung to him, astounded by what was happening.

"Oh, King," she whispered achingly, lifting her eyes.

He eased her upward then, holding her gaze while he positioned her hips against his. His face was that of a stranger, utterly sensual, slightly threatening, but there was something in his dark eyes that held her spellbound. He bent, his breath mingling with hers as he brushed his mouth over hers in lazy, comforting sweeps that eased her fear.

While his lips toyed with hers, his hands were learning the silken contours of her body. He teased her breasts, nudging their hardened tips, making her tremble with the sensations he aroused. He nipped her lower lip and trailed his mouth over her throat, her shoulders and, finally, the soft swell of her breasts.

She could hardly breathe. She held his arms for support, her eyes closed, the air cool at her back. He moved then, and she felt the sudden contact with his thighs, the ripple of muscles as he probed her softly. She gasped, looking up, her breath stopped in her throat.

He moved against her, very slowly, holding her eyes. His hands made their way to her hips, moving her against him in a slow, lazy, arousing rhythm. She didn't understand what was happening to her. She felt her body begin to tremble, and she gasped when he increased the gentle rise and fall of his hips against her. She clutched at him, overwhelmed by the intimacy of the gesture.

"King…sitting up?" she gasped, her voice scarcely recognizable to her own ears.

"Shh," he whispered, lowering his mouth over hers in delicious teasing motions. "Just relax, little one. I wouldn't hurt a hair on your sweet head for all the cows in Texas."

"But...like this?"

He laughed gently, even though his body was shuddering with his need of her. He looked down at her taut breasts and deliberately pressed his hard, hair-roughened chest against them. She moaned, and the sound fired his blood.

"Are you going to get noisy?" he whispered into her mouth. "I won't mind." He bit her lower lip delicately while one hand teased her swollen breast and moved down slowly to her hips, her thighs and into a sudden, wildly shocking intimacy that she instinctively protested. But after a minute, when her body demanded that she let him do it, she gave in and held on, crying out softly at the delicious pleasure he was giving her. She felt tears sting her eyes and run down into her mouth.

He tasted them and lifted his head to watch her fevered eyes, her flushed face, while he savored her sweet body. "It won't be hard for you," he whispered, and he shifted, just a little, holding her hips. "It won't be hard at all. Don't tense up. I'm going to show you the mystery, Elissa. I'm going to make a woman of you now."

She felt him arch slightly, and her lips parted on a soft gasp. She looked into his eyes, frightened at the first burning stab of sensation.

His hands framed her face as he moved again, and she jerked a little. "Another few seconds," he whispered, his voice soft and slow and intimate. He smiled. "Relax for me. It won't ever hurt again, I promise," he breathed brokenly, his hands bringing her down to him.

He kissed her softly as he took her completely, and her nails bit into him. She started to stiffen, but she bit her lip and laid her forehead against his broad, damp chest and forced her body to admit him. There was only a small stab of pain, and then she sighed in relief.

His hands moved on her, stroking her, doing impossible things, moving her, shifting her. He bent to her mouth again, probing it with his tongue. He took it, and his hips began to move, and she felt a savage ripple of pleasure that took her by surprise. Surely, she thought dazedly, she'd only imagined it. But he moved, and it came again. And again. She bit his shoulder, shuddering. He shuddered, too, and she felt his body surge powerfully.

He lifted his mouth just enough to look at her. "Exquisite," he whispered, studying her. "That expression, wild and tortured, as if I were hurting you. But I'm not, am I?"

"No," she whispered. His hand moved, and she cried out, biting her lip.

"Don't stop yourself," he gasped as he increased his rhythm, his eyes stormy and dark. "There's no one to hear you. Let it out. Make noise," he whispered. "Make as much noise as you want."

His hands bit into her thighs, holding her down to him. Her eyes dilated, because she'd never expected that it would be like this. Her head fell back, and she gasped as he arched under her. His face was a mask of passion, tight and flushed, his eyes black as night and glittering, exultant.

She cried out, and her fingers bit into his shoulders as she shuddered with unexpected, total completion, his name a hoarse sound torn from her throat.

He felt her convulse, stunned that it should happen for her the first time. And then he felt the familiar stab of fulfillment racking him, and he cried out her name over and over.

A long time later, she wafted back to earth. Under her, his body was damp and shuddering in the aftermath, his hands protective now, soothing, tender. He lifted his face to hers and began to kiss her, his hard mouth so tender and cherishing that she wanted to cry. He whispered her name over and over again, his voice awed. He'd never experienced anything like this in his life. With Elissa, he'd attained heights he hadn't touched before. Whatever this was, it wasn't simply sex.

His body still trembling, he kissed her closed eyes warmly and then her face again, in soft, searching caresses. She felt loved, cherished, and she smiled against his damp throat.

He nipped her ear. "I felt it happen to you," he murmured. "It almost never does the first time."

"My body didn't know. I'll make sure I tell it."

"Imp," he drawled. He looked into her eyes and shifted his hips, his eyes hot and wicked when she gasped. "Shocking, isn't it?" he whispered. And then his gaze softened, and his smile faded. "I hope you aren't having second thoughts," he said quietly.

She opened her mouth to tell him that she wasn't protected, but his opened against it, and his hips rose and fell, and the pleasure came stabbing back in a rhythm that was already familiar.

"Angel face," he whispered softly. "I've dreamed about this for so long, about how it would be with you. It was beyond my wildest dreams. It was perfection," he breathed, touching her face reverently. "My God, it's never been like that for me. Never."

She stared at his hair-roughened chest and touched it tentatively, liking the feel under her fingers. He stiffened a little, and she smiled at him. "You're very good at this," she said shyly, wondering how many women there had been before her. The thought disturbed her a little, and her conscience was twinging. He didn't love her, she knew, but she loved him. Was that reason enough to covet this oneness with him? This one night out of a lifetime, when she could lie in his arms and pretend that he loved her? She refused to think. She leaned forward and kissed his chest softly. "You'll have to show me what to do to make it good for you," she whispered.

"The mind boggles," he whispered back, sliding his mouth softly over hers. "Come on. We'll have a shower, and then we'll go to bed." He lifted his head, searching her eyes. "If you still want to."

She returned that intent look. "I want to," she assured him.

He carried their things upstairs to his bedroom and led her into the shower. For the next few minutes, they soaped and explored each other and kissed until her mouth was swollen and his body was making new and urgent demands.

"I'm not protected," she whispered as he laid her down on the bed. "I should have told you before."

"I don't give a damn," he breathed. He was on fire for her, burning. Consequences didn't seem to matter anymore, and they were engaged, so what the hell. "A baby wouldn't be the end of my world or yours."

"How would you make love to me if you wanted a baby?" she whispered, her eyes soft with love.

He smiled as he brushed her mouth with his. "Very much as I did downstairs," he murmured against her lips. "As if you were innocent all over again. We'd be exquisitely tender with each other, like two people desperately in love. Like...this."

It was tender. And profound. He drew it out, exploring her body like some delicate treasure that might break with a harsh breath. Even when he began to take her, it was still gentle, their eyes openly cherishing each other, their voices hushed. When the tide came and washed them into the blinding heat of fulfillment, they were still looking into each other's eyes, and it was a gentle violence, rocking them with exquisitely tender shudders and warm convulsions that were even more beautiful than those of wild passion.

When it was over, she cried helplessly, and he held her, kissing away the tears, cradling her against his damp body.

"You make it so profound," he whispered shakily. "It isn't even physical with you. It's a thing so much of the spirit that it makes me tremble. I never dreamed of such fulfillment."

"You make love beautifully," she breathed.

"So do you, baby." He curled her into his body with a weary sigh. "I want to sleep with you, Elissa. I never want to let go of you."

She cuddled close to him, savoring his strength, feeling secure and adored and totally fulfilled. At the back of her mind, a tiny voice nagged that it wasn't right or proper, but she was too tired to listen.

"Don't hate me," he breathed.

"How could I?"

"I took you out of wedlock."

"I offered myself."

"Did you? Or did I simply back you into a corner and take the choice away from you?" He lifted his head to search her eyes. "Will you mind if I made you pregnant?"

"There probably wasn't much risk," she murmured shyly.

"The way we made love that last time, there was most definitely a risk," he said.

She nuzzled her face against him. "Will you hate me if that happens?"

"Never."

"Babies can create problems."

His arms tightened. "Babies are little tiny breathing miracles. Now shut up and go to sleep. I'm so tired, it's all I can do to breathe, you insatiable little witch."

"*I'm* insatiable?" she burst out.

He only grinned and folded her closer. "Go to sleep. If you're able, I'll make love to you again when we wake up."

She sighed. "What a delicious incentive to sleep."

"I thought so, too."

It seemed like no time at all before the sounds of farm equipment outside the window brought her eyes open. She looked down at King, smiling at his nudity, at the vulnerability of his powerful body in sleep.

"It's morning," she whispered in his ear.

"Is it?" he whispered back, smiling. He opened his eyes and reached for her, his intentions obvious. "Are you up to this?" he asked solicitously.

She pressed down against him. "I want you," she whispered before bringing her mouth to his.

He took a long time with her, despite his overpowering hunger, and it was late morning before he was satisfied enough to get up. He stretched grandly and looked down at her sprawled facedown on the bed.

"You miracle, you," he breathed. "Roll over. I want to look at you while I dress."

She did, smiling at him, watching him open drawers and the closet and get into jeans and a chambray shirt. "It's even exciting to watch you put clothes on," she confessed, laughing.

"I'd rather watch you with yours off, angel," he murmured, bending to brush hungry kisses on her breasts. "I want you all the time, lately. It's all I can do to stop." He lifted his head, searching her eyes. "You flinched a little that last time," he said gently. "It wasn't comfortable, and you should have told me in time. I'll leave you alone until you're sure it won't be an ordeal instead of a pleasure."

"You're very perceptive," she murmured.

"You're very generous," he whispered. "So eager to please me, to put my desire first. But that isn't what I want. It gives me no pleasure unless you share it."

"Oh, but I want to give you everything, to make it sweet for you," she said fervently. "I don't care what I feel—"

He stopped her tirade with his mouth, smiling against it. "*I* care. Come on downstairs when you're dressed, and I'll take you for a nice, comfortable ride in the Lincoln. No horseback riding just yet." He grinned, and she flushed.

"Okay."

He lifted her hand to his lips, studying her over it. An innocent, and with all her inhibitions, and yet she'd given herself to him with wild abandon. She cared more than a little; he was almost sure she loved him. That thought was sweetly disturbing. Could she? He looked at her hungrily. All night, and still he wanted her. She was under his skin, driving him mad. Bess and his problems with her had faded to insignificance. Whatever he and Elissa had, it was something far removed from lust or infatuation. He wanted to take care of her, to be there when she cried. He sighed softly. What was he going to do about Bess? Or did he need to do anything, now that he was marrying Elissa? He thought about marrying Elissa and smiled slowly. She'd be in his bed every night, making magic with him. His chest began to swell.

She saw that look and smiled at him. "Don't feel guilty," she whispered. "I don't."

"Don't you?" he asked quietly.

"Not in the least," she said, ignoring her conscience.

"Anyway, I wasn't thinking about guilt," he confessed. "I

was wondering if you loved me," he added bluntly, watching her flush. "Somehow, I don't think you'd be able to give yourself to a man you didn't love. You're not the type." He touched her cheek, teasing her face up to his. "Don't hide it," he whispered, finding the evidence of love in her face wildly pleasing, exciting. His breath caught in his throat, and he wondered why it should suddenly matter so much that she loved him. "That was why you were so uninhibited, wasn't it?" he asked slowly. "That was why I gave you pleasure the first time. And you did enjoy it."

"More than you'll ever know," she confessed. "Do you mind?"

He shook his head. "You're very special to me."

"Even when we aren't lovers anymore," she began, her eyes wide and worried, "will you still be my friend?"

That hurt. He sat down and lifted her across his knees, cuddling her close. "My God," he ground out, his arms wrapped tightly around her. "You little fool. You don't have some crazy idea that I was just satisfying a whim last night, do you?"

"I hoped it wasn't that."

"I'm going to marry you," he whispered. "This isn't a one-night stand. For God's sake, Elissa, you're part of me now."

She trembled a little at the urgency in his voice, at his warmth and fervency. She turned her mouth against his throat and kissed him. "Thank you," she said.

"I don't want thanks." He lifted his head and looked into her eyes, his expression both thrilling and puzzling. His dark gaze went over her slowly, lingering on her breasts. "I'm more old-fashioned than I realized," he said unexpectedly. "If you ever let another man touch you like I did, I'd break his neck!"

"Well!" she gasped, but his mouth covered hers fiercely, blotting out the world.

"You're my woman," he whispered against her responsive lips. "You belong to me. We're going to get married and enjoy each other for the next eighty years or so."

Her arms linked around his neck, and she savored the pressure of his mouth for a long, spinning minute until he finally satisfied his hunger and lifted his head.

"Get dressed," he whispered. "I can't take much more of that without laying you down and ravishing you again."

She smiled softly. "I adore you."

"I adore you," he whispered. He smiled at her, new to possession, new to that look in her eyes, that total fulfillment his loving had given her. It made him proud that he could fulfill her, that he'd done it her first time.

"You look smug," she mentioned.

He dumped her onto the bed, looming over her to press a hard kiss on her mouth. "I feel smug. Now get up."

"Yes, Your Worship."

He glanced at her on his way out the door and smiled again as he closed it behind him. He couldn't remember a time in his life when he'd felt so pleased with himself, so satiated with happiness that he felt as if he could do anything.

She dressed quickly, taking time to sneak down the hall to her room and mess up her bed—only to find that he'd already done it. She smiled to herself as she went downstairs, wrapped in the sweet illusion of loving and being loved.

He was sipping coffee when she got to the kitchen, and his eyes when they met hers were dark with acquisition. His chin rose, all male arrogance in the smile he gave her. His eyes ran down her body with remembered possession, and they kindled like dusky fires.

She tingled all over as she joined him, her mouth softening at his welcoming kiss.

"Here," he whispered.

She opened her eyes to find him sliding a solitary emerald onto her ring finger. It was in a delicate antique filigree setting, and a perfect fit. She caught her breath, her eyes searching, questioning his.

"It belonged to my grandmother," he said, his face solemn. "You can give it to our eldest son..."

"King." Tears fell like rain from her eyes. She went into his arms, trembling all over. If only she could stop wondering if it might be guilt and a sense of responsibility that had led to this. She knew he didn't love her, although he was fond of her and he did enjoy her body. But maybe in time he might learn to love her. She clung to him. "I love you so much," she said shakily, her eyes closed so that she missed the delight on his dark face. "So much."

He held her, his expression one of contentment, rocking her softly against him. God, she was soft. Sweet. Deliciously female. She smelled of flowers, and he wanted to hold her all day. She felt just right in his arms. He smiled, closing his eyes.

"Now, ain't that pretty?" Margaret sighed from the doorway, smiling benevolently at both of them.

"Look," Elissa said tearfully, sitting on King's lap to extend her slender finger with the emerald ring on it.

"Glory be!" Margaret exclaimed. "We really are having a wedding!"

"Looks like it, doesn't it?" King said affectionately.

"I'll go tell Ben." Margaret grinned and walked away.

Elissa was just starting to speak when the phone rang.

"I'll get it," he said as he set her on her feet. He walked into the hall and picked up the receiver, listened for a minute and took a sharp breath. "What the hell was he doing on it in the first place?" he demanded. "No, honey, don't, don't. I'm sorry. God, I'm sorry. Listen, sweetheart, you just sit tight, you hear? I'll be right there. Everything will be all right. I'm on my way."

He hung up and dug into his pocket for his car keys. "Bobby's been thrown from a horse," he said tersely. "Bess came in last night, and they went riding together this morning. He's got a concussion and a broken leg, at least. I'll have to go to the hospital, honey. Bess was pretty upset. She needs me."

Elissa just sat there, stunned, as he turned away without another word. She watched him rush out the door, on his way to Bess, without a backward glance toward the woman he'd just asked to marry him. She closed her eyes, feeling the tears start. If this was a glimpse of the future, she'd just looked straight into hell.

CHAPTER TEN

MARGARET CAME BACK minutes later to find Elissa cupping her hands around a cup of cold coffee, a look of utter defeat on her face.

"Where's he gone?" the older woman asked curtly.

"Bobby was thrown from a horse," Elissa said quickly, looking up. "He's got a broken leg and a concussion. King's gone to the hospital."

Margaret whistled. "I knew it would happen one day.". She shook her head. "Bobby isn't a rider, for all he keeps trying. Will he be all right?"

"Bess didn't say, apparently," she faltered.

The older woman sat down, staring at Elissa. "That young madam has too much time on her hands and not enough husband," she said bluntly. "I've known both them boys for a long time—watched them fuss and fight and grow into men. Bobby's too eaten up trying to compete with his half brother to be the man he could be. All business, even when he comes to dinner over here. Bess sits there watching him so sadly, and he doesn't see her at all. I understand why he's doing it, mind you, but Bess isn't the kind of woman a man should treat that way. God knows she had a hard enough life, what with her family."

Margaret was good for half an hour on that subject. By the time she got through the alcoholic father and eternally pregnant mother and the abject poverty Bess had grown up in, Elissa felt sorrier for the blonde than she'd ever dreamed she could. But King had gone running when Bess needed him, and that fact stood out above all the rest. Was he simply sorry for Bess and protective of her, or was it something more?

"You don't mind that he went to see about Bobby?" Margaret asked suddenly.

"Oh, heavens, no!" Elissa said. "I would have gone, too, if he'd asked me." She shrugged, biting back tears. "I guess he was thinking that Bess would need some support."

Margaret's eyes narrowed. "Bess loves Bobby," she said quietly. "Sometimes she may flirt with other men, but that's all it ever is. And Kingston asked you to marry him, didn't he?"

"Yes, but that was because we—" Elissa looked up wildly and bit her lip. Her face grew suddenly hot as Margaret pursed her lips and lifted an eyebrow. "Because he knows I'm in love with him," she amended quickly. "He feels guilty."

"Good. I raised him to have a conscience," she said curtly. "That's right, I was with his mama since he was just a boy. What morals he's got, I put there, no thanks to her. I took over where his dad left off. Poor old fellow, he couldn't take her everlasting roving eye. He was a good man."

Elissa studied her silently. "Is his father still alive?"

Margaret smiled gently. "Very much alive. He's in a nursing home in Phoenix—a good one. We correspond, and I tell him all the news about once a month."

"Oh, shouldn't you tell King?" she asked worriedly.

"Honey, Kingston would go crazy. He thinks his father deserted him, and he's never wanted anything to do with him. I wouldn't dare confess what I've been doing."

"But his father will die one day," Elissa argued.

"It's not my place to say anything," Margaret replied. She searched Elissa's pained eyes. "You could, though. He might listen to you."

Elissa laughed weakly. "I wonder." She stared at the emerald ring on her finger. It felt cold, an empty gesture to appease his guilt, to satisfy his sense of responsibility. Her eyes closed. Last night it had all seemed worth it. In the cold light of reality, with her mind back in control of her body, it seemed wrong. How could she have done it?

It had been a last desperate gamble, she thought miserably. To make him so enslaved that he'd get over Bess. But it hadn't worked. Bess was still number one in his thoughts. It seemed that she always would be.

"If you want him, fight for him," Margaret said gruffly. "You've got an advantage she doesn't. He likes you. All he really feels for her is pity and some leftover affection. She was like a child when she and Bobby got married. Kingston helped her over those first few quarrels."

Elissa studied her slender fingers. "Liking isn't enough."

"Neither is pity," Margaret said, and got up. "Now, you eat a good breakfast. We've got to build up your strength. If Bobby stays in the hospital for any length of time, we'll probably have ourselves a houseguest."

With a sinking feeling, Elissa watched Margaret's broad back disappear. She hadn't considered that King might bring Bess here. But on second thought, of course he would. And what a perfect opportunity for Bess to get through his defenses. And what in the world was Elissa going to do to prevent it?

Sure enough, a few hours later, King came in with a weeping, pale Bess in tow. Bess was still in jodhpurs, gloriously sexy in the expensive silk blouse she wore opened to the deep cleavage between her breasts. Her honey-blond hair was in a delicious tangle around her shoulders, and she was clinging to King as if he were a lifeline.

"I'll take her upstairs," King said, glancing at Elissa. "Call Margaret to help her undress, would you? Have you got a nightgown she can borrow?"

"Yes, of course," Elissa said dully, following them. "How's Bobby?"

"He'll be all right," he said, his arm protective around his sister-in-law. "His leg's broken, and he's got a hell of a headache, but he'll be out in a few days."

"Thank God." Elissa sighed. But nobody seconded that, least of all the two people in front of her.

She had only two nightgowns with her, but she spared the blue one for the opposition. Margaret gave it a sinister look as she carried it into the second guest bedroom to the tearful blonde.

Elissa slowly wandered back downstairs. Margaret was getting Bess some soup, and King, forgoing all the pressing business he'd been attending to without a thought to Elissa's lack of company, was proving he had all the time in the world for Bess. And why not? Elissa thought miserably. He loved Bess.

King ate his supper on a tray in Bess's room, to Margaret's blatant fury, leaving Elissa to eat alone or with the housekeeper.

"Idiot!" Margaret flared as she put a bowl of stew in front of Elissa. "Blind man!"

"Don't start feeling sorry for me," Elissa murmured. "I went into this with my eyes open. Nobody dragged me here. On the other hand," she added quietly, staring at the empty symbol on her ring finger, "I think I might see about a flight back to Miami. I'm only going to be in the way here."

"You can't go," Margaret huffed. "If you do, they'll be

here alone, and I won't have that kind of gossip." She glared at Elissa. "Your parents wouldn't appreciate your doing that kind of thing, either. No, ma'am, you're stuck. I'm sorry, but there isn't a thing you can do and still live with your conscience."

Ah, Elissa thought, *but you don't know what I'm already living with. You haven't a clue.* But she didn't say it. Conventions or no conventions, she was getting out of there. If she didn't, seeing King and Bess together was going to kill her. She was brave but not suicidal. Her heart was already breaking.

King still hadn't come out of Bess's bedroom when Elissa went upstairs. Gritting her teeth, she looked in the door, which Margaret had apparently left open.

King was sitting beside the bed, holding hands with a radiant Bess, and they were talking about Bobby. Elissa felt sick all the way to her toes just looking, and then she heard what they were saying.

"I feel so guilty," Bess was saying. "But I couldn't help it, Kingston. You know how he treats me. I'm so alone. He's never going to change, we both know that."

"The horse was a stallion. I've warned him not to try to ride it," he told her.

"But it was because I told him I wanted a divorce," Bess burst out, and Elissa felt her blood run cold. "Oh, Kingston, I can't go on living with a man who doesn't love me anymore. It's so much worse now, and when I'm with you—"

Elissa knocked abruptly on the door; she couldn't bear to hear any more, and it would look as if she were eavesdropping if she waited any longer. They both jerked around, looking stunned by her unexpected appearance.

"How are you feeling?" she asked Bess, schooling her

voice and face to show nothing but polite interest and friendliness.

Bess moved restlessly and pulled her hand from King's. "Oh, I—I'm feeling much better, thank you," she stammered. Her face colored. "I'd forgotten you were staying here."

"Under the circumstances, that's quite understandable," Elissa said gently, forcing a smile. "I'm sorry about Bobby, but I'm sure he'll be fine."

"They'll let him go home in a few days, they said." Bess sighed, then grimaced. "Back to his papers and business calls. He was already raving because they wouldn't let him have a telephone."

Elissa hesitated, unable to look at King. "Well, take care. I'll say good-night."

She went out, feeling her heart breaking inside, and stiffened when she heard King murmur something to Bess and follow her. She stood in front of her door, waiting for him, her back carefully straight.

"I'm glad she's going to be all right," she said, smiling, but she wouldn't meet his eyes. It was just as she'd predicted when she'd said back in Florida that she wouldn't marry him. She'd said that Bess might be free one day, and now it was going to happen. Elissa had represented an urge he couldn't control, but now she was an embarrassment, an obstacle. She stared down at the ring on her finger and knew how he felt and what he was thinking. If only he'd waited a few hours…

"She wasn't hurt," he said curtly. "Just upset. But I had to go to her."

Her, not his brother. She noticed the wording even if he didn't. "Of course."

He hesitated, which was unusual. "Elissa…"

She turned, forcing a smile. "Yes?"

"About last night..." he began slowly.

"Oh, yes. Last night." She pulled off the emerald ring and, taking one of his hands, pressed it into the palm. She stared at his closed fingers, feeling their strength and warmth and remembering all too well how they felt on her bare skin. She closed her eyes and wanted to die of the shame. "This is what you wanted, isn't it?"

He took a sharp breath. What did she mean, what he wanted? For God's sake, they'd made love. She'd told him she loved him. They were going to be married. So he'd brought Bess home—what else could he do? Surely, after what they'd shared the night before, Elissa didn't think he was still struggling with a hopeless passion for his sister-in-law?

"What I wanted?" he shot at her angrily. "Did I ask for the damned ring back?"

"Don't tell me the thought hasn't crossed your mind," she returned, staring at him accusingly. "I heard what Bess said, King," she confessed. "About divorcing Bobby. And maybe it's for the best. If they can't get along, and the two of you are... Well, I'm sure it will all work out," she added, lowering her eyes to his broad chest. The first few buttons were open, and involuntarily she wondered if Bess enjoyed touching him there as much as she did.

She turned away. She was about to burst into tears, and that would never do.

He stared at her as if she'd lost her senses. She'd agreed to marry him, and now she was backing out. Of course, he'd thought he wanted Bess, and now Bess was talking divorce. The obstacles to their union would be removed. And yes, he'd once thought he wanted that. But not now. Not anymore. He wanted Elissa, desperately, and here she was, throwing his ring back in his face. He felt suddenly, unreasonably angry.

"And what about you?" he demanded, hands on his hips.

Her chin lifted as she opened the door to her room. "What about me?" she asked curtly.

"You could be pregnant," he said bluntly. He sounded as if he wanted to throw things, starting with her.

"If I am, it's my problem, not yours."

"To hell with that!" he burst out. "It's my problem, as well, and don't you forget it."

His sense of responsibility, she thought miserably. "All right," she said quietly. "But there probably won't be a problem. I'd like to leave tomorrow."

He had to take deep breaths. His eyes flashed at her. "So that's it, is it? A quick one-night stand and you're off? You agreed to marry me, remember?"

"That was before," she threw back. "I don't want to marry you anymore. I don't want to become like Bess, tied to a man who doesn't love her, who barely notices she exists! No, sir, not me. That isn't what I want to do with my life. What kind of marriage would it be if every time Bess calls, you go running?"

"Bobby was injured," he reminded her. "I had to go."

"To her," she agreed, lifting her head. "You didn't even ask if I wanted to come. Bess needed you, so you went."

"Of course I went," he ground out with failing patience. His dark eyes flashed at her. "Bess falls apart in a crisis. And if my little brother can't take care of her, I feel responsible for her," he added, recognizing without quite realizing it that he was articulating what had been his own feelings all along. "Anyway, damn it, you aren't making sense."

"On the contrary, I'm finally making perfect sense. I've finally opened my eyes," she snapped. "I can see what's ahead, and I want no part of it. Bess is frail and helpless and needs protecting, is that right? And I'm tough and insensitive and I don't need anybody?"

"That's how it seems to me, lady," he bit off, totally confused now and losing his temper. "You handle yourself just fine without help. You always have. You're too damned independent."

It wounded, but she smiled so that he wouldn't see. "It beats begging people to notice you," she said with a poisonous smile.

"When did you ever have to?" he demanded.

"The minute Bess got within thirty miles of you," she shot back. "And if you're bothered that I might die of love for you, you can forget that, too. I'm *un*infatuated! Why don't you go and let Bess cry on you some more? I've got packing to do."

Elissa's blind stubbornness was making him see red. "What will you tell your parents?" he asked coldly.

She took a deep breath. "That I got homesick. What else?" She closed the door behind her and, as an afterthought, locked it. When she heard him stomp off down the hall, she blushed at her own conceit. As if he'd try to come to her, with Bess so handy. She crawled onto her bed, still dressed, and cried until there were no tears left.

By morning, she'd salvaged a bit of her pride. She dressed in one of her own flamboyant creations, a stunning white pantsuit with a red silk blouse. She wore heels, as well—red, to match the blouse—and carried a stylish white purse. Her long hair was pulled back into a bun, her makeup carefully applied. She looked sleek and sophisticated, a woman of the world. The fantasy was finally real, but now that she had it, she no longer wanted it. She wore rose-tinted sunglasses to camouflage the ravages of tears.

But she was a trouper. She'd learned from her parents that it always got darkest just before the dawn, so she glittered like sunlight as she joined Bess and King at the breakfast table.

"Well, good morning, glories," she bubbled, glancing from King's dark, shocked face to Bess's pale one. "Isn't it gorgeous traveling weather? Margaret, I'll just have toast and coffee, thanks. I don't manage airplanes very well on a full stomach."

Margaret sighed. "You're still going, then?" she asked, revealing that she knew what was going on.

"Of course," Elissa said brightly. "I made reservations a half hour ago. I've got two hours to get to the airport, and I've ordered a taxi to take me there. Fortunately Jack's Corner is large enough to have one."

"I'll drive you to the airport," King said curtly.

"You will not," Elissa told him. She even smiled. "Don't be silly. You'll have to go to the hospital and see your brother."

"I'm getting a divorce," Bess said quickly to Elissa.

"Yes, I heard," Elissa said, as if it didn't bother her in the least. "It's probably the best thing for both of you, too. I'm sure you'll find someone much more attentive than your husband. He did seem rather too busy for you."

"He works very hard," Bess said defensively, and King glanced at her curiously.

Elissa only smiled. She thanked Margaret, who had deposited a cup of black coffee and two honey-brown pieces of buttered toast at her elbow.

"Do you have a headache?" King asked Elissa.

"Yes," she replied, touching the sunglasses. "But nothing bad enough to prevent me from leaving, if that's what's bothering you."

"For God's sake!" He hit the table with his fist, and Bess jumped. "I haven't asked you to leave!"

"Like hell you haven't!" Elissa gave as good as she got, glaring across the table at him. "I'm not blind! I'm nothing more than an embarrassment to you now. You can't wait to get rid of me!"

"I asked you to marry me!" he said shortly.

Bess's eyes widened, and her mouth flew open.

"Marry you? I'd sooner have—have Blake Donavan!"

"Then go get him, honey. He's available!"

She got up, shaking all over, wanting nothing more than to pick up a chair and hit him over the head with it. Black-eyed devil, sitting there as arrogant as king, bursting with bad temper. Well, hers was just as bad, and he wasn't bull-dozing over her ever again.

"Thanks, I might just do that," she said, her voice shaking. She turned and stormed back upstairs to finish packing. She'd left the coffee and toast untouched, unable to bear seeing King and Bess together again.

Margaret came up to get her when the taxi arrived. "I wish you wouldn't go," she grumbled.

"I can't fight her," Elissa said simply. "He cares about her in a way he'll never care about me. It isn't something he can help."

"But, honey, what about you?" Margaret asked gently, her eyes so caring that Elissa burst into tears and was gathered up like a child to be comforted. "There, there," Margaret cooed. "He'll come to his senses one day. Men get a little blind sometimes, and Bess has always been special to all of us. He's a little sidetracked right now, but once he's had time to miss you a little, he'll be along—you mark my words."

"Think so? I don't." Elissa wiped her eyes and nose on

a handkerchief and crumpled it back into her purse before she readjusted her dark glasses. "There. Do I look terrible?"

"Not at all. Keep your chin up," Margaret advised. "Don't let them see you break down, even if you have to bite your tongue through. Poor Bobby, helpless in the hospital..."

"Poor Bobby may see the light if he can't get to his business for once," Elissa muttered. "What a pity he didn't look sooner. He might have saved himself some heartache."

"I suppose so. Well, you have a safe trip."

"I will. Thank you for being so good to me."

Margaret studied her quietly. "It's easy to be good to nice people. I hope we meet again someday."

"We probably won't," Elissa said, "but thank you for the wish."

She grabbed up her carryall and started downstairs. When she reached the hall, she heard voices in King's study. They stopped, quite suddenly, as she started past the open door, and a moan drew her attention. She glanced into the room and saw Bess in King's arms, smiling up at him.

It hurt, if possible even more than what had already happened, and she hurried past the room to the front door.

"Who was that?" King said, frowning as he heard the front door slam.

He moved away from Bess to open the curtain and look out, just in time to see Elissa dive into the waiting cab and slam the door before it roared off down the driveway.

"Oh, for God's sake," he grumbled. "I've got to go."

"Must you?" Bess asked, uncertainty in the soft eyes that looked up at him. "We were just going to talk."

"And we will. Later," he replied. He let out a slow breath, sensing that she'd already come to the same conclusion that he had; that his near involvement with Bess had been a sense of responsibility and tender affection on his part and desperate loneliness on hers. They'd work it out later, he was sure, without any hard words being spoken. He touched her blond hair lightly. "You're a lovely woman, Bess," he said gently, "but I've got a bad case of the woman who just walked out the door."

Bess sighed. "I guess I knew that already." She looked up at him. "It's just...well, I..." She faltered, trying to explain her own confused intentions.

"Don't fret," he said, smiling at her. "When I get back, we'll have that nice, long talk, and then we'll go see Bobby. Okay?"

She smiled wanly. "Okay."

He got into the Lincoln and proceeded to set new speed records driving to the airport. Damn. Elissa had probably seen him with Bess and drawn all the wrong conclusions. He was going to have to do some fast talking to smooth over this misunderstanding. He could only imagine how much her conscience was smarting over what they'd done together. Vividly remembering, he went hot all over.

Almost two hours later, he caught up with Elissa while she was waiting to board her flight.

She looked up, her broken heart cracking all over again at the sight of him, ruggedly jean clad and visibly impatient. The image almost shocked her into smiling, but the pain was still too sharp. She didn't get up. She sat there, her dark glasses in place, and looked at him as if he were some insect.

He sat down beside her, glancing at the flight attendants who were just entering the walkway to the plane. "I have to talk to you," he said curtly.

"We've talked," she said calmly.

"What you saw wasn't what you think," he began.

"Your private life is none of my business," she said simply. "I'm not interested."

"Will you listen," he gritted. "We've only got a few seconds."

"Then you'd better make your speech short," she replied.

He drew in a steadying breath, gripping his temper tightly to keep it from exploding all over again. All in all, his patience was being sorely tried. He seized upon the first thing that came to mind. "If you won't marry me, fine. But if you find yourself pregnant, I want to know immediately," he told her. "Promise me this minute that you'll get in touch with me, or so help me, I'll phone your parents and tell them the whole sordid mess."

Sordid. So that's how he thought of it. Perhaps it was sordid. A little back-alley overnight affair that he'd forget soon enough when he and Bess were married. Her heart was breaking. She had only a little pride left, and it was in tatters. He knew that she loved him, and that hurt most of all.

"I'll get in touch if anything happens," she said finally, the words dragged from her. "And in case you're afraid I'll be eating my heart out over you, save your pity. Whatever I felt for you, it certainly wasn't love."

He stiffened and felt himself going cold. "That's a lie," he said, his voice quiet and deep.

"Love isn't part of sordid affairs," she said, her voice starting to break. "That's all it was, just a…a cheap little roll in the hay!"

"No," he said softly, his eyes fierce. "Never that."

She turned away, clutching her bag. They were calling the first-class passengers aboard. She was next. She got to her feet. "I have to go."

He caught her arm, but she moved away and wouldn't look at him. "Elissa, damn it…"

"I have to go," she repeated. "So long, cowboy."

"For God's sake, will you listen to me?" he demanded, oblivious to the curious stares they were getting as they faced each other.

"No." She laced the single word with mocking contempt, and her blue eyes dared him to make her change her mind.

He let go of his temper with a word that turned her ears red, and she walked away without looking back. He took off his hat and slammed it to the floor, damned it to hell, damned her with it and stomped back down the concourse. Let her go. What did he care? She didn't love him—she'd said so. It was just a "cheap little roll in the hay." His dark eyes got darker, and his pride felt lacerated at her careless reference to the most beautiful experience of his entire life.

Still cursing, he came home hatless and ran head-on into Margaret, who looked like an entire invading army about to launch an attack. "So you ran her off, did you?" Margaret glared at him. "Congratulations. The first woman who ever cared anything about you and not your money, and you get rid of her. I don't know what's come over you. And here's Bobby's wife, and—"

"Shut up!" King threw at her, his eyes dangerous.

"Jackass!" she tossed off. "You don't cow me! Maybe Bess is scared stiff of you, but I ain't!"

He glared back at her. "What do you mean, scared stiff of me?"

"She took off upstairs the minute she saw you walk in the door. And she never once opened her mouth at the breakfast table when you and Elissa got into it." She harrumphed. "That poor little thing's got no spirit at all. Not like Elissa. You'd have Bess crawling in a month's time, if she didn't cut and run first. Or don't you remember what a hell of a mean temper her father had when he drank? Of course, you can control yours, most of the time, but that child is carrying deep scars. A man like you is the last thing she needs!"

As if he hadn't realized that already, he thought furiously. Elissa was gone, and he felt sick, and here was Margaret, giving him hell. He glared at his housekeeper with black frustration.

"And where's your hat?" she demanded.

"At the airport," he retorted. "Catching mice."

"*Your* hat probably could," she muttered. "It would have to be pretty damned mean to sit on you!"

He sat down with a cup of black coffee, which he wished were whiskey. He felt empty and hollow and cold. Bess was still upstairs, and he thought about what Margaret had said. Perhaps Bess was afraid of his temper, he thought idly. But Elissa wasn't, he recalled with a faint smile. She was more than equal to his angry outbursts, most of the time. She was equal to him in other ways, too. He closed his eyes and saw her, felt her, as she was that night, her body lifting to his, her eyes wild and passionate, moaning as he held her to him, crying out his name in aching fulfillment.

He got up, his body on fire. Bess paused at the doorway, hesitating. He glanced at her. She was blonde and beautiful, but when he looked at her, he saw only Elissa's laughing blue eyes and black hair.

"Well?" he asked curtly.

She hesitated. "Are you angry with me?" she asked.

The harshness left his face. She was a child, after all, in so many ways. He went to her, taking her gently by the shoulders, smiling.

"No, of course I'm not," he said gently. "I couldn't stop Elissa. She thinks I'm out of my mind over you and that you're leaving Bobby to marry me. I couldn't make her listen, and I'm frustrated, that's all."

"It's my fault, isn't it?" she asked, searching his eyes. "I'm sorry. I was so lonely. And you took me places and talked to me and even listened," she added with a wistful smile. "I guess I got drunk on attention. But I'm sorry if I've messed up your life."

"Don't worry. I'll sort it all out somehow," he said.

She stared at his shirtfront. "Elissa loves you, doesn't she?"

"I thought she did," he replied quietly. "Now I'm not sure."

She looked up again, smiling at him. "I liked her. She isn't the least bit afraid of you. She bites back."

He laughed. "Yes. She gives as good as she gets. That's one of the things I like best about her." He searched her face. "Do you really want a divorce?"

She sighed. "No," she said finally. "I love the stupid man to distraction. If only he'd wake up and realize that I never married him for money. I wanted *him*—I still do—and he's too busy making money to notice."

"Then why," he asked slowly, "don't you tell him?"

She blinked. "Tell him…that?"

"Of course."

She shifted restlessly. "Well…"

"Chicken," he taunted, his dark eyes sparkling.

She burst out laughing. "All right. Why not? Things can't get any worse, can they?"

He took her arm. "Where there's life, there's hope," he muttered. He was still wondering how to deal with Elissa's defection. She'd tried to reduce what they did together to something sordid and wrong, and he wished he'd gone about things in a more conventional way. He should have picked her up and carried her off to a minister. Now she was determined not to care about him anymore, was determined to put him out of her life. Did she still think he wanted Bess? How could she be so crazy?

He followed Bess out the door, frowning fiercely. He'd have to give her some time to cool off, to figure out that they couldn't live without each other, that they needed each other. And knowing Elissa, she'd have to come to those conclusions her own way in her own sweet time.

CHAPTER ELEVEN

ELISSA DIDN'T GO home to her parents. She wasn't quite ready to face them just yet. Instead, she boarded the next flight to Jamaica. Since King was going to be busy with Bess now, it looked like the best time to tie up a few loose ends.

She went to his villa first and got Warchief, then left without a backward glance. She wasn't ever going to see the villa again. She'd made plans.

Warchief made eyes at her and flapped his wings while she packed. She couldn't accomplish everything in one day, so she took her time. There were forms to fill out to allow her to take Warchief back to the States, and there was the real-estate agent to see. She was going to put the cottage up for sale. After what had happened, she never wanted to come to Jamaica again.

It was like leaving home, because she'd grown to love it, but she'd have to find someplace else for a second home. Especially since pregnancy was a real possibility. She still hadn't decided what to tell her parents. She just couldn't bear telling them the truth.

She stayed in Jamaica for three days. Then, with the necessary forms filled out, she took Warchief to the airport in a sturdy pet carrier and left the island behind. Warchief was the one reminder of the past that she couldn't bear to give up.

Hours later, she pulled up in front of her parents' home.

Her father was busy in his study, working on his sermon, which he always started on Fridays. Her mother was in the kitchen, and her head jerked up when she saw what Elissa was carrying.

"Oh, no!" Tina wailed. "It's the green mosquito!"

"Now, now," Elissa said gently. "He grows on you."

"That's what I'm afraid of," Tina muttered, nibbling her lip and frowning.

Elissa set his carrier on a chair. Warchief took one look at Tina and began to whoop and blaze his eyes and make cute little parrot noises.

"I love you!" he cried. "Cute, you're cute!" He gave a wolf whistle, and Tina, who'd never seen a parrot except in exotic pet shops, was charmed.

She dropped to her knees and peeked into the carrier. Warchief wolf-whistled again and blazed his eyes, and Tina laughed.

"You gorgeous bird," she enthused. "I'd love to hug you."

"I wouldn't," Elissa murmured drily. "He gets excited when he's close to people. You could lose an ear, a nose—"

"I get the idea." Tina chuckled and rose. "What about his cage?"

"It's outside, in the car."

Tina looked out the window. "How did you squeeze it into that subcompact rental?" she asked.

"With great difficulty," came the reply. "But I did."

Tina cocked her head and stared at Elissa. "Wait a minute. He was in Jamaica, wasn't he?" she asked, nodding toward the parrot. "So how is it that he's with you, when you were in Oklahoma? And where's Kingston?"

"This is going to be an interesting story," Elissa said. "So do you mind if I get the things out of the car and change clothes? You can make coffee, and then we'll talk."

Tina sighed. "Uh-oh."

Elissa nodded. "That's one way of putting it."

"I'm sorry, darling."

"It's just as well I found out now," Elissa replied, looking and sounding worlds more mature than she had when she'd left. "I might have married him and ended up ruining his life."

"He asked you to marry him?" Tina asked.

Elissa nodded. "He gave me a ring," she said, smiling at the memory of the fragile thing. Then she burst into tears. "Oh, Mama, I had to give it back," she wailed, going into the taller woman's outstretched arms. "He's in love with his sister-in-law, and she's getting a divorce, and he only found out after he'd given me the ring. I had to let him go—don't you see? He'd have hated me for tying him down!"

Through all that muddled speech one thing was clear: that Elissa loved her man desperately and had given him up for love of him. Mrs. Dean smiled. "There, there, darling," she cooed, "you did the right thing. Loving isn't loving unless you have the strength to let go when you have to."

"I'm so miserable," she said brokenly. "I went to Jamaica and arranged to sell the cottage and got Warchief. Is it all right if I stay here for a while?"

"Honey, of course," Tina said, shocked. "Why wouldn't it be? This is your home."

Elissa lifted her tear-stained face to her mother's. She wanted to tell all, but she didn't know if she could bear to. Her eyes filled with new tears.

Tina Dean brushed the damp hair from her daughter's eyes. "I think this would be a very good time for you to have a talk with your father," she said with a smile. "Do you know the old saying that you never really know people until you're in trouble? Well, you're about to get an education in human frailty. Come on."

Elissa puzzled over that on the way to the study, where her father was sitting behind a desk, glaring at a legal pad and frowning.

"Look who's home," Tina said brightly, exchanging a pointed look with her husband.

"Hello, my darling." Her father beamed. "Home for a visit?"

"Maybe to stay awhile," she said. And then she burst into tears again.

"Uh-oh." Mr. Dean sighed and glanced at his wife. "Trouble in paradise, I guess?"

Tina nodded. "I thought it might help if you told her about that young minister and the unmarried couple. You know the one?"

He smiled, reminiscing. "Oh, I do indeed. Make some coffee, will you, dear?"

"I'll do that little thing." She went out and closed the door.

Mr. Dean came around the desk to hug his daughter and deposit her in an easy chair. He perched himself on the edge of his desk and studied her wan, tear-stained face. And then he smiled warmly.

"Elissa, I want to tell you about a young man I knew, oh, about twenty-five years ago," he began. "He was a cocky young brute, just twenty-three at the time. He was good with his fists and not very concerned with the world or even his own future. He came back from Vietnam half out of his mind on alcohol, and he robbed a grocery store and had the bad fortune to get caught."

He studied his neatly shined black shoes. "Well, to make a long story short, he went to jail. And while he was there,

sure that God and mankind had given up on him, a young
visiting minister took an interest in him. Now this young
hoodlum," he added brightly, "had an eye for beauty, and
he liked the ladies. And there was a lovely young girl with
whom he was deeply in love. They'd gone, as the saying
goes, a bit too far of an evening, and she'd gotten into a
family way. So there she was, all alone, her lover in jail
and a baby on the way."

He sighed. "The young minister found a capable law-
yer to defend the young man. He got him off, since it was
a first offense, then proceeded, in turn, to find the young
man a job, get him married as quickly as was feasible to
the young lady and move them into a small apartment."

Elissa smiled, her tears drying, sure that the young minister had been her father. "What a nice fellow," she murmured.

"Yes, I thought so, too." He sighed, returning the smile.
"To finish, the young man was so grateful for what the minister had done that he entered a seminary and undertook to
repay the man by carrying on his good work."

"And the minister, I daresay, was delighted with his
handiwork."

Her father had a sad, faraway look in his eyes. "Well,
not exactly. You see, the minister was in a reserve unit, and
it was called up for duty in Vietnam. The young hoodlum
I mentioned came out of combat without a scratch, but the
minister stepped on a land mine the very first day he was
in Da Nang." He sighed, a sound resonant with regret. "He
was killed before that young man he'd rescued could get
in touch and tell him that he'd decided to take the cloth."

Elissa felt a chill down her spine. "It was you," she whispered.

He nodded. "Me and your mother. I was twenty-three,

she was twenty." He leaned over and took her hand, holding it tightly. "And now you know why we've sheltered you, don't you, my girl? How well we understand the passions of youth. All too well, I'm afraid." He smiled at her gently. "Now tell me all about it, and maybe I can help."

She burst into tears. In all her life, she'd never been so proud to be his daughter. "I didn't know," she whispered.

"Sometimes," he replied, "we have to fall into a hole to touch the sky. The important thing is to realize that we're never out of God's heart, no matter what we do. And very often it isn't until we hit bottom that we reach out for a helping hand."

She hugged him warmly and sighed, feeling at peace for the first time in days. "I could use a helping hand."

"Here's mine. Lean all you like."

After she told him what had happened, he took her into the kitchen, where they joined her mother for a cozy supper of cold cuts and iced tea. Not one word of censure was spoken.

Her mother seemed to know it all without a word from her husband. She smiled at Elissa with loving warmth. "Don't worry," she said gently. "There's nothing to be afraid of."

Elissa cupped her hands around her glass. "I could be pregnant," she said, putting her most delicate fear into words.

"Does he know?" Tina asked.

"Oh, yes," she said, looking up. "He made me promise to get in touch with him if that happened. But I can't see that it would help, to back him into a corner. He loves Bess. I can't tie him to me for all the wrong reasons."

"A wise decision," her father remarked. "But I think you underestimate the gentleman's feelings. Infatuation dies a natural death without anything to feed it. He'll get over Bess soon enough—if he's even still interested in her, that is."

"But he's got her now. She's going to divorce her husband," Elissa protested.

"Is she?" Mr. Dean looked at her over his glasses and grinned. "Well, we'll see, won't we? Eat your ham, darling."

She glanced from one to the other. "Aren't you upset?" she began hesitantly.

Tina lifted her thin eyebrows. "About what, dear?"

"The baby, if there is one!"

"I like babies," Tina said.

"So do I," her father seconded.

"But it will be..." Elissa hesitated.

"A baby," Tina finished for her. "Darling, in case it's escaped your notice, I've brought quite a number of unwed mothers into the congregation in years past, and the children have been raised in the church. Little babies aren't responsible for the circumstances of their birth. They're just babies, and we love them. Now do eat your ham, Elissa. For all we know you may already be eating for two."

Elissa sighed. She'd never understand them, but she certainly did love them. "What's your sermon going to be on?" she asked her father.

He looked at her gently. "On learning to forgive ourselves, after God has. Sometimes he punishes us much less than we punish ourselves, you know."

She flushed, wondering how he'd learned to read her mind so accurately. "I imagine we'll all learn from it, then," she murmured.

He winked at his wife. "Yes, I hope we will," he replied, and then he concentrated on his meal.

Warchief was back in his cage soon afterward, making

enough noise to wake the dead. Elissa carried him into her room, saying a quick good-night before she closed the door.

"Be quiet, or you'll get us thrown out!" she raged at him.

"Hellllp!" he screamed. "Let me out!"

"Go to sleep," she muttered, pulling his beak toward her to kiss his green head. He made a parroty sound and wolf-whistled softly. She kissed him again, putting the cover over his cage.

As she slid into bed, minutes later, she wondered how King was and if he was happy now. She hoped he was. She hoped, too, that she wouldn't be pregnant. Despite the fact that she wanted his child very much, it wouldn't be fair to tear him between Bess and her own baby. For his own happiness, she had to let him go. She turned her face into the pillow, thanking God for loving parents and the hope of a new beginning.

But hope wasn't a good enough precaution. Six weeks later, after horrible bouts of morning sickness and fatigue, she went to her family doctor to have the necessary tests. And he confirmed her pregnancy.

She didn't tell her parents. Despite their support, which she knew she could count on, she had to come to grips with her situation alone. She went downtown to a quiet restaurant and drank coffee for two hours, until she remembered that coffee wasn't good for pregnant women. She switched to diet drinks and then worried about the additives in them. Tea and coffee and most carbonated drinks had caffeine, herbal tea nauseated her and she hated plain water. Finally she decided that her choices had to be decaffeinated coffee, milk and Perrier. Those should carry her through the next several months.

The thought of the baby was new and delicate, and she sat pondering it through a fog of confusion. Would it be a boy or a girl? Would it have her coloring or King's? She smiled, thinking about dark eyes in a dark complexion and holding the tiny life in her arms and rocking it on soft summer nights.

The more she considered the future, the more appealing it became. She wouldn't have King, but she'd have a tiny part of him. Someone to hold and love and be loved by. Maybe that was her compensation for a broken heart. She smiled, overwhelmed by tenderness. She could still work; pregnancy wouldn't hamper designing clothes. And her parents weren't going to throw her out in the street, although she worried about the impact her unwed-mother status was going to have on her father's congregation. She might get a cottage farther up or down the coast to prevent any gossip from harming his career. He'd find it hard to get another job at his age, despite his protests. He loved her, but she loved him, too, and she wasn't going to be the cause of any grief to her parents. Well, she'd think about that later.

Right now, the thing was to get back on her feet. She'd grieved so for King that she could hardly function. She had to learn to live with the fact that he wasn't coming after her. She'd spent the past few weeks gazing hopefully at the telephone and jumping every time it rang. Cars slowing down near the house threw her into a tizzy. She checked the mailbox every day with wide, hopeful eyes.

But there were no phone calls from Oklahoma. No visitors. And no letters. Eventually even her stubborn pride gave up. King finally had Bess, and Elissa was well and truly out of his life. So she began to make plans of her own. She was going to move someplace far away, and she wasn't going to tell anyone where she was going, not even her parents. She'd write to them, but she'd find one of those forwarding-address places that would confuse the postmarks. Yes, she had to do this on her own. She and the child would grow close over the years, and someday she'd tell him about his father.

That was when she remembered that King didn't know where his own father was and had always blamed the man for running out on him. She'd decided when Margaret told her about it that one day she'd tell King where his father was and make sure that he got to sit down and talk with him, to hear his side of it. But for now, she didn't have the right to deny King at least the knowledge of this child. She'd promised.

She went home, resigned to do the right thing, no matter how much it hurt. Bess would be there, surely, whether or not the divorce was final. Maybe they were preparing for the wedding already. She hesitated, but in the end she reached for the phone and called the number King had once given her in case she needed to reach him at the ranch.

Her parents were visiting a sick member of the congregation, so it was a good time to make the call. She didn't want them to see her go to pieces when she tried to tell King what had happened.

It rang once, twice, three times, four. She was about to hang up when a breathless, familiar voice came over the line.

"Hello?"

"Bess?" Elissa faltered.

"Oh, it's Elissa, isn't it?" came the enthusiastic reply. "Kingston isn't here right now, I'm afraid, but…"

Elissa paused. "Do you know where he is?"

"Not offhand, but I can take a message."

"No. Thank you." She hesitated, desperate to ask if the divorce had gone through. She settled for, "Is Bobby doing all right?"

"He's already back at work," Bess said, her voice oddly soft, "cast, crutches and all. I... Are you sure I can't take a message for Kingston? I'm not sure he'll be home tonight, but I could—"

"No. I'm glad your... I'm glad Bobby is doing well. Goodbye."

"Wait!"

But she hung up, trembling all over. So now she knew. Bess was living with King.

She almost let it go at that and made her plans without trying again. But that was the coward's way out. She phoned his office, only to be told that he wasn't in and they didn't know when to expect him. She left word, but the secretary didn't sound reliable. As soon as she hung up, she wrote a terse note and dropped it in the mail, addressed to his Oklahoma City office. Perhaps he could find time to read it, she thought unreasonably, and went back to her designs.

She'd finished her collection, mailed the completed designs to Angel Mahoney and picked out a nice town near Saint Augustine to move to. She packed her things, careful not to let her parents see the baggage. She'd leave in the morning. It had been over a week since she'd mailed that note to King, and she was sure he'd seen it by now. Perhaps he didn't want any complications and was going to ignore it. That wasn't like him, but men in love weren't always rational, she guessed. He'd wanted Bess for a long time, and now he had her. It wasn't his fault that he wanted to look ahead and not behind him.

Warchief was quiet these days, almost as if he knew he'd lose his home if he kept being noisy. He purred at Elissa and talked to her, but he'd stopped making such wild noises at dawn and dusk. She wondered if he was sick.

Heaven knew, she was. The morning sickness hadn't let

up, and she was beginning to feel pregnant. Her slacks were tight, and her breasts were sensitive. She grinned at all the little disadvantages. None of them mattered, because she was going to have a baby and love it so much that it would feel as wanted as she always had.

She settled down to bed that night, leaving her parents sitting up to talk. There was a full moon and a scattering of stars, and she closed her eyes with a sigh. King would be seeing that moon out his window in Oklahoma, probably with Bess lying beside him. She hoped Bess would be kind to him. Tears stung her eyes. Instead of getting easier, bearing the knowledge that she'd never see King again was getting harder every day. But she'd better get used to it, she chided herself. Forever was a long time.

About two o'clock in the morning, she and Warchief were awakened by a thunderous knocking on the front door. With a white chenille bathrobe thrown hastily over her nightgown, she rubbed her sleepy eyes and stumbled to the door, calling, "Who's there?"

"Kingston Roper," came the gruff reply.

She fumbled the door open. With his jacket slung carelessly over his arm, his tie hanging haphazardly around his neck, and his face hard and drawn and in need of a shave, he looked haggard and weary but devastatingly handsome. And Elissa wouldn't have cared if he'd been covered in mud.

"Come in," she said, fighting down the impulse to throw herself at him, trying to appear calm when her heart was beating her to death and her breath was stuck somewhere below her collarbone.

He stood looking at her as she shut the door again, his eyes dark and troubled and oddly hungry. He didn't move, as if riveted to the spot, staring.

"What was that noise? Oh, hello, Mr. Roper," Tina said, smiling at him from the door of their room off the living room. "You look exhausted. Elissa, there's some decaffeinated coffee you can reheat, and some of that cake I made. You can put Mr. Roper in the spare room if he's staying. Good night, dear."

She closed the door again, and King turned back to Elissa.

"I'll heat the coffee if you'd like a cup," she said quietly.

He searched her face, looking for any sign of welcome, but there was none. His eyes dulled. He'd hoped so desperately that she might have missed him even a fraction as much as he'd missed her. He'd stayed away deliberately, denying himself the sight and sound and feel of her all this time to try to make her miss him, to make her see the light. And he knew that it hadn't worked. He looked at her and thought he'd die of emptiness if she sent him away. He followed her into the kitchen without another word, as cold inside as an empty tomb.

CHAPTER TWELVE

KING SAT DOWN in the chair Elissa indicated and watched her move around the kitchen, slicing cake and heating cups of coffee in the small microwave oven. She looked delicious. Glowing. Wait a minute—didn't they say that pregnant women glowed? He took a slow breath, feeling warm all over with the possibility of it, with possession in his eyes as they followed her. He'd win her back somehow. He had to.

"I didn't expect you," she said.

"I went back to the office tonight to check some figures," he said as she placed mugs of steaming coffee on the table, along with saucers and forks and slices of cake. "I've been in Jamaica," he added, glancing up.

"Have you?" She nibbled at her cake.

"Your cottage had a young redhead in it," he remarked. "She said her parents had bought the cottage from you. Warchief was gone, too."

"I have him here," she said. She took another bite of the cake, still without looking at him. "You found my letter tonight, I guess?"

"Buried in a stack of bids," he confirmed. He left half his cake uneaten and leaned back in the chair with his coffee cup in his hand, studying her. "Was that note the best you could do?" he added. "A terse 'Need to talk to you when you have time. Best wishes, Elissa'?"

She flushed. "I'd already tried your ranch and your office. Nobody seemed to know where you were."

"Nobody did, for a while," he said. He didn't mention that the past few weeks had been pure hell. His temper had become so vile that it had already cost him two of his best junior executives. So much for testing that absence-makes-the-heart-grow-fonder business, he thought angrily. She didn't look any the worse for wear, but he sure as hell did. He stared at her coolly. "Are you having any morning sickness?"

She almost dropped the coffee cup.

"Well, why else would you bother to contact me?" he chanced. "It wasn't out of love. You told me how you felt when you left," he said curtly, his dark eyes glittering at her across the table. "The only possible reason was that I'd made you pregnant. So here I am." He didn't mention that he'd practically bought an airline to get here that fast.

"There was no rush," she said. "I've got everything worked out. My parents know," she added softly. "They didn't make accusations or rage at me or even try to shame me. They said..." She bit back tears. "They said people are human."

"Oh, God," he whispered roughly. Though he himself was delighted—surely she'd reconsider and marry him now—he hadn't thought about how her parents would take the news. He wasn't surprised that they'd stand by her, though. They were good people, and they loved her.

"It's all right. I make more than enough money to take care of myself and the baby. And you can visit if you like," she told him. "But I'd rather you waited a while," she said, lifting tired eyes to his. "I don't want people gossiping, and it's the last kind of complication you need right now."

He stared at her blankly. Bess said Elissa had called, so

didn't she know that Bobby and Bess were back together? "It's my baby," he said simply. "I want to take care of you both."

"I don't need taking care of, thank you," she said with forced calm, remembering that he hadn't bothered to make a move toward her in seven weeks and that Bess was now living with him.

He exhaled angrily, leaning forward to pin her with his dark, quiet eyes. "I'm responsible for you," he said. "This is all my fault."

"I'm not blaming you," she replied. "That isn't why I contacted you. I gave my word that I would, if it happened."

He stopped breathing for an instant. "That's the only reason you got in touch with me?"

Her eyebrows arched with practiced carelessness. "What other reason would I have had?"

He wanted to throw something. "You loved me once," he growled.

"Oh, I've gotten over that," she assured him, rising to put the empty cups into the sink and praying that he wouldn't see through the fiction of what she was saying to the agony underneath. She swallowed down tears. "It was just infatuation. I was pretty naive, you know, and you were very experienced. Any girl can lose her head with a sexy man. I just happened to be a little too naive. You see—" She turned to tell him a few more choice lies, but he wasn't there. Seconds later, she heard the front door open softly and close. Then a car engine roared once, and she heard the vehicle drive away.

It had no sooner pulled away than the phone rang. What a night, she thought miserably. At least, thank God, she'd kept her composure. King hadn't guessed how she'd grieved for him, and that was something. He'd leave her alone now, and she and the baby would be each other's world. King wouldn't have to sacrifice his happiness with Bess on Elissa's account.

She lifted the receiver on the second ring, hoping her parents hadn't been disturbed again. "Hello?" she said, wiping away a tear.

"Elissa?"

It was Bess. Elissa glared at the telephone. "If you're looking for King, you're too late. He's on his way back to you—I made sure of that—and you don't have to worry. I won't bother him again. The baby and I will manage just fine."

"Baby?" Bess sounded shocked.

"King will tell you all about it, I'm sure. It's no concern of his anymore."

"Please don't hang up," Bess said suddenly.

"I can imagine what you have to say to me, but—" Elissa began quietly.

"No, you can't," Bess interrupted softly. "I'm sorry. I'm so sorry. I've loused things up for you and Kingston, and I almost destroyed my own marriage, all because I couldn't tell Bobby the truth, couldn't tell him what I really wanted. Elissa, Bobby and I aren't getting a divorce. I finally got up enough nerve to swallow my pride and say what I felt, and now we're staying together. I was sure Kingston would have told you by now. He was the one who convinced me to talk to Bobby," she added, stunning Elissa into silence. "I tried to tell you when you phoned that time, but you hung up. Bobby and I were visiting him."

Elissa could hardly breathe. "Visiting?" she echoed hoarsely.

"I guess you had a pretty good idea what was going on all along, but most of it was just in my mind. Poor Kingston was truly caught in the middle, all because he felt sorry for me. Well, he's big brother again, and I do adore him. But if you'd seen him these past weeks, you'd know that he didn't give a hang about me—not the way you thought. He's nearly worked himself to death, taken crazy chances with the live-stock and that new sports car of his—he's gone hog wild, Margaret says. Margaret tried to get him to go see you, but he wouldn't. He said he couldn't go until you asked him to, because that would mean you still loved him. Margaret says he loved you all along, only he didn't know it. I think he knows it now. I just hope I haven't done anything to take his last chance away from him. I think he'll go crazy with-out you, and that's the truth."

Elissa was still trying to find her voice. "I sent him away," she whispered tearfully. "I thought you and he were getting married. I couldn't let him sacrifice his own happiness…just because I was pregnant."

"Oh, Lord, I hate myself!" Bess groaned. "Listen, can't you go after him?"

"I don't know where he's gone," Elissa wept.

"Well, if he comes here, I'll send him back," Bess prom-ised. "Now you go get some sleep. Don't worry too much, it isn't healthy for the baby. My gosh, Bobby and I will be uncle and aunt. That sounds so nice. Get some sleep, honey. Everything will be okay—I promise."

Elissa's heart warmed at the compassion in that soft voice. "I'll be all right," she said. "You'll let me know if he shows up there?"

"Of course I will. And good luck."

"Thanks." Elissa hung up with a sigh. Lately, all her luck seemed to be bad. She went to the sink and bathed her flushed face. It didn't help a whole lot, so she went out the back door and onto the quiet beach. Maybe a walk would help clear her mind.

She wandered along in her robe, hardly seeing where she was going for the pain. What irony, she thought miserably. She'd sent him away, and for what?

She didn't notice the silent figure near the dune until he spoke. "You'll catch cold," he said, his voice deep and lazy.

Elissa whirled, catching her breath, to find King sitting there, smoking a cigarette. He was in his shirtsleeves, his chest bare where the white shirt was unbuttoned, his dark hair untidy.

"What are you sitting there for?" she asked shakily. "I thought you'd gone."

"Oh, I started to," he agreed pleasantly. "And then I realized I had no place to go."

"There are hotels in Miami," she faltered, wrapping her arms around herself as she drank in the sight of him, her eyes adoring every hard, powerful line of his body in the darkness.

"You don't understand." He put out the cigarette. "You're the only home I have, Elissa," he said quietly. "I don't have any other place to go."

Tears stung her eyes. She'd never dreamed, even when Bess was telling her those things, that he cared that much. Trembling a little with mingled excitement and fear, she went to him and dropped to her knees in front of him.

"I thought it was Bess," she said simply.

He looked up at her, his eyes dark with possession. "So did I, at first," he returned. "Until you started taking me over, that is. First my body, then my heart. In the end, all I felt for Bess was compassion and responsibility. I could have told you that when you left, but you wouldn't listen," he said gruffly. "Seven weeks I've stayed away, hoping against hope that you'd miss me. I broke speed records

getting here tonight, and for what? To be told you didn't
give a damn!"

She stopped the tirade with her mouth. Poor wounded
man, she thought. She slid her arms around his neck and
felt him tremble as she pushed, gently unbalancing him.
He fell against the dune, and she fell with him, her softness melting over him, her eyes red from crying, her mouth
tasting of salty tears.

"Will you listen?" he ground out against her lips. Then
he groaned and captured her, enfolding her against the
warm strength of his body. His mouth opened under hers.
She felt the deep penetration of his tongue, the throb of his
heart. He was hers.

She nibbled his lower lip, lifting her head to stare down
at him, her eyes adoring, sure of him. Her hands smoothed
back his hair, and she smiled as she touched him with confident possession.

"Are you, by any chance, trying to seduce me?" he whispered. His heart was pounding, and his body was making
insistent statements about what it wanted. He tried to shift
her so that she wouldn't feel how vulnerable he was, but
he couldn't budge her.

"Just lie still," she chided. "I know you want me, so
there's no use trying to hide it."

He glared up at her. "Rub it in," he muttered.

She bent and kissed his eyelids with aching tenderness.
"Were you going to sleep on the beach?" she whispered.

"If that was as close to you as I could get, yes," he said
angrily.

He was a hard man, she thought lovingly, lifting her head
to look at him. A real handful. But she could manage him.
They'd been friends a lot longer than they'd been lovers,
and now she knew how to throw him off balance, as well.

She sat up, opening her robe. "I want to show you something," she said without the least bit of self-consciousness, although she peeked down the beach, knowing her parents were eventually going to come looking for her. Under the robe, she was as she slept, bare except for a tiny pair of blue briefs.

He stared at her, stunned, as if he couldn't believe what he was seeing.

"This is what you did to me," she whispered tenderly. She took his hands and held them to her minutely swollen waistline, watching the incredible expression that tautened his face as he touched her.

"My child..." His voice was soft, deep, reverent.

She gathered his head against her sensitive breasts, tears stinging her eyes as she rocked him, cradled him, feeling his lips touch her, though not in a sexual way. His hands smoothed over her under the robe as he brought her against his body, holding her so close that she could barely breathe. And she cried, because he cared and because she loved him.

"You little imp," he whispered, nuzzling her warm throat. "I'm so crazy about you. I would have carried you home to Oklahoma in my arms, walking."

Her lips touched his face, her breath catching as he turned and put his mouth with aching tenderness to her breasts.

His hands came up to touch them, to cup them. He moved, laying her down gently on the robe so that he could look, could explore the new contours of her body with his child tucked under her heart.

"Our baby," he whispered, his fingers trembling as he lay beside her in the darkness with the surf crashing behind them.

She trembled with the profundity of the moment. "I know exactly when we made him," she whispered.

He met her eyes. "So do I, to the very second. I meant to, even though I was temporarily confused about Bess. Do you know that the minute I got home from putting you on that plane, I patched up her marriage? She admitted that she loved Bobby, that she was just lonely. She'd never stopped loving him, but she was afraid to tell him how she really felt. She did, though, and now they're closer than ever. They're even talking about having babies."

She laughed. "She called me a few minutes ago. She wanted to clear the air."

"Nice woman. I'm glad she and Bobby have finally gotten their act together." He looked down into her eyes, searching. "Do you know how I feel, or do you want the words?" he asked gently.

"Have you ever said them before?" she countered.

He smiled ruefully. "No. But I never wanted to before, either."

"When did you know?" she asked.

"I knew how *you* felt when you were willing to give yourself to me in Jamaica." He laughed at her startled expression. "That's right, tidbit, I knew before you did. But there was Bess, and I didn't think I wanted that kind of involvement. But when I saw you lying in bed in that sexy nightgown, and I got hot and bothered like I never had before..." He bent and brushed his mouth over hers, reveling in its soft, trembling response. "After that, bad went to worse. I didn't really want to seduce you at the ranch, but my body got the best of me."

"Yes, so did mine." She sighed, nuzzling his cheek. She closed her eyes. "It's been hard living with it, King," she whispered.

"How do you feel about starting over again?" He touched her abdomen. "And decide quick, would you? I think he's already growing."

She grinned at him, drunk with happiness. "As if I could have stopped loving you." She laughed. "Seven weeks, damn you!" She hit him.

He crushed his mouth down on hers, suddenly all man, all domination, burning her with his ardor. "Damn you, too," he growled, his lips hard against her mouth. "Calling it a 'cheap little roll in the hay,' when I'd never loved a woman that way in my life. Sticking a knife in my pride, my heart. I went off like a wounded animal to lick my wounds, then went to Jamaica with my heart in my hands to offer to you…and you'd gone. You'd sold the cottage and taken Warchief, and the real-estate agent said you hated the cottage and everything connected with it." His eyes narrowed. "I guessed that meant me, too. So I went back to Oklahoma and drank myself into a stupor, then set about working myself to death."

"While I was sure you were going to marry Bess," she murmured. "I knew how you felt…"

"How you thought I felt," he corrected. He kissed her softly. "I slept with you for one night, and it ruined me for any other woman. You've haunted my dreams ever since. An innocent, and you gave me the first total fulfillment I've ever had."

She smiled against his mouth, bristling with pride. "Sitting up, too," she murmured, and she blushed wildly.

"Don't smile about it, you brazen hussy," he taunted. "I needed my head examined. I prayed every night that you'd end up pregnant," he confessed, "because I knew you'd send for me. Your sense of honor would force you to. And then I'd come to you and take care of you and find some way to make you love me again." He traced her breasts, watching them tauten in the moonlight.

"Don't forget," she whispered, loving the sensation, "that my parents are just down the beach."

He kissed her softly. "I hadn't forgotten," he said with a rueful smile. "I'm not about to give them any more cause to resent me."

He helped her back into her robe and pulled her onto his knees, cradling her.

"How could they resent the father of their very own grandchild?" she whispered, her mouth brushing warmly over his. "He's going to be just like his daddy." She smiled. "Tall and dark and handsome and gentle."

"Blue-eyed," he whispered, tilting her warm mouth up to his.

"Brown-eyed," she whispered back, and drew his lips over hers.

A long time later, he lifted his head. "Elissa?"

"What?" she murmured dreamily.

"I think we have company."

She looked up. Her father was sitting on one side of them, his knees drawn up under his bathrobe, watching the surf. Her mother was on the other side, similarly clad, humming.

"Lovely night," Mr. Dean remarked.

"Lovely," his wife agreed.

King and Elissa burst out laughing. "The marriage license and the rings are in my jacket pocket," King told them. "All we need is a quick blood test and a quiet little ceremony, which we hope you'll perform. You, uh, might have noticed that we've rather jumped the gun," he added with a sheepish smile.

"She likes kosher pickles in her corn flakes, and he wonders if we've noticed that they've rather jumped the gun," Mr. Dean addressed his wife.

"Yes, dear, I heard." Mrs. Dean grinned.

"And in case it crossed your mind," King murmured, glancing wickedly down at Elissa, "we've been controlling those interesting impulses that led us to this delicious complication. We've just been trying to decide what color his eyes will be."

"I like girls," Mr. Dean suggested.

"What's wrong with a boy?" Tina asked innocently.

"Maybe it will be both," Mr. Dean remarked. "Her appetite has been extraordinary."

"I'd like twins," King murmured, his eyes shining with everything he felt as he looked at the slender, beautiful woman in his arms. He glanced up at her parents, who were on their feet now. "I'm sure you'd rather things had worked out a little more conventionally, but I guess I had to learn how to love."

"You seem to have the hang of it now, son," Mr. Dean said drily.

"It's not all his fault," Elissa muttered. "I sort of forced him into it."

"You did not," King flashed.

"I thought you told her the facts of life," Mr. Dean murmured to his wife.

"I thought you did," came the dry reply.

"Well, we might try again. Come on, children, we'll have coffee and discuss some details," Mr. Dean said, sliding an arm around his wife's waist. "Nice boy."

"I think so, too." Mrs. Dean stopped, glancing behind as King gently helped Elissa to her feet. "There's just one thing, Kingston," she murmured, frowning. "I shouldn't really ask, but can you support her, working in a garage? If you need any help, we'll do what we can."

King burst out laughing. He drew Elissa close to his side and fell into step beside her parents. "While we have that coffee," he told them drily, "we'll have a little talk about the oil business."

TWO WEEKS LATER, King and Elissa were back in Jamaica at his villa, Warchief happily installed in his cage while his owners set out for a new and delicious experience on the beach. It had been a learning period for them both, getting to know each other without the barriers of uncertainty and mistrust.

Just before they'd left for Jamaica again, Elissa had even found a way to tell King about his father, still alive and in a nursing home. King had listened to her, then sat staring into space for a long time. Minutes later, he'd gone off to use the phone. When he came back, he'd looked thoughtful and pleased. She'd later learned that he'd spoken to the old man and had promised to go and have a long visit with him after the honeymoon. It was a milestone, Elissa had thought.

And speaking of milestones... She hesitated as they walked out onto the damp sand.

"Someone will see us," she squealed as King stripped her out of her robe and nightgown, leaving her bare and beautiful on the white beach.

"The only person who might lives in the cottage, and she's away for a week. I checked," he said, chuckling and pausing to strip out of his own robe. "Come on. You'll love this."

He led her into the warm, rippling water, and she felt it swallow her up like a satin embrace. She gasped at the exquisite freedom of it while she swam and floated and finally wound up close against a smiling King.

"Now I see why you like it," she whispered. "It's… incredible."

"Yes, isn't it?" But he wasn't looking at the water. His hands were busy under its surface, doing things to her body that made her gasp and cling to him and cry out.

He took her cry into his mouth, taking full advantage of its position to explore it in a silence that quickly grew hot and hungry. He lifted her into his arms and carried her out onto the beach, putting her down gently in the center of a huge beach towel. He stood over her, his body fully aroused, his eyes, dark and wild, devouring her as she lay there. "I want you," he whispered hoarsely.

"Then why don't you come down here and do something about it?" she whispered huskily, stretching in a way that made her tremble.

He eased down completely over her, his hands gently tangling with hers, letting her have most of his weight, feeling the bare saltiness of his skin over every inch of hers.

"You look like you did the first time," she said softly.

"I was hungry then, too," he murmured, finding her mouth. "Starving for you, by then. I still am. But it's…hard to describe." He lifted his head, shifting his hips to make her gasp. "Patience," he teased softly. "I want to talk first."

"Talk fast," she pleaded.

He nipped her lower lip and teased it with his tongue. His hands were on her waist now, her hips, moving her body against the hair-roughened contours of his in a kind of love play he'd never used with her before. She caught her breath, clutching at the broad shoulders above her, the fires kindling deep in her body.

He looked down the length of them, smiling at the tremors claiming her long, slender legs, shudders that he could feel along with her changed breathing. "There are hundreds of paths to fulfillment," he whispered, moving his eyes slowly back up to catch hers. "This is a new one." He bent, putting his mouth to her breasts.

"I thought...you wanted...to talk," she gasped when he took a hard nipple into his mouth.

He laughed huskily. "I'm not sure I can just now. Oh, baby," he breathed, positioning her, hungrily assaulting her mouth, dragging his body against her until she was on the verge of tears with the sensations he was arousing.

Her nails scored him, and she moaned. "I'm sorry," she whispered shakily. "I didn't mean to..."

"Bite, claw, scream," he ground out against her mouth. "Whatever you need, whatever you want, I'll give you. Tell me."

She did, astonishing herself with her own shameless whispers. She looked up at him then, seeing his eyes blazing with love, his face taut with passion but tenderness, as well. She threw back her head and nearly wailed as the first wave hit her and she went into spasms of hot, almost unbearable pleasure.

Somewhere in its midst, she felt him move, felt him still, heard him cry out above her and then shared the delicious echo of her own shudders.

It was a long time before she could breathe again. The stars came back into focus over his shoulder, and she felt the warm wind off the ocean on her damp, bare skin.

"The first man and woman—it must have been like this for them," she whispered in his ear. "Alone in the world, under the sky, joining."

"Joining," he whispered. "Cherishing. Becoming one." He lifted his damp head and searched her rapt eyes. He kissed her softly, touching her belly. "Is he all right?" he whispered. "I didn't mean to get so rough."

"He's fine," she whispered back, smiling.

"It excites me," he said quietly, "having my child inside you, knowing I helped create him." He breathed deeply. "What I wanted to say to you," he murmured, resting half his weight on his forearms without moving away from her, "is that when we make love, it isn't just sex."

She smiled. "Yes, I know." She adored him with her eyes, the excitement growing again. "It's an expression of love, isn't it, King? It always was, even the first time."

"Reading my mind again," he murmured contentedly. "I've noticed that even your parents seem to do that."

"I think they're pretty super," she said.

"So do I. That being the case, it might not be a bad idea if we adopted them." He toyed with her lower lip. "What with his lizards and her crime busting, they need looking after."

"Mother almost wept with relief when she found out we were bringing Warchief back with us, did you notice?" She grinned. "She thinks he's a giant green mosquito."

He grinned, too. "He bites, all right. But he's learning to sing lullabies—have you noticed?" he added on a frown.

"I'm teaching him," she confessed. "I expect to have more than one child, you know. He can sing babies to sleep while I rock them."

His powerful frame trembled a little. "I like babies."

She shifted her hips very slowly, her lips parting, her eyes come-hitherish, feeling him begin to tauten. "So do I," she whispered. "And this time," she added, pushing at his shoulders until she got him onto his back and moved over him, "I'm going to show *you* something new."

"Elissa…" He held her hips, hesitating.

"Just relax," she whispered, looking like an imp, her eyes sparkling. "I won't hurt you."

She moved, and he groaned harshly. And then it was too late to protest. He felt his body being flung up against the sky, hearing her soft laughter, dying in the throes of a feverish struggle for control that even as he fought, he lost.

When his eyes opened, her face was there, smiling at him, loving him. He sighed. "Well, I guess there had to be a first time," he teased, exhausted. "And we are married, and it's a new world."

"Prude," she whispered, putting her mouth softly on his. "You're just afraid you'll get pregnant in this position."

He burst out laughing, holding her to him. "You enchant me," he whispered. "Tease me, torment me, burn me up. I love you so damned much, I can hardly breathe for it."

That was the first time he'd actually said it. Tears burned her eyes, and she buried her face against his chest, hugging him to her. "I love you, too," she whispered. Her eyes closed. "I always will."

His arms closed around her, and he sighed. "Have you ever noticed how close heaven seems when you look up at the stars?"

She smiled against the rough hair over warm, pulsating muscles. "I know how close it feels," she murmured, nuzzling his chest.

"Yes," he said gently, pressing his hand to her stomach as he folded her against his side. "So do I." He kissed her forehead with aching tenderness. "So do I, my darling."

Above them, a silvery drift of clouds passed over the waning moon. And back in the villa, a gravelly parrot voice was crooning the opening bars of Brahms's "Lullaby."

* * * * *

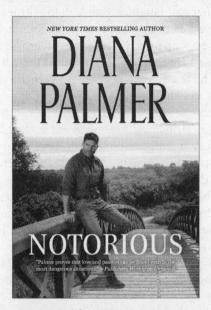